The Gamma Effect

Countdown to Epsilon Book 2

James Pelkmans

Gamma Publishing

GammaPubs.com

ISBN Paperback: 979-8-9858144-3-9

ISBN eBook: 979-8-9858144-2-2

Chapter 1

THE CAFETERIA AT THE Center for Sustainability Research was nearly empty aside from the staff cleaning up after the breakfast rush. Andrew Jorgensen sat alone at a table in a quiet corner of the lanai, as far as possible from the chattering workers carrying their bins full of clanking dishes to the kitchen. While he'd never been a morning person, the main reason he ate at off-peak hours was to avoid the crowds. Eating alone in a deserted cafeteria made him feel less self-conscious than doing so amid a throng of colleagues.

It wasn't as though Andrew didn't welcome a bit of company. Every time a group of new recruits arrived at the Center, there were a blissful few days when they hadn't yet been informed of the social pecking order. As the IT guy, the gangly redhead was among the first to meet the new arrivals, giving them their hardware and setting up their system access. He took care in his interactions, remembering everything he'd learned from his only friend, Samaira, before she'd disappeared.

It had worked, too. Once she'd helped him realize he was pushing people away with his mean-spirited practical jokes and inappropriate sexual innuendo as a self-defense mechanism, he'd been able to keep his behavior in check and connect with people. The newest team members were always happy to make small talk and share meals with him in the cafeteria. Then, after a few days at the Center, they gradually migrated from his table into new social groups as they learned of his reputation.

Sipping his lukewarm coffee, he recalled the day he and Samaira had last shared a meal together. It had been at the same table where he now sat alone—on an uncharacteristically chilly, wet day four months prior. They could both sense his transformation, and had agreed that maybe a fresh start was in order. He could move away from O'ahu and find a new job where he wouldn't be saddled with such an odious reputation. He'd make friends, and maybe even find a girlfriend. Andrew had felt his life was about to change. Unfortunately, it had changed rather suddenly—and not for the better.

The last thing Samaira had done before vanishing forever was to slip him a note and kiss him on the cheek. He still remembered the warmth of her lips touching his face, and how it spread throughout his whole body, banishing the chill of the damp air. The note, which she'd instructed him not to read until two days later, imparted a new chill he'd never quite managed to shake.

From it, he'd learned the real purpose behind Anton Kamaras's Center for Sustainability Research. It wasn't about saving the world at all. It was about abandoning it as a lost cause and escaping to a new one. Samaira and Jayson, along with over two dozen other scientists, were among the first in a multi-generational effort to prepare a pre-industrial version of Earth for Kamaras and a group of his hand-picked guests.

Samaira had uncovered evidence of a secondary mission kept hidden from her and the other recruits. Though the Navy team accompanying them to their new world for protection had bona fide credentials as engineers, doctors, and various other useful specialties, she remained suspicious their primary objective wasn't the same one she'd been preparing for. In the note, she described subtle signs she'd been shepherded into an engineered relationship with a SEAL masquerading as a fellow researcher. Most damning of all, she'd expressed a suspicion one of their colleagues had been murdered when she'd tried to back out of the mission.

That was the reason Andrew was still at the Center, sitting in a corner of the lanai finishing up his breakfast alone. He'd verified Samaira's suspicion using a burner phone to pose as a fictitious college friend of their missing colleague. The bot pretending to be materials scientist Hitarthi Srinivasan took the bait, and Andrew knew the Center's wealthy benefactor and his ubiquitous social media app were behind the deception. When Hitarthi's body washed ashore a couple of weeks later, it confirmed what Samaira had expressed in her note—leaving the Center was suicide.

The designation for Samaira's mission was Gamma. So, when the Center's managing director, Dr. Richard Vandergroot, informed Andrew he'd be part of the Delta mission, he knew exactly what it meant. Though he hadn't yet been told officially, he knew he would follow the others through some sort of portal to another reality. The thought terrified him, but at least it might be a chance to reconnect with a real friend—and maybe not feel so alone all the time.

By now, his coffee was cold. He downed the last gulp and grabbed his phone, timing his departure for a lull in the cleaning activity so he wouldn't have to acknowledge anyone on the way out.

***

Dr. Richard Vandergroot was late getting to his office. His daughter was home from med school for spring break, and he'd lent her his car so she could run errands and get together with friends. He'd started the morning working from home before catching a ride in with his wife. After stealing a quick kiss, she'd dropped him off in the circular drive by the main building just after 9:30.

He didn't feel guilty about arriving late. The Center had already demonstrated what little regard they had for his years of loyalty and hard work. Anton Kamaras had personally recruited him out of the Office of Naval Research eighteen years earlier to develop the quantum computing capabilities that had made Hitz-It.com the world's dominant social media platform—and made Kamaras a billionaire many times over. When the implications of their research suggested more exciting possibilities, it had been Richard's relationship with Admiral Spencer Daniels that gave Kamaras access to the Navy resources that had brought those possibilities to life. After all of that, one mistake was enough to lose his favor.

Gamma had been a shit show. There was no denying it. But there was plenty of blame to go around. Neither the psychologists nor the algorithms had predicted Samaira's sabotage, which had almost certainly compromised the mission. Video replays of Gamma showed that Jayson Reilly, the young native Canadian sustainable agriculture researcher, had witnessed her attempt to stop Aiden from going through the portal. Countless simulations revealed the mission's success now hinged on whether or not he would tell the others when he got to the other side. Based on the data, it wasn't looking good. The algos said he was too loyal to her.

They'd pinned the failures on Richard. All of them. Instead of arriving triumphantly in the new world alongside Kamaras in Epsilon, Richard had been relegated to Delta. He would arrive centuries before his wife and family—assuming they'd still be included at all—to contain the fallout from Gamma.

And that arrogant prick, Dr. Akindele—Jimi—the 'genius' physicist, was now getting all of the credit for what Richard had started. He'd reveled in Gamma's failure, suggesting the smoking remains of the capacitor network should remain onsite at Pai'olu'olu Point as a monument to Richard's incompetence. Even more than Anton Kamaras and his right-hand bitch, Richard wanted Jimi to pay for his disrespect and condescension.

Arriving at his third-floor office, Richard sat at his desk and spun around to face Joint Base Pearl Harbor-Hickam on the far side of the harbor, wondering if his life would have been better had he just stayed in naval research. No, he realized. It wouldn't. His struggles over the last few months notwithstanding, working for Kamaras had made him part of something incredible—a party to the greatest scientific achievement in the history of mankind. He turned to his desk and flipped open his laptop, determined to get the credit he deserved, and reclaim his place on Epsilon.

Chapter 2

JASMINE'S HOPE SLICED THROUGH the low rolling waves of the South China Sea five kilometers off the Ca Mau Peninsula. Though sleek, the thirty-five-meter single-mast sailing ship was a study in design compromise. She had to be spacious enough to transport a reasonable amount of cargo, sturdy enough to voyage across the open ocean, and fast enough to evade anyone who might want to follow her home. A year into the first mission, she'd proven more than adequate in all respects. Though burdened with a heavy load of gold, jewels, and spices, she maintained a comfortable ten knots, even with the jib stowed.

The crew had a uniquely intimate relationship with Jasmine's Hope. They didn't just sail her, they'd built her with their own hands. Arriving on O'ahu through Kamaras's portal with only a limited amount of modern parts and equipment, the sailors had harvested their own trees, milling them into planks and beams before building their ship using the nearly-forgotten techniques of centuries past. Then, leaving a pair of their colleagues behind to babysit the geeks, ten Navy crewmen departed Honolulu Harbor for China on the last day of May, 1175. After a year aboard Jasmine's Hope, their mission nearly complete, the weary sailors were looking forward to going home.

Having spent most of the northward journey out of Singapore towards Guangzhou tacking their way against gusty headwinds, her crew was enjoying a respite, taking advantage of a light crosswind to follow an unhurried straight-line course parallel to the coastline of Vietnam. Of course, it wasn't really Vietnam. Not yet. The land to the west was still under control of the Khmer kingdom of Angkor, and the Singapore they'd left behind a few days earlier was still known by the Malay name of Temasek.

That didn't matter to Josh Talbot, the man at the helm. He didn't worry about keeping the names straight, referring to the places they visited only by what was written on his twenty-first-century navigational charts. He viewed the wonders of his new world with a sense of detachment—as if isolated from it by some unseen barrier.

In a way, the experience wasn't that different from his countless childhood school outings to Colonial Williamsburg or Jamestown—such trips being the curse of any kid growing up in coastal Virginia. Josh couldn't remember how many times he'd watched some bored cosplayer halfheartedly demonstrating colonial candle-making or the wonders of the flying shuttle. He couldn't shake the sense he was trapped in some large-scale version of that. Ducking into a back alleyway of some port city along their route, he half-expected to catch a group of re-enactors on a cigarette break, silently scrolling through their social media feeds before returning to roles as merchants or shopkeepers.

Although that had never happened in any of the dozens of places they'd stopped, Josh still didn't feel guilty about ignoring the often unpronounceable place names or the arbitrary borders of fleeting empires. Most of the people they'd encountered there would soon be dead, and none of these places would matter anymore.

Their first port of call after leaving the geeks behind on O'ahu was Guangzhou, China. Arriving in August, they'd wasted no time negotiating a small amount of their imperial jade for silk, steel, and fine porcelain they could trade at other stops along their route. At the busy port, the unique design of Jasmine's Hope, with her carbon fiber mast towering over the other ships, brought more attention than they were comfortable with, along with many questions about the diverse crew's origin. They described their home as a large Island in the expansive waters east of Africa called Atlantis. It was a fun inside joke—and harmless enough.

Before leaving Guangzhou, they'd told their new contact to expect their return early the following spring, when they'd purchase a significant quantity of the highest quality steel, copper, zinc, lead, and saltpeter he could find. After getting assurances their cargo would be ready to go upon their return, they'd set sail on a six thousand-kilometer trip to the Chola Empire port city of Poompuhar at the southeast end of the Indian subcontinent. There, they'd traded silk and steel for gold, spices, and other agricultural products grown in the rich soil flanking the Kaveri River. Engaging in trade was an essential part of their cover, and an opportunity to multiply the value of the jade they'd brought with them through the portal.

As with the stops that followed, their last act before departing Poompuhar had been to plant the seeds of the deadly Scylla outbreak. They'd been instructed to seek out the vulnerable and unvalued in the places they visited, and those most likely to amplify the early stages of an outbreak. That usually meant prostitutes. Not only did they often live in close quarters with one another, they were also sought out by travelers and silk road merchants who would spread the infection even further.

However, it was a tactic that could easily backfire by exposing their new society to some ancient venereal disease if anyone on the crew got careless. Former SEAL medic Dr. Martina de la Cruz made it clear she'd be subjecting the team to regular inspections and would cut the dick off any of her crewmates dumb enough to stick one of their victims with anything but a syringe.

After Poompuhar, they'd worked their way northward along the east coast of the subcontinent over several weeks, stopping at the major Chola and Sena empire ports to trade in both goods and death. From there, it was south along the Malay Peninsula, making their way to the most recent stop at Temasek. There, they'd experienced their first close call with local authorities.

The city of Temasek profited more from its location at a chokepoint on the shipping lanes of the silk road trade routes than it did from producing anything of real value. In modern parlance, they ran a protection racket. Merchants could either stop there to pay a fee, or be attacked by the privateers under the city's control patrolling the waters on either side of the peninsula. Although it would have been easy to overpower any pirates with their modern weapons, the crew of Jasmine's Hope preferred to play by the rules and keep a low profile. They hadn't managed to do so on their return trip to Guangzhou.

As Paul Suryana was negotiating the toll, a commotion caught the attention of the toll collectors on the dock. Ted Park, chased from a brothel near the port by a gaggle of irate prostitutes, sped past them and scurried up the ladder onto the ship. The women complained to the port officials while Paul tried desperately to make out what they were saying. Though their dialect was unfamiliar, it was clear they were upset about some kind of mistreatment, and wanted the officials to drag Park off the ship so they could mete out their own justice. Paul apologized profusely, distributing a few extra gold coins among the officials and the angry women to calm the situation. Finally agreeing the payment was adequate, they'd suggested Jasmine's Hope and her crew should depart immediately.

That had been four days earlier. In six more, they'd be back in Guangzhou to trade their haul and load up their cargo before heading home to O'ahu. As they made their way north, former Navy SEAL Luong Vu stood by the railing near mid-deck, gazing at the distant shoreline.

"Is that home?" asked Josh.

"Dude, I'm from San Jose," replied Vu, turning around.

"You know what I mean."

"Yeah. I do," he laughed. "Just messing with you. See that point of land over there?"

"Yeah."

"My dad was born about fifty miles northwest of there—in Ho Chi Minh City. He was just a kid when they got out in seventy-nine. Crazy to think my ancestors are somewhere over there right now."

"I've given up trying to wrap my mind around it," admitted Josh.

"The craziest part is what we're doing now—what it's going mean for all that."

"The butterfly effect," replied Josh with a nod.

"Sledgehammer effect, you mean?"

Josh laughed.

The crew aboard Jasmine's Hope understood their mission was to reshape their world. Whatever quantum level changes Dr. Akindele had made to initiate the superposition for Alpha, Beta, and Gamma would eventually cause this world to diverge from the one they knew. By themselves, those changes would probably be too subtle to save them from the ecological disaster looming centuries ahead. That's what Scylla was for. Planted in the major port cities of the silk road, the pathogen already spreading across the Indian subcontinent and the Malay Peninsula would find its way by land and sea all the way to the Atlantic Ocean, cleansing the world and changing everything it touched.

The Navy recruits had done the first part of their job, and would spend their lives keeping the human population in check while isolating the geeks back home from the rest of the world. Then, they'd teach their children to keep doing the same thing until the Delta team arrived to start the next phase.

"We've got company," called Ted Park from his post at the bow.

He joined Josh at the helm and handed him a set of binoculars, pointing to a ship running a parallel course a few kilometers ahead of them farther offshore.

"Doesn't look like anything to worry about," he replied after a few moments of observation. "Keep an eye on it."

Park noticed Vu leaning on the port railing, staring at the distant shore.

"I'd like to have seen Korea," he said.

"We're not tourists, Park," admonished Josh.

Though it was essentially the same conversation he'd been having with Vu, his reaction was different. There was something about Park that got under Josh's skin. He tried too hard—like the annoying little brother constantly trying to hang with his older brother's friends.

"Yeah. But I can imagine what he's feeling right now, being so close to his people," continued Park.

"This isn't our world, and those aren't his people. You need to keep that shit straight."

"You know what I mean."

Josh didn't respond.

"So, back by August?" asked Ted, changing the subject.

"That's a safe bet. Maybe sooner if we get some favorable winds."

"What do you think they're doing back on O'ahu?"

"Sticking to the plan. We should come back to better infrastructure—and better food, I hope."

"I think it'll be time to start a family when we get back. I hope Kailani hasn't hooked up with anyone."

"She's out of your league, Park," assured Josh.

"What makes you say that?"

"Because they're all out of your league," he replied with a laugh.

"Fuck you."

"You wish. I'm out of your league, too."

"Now I *know* you're full of shit," replied Park, doing his best to stay in on the joke instead of being the butt.

"You're not going to have much time to get something going with Kailani, anyway. Next year, we hit the Americas."

"What's the plan?"

"Head for Ecuador and then make our way up to Vancouver Island. No point going any farther than that. We'll be gone another fourteen or fifteen months."

"Again? Shit."

"You joined the Navy, Park. What did you expect?"

"From what my recruiter said? Thai hookers and tropical beaches."

"Recruiters are all full of shit, man. Sorry to be the one to tell you."

"Still, six months is plenty of time to get to know someone before we head out again."

"Yeah," agreed Josh. "That's part of the plan for all of us eventually, I guess."

"And we won't be working our asses off building a goddam ship all day and night."

"Still lots to do."

"But none of this dawn-to-dusk shit, right?"

"No," agreed Josh. "I think we can settle into a more normal routine now, depending on how the geeks behaved while we were gone."

"How bad can it be?"

"Not that bad, I guess," he said with a shrug. "Nothing Jen and Farzin can't handle."

"And sure-as-shit, nothing Olena can't handle."

"Yeah," snorted Josh. "I hear that."

Isiah O'Neal and Miroslava Sirotkin stepped onto the deck from the crew quarters, joining the pair at the helm.

"Time for our shift," said O'Neal. "There's some chow waiting for you below."

Josh looked back and forth at the pair through narrowed eyes.

"Something wrong?" asked Sirotkin.

"Just wondering how I got stuck with Park," he said, breaking into a grin.

"Short straw, man," said O'Neal with a laugh. "Short straw."

"Fuck all you guys," replied Park, extending a middle finger at the new arrivals.

He raised the binoculars for one last check before handing over watch duty to Sirotkin.

"Shit," he said. "Looks like they've adjusted course."

"Intercept?" asked Josh.

"Sure looks that way."

"A couple behind us now, too," added Sirotkin.

"Where'd they come from?" wondered Park, jerking his head around to get a look.

He trained the binoculars on the trailing ships.

"Triple mast. Square sails. Same configuration as the one off the starboard bow."

"Pirates?" asked Josh.

"Could be Japanese Wokou," interjected Vu, still leaning casually against the railing. "But we're pretty far south for that."

"Doesn't matter who they are," said O'Neal. "They're trying to corral us."

Park disappeared below deck, returning a few minutes later carrying a crate of rocket-propelled grenades. The launcher was slung over his shoulder.

"What the fuck are you doing?" asked Josh.

"Getting ready to engage."

"Put your toys away, man. I'm not getting outmaneuvered by these assholes."

Park sighed and retreated below deck.

"Let's see how they feel about this," said Josh with a grin.

He cranked the wheel, changing their heading a few degrees starboard—directly toward the ship ahead.

"What are you doing?" asked Sirotkin.

"Going after them," he shrugged. "They want to intercept? Let's force the issue and see what they wanna do."

If there were any doubts as to the intentions of the nearby ships, they didn't last long. Almost immediately, one of the trailing pair turned in pursuit, while the other maintained its original route parallel to the coastline. The ship ahead took longer to react, eventually coming about in a wide starboard turn.

"They're not going to let us break to the outside," cautioned Sirotkin.

"I can see that," replied Josh. "But they've opened themselves on the shore side. O'Neal? Ready about."

Isiah O'Neal nodded, then quickly moved to bring the boom across.

"Not so fast," cautioned Vu, pointing to the northwest.

"Clever bastards," said Josh with an appreciative nod.

Another ship had appeared from the bay ahead, running on a northeast heading parallel to their own.

"Well?" demanded Park.

Josh surveyed the sea around Jasmine's Hope, realizing it was about to become a battle zone.

"Fine," he conceded. "But light arms only—you and Mira. I don't want this to be any more of a spectacle than it needs to be."

"Should I wake the others?"

"Let 'em sleep. This shouldn't be much of a contest."

Park offered a curt nod before disappearing below deck again.

"What can we expect from these guys, Vu?"

"Can't say for sure," he shrugged. "We don't even know who we're dealing with."

"Worst case?"

"Deck-mounted crossbow harpoons. They'll try to stick the hull, haul us in, and engage with melee weapons."

"Range?"

"Hundred meters, at most. Probably not even that."

"Alright," replied Josh. "Let's do this."

The ship ahead finished coming about, trimming its sails to slow to a near-dead stop. The onshore wind meant there was no leeway to evade it to the east without turning back into the path of the ship now trailing behind. Their pursuers had them boxed in.

"What are we doing, man?" asked O'Neal.

"Hold steady."

Jasmine's Hope closed the distance to the nearest ship at a rapid pace now that it was almost stationary; the captain waiting for Josh to make the first move before committing himself to the chase. Its companion, charging out from shore farther ahead, cut off escape to the north while the two in pursuit covered any attempt at a retreat southward. They'd sprung their trap perfectly.

The distance to the ship ahead was now less than five hundred meters. O'Neal eyed Josh nervously, waiting for the order to change course.

"Josh? We're getting close, man," he cautioned.

Park took up station along the starboard railing and released the safety on his assault rifle.

"Hold your fire," reminded Josh. "Vu, get ready with the jib."

Vu nodded and moved into position.

With just about two hundred meters left, Josh made the call.

"Hard a port!"

Everyone braced as he spun the wheel to the left. O'Neal released the boom, allowed it to swing under his control to the opposite side of the five-meter-wide deck, and had it secure again in just a few seconds.

"Unroll the jib!"

Vu already had the halyard in his hands by the time the command came and immediately began hauling it in. The acceleration was noticeable as he tightened the working sheet, and the wind caught hold of the extra sail.

They were close enough to hear the shouts from the nearby ship's captain. At his command, the crew scrambled to raise their sails, surprised by their quarry's sudden and unexpected burst of speed. Josh eyed the outbound ship, still at least a thousand meters to the northwest, to see how the captain would react. If he was too slow to figure out what was happening, there would be a chance to slip between him and the shoreline to the west, escaping the trap.

The outbound captain quickly realized the plan. Leaving his companion to cover off an eastward escape, he turned hard to his port side to loop back towards shore.

"Hard a starboard!" called Josh in response, cranking the wheel again in the opposite direction.

O'Neal manned the boom while Vu worked the jib sheets with perfect timing.

There was no time for the captain of the nearest ship to react. Jasmine's Hope was already dodging past, moving too fast to catch. The captain of the vessel ahead came about quickly to starboard, resuming his original outbound line, upon realizing his quarry was now committed to a north-easterly escape. He'd lost considerable time getting turned around by Josh's bluff, but was now back on his intercept course.

"Yes! How do you like that?" asked Josh of no one in particular.

"Awfully proud of yourself, aren't you?" replied Miroslava with a grin.

"Anything he can do to ruin my fun," added Park as he re-engaged the safety and crossed over to the port side to prepare for the next encounter.

"We're not out of this yet, Park. You might still have a chance to be useful."

Both ships were now heading northeast, away from the coast of what would one day be Vietnam. Though the pirates had the advantage of being ahead, they were also closer to shore. They'd had to set a course slightly more into the wind to intercept Jasmine's Hope, compromising their top speed and giving their prey a decent chance at escape. As the distance closed, the navy crew could see the pirates gathered along the nearside of their deck. Sirotkin raised her binoculars.

"Looks like Vu was right about the crossbows," she said. "There's one mounted on the stern and looks like another on the bow."

"How sure are you on the range of those things, Vu?" asked Josh.

He shrugged and shook his head in reply.

"Be ready, Park. Harpoon crews only. You too, Mira."

Park nodded without taking his eyes off the target. Sirotkin raised the weapon slung over her shoulder and flicked the safety.

"What do you think, O'Neal? We getting past them, or what?"

"Gonna be close, man."

Close was right. While they had the edge on speed, the attackers were still ahead, and steadily converging on the path of escape. The gap continued to close, but it seemed Jasmine's Hope had the pace to slip past the approaching ship.

It was now only two hundred meters off the port bow on a near-parallel course. The pirates aboard brandished their weapons in anticipation, their grim faces betraying no hint of fear. By the time Jasmine's Hope had pulled even with their attackers, the distance between them was down to a hundred meters. The crew manning the aft harpoon swung it around, preparing to fire as soon as they were in range.

"Come on, man," pleaded Park. "You wanna wait until we're eating that fucking harpoon before we do something, or what?"

"Okay, hit 'em."

Park squeezed the trigger, tracing an arc of splintering wood across the side of the ship as he homed in on the crew manning the massive crossbow. Misty clouds of blood erupted around a pair of men as they fell to the deck. The triggerman panicked, loosing his bolt before he, too, was taken down by gunfire. The harpoon sailed through the air towards Jasmine's Hope, trailing a line of thick rope. It hit the side of the ship with a loud thud.

"Shit!" yelled Josh. "They got us?"

"I think so," answered Sirotkin, watching the rope between the two ships go taut as they moved ahead of their pursuers.

The rope sang out with rising frequency as the tension increased until it finally let go, sending the harpoon whistling back toward the pirate ship before it splashed harmlessly into the water. Park ran to the stern and quickly zeroed in on the forward crossbow station, dropping the crew before they could take aim. The triggerman let the harpoon fly as he fell to the deck, sending it high into the air and off-target.

The pirate ship adjusted course and fell in behind Jasmine's Hope, trying to keep pace long enough to reload. It was no use. They were soon out of range.

"Sayonara, motherfuckers!" called Park, gripping his crotch in an emphatic display of contempt.

Then he raised his middle finger, holding it aloft for them to see as they fell farther and farther behind.

"Real mature, Park," said Sirotkin, rolling her eyes.

"Alright, Josh. I'll take the helm," offered O'Neal. "Go down and get your dinner—if it's not all over the floor by now."

"Thanks. I think I will," he replied.

"You want us to lower the jib and trim out for a smoother ride once we drop these assholes?"

"No," replied Josh, shaking his head. "Let's keep the pace so we can finish up in Guangzhou and get home."

Chapter 3

THE PRINCE KUHIO FEDERAL Building, home of the U.S. District Court of Hawaii and several federal agencies, commanded majestic views of Honolulu Harbor from its position along the water at the base of Punchbowl Street. Jessica Reyes believed you could tell a lot about the importance of an agency from the building where it was housed. Her employer, the Occupational Safety and Health Administration, occupied a squat, ugly building across the street from the District Court, and the only view offered from her office window was a parking garage. That seemed about right to her, considering every other administration threatened to shutter the agency entirely, deeming it too unfriendly to business.

Still, it was hard to complain. Plain and uninspiring as her office was, she lived in the most beautiful place imaginable, and wouldn't trade her drab little office for a corner suite anywhere else in the country. Nor did she belong anywhere else. Though considered by some a haole—an outsider, she traced her roots back to the Puerto Rican immigrants who'd come to work on the sugar plantations almost sixty years before Hawaii was even a state. Left homeless and jobless by a massive Atlantic hurricane, her great-great-grandparents had come to Hawaii with hundreds of others from their Spanish-speaking island for an opportunity to start over.

Like many descendants of those Puerto Rican laborers, Jessica made her living far from the plantations, spending much of her time staring at a computer screen. Working on a report detailing the circumstances of a grisly accident at a new high-rise construction site, she was interrupted by the ping of a notification from her phone.

"Shit," she huffed under her breath.

Ordinarily, the arrival of her lunch break wouldn't be a cause of distress. Today was different. She grabbed her purse and headed for the stairs, walking past the bank of elevators in a conscious effort to take the stairs for exercise.

Pausing outside after exiting the aggressively air-conditioned lobby a little after noon, she closed her eyes and absorbed the sun's warmth. The light fragrance of a flowering tree wafting in from nearby combined with the salty air to trigger a memory. Well, not exactly a memory; more a vague sense of comfort. It felt good. For a moment, she almost didn't mind that she was going to meet local building inspector Don Lee. Downer Don, she called him. At least it was an excuse to get outside. She'd received a hit from him the day before, asking to meet after work to discuss a 'mutual issue.' Dreading the company, she'd insisted on meeting over lunch instead to avoid any possibility of a lingering encounter.

The only mutual issue they had was the Center for Sustainability Research. The previous fall, she'd agreed to help him shut down their construction project on Pai'olu'olu Point at the southeast tip of the island following the accidental death of a local contractor. Though it was within her purview to do so whenever she had concerns about safety, she'd been slapped down hard by her superiors within minutes of her decision. The message was clear; Richard Vandergroot and the Center were untouchable.

Pushing thoughts of the unpleasant encounter aside, she walked a few blocks west along Queen street to her favorite nearby sushi restaurant. Don was buying. If she had to endure him for a full hour, there was no reason she shouldn't at least enjoy the meal. When she arrived, he was already waiting. Sitting at a quiet corner table, he was a caricature of a midlevel government employee. Balding and skinny—except for a protruding pot belly—he sported a wrinkled short-sleeved white shirt and blue Dockers. He either had a closet full of identical shirts, or wore the same one every day.

"Hey, Don," she offered with as much enthusiasm as she could muster.

"Jessica. Hi. Thanks for coming."

"Of course. You order yet?"

"Waiting for you to make a recommendation. This is your favorite place, right?"

"Near the office, yeah. It's as good as it gets in my price range."

She downplayed it, hoping he wouldn't make a habit out of eating there. Not likely, she realized, judging him a sacked lunch kind of guy.

"What's good?"

"Can't go wrong with a bento," she said with a shrug.

"Listen," he started, looking up from the menu, "I just wanted to thank you for going to bat for me last summer with that whole Pai'olu'olu Point shit show. Sorry about how it turned out."

"I got reamed for that," she reminded him.

"Yeah. I know. But you did the right thing."

"I'm not sure about that. It warranted a look, for sure. But shutting them down?" she said, shaking her head. "That was probably too far."

A waitress arrived, and Jessica ordered the sushi bento. Don followed her lead, handing over his menu with a polite nod.

"They took shortcuts on every permit," he reminded her. "I'm sick of them—and that arrogant prick, Vandergroot."

The hairs on the back of Jessica's neck stood at the invocation of Richard's name.

"Permits are your issue, not mine. I should have just done it by the book."

"But you knew it, right? You sensed something was wrong over there—with that whole operation."

"Dodgy as hell," she admitted. "But that's not my problem if there're no safety issues."

"You hear one of 'em died?"

"Who?"

"One of their scientists. Drowned paddle boarding off Waikiki."

"Hardly sounds like a work-related accident, Don. Someone drowns out there almost every week."

"It's just suspicious, that's all," he whispered, leaning in towards her. "Especially with other stuff I've been hearing."

"Like what?"

"I know someone on the inside. A friend of a friend," he said vaguely. "Apparently, there's a bunch of 'em missing."

"A bunch of who?"

"Scientists. They just vanished around Thanksgiving. Supposedly some kind of biodome thing."

"That sounds pretty reasonable, considering the kind of research they're doing."

"Maybe," he allowed. "But I couldn't find a record of a permit application for it on any of the islands. Nothing like that could go under the radar."

"You said yourself they're not above board on permitting, Don. Besides, if something was up, we'd have a bunch of missing persons reports."

"How do you know we don't? Who gets those?"

"Local police? Maybe FBI?"

A sudden realization struck her, and she narrowed her eyes at him.

"Christ, Don. Is that what this is about?"

He broke her gaze and looked sheepishly down at the table.

"Christ," she said again with disbelief. "I thought this was an apology lunch, but you want more from me, don't you?"

"You still talk to her?"

"She doesn't go out of her way, but we're civil when we run into each other."

Jessica had been divorced from Special Agent Shannon Boucher for a little over a year, and it was still a touchy subject.

"That's good. Since my ex-wife moved to Colorado, we haven't spoken more than a couple of times—and it wasn't exactly friendly."

She didn't care about his personal life.

"What do you want, Don?"

"Just ask if she's heard anything," he pleaded. "Or if they have any suspicions."

"She's not going to tell me anything."

"Well, if they *do* have suspicions, maybe hearing from you will encourage her to get more aggressive."

She shook her head and sighed.

"I got my ass handed to me last time I did you a favor."

"I only want you to ask a couple of questions. That's all. You don't need to stick your neck out this time."

"No promises," she replied.

She'd already decided she'd do it. Not to help Don. It was because of Richard; that smug, condescending prick from the Center. Even if nothing came of it, the slightest chance she'd be able to piss him off was worth what little effort it would take to pull out her phone and make a call.

***

The data on the screen was mindboggling from any perspective; the sheer amount, the detail, and, of course, the highly sensitive—probably classified—nature of the Columbia ballistic missile submarine digital mock-up. Andrew had been analyzing it for days, working on the optimization Richard had requested. He'd asked him to distribute the mass of all moveable equipment and crew, along with several tons of unidentified cargo, to achieve an even weight distribution from bow to stern. Although Richard had provided no details on why the optimization was necessary, Andrew had already figured it out based on the secret letter he'd received from Samaira before she and the others had vanished.

He knew he'd be following her into the unknown as a passenger aboard the Columbia for the Delta mission. Initially, it had kept him awake at night with worry. But, as he had done with his once-crippling existential dread, he'd finally managed to program his brain to preempt any examination of the facts he'd find too discomforting. He accepted his fate—still too distant to cause immediate panic—to be as inevitable as his own death. Luckily, he'd found plenty of distractions in his work to keep his darker thoughts at bay.

It wasn't that hard to make an algorithm to redistribute the people and objects onboard to spread the mass evenly. Once he set it up, it was just a matter of letting the data crunch. He spent the rest of his time exploring the other aspects of the dataset Richard had given him. As a kid, he'd wanted to be an engineer, but his father had talked him out of it—explaining it would be too challenging, and probably less rewarding than computer science. He observed with jealous regret the work that others were doing at the Center, and realized how wrong his father had been. The incredible feat of engineering that was the Columbia only exacerbated those feelings.

The most fascinating aspect to him were the results of the finite element analysis. How was it possible, he wondered, to accurately predict how something so complex as a submarine would react when exposed to outside forces like water pressure, or even an explosion? The answer turned out to be easier than he'd imagined; nobody can predict how such a complex shape will react under a given set of parameters. However, straightforward rules govern *exactly* how simple shapes like rectangles and triangles react to applied forces.

In the finite element analysis, the outer hull of the Columbia was first replicated by algorithms as a two-dimensional mesh of millions of small rectangles. Then, the bulkheads and other structural components were modeled as three-dimensional meshes of cubes. Instead of analyzing an impossibly complex shape, it was only a matter of analyzing a collection of millions and millions of simple shapes. Usually, all that took was computing power—and a lot of time. Using the quantum stack for the job, it took hardly any time at all.

The analysis results were mesmerizing. In one animation, the simulated Columbia dove from the surface to a depth of five hundred meters. As it did so, the finite element mesh began changing color from blue to cyan, to green, and then to yellow, with red hotspots indicating where the metal hull was stressed beyond the yield point. In a simulation of how the Columbia would react to an enemy depth charge, Andrew adjusted the setting that exaggerated the deformation of the skin so the tiny distortions were magnified enough to appreciate with the naked eye. The submarine's skin rippled with waves, as if the percussive blast of the depth charge was a stone hitting the surface of a pond. The color scale showed the stress levels, revealing where the material was most likely to suffer a catastrophic failure under continued enemy attack.

"Cool," he whispered to himself.

Startled by a knock at his door, his head jerked up suddenly. Dr. Akindele walked in without waiting for an invitation.

"H—hello, sir," stammered Andrew.

Akindele never visited Andrew's office. He just sent out a terse hit or an email demanding immediate attention when he needed something.

"Hello Andrew," he replied, looking oddly uncomfortable. "I have something for you."

He hesitated momentarily before walking over to the desk, holding an envelope in his extended hand.

"What's this?"

"It's an invitation—to tea."

Andrew cocked an eye at his unexpected visitor.

"You're inviting me to tea?"

"No. Not me," he clarified. "My mother."

Andrew stared—first at the letter, then at Akindele. He had no words.

"There is an RSVP card inside," continued the physicist.

"I don't know what to say," said Andrew as he took the envelope. "This is—unexpected. And unnecessarily formal."

"All of this is very proper," assured Akindele.

"Are you sure this was meant for me?"

"Believe me, Andrew. I spent a great deal of effort verifying that myself."

"Well, okay then. Thanks."

"I trust you won't disappoint her with your response?"

"I wouldn't dream of it, sir."

Akindele nodded and left without another word.

"What the hell just happened?" wondered Andrew aloud as he stared at the invitation in his hand.

He placed it on his desk without opening it, returning to his review of the analysis results. The next one showed the effect of a pair of depth charges detonating on either side of the Columbia. Again, the submarine's outer hull rippled under the impact of the concussive blasts, with wave interference patterns emerging all over the surface, and stress concentrations developing where the sail met the rest of the structure.

A second knock landed on his door.

"Jesus Christ. What now?" he muttered.

Richard stepped in, and Andrew's eyes widened in horror.

"Sorry," he blurted.

"It's okay, Andrew," assured Richard with a dismissive wave. "A lot of interruptions today?"

Andrew quickly toggled to another window where the people and objects on the Columbia were incrementally shifting their positions as a graph below charted the weight distribution along the center axis. He spun his laptop around to show the progress.

"I'm just running through the optimization to make sure the numbers make sense."

"I saw Akindele in the hall," said Richard, ignoring the data on the screen. "He doesn't get over here much."

"Yeah. He wanted me to create another segregation on the stack."

It was an easy lie. Creating a clean space to run new simulations accounted for well over half of the requests he got from the research teams.

"What's he up to?"

"He didn't say. Never does," said Andrew with a shrug.

Richard sat down, still ignoring the laptop.

"Listen, Andrew," he began. "I need a little help with something. An internal security audit."

"You think we got hit?" asked Andrew, wrinkling his brow. "Who would even have the tech to do that?"

"I don't think we're vulnerable from the outside," assured Richard, "but Rebecca has asked me to evaluate the danger of insider espionage. Someone could get a big payday selling what we've developed here—not to mention the classified stuff we're looking at for the Navy."

Andrew gulped. He'd probably been digging through the data more than he should have. Perhaps Richard was on to him.

"How are we vulnerable?"

"You tell me. You're the expert."

"Well," started Andrew, leaning back and looking at the ceiling, "anybody with an account can just put whatever they have access to on a memory stick. That's our biggest weakness. But I'd get a notice from the system—and so would you—if anything sensitive got transferred. We'd know who, what, and where within seconds."

"What if someone hacked another account?"

"Our password quality rules are pretty good, and we don't have a lot of morons working here. I doubt anybody's got them written on a sticky note on their monitor."

"What about brute force? Someone with your skills could create a quantum code breaker, right?"

Andrew gulped again. Someone with his skills *could* do that. In fact, it's how he'd accessed the deleted file system where Richard had uploaded the videos of the recruits saying goodbye to their families.

"We've got checks in place to stop that," he protested. "After five tries, the target account would be locked out."

"Yeah. But *you* could disable that, right?"

"Sure," he tried to say in a way that would convey such a thing had never occurred to him, "but someone would need to hack my account first. It's chicken and egg."

"Can we run a test to see how long it would take?"

Four hours, three minutes, and twenty-seven seconds, for Richard's account, he knew.

"Theoretically, yes," he allowed. "But there's a huge risk."

"What do you mean?"

"You warned me yourself at my onboarding. We have an agreement with the NSA that we don't use our tech against encryption, and they don't come in here, box everything up, and take it away."

"This is purely internal," assured Richard. "And it would be in their interest as much as ours to test the security."

"What are you thinking?"

"Well," prompted Richard, "who around here has access to the most sensitive stuff—other than us, of course."

"Ms. Steinman?"

"You want to get us both fired?" laughed Richard. "That's out of the question."

"I guess it's Dr. Akindele, then."

"Of course!" agreed Richard. "Tell me the moment you crack it."

"What? I've got this optimization to do," protested Andrew.

"This security audit is my top priority—and Rebecca's. I need you on this now."

"Okay," he sighed as Richard got up to leave.

"Oh, and not a word of this to anyone," cautioned Richard. "You report only to me."

"Got it."

"Thanks," said Richard with a nod before leaving the office.

Andrew exhaled and slumped back in his chair. The last thing he wanted was another reason to talk to Richard, but at least he had an excuse for snooping around in the system. Maybe he'd be able to find something to help Samaira and the others.

***

Richard smiled as he slipped out of Andrew's office, pulling the door closed with a click. The geek was as naïve as he was gifted. It had taken no time to shepherd him into identifying Akindele's account as the one he should hack for the fake security audit. Once Richard had access, he'd be able to frame him for espionage, or any number of things that would get him out of the way. Without Akindele to manage the physics, Richard would be far too valuable to waste on Delta. Of course, he still needed to make sure Delta was successful—whether he was going or not. He couldn't afford another screwup.

His next stop after visiting Andrew was on the second floor, where psychologists Cal Young and Denise Bertrand were reviewing an analysis of Columbia's crew.

"What are we learning?" he asked without preamble or pleasantries as he strode into the room.

"Nothing earthshattering," replied Cal.

"Just debating about replacing a couple of Delta candidates on the margin," added Denise.

"Getting a little close, isn't it?"

"Not really," replied Cal. "Since the crew doesn't know what's going to happen, the only thing that matters is the reaction. That's a lot easier to deal with than getting our Gamma recruits to go through the portal voluntarily."

"So, what's the issue?"

"We're looking at one in twenty simulations where some potential outliers lose it after the transfer."

"Lose it?"

"You know. Flip out."

"In one out of one hundred simulations, it leads to a minor mutiny," added Denise.

"Minor mutiny? What the fuck does that mean?"

"We define that as between three and ten crew members openly opposing the captain."

"And Captain Ibarra knows this?"

"He's keeping a close eye on things. A one percent chance doesn't seem to bother him much."

"Don't forget, I'm supposed to be on this mission, too," cautioned Richard, wagging a finger at them. "I think I deserve a little say in what's acceptable."

The two psychologists looked at one another—then glanced uncomfortably at the floor.

"What is it?" demanded Richard.

Cal looked up first.

"Uh, you're one of the variables impacting the outcome."

"What?"

"Don't get me wrong," he added. "We can get the odds down by making some crew changes—but you seem to be the biggest factor."

"Are you questioning my loyalty?" asked Richard, narrowing his eyes.

"We don't question anything," interjected Denise. "We just run the simulations."

"Good. It may be Ibarra's sub, but it's *my* mission. If *I* have to intervene, it's not a mutiny. Does anyone else know about this?"

"No."

"Keep it that way," he spat. "And fix your inputs. If you're this far off, it's no wonder Gamma was such a disaster."

They looked at each other again as he turned to leave the room. Halfway out the door, he paused and glanced back.

"Swap out anyone posing more than a tenth of a percent risk—and not a word leaves this room."

"Yes, sir," they agreed in unison.

He shook his head as he left the room, closing the door behind him.

"Shit," he muttered.

Somehow, the algorithms had picked up warning signs and applied them to the missions simulations. If Rebecca found out, there was a good chance he'd get his wish to be taken off Delta. Unfortunately, the repercussions likely wouldn't stop there. He'd have to figure out what was happening and reverse engineer some modified behaviors to get back in the algos' good graces.

Chapter 4

An uneasy peace had settled over the Island of O'ahu in the months following the dramatic arrival of Kai's people among the Gamma Recruits. While daily life continued as normally as possible, twin threats loomed ominously. The risk of another attack from Pa'ao warranted a constant presence at the summit of Diamond Head, where pairs of volunteer sentries rotated in and out every two days to keep watch for war canoes coming in from the southeast. With enough warning, it was unlikely Pa'ao's forces would be a threat. Only given a chance to land and disperse into the jungle could they cause any actual harm.

The greater concern remained the security team. It had been fourteen months since they'd left for the orient, and every new day marked an increased likelihood of their return. To ensure advanced warning, a pair kept watch from the mountains overlooking the southwest corner of the island. The challenging terrain made the trek back and forth from Honolulu a significant challenge. As a result, the shifts were long, and watch duties were limited to those experienced in mountaineering or adventurous enough to learn the essential skills required for a safe ascent.

To ease the burden of the western watch assignment, they'd constructed a weatherproofed cabin commanding impressive views from a small lanai extending over the cliff on the west side. It had comfortable bunks and even a stone fireplace to ward off the chilly night air that often came with such altitude. For some, a few days of peace in the mountains was a welcome break, and there was never a shortage of volunteers.

Of course, the real question was what they'd do when the Navy recruits returned—if they did at all. The equipment they'd taken, the ship, and the manpower they represented had tremendous potential value to their nascent society. Still, some recruits thought they'd all be better off if their colleagues had been swallowed by the sea and never returned at all. Wishful thinking aside, they had prepared a plan and were ready to enact it when word of the ship's reappearance came down from the mountaintop at Akupu.

They'd not neglected their other duties while waiting for threats to materialize. Several crops, having been through a few growth and harvest cycles, were now abundant enough for regular consumption. West of Punchbowl, the recruits had built a threshing and milling facility—powered by harnessing the water of Pauoa stream. Wooden shafts, cogs, and gears lubricated with tree oils were more than up to the task of making flour, so they'd managed not to consume much of their technology in the effort.

Back at the settlement, a bakery sat alongside the adjoining storage building, with two small empty apartments occupying the second floor, waiting to be claimed as their numbers grew. They'd constructed a large stone oven for baking bread every morning, delighting the recruits and their native companions alike by making a few cookies and other treats using sugar from their successful crop of cane and beets.

They even served fresh pizza one evening a week. Topped with tomato sauce, fresh vegetables, and whole basil leaves, Jayson felt it was only one ingredient short of perfection; it was missing the giant globs of fresh mozzarella cheese.

"Where do you think the closest cow is right now?" he asked, taking a bite.

He and Matteus sat outside at one of several small tables occupying a section of the central plaza in front of the bakery.

"I would say Japan," replied Matteus with a shrug. "I'm not really sure."

"Hmm," said Jayson, as if mulling over the logistics of getting his hands on one.

"I can't believe I'm eating a pizza, even without cheese," said Matteus.

His nostrils flared as he took in the scents of the roasted vegetables and fresh herbs.

"True," allowed Jayson. "If I close my eyes and sit back, I can imagine I'm sitting at an outdoor café back home."

"Except for the coffee, of course."

"Still a few years away, I'm afraid. You'll need to rebuild your addiction from scratch."

Jayson glanced across the plaza and quickly wiped the corners of his mouth with a knuckle to clear away any sauce that might still be on his face. Matteus looked over his shoulder to see what had suddenly captured his companion's attention.

"Ah," he said with a smile.

Luni and her younger sister were walking towards the bakery, hand in hand.

"What's that supposed to mean?" demanded Jayson.

Matteus raised an eyebrow, but said nothing.

"Hi Jayson. Hi Matteus," greeted Luni with a broad smile as she approached.

"Hey Luni, Palila," replied Jayson. "How are you?"

"Very well, thank you," answered Palila.

"Wow," remarked Matteus. "Your English is excellent, young lady."

"She is a fast learner," beamed her older sister.

"I'd say you both are."

"Jayson has been helping me," said Luni.

"I'll bet he has," said Matteus, glancing at Jayson with an approving nod.

"Yes," she continued, seemingly unaware of the inference. "Many evenings, we watch movies together on his tablet, and use the translator to make sure I understand."

Jayson fought vainly to suppress a blush, which only made it worse. He felt his face burning with embarrassment.

"I'm taking Palila for a treat from the bakery," explained Luni. "It was nice seeing you both."

She was looking only at Jayson as she spoke.

"Way to put on the moves," said Matteus in a hushed voice as Luni and her sister walked away.

"It's not like that. I'm just being friendly," he lied.

"Then you're an idiot."

"What?"

"She's obviously into you, man."

"I think she just feels more at ease with me because I look like one of her people."

"Are you really that obtuse?" marveled Matteus. "Didn't you see how she was looking at you? And exactly how much time do you spend with her?"

"Maybe three or four evenings a week. And when she helps in the fields."

Matteus shook his head.

"What?" demanded Jayson.

"This is going to be Samaira all over again if you don't get your head out of your ass."

"What's that supposed to mean?"

"It means you better make a move before she gives up on you."

"So now that you're dating someone, that makes you some kind of expert?"

"I'm only an expert compared to you."

Jayson took another bite of pizza, mainly as an excuse to end the conversation.

"Sorry," said Matteus, clutching at his heart in jest. "It's just that watching you flail around is causing me physical pain, you know?"

"I'll show you physical pain," replied Jayson between bites.

At a nearby table, Dr. Kitzinger sat fiddling with his guitar. He'd brought the tuning pegs, frets, and other bits of hardware, along with some strings, as his luxury items when Dr. Akindele had given them the unexpected weight bonus. After months of carefully shaping the wooden pieces during his spare time, he'd finally managed to put everything together and strum out the first tentative chords. He had a tablet with some beginner lessons resting on the table in front of him as he tried to play something.

"When you started making that thing, I assumed it was because you already knew how to play," said Jayson, still chewing.

"Sorry," he said with a grimace. "Is it bothering you?"

"It's fine, doc," assured Matteus. "He's just trying to change the subject because he's embarrassed."

"Oh? Do tell."

The doctor dragged his stool over to the pair and grinned.

"He's missing all kinds of hints from Luni," explained Matteus. "Obliviousness personified."

"She's just a friend," insisted Jayson.

"You should learn to play," suggested Kitzinger, holding out the guitar. "Women love a man with musical talent."

Jayson set aside his pizza to take the instrument, strumming out a few chords.

"You can play?"

"Not really," he replied. "I tried to learn once—to impress a girl."

"How'd that work out for you?" grinned Matteus.

"I'm here, aren't I?"

"Sounds pretty good to me," shrugged the doctor. "Can you show me a few things?"

By now, the rest of the people outside the bakery had stopped what they were doing to listen. Zaina and Herman rose from a nearby bench and walked over, hand in hand, to join them.

"That is incredible," marveled Luni as she emerged from the bakery.

Palila stood wide-eyed, silently munching her cookie as Jayson continued to play.

"Told you so," said Kitzinger with a wink. "You can borrow it any time you like."

Jayson, turning red with embarrassment again, tried to hand the guitar back.

"No. Keep going," insisted the doctor, waving him off.

"Yes," agreed Luni. "I want to hear more."

"I don't really know any more," he protested.

Sounds of excitement rose from nearby. They turned to see Kai sprinting from the common building where he'd been enjoying dinner with the others. He was heading toward them with Samaira, Jen, and Malo right behind.

"What's up?" called Jayson as he ran past.

"Ke hele mai nei lākou," he yelled back without slowing his pace.

"Who?"

But Kai kept running without reply.

"What's going on?" he asked Samaira as she slowed to a trot and approached their table.

She held her newborn baby boy, Keanu, in a sling, cradling him against her body with one arm.

"Mano and Serge reporting in from Akupu," she explained. "They've got something incoming."

"Shit. The security team."

"We knew this day was coming—and we've planned for it," said Matteus with a sigh as he rose from the table.

"Yeah," agreed Jayson. "But I had more faith in the plan when we were dealing with a hypothetical."

"We all know the drill," reminded Samaira. "Let's get to it."

Jayson pushed the guitar back to Dr. Kitzinger and, loathe to waste any of his meal, shoved the last bite of pizza into his mouth as he stood to follow Kai and the others to the hidden armory in Punchbowl crater.

"Be careful," said Luni.

"I will," he assured with a nod. "Everything will be fine."

Chapter 5

THE UPDATE FROM MANO eased the sense of dread among Honolulu's inhabitants, downgrading it instead to a sense of mild unease. They'd assumed any approach from the west could only mean the return of the security team and the start of a very tense, possibly deadly, confrontation. When Mano reported down that the approaching craft was close enough to determine it was a large outrigger canoe with about a dozen people onboard, they realized it was more likely an unexpected visit from their neighbors on Kaua'i. Some of Kai's people and the refugees from Maui and Moloka'i must have escaped Pili's attack and sought safety with the Nanaulu people of the island.

Around sunset, the canoe disappeared from sight behind a hilltop as it approached Mākua Beach on the northwest side of the island. Kai sent a party of his warriors by canoe with food to meet them. Going by foot would have taken too long, and they'd need to wait until morning to get started. By canoe, they could set off immediately to make contact at first light. Jen reluctantly stayed behind, agreeing that encountering familiar faces would be the best way to diffuse—or at least mitigate—any initial tension. She and the others settled in for a night of uneasy sleep.

The following day, the community began preparing a welcome feast in the plaza. At Samaira's suggestion, they moved the tables and chairs outdoors. Aside from the fact it was a beautiful day, she felt it might help keep their guests more at ease if they were out in the open rather than confined in the common building among strangers.

She also suggested a balanced approach toward showcasing their technology, saying it should appear inspiring but not threatening. She set up some lights that would gradually turn up as the sun went down, and convinced the others to only use the tablets as essential to facilitate communication. Most of the recruits could converse somewhat in the language of their native colleagues, and all could handle the basic greetings and pleasantries. Only more intricate discussions would require the translator app.

It was late afternoon when Kai's warriors, followed by their guests from Kaua'i, paddled into Honolulu Harbor and beached their canoes near the slipway that had launched Jasmine's Hope on her maiden voyage more than a year earlier. The men chattered excitedly as they waded out of the water, their old friendships readily rekindled after sharing the last stage of the journey.

Kai, Jen, and Samaira waited for them at the bottom of the pathway to the Punchbowl settlement. Samaira had convinced Jen to come unarmed, and she'd relented only on the condition that Farzin position himself out of sight nearby with a sniper rifle.

"Welcome, my old friends," greeted Kai in the language of his people. "Kameha is not with you?"

"He sent us as his emissaries," explained the nearest warrior.

"You are his emissaries, Huaka'i? He must be an important man now."

"An honored guest," shrugged Huaka'i.

"No matter. I am pleased to have you here among our new friends."

"I remember him," said Huaka'i, pointing to Jayson.

Jayson nodded and approached.

"Aloha," he said, extending a hand.

The warrior eyed him doubtfully for a moment before offering a handshake.

"This is Jen, one of our warriors," continued Kai, "and my wife, Samaira."

"The kupua 'ele'ele," nodded Huaka'i, furrowing his brow.

Samaira snorted, covering her smile with her hand as the translation emerged.

The dark witch.

"Ouch," whispered Jayson.

"Please, I'm from the south," she replied. "I've been called worse."

"I'm sorry if I offended you," said Huaka'i, noticing their side conversation. "Word of your power has spread to Kaua'i."

"I'm not offended," she assured, still smiling.

Huaka'i regarded the infant nestled in the sling across her chest and eyed his old friend.

"You must be tired and hungry," realized Kai. "Please, come with me to our home. We have prepared a feast."

Huaka'i nodded and motioned his companions to follow.

As they approached the settlement, the visitors marveled at the high-roofed common building with its expansive lanai extending over the slope.

"Is this your temple?" asked Huaka'i.

"No," explained Kai. "This is the place where we share meals and gather to talk."

Huaka'i and the other warriors seemed equally in awe of the view greeting them at the top of the stairs. The central plaza, with its tree-lined stone paths and gardens, was a flurry of activity as people prepared tables for their guests. The aroma of unfamiliar foods and spices wafted from an ad hoc buffet table.

"Have we arrived at a time of celebration?"

"Your arrival *is* the celebration," explained Samaira in his native language.

Huaka'i smiled and bowed slightly, a sign her language skills were improving.

"We are honored," he replied on behalf of the others.

Behind them, Farzin slipped through the group and approached Jen.

"I checked their boat. Just a few spears that look more like fishing gear than weapons," he whispered.

"I'm not surprised. They seem to know about our little encounter at the beach with Pa'ao, and probably realized weapons would be useless."

"Well, at least we can relax a bit now."

"I'm not relaxed at all," replied Jen. "What do we know about any poisons they might have?"

"Nothing," he said, shaking his head.

"Take a look?" she suggested. "I'll stay here to see if any of them start sniffing around the food and water."

Farzin shook his head again.

"You ever lighten up?"

She raised an eyebrow but said nothing. Farzin sighed and trotted off to find a tablet to do some research.

The guests from Kaua'i were given water and shown to the facilities before their hosts invited them to sit at a few tables nearest the common building. There they dispersed among the recruits already seated. Samaira invited Huaka'i to sit opposite herself, Kai and Jen. As people continued filing down from their apartments along the crater wall, they filled most of the remaining tables. At Jen's insistence, they'd set several extra spaces to disguise the exact number of people on the island.

Jayson observed as Luni and her younger sister scanned the crowd of guests. A sudden, broad smile revealed she'd recognized someone. She scurried toward one of the tables, leading Palila by the hand. Jayson started as casually as possible for the same one, managing to claim the seat next to her. A broad-shouldered warrior sat across from them. His stern look melted into a smile the moment he noticed Luni and Palila.

"Luni," he said with a nod. "I'm happy to see you are safe and well."

"Thank you, Ino. It is good to see you escaped Moloka'i. How are my brothers and my father?"

The man's smile faded.

"Kameha is well on Kaua'i, but—"

He paused—the corners of his mouth turning down.

"What is it?" she demanded.

"Your father did not make it to the canoes, and we do not know what became of him."

"And Olakino?"

Ino closed his eyes and took a deep breath before delivering the blow.

"He fell defending our retreat to the canoes. He saved many lives."

The speed and nuance of the conversation required Jayson to follow along with the translator, which he'd muted to avoid distraction. As the terrible words appeared on the screen, he put his arm around Luni to comfort her. Ino glared at him for a moment before softening again to address Luni.

"Any warrior would be proud to die in such a way," he offered.

"But he wasn't any warrior, was he?" demanded Luni as tears streamed down her face. "He was my brother."

Palila was crying as well. Luni broke away from Jayson to embrace her sister, and the two rose from the table.

"Please excuse my sister and me," she said before hurrying away.

Jayson watched helplessly as they disappeared on the pathway leading up to the apartments. Turning back to the table, he found his guest drilling holes through his skull with his eyes.

***

At another table, Kai and Huaka'i were past the pleasantries, already discussing the reason for the visit. Jen, whose language skills were a bit behind many of the others, followed along on her tablet while Samaira tried her best to stay abreast of the conversation unaided.

"When Pa'ao returned to the beach at Hālawa, his men told the story of the—"

Huaka'i paused and looked at Samaira uncertainly.

"Kupua 'ele'ele," she said with amusement.

"Yes. The dark witch," he continued. "Their koa shields were shattered to pieces—and so were the bodies of the dead and injured among them."

"How did you learn this?" asked Kai.

"From the locals who stayed behind. Their legends say that when provoked, the demon of O'ahu will venture out to seek revenge. They feared Pa'ao had doomed all who remained on Moloka'i to death, and many slipped away in the night to join us on Kaua'i."

"If you are here, you no longer believe the demon is real."

Huaka'i eyed Samaira warily.

"We knew that you, and those you took, did not suffer the fate of Pa'ao's warriors. If there is a demon here, you have its favor."

"And you knew it was safe to come," concluded Kai.

"Safe or not, we knew we must come to O'ahu."

"Why?"

"Kameha sent us to forge an alliance—and to find his sisters for him," said Huaka'i. "He could not find them on the morning of the attack, and believed they might be safe here with you."

"They are safe," confirmed Kai.

"And he will be forever grateful to you. He lost his father and brother in the chaos of the retreat from Moloka'i. When we return with Luni and Palila, it will ease his grief."

Samaira squeezed Kai's thigh under the table before he could continue the conversation, motioning for Jen to unmute the tablet. The message she wanted to convey was too critical to allow misinterpretation.

"Whether you return with them or not, I'm sure Kameha will be relieved to know they are safe."

"Do you mean to hold them here?" asked Huaka'i, suddenly rigid in his seat.

"Of course not," assured Samaira. "Nor will we allow you to take them against their will."

Kai turned to her with a look of surprise, but she continued, undeterred.

"Everyone in our community has the right to self-determination," she said, placing her palm deliberately on the table. "We will defend that right for Luni and Palila."

"And if they choose to return to Kaua'i with us?"

"Then they will return with you."

Jen met Kai's gaze and raised an eyebrow, but neither spoke. Offering a nod of acknowledgment, if not acceptance, Huaka'i turned his attention to the food.

***

Following the feast, the exhausted visitors opted to make camp in the clearing just south of the settlement. They'd been offered the empty second-story apartments, but had politely declined. It was unclear whether they were wary of the enclosed space or the unfamiliar concept of a second floor. No sentry kept watch. They were all too tired—or simply resigned to the fact that no amount of warning would save them from the magic of O'ahu if their hosts decided they were unwelcome.

Farzin sat on a chair in a dark corner of the lanai overlooking the camp, certain he was wasting his time. He was only there to appease Jen. She'd promised to relieve him after discussing the offer of an alliance and the requested return of Kameha's sisters with the others inside.

"You had no right to make that kind of unilateral decision on our behalf," started Jen, waving a finger uncomfortably close to Samaira's face.

Usually seeking to diffuse tension, Samaira was uncharacteristically aggressive.

"This point is not up for negotiation. We're not trading our people like cattle."

"They're not our people. These are Kameha's sisters."

"And that makes them his property? What is it, then, that makes someone 'our people?' You want to set up an immigration bureaucracy? Maybe a citizenship test?"

"Please," interjected Kai. "Let's speak calmly."

Jen huffed and took a step back. Samaira was still regarding her through narrowed eyes.

"We need to consider Kameha's offer of allegiance," he continued. "If we hold his sisters, we will have three enemies to consider instead of two."

"We're not holding anyone," insisted Samaira, throwing her hands in the air.

"And the security team—*my* team—is not an enemy," added Jen. "We just need a chance to update them on—on the evolving situation."

Jayson watched the argument with detachment, slumped in a chair, as the two redirected their anger at Kai.

"We can't let them go," he said, mostly to himself.

"What?" asked Samaira, spinning around.

"I said we can't let them go."

"That's just as bad as forcing them to stay, Jayson," she replied. "It's their choice."

"But they have so much more opportunity here. Luni has an independent streak, and Palila is smart as hell. They could choose to do anything they want here."

"Including sacrificing some of their freedom for the good of their community," insisted Samaira. "We'll give them all the information we have and allow them to choose."

It was a pronouncement rather than an invitation to further debate, and neither Kai nor Jen had the will to keep the argument alive. Jayson slipped out quietly to find Luni as the others discussed the potential fallout from whatever decision she and her sister eventually made.

Volunteers were still cleaning up after the celebration, working together and chatting in small groups as they carried tables and chairs back inside and swept up the plaza. Jayson wandered nonchalantly to the north side by the clinic so as not to attract attention. Once out of sight, he picked up his pace, hurrying along the pathway to Luni's door. He knocked.

It took a moment for her to answer, cracking the door open just enough to poke her head out. Her eyes were red from crying.

"Hi Jayson. I'm not really in the mood for a movie tonight."

"I'm not here for that," he said in a hushed voice. "We have to talk."

"Can it wait until tomorrow? Palila's not handling the news of our brother very well."

Jayson could tell it wasn't just Palila having a difficult night, but insisted anyway.

"I wish it could wait. But it really can't. Something terrible is happening."

"Is there a fight?" she demanded, opening the door a bit more before stepping outside.

"No. Nothing like that," he replied with a glance over his shoulder. "Please. Can I come in?"

Luni relented and invited him inside.

"What's wrong?" she asked.

"Your brother sent Ino and the others here to take you back to Kaua'i," he said, taking her by the hand. "But we're not going to let them."

"What?"

"He wants to trade you for an alliance like you're some piece of property," he spat. "I won't allow it."

"I—I don't know what to say."

"It's okay, Luni. Just remember you don't have to do anything Ino tells you tomorrow, okay? You're one of us now."

Luni stared at him in silence as she digested the news. Palila walked into the room with fresh tears running down her face.

"What is it?" she asked.

"Nothing," said Luni. "We're just talking about our visitors."

"I can't sleep. Will you come and hold me?"

"Of course I will," she assured before turning back to Jayson. "Thank you for telling me, but you should go now."

"I understand. And I'm sorry to hear about your brother."

"Thank you, Jayson. Good night."

Outside of her door, Jayson breathed a sigh of relief, thankful he'd gotten to her before anyone else could spin the news.

***

The following morning, the people of Honolulu brought a traditional breakfast down to their guests, along with some novelties like sweet pastries and mixed non-native berries. They had their own breakfast separately to discuss Kameha's offer of allegiance, and the implied quid pro quo of returning his sisters. Though Luni and Palila were the subjects of the discussion, they'd said little. Neither had slept well. Black bags hung under their red, puffy eyes, and they mostly stared absently at the floor.

"While an alliance with Kameha and the rulers of Kaua'i would be a benefit," explained Samaira, "we can't just hand people over. We won't."

"It's a bullshit demand anyway," added Farzin. "Without our help, Pili is going to roll right over them. They'll agree to an alliance, no matter what."

"For sure," agreed Jayson. "We don't need to give them anything besides protection."

"Who said anything about giving them protection?" demanded Jen. "I thought we were talking about a non-aggression pact. We can't spare the manpower to watch over two islands."

"They don't need people. Just weapons," said Jayson.

"No fucking way," said Jen, shaking her head. "That's out of the question."

"The point is," reminded Farzin, "they have nothing to offer that would justify forcing Luni and Palila to leave with them."

"That's off the table," said Samaira. "No matter what benefit it might bring, only Luni and Palila can decide what to do."

"It's not fair to put that burden on them," insisted Jayson. "It's—it's coercion."

"Being part of a society isn't about unlimited freedom, Jayson," scolded Samaira. "People make sacrifices for what they believe in, too. We can't deny them the opportunity to decide for themselves."

"Palila's just a kid. A bit young to be talking about sacrifice, don't you think?"

"I am not!" she protested.

It was the first thing she'd said all morning. They stopped talking and looked at her.

"Besides," added Luni, raising her eyes from the floor, "we have already decided what to do."

There was something about the way she said it that twisted Jayson's stomach into a knot.

"Last night," she continued, "when Jayson told me you would never let Huaka'i take me, it reminded me how much you have done for us. Palila and I spoke about it for hours—how you helped Kai, and how your friend Kailani gave her life for him."

"No," said Jayson, shaking his head. "You don't have to do this. You heard what Farzin said."

"Kameha mourns the death of our brother and our missing father alone," she added, turning to Jayson. "We will go, knowing we will see you again soon."

"You can't!"

"Jayson," said Samaira as she placed a hand on his shoulder. "If this is their choice, we'll respect it."

"Was it their choice?" he demanded. "Or just more manipulation? Haven't we all had enough of that?"

"No, Jayson," assured Luni. "Kameha needs what is left of his family right now. And so do we."

Jayson rushed out ahead of everyone else as the meeting ended. He felt like he was going to throw up, even though he hadn't eaten a thing. He kept walking without looking back, afraid he might start crying at any moment. How would that look to Luni? Ino, the warrior who had sat across from them at dinner the evening before, probably never cried. He quickened his pace as footsteps closed in from behind.

"Jayson. Wait."

It was Luni. He steeled himself, choking back his emotions as he turned around.

"I've got work to do," he said.

It came out sounding colder than he'd meant. Maybe that was a good thing.

"Please. Don't be angry. If I can be your ambassador to Kameha and the people of Kaua'i, I can repay the kindness you have shown."

"I'm not angry. I'm—. I don't know what I am. I just don't want to see you go."

"I don't believe this is the end for us, Jayson. It is a new beginning for *all* of us."

She took his hand and smiled with hopeful eyes.

"I get it," he assured, fighting to stay composed, "but I've really got to get some stuff done."

He slid his hand from hers and headed for the fields without looking back.

***

By late morning, Luni and Palila had gathered what few possessions they needed to join Huaka'i, Ino, and the other emissaries from Kaua'i at the harbor. Their hosts provided food and water for the long journey that would not see them arriving until the following evening.

Everyone was there to see them off, even Jayson. Samaira had sent Jen to fetch him from the grove of fruit trees he was tending to convince him he'd regret not saying goodbye. Even so, he stayed mostly hidden behind the others in case his emotions got the better of him. Palila scanned the crowd desperately as the men prepared the canoe. Her eyes lit up when she finally saw him.

"Jayson!" she yelled, running over.

She threw her arms around him, and he picked her up.

"Thank you for being our friend and teaching us so much. I will miss you."

"I will miss you, too," he said.

After a final squeeze, he set her down and kneeled before her.

"Be good. And listen to your sister."

His lip quivered. It was impossible to fight the tears welling up, and they streamed down his face. Luni came over to join them. Jayson sniffled, trying desperately to recompose himself. She started crying, too, as they embraced.

"Luni. It's time to go," someone called.

Jayson looked up and saw Ino sneering at him. He let go of Luni and quickly wiped his face, imagining the warrior must think him pathetic.

"You've got to go," he sniffed.

"I will see you again soon," she promised.

She took Palila by the hand and led her to the waiting canoe. Wading into the harbor, they turned to wave one last time before getting in to find a seat among the warriors, who started paddling immediately. The crowd of onlookers slowly thinned as the canoe grew smaller into the distance until only Jayson and Jen remained—just as it had been the day they last saw Jasmine's Hope.

"That was tough for you," observed Jen.

"Yeah," he admitted. "It was."

"Will Jayson ever get the girl?" she asked as if narrating a cheesy romcom.

He snorted, shaking his head with a wry smile.

"Who knows?"

"Listen," she said. "I know this probably isn't the best time, but I'm up for some fun if you are."

Jayson took a deep breath.

"Yeah," he shrugged finally. "Why not?"

Chapter 6

SHANNON BOUCHER'S PHONE BUZZED again as it slid a few millimeters across her desk. It was her personal phone, not the secure FBI-issued one she kept clipped to her side at every waking moment. She wouldn't have ignored that one. It was probably just Jessica again, asking if she'd looked into that thing with the Center for Sustainability Research. Shannon didn't want to get involved. She'd listened sympathetically when Jessica had vented about her encounter with one of their people a few months earlier, and assumed it was some kind of personal vendetta that had prompted her recent inquiry.

In the end, she'd relented and agreed to investigate. Jessica could be manipulative, and had a way of making Shannon feel like she owed her something. As it had been when they were married, it was often less exhausting to just give in. At least now, it was only a random favor rather than the draining daily ordeal it had been before she'd gotten her freedom back.

She'd agreed to run a few queries through the system to placate her ex-wife, and then planned to assure her nothing was going on. Now, Shannon wasn't so sure of that herself. Taken individually, there was nothing remarkable about the reports on file. But, as a whole, it was a bit more troubling. A pattern of abuse—corruption, even—emerged from the data on the FBI system; one so blatant their algorithms should have flagged it.

There were a few complaints from a local building inspector about circumventing the permitting process. Stopping short of an outright accusation of bribery, it was heavily implied in the reports. Then, there was the odd missing person's report from the Los Angeles field office. The Srinivasan family insisted their daughter was missing, despite returning text messages and leaving a couple of voicemails. Something subtle about the things she said and how she'd said them gave her mother chills.

An analyst had been reviewing the complaint as a possible abduction, and was about to ask the Honolulu field office to follow up when the body washed ashore. The autopsy showed nothing out of the ordinary, so the case was closed. The order to drop the follow-up visit to her employer hadn't come from the analyst in LA, but straight from Washington. There was an eerie parallel to Jessica's story. Shannon had written it off to her penchant for drama, but in both cases, the cease-and-desist had come from somewhere high in the D.C. bureaucracy.

As she dug beyond the FBI documents, she found that even the land deal for The Center for Sustainability Research made little sense. The U.S. government leased land to private companies all the time—especially when their technology had military applications. There was no sign the western part of Joint Base Pearl Harbor-Hickam was even under consideration for lease, and then, suddenly, it was a done deal. Stranger still, there was no evidence that the Navy had undertaken the requisite due diligence prior to handing it over. There was a process, and it wasn't just a suggestion. It was written into law. Those kinds of strings couldn't be pulled by just anyone. Investigating the Center for Sustainability Research had 'career limiting move' written all over it, and she wasn't going to poke at it. Whatever was going on, she resolved to downplay it with Jessica and walk away.

Her personal phone buzzed again. This time, Shannon finally looked. As expected, it was a hit from Jessica.

"Goddammit, Shannon, is that your phone or do you have a vibrator over there?"

"Eat it, Tanaka," she replied, tossing a rubber stress ball over the divider that separated her desk from Special Agent Daniel Tanaka's.

"It's been buzzing nonstop for five minutes."

"Mind your own business."

"But my business is boring," he complained, standing up to peer over the divider. "Your drama is the most excitement I get in a day."

She shook her head, flipping her middle finger at him.

"So it *is* her," he chuckled. "What is it this time? Shared custody of a cactus?"

She raised an eyebrow, but and said nothing.

"Fine," he allowed, sinking back into his chair. "None of my business."

She smiled to herself and shook her head before turning her attention back to the phone.

U there?

Yeah. Just busy
What's up?

U tell me

Not much

Meet me Saturday AM?
It's important

Shit.

Where?

Pearlridge market
Usual place @ 8:30

Ok

The weekly farmer's market near the townhouse they'd shared was one of the happy memories of their time together. Choosing to meet there—at their favorite coffee shop—was a classic manipulation tactic. That was okay. Shannon was stronger now, and knew how to handle the situation.

***

Every Saturday morning, from 8:00 until noon, the parking lot at the southwest end of Pali Momi Street on the north side of Pearl Harbor filled with the sound of traditional Hawaiian music as vendors gather to sell local produce, meats, and flowers. Once a ritual for her and Jessica, it was the first time Special Agent Boucher had been there in months. She'd arrived early to buy a few groceries when the vendors were still setting up. A lot of groceries, actually—more than she could eat in a week. The unwieldy collection of bags was part of a plan to preempt any suggestion by her ex that they should go shopping together after getting coffee.

Shannon arrived at the coffee shop with a few minutes to spare, lucky to find a table among the growing crowd of market-goers. The smell was intoxicating. The fresh fruit in her bags, the coffee and toasting bagels—it was like traveling through time to a place that didn't exist anywhere but in memories. She considered getting a coffee while she waited, but couldn't decide how that would go down. If she bought Jessica's favorite, she might take it as a sign of a reconciliation that wasn't going to happen. If she just got one for herself, it might seem like she was being a bitch. By the time she was done overthinking, it was too late. Jessica waved and joined the lineup, bringing an imaginary cup to her lips to let Shannon know she'd grab them both a coffee before coming over.

"Hey," she greeted as she set two steaming cups down on the table and nodded at the collection of bags at Shannon's feet. "You've been busy this morning."

"Needed a few things," replied Shannon with a shrug.

"So what you got for me?"

No small talk. It was a good sign.

"Not much. Your friends at the center might be assholes, but we don't have any reason to think they're criminals."

"Assholes, for sure," she agreed. "Nothing else?"

"Not really," she replied, shaking her head.

"You asked me to meet in person to tell me that?"

"What? You asked me."

"Don't try to gaslight me, Shannon. What do you want?"

Agent Boucher sighed and leaned back in her chair.

"Whatever game you're playing, I don't have the energy."

She opened the Hitz-It app and set her phone on the table in front of Jessica to show her there was no point in lying.

Jessica stared at it for a few moments before pulling out her own phone to examine them side by side.

"What the hell is this?" she demanded. "Some kind of new FBI tech you're using to fuck with me?"

She spun both phones around and sat back with her arms crossed. Shannon snorted, determined to put an end to whatever kind of game this was. After examining them herself, she shook her head in disbelief.

"I didn't write this. I'm here because you asked me."

"Fuckers!" spat Jessica, slamming a fist on the table and spilling some coffee over the side of her cup.

An old couple at a nearby table glared at her.

"Don't you see?" she said, leaning in and lowering her voice. "It's their app. It's their fucking app!"

"Watch my stuff," said Shannon as she rose from the table and took out her work phone.

She was willing to ignore things she could pretend she hadn't seen, but if they were really going after her directly? Then it was game on.

***

Charlie Hoang was a lucky man. He and his wife were in good health, and did not want for anything. More importantly, they'd raised two fine sons and a beautiful daughter, all with college degrees and healthy children of their own. Only the unfaithful would be so blind as to ignore the role of God in providing such a blessing. God had given him everything a man could want—and every Saturday, he gave back.

He left his home a little after 8:00, as he always did, driving to the market to pick up fresh food for those in need. He'd started small years earlier, doing what he could and buying a couple of bags of groceries every week before walking them over to his nearby church and helping to distribute them among parcels of donations from the other parishioners.

As his income grew over time, so did his generosity. Eventually, some of the vendors learned what he was doing and began offering him discounts and free surplus produce when harvests were good. Gone were the days when he could walk his haul the few blocks to the church. Now he had an honorary parking spot for his hybrid-electric SUV between two vendor stalls, and someone even hung a tongue-in-cheek plywood sign every Saturday morning to ensure it was available. 'Reserved for St. Charlie,' it read.

Rounding the corner from Moanalua Road to Pali Momi Street, he felt a tug on the steering wheel. The fancy driver assist options on his new SUV were hard to get used to. He didn't like the idea of having less than total control of the vehicle, but it's not like they sold them without it anymore. Just as he started to relax after the unexpected input, his SUV lurched forward under the full power of its dual five hundred horsepower electric motors, pressing him back into his seat. He pounded on the brake pedal, but it was unresponsive. Instinct took over, and he began looking for a break in the foot traffic on the sidewalk to his right so he could stop himself against the trunk of a palm tree before he slammed into another vehicle and killed someone. The driver assist fought his efforts, and the SUV continued accelerating southwest on Pali Momi.

As it approached the next intersection, it veered to the right, heading for the building on the corner at nearly seventy-five miles per hour. Charlie could see the people standing in line getting coffee, an elderly couple sitting by the window, and a woman staring at her phone. Even though he only had fractions of a second, he absorbed the most minute details of the lives he was about to destroy. The elderly woman was talking. Her lightweight scarf had butterflies on it. Her husband was pretending to listen, but his mind was elsewhere. The woman with the phone was angry. A purse and another phone were on the table in front of her. Bags of groceries were arranged at her feet.

Then, his SUV hopped the curb as the customers inside began turning their heads toward the street. His last sensation was a millisecond of odd comfort, knowing they'd have no time for even a moment of terrifying recognition before the end.

***

Shannon's world exploded in a shower of broken glass. The body of the elderly man slammed into her, knocking her to the ground. Her phone flew from her hand and skipped along the floor. There was no more than a second of eerie silence before the coffee shop erupted in screams. She scurried forward on her elbows and knees, cutting herself on the glass littering the floor. Grabbing her phone, she fumbled to dial 911 with shaking hands. It took three tries to punch it in correctly.

"Nine-one-one. What is your emergency?"

"This is Special Agent Shannon Boucher of the FBI. Multiple fatalities and injuries at the corner of Pali Moma and Haukapila. Send fire and ambulance now!"

"Agent Boucher, I'm going to—"

Shannon ended the call and struggled to her feet. Pain shot through her right side, intensifying with every breath. Probably broken ribs, she realized. A crushed SUV with its deployed airbags hanging out of the broken driver's side window was lodged in the pastry display, which had itself been pushed up against the far wall, crushing an employee against the row of coffee machines. An elderly man was slumped motionless against the steering wheel. The speeding vehicle had obliterated everything in its path, including the table where she'd been sitting moments before.

"Jessica?" she called in vain, realizing there was no hope for anyone who had been on that side of the coffee shop.

By now, people were rushing into the building to see who needed help.

"Are you okay? You're bleeding."

Shannon turned with a start. A man in a ball cap took her by the arm.

"I'm fine," she replied, looking around in shock.

Still, she didn't resist as he guided her from the building to sit her in the shade against the undamaged side of the building among a growing number of survivors. The initial rush of adrenaline that had allowed her training to guide the first few minutes after the crash was subsiding, and she shook uncontrollably. She had almost died. An FBI agent—and she'd almost died at the hands of some senile old man who probably shouldn't have been driving in the first place instead of in the line of duty. How ironic would that be? And Jessica was dead. There was no denying it. She knew it was true, even if she was still in too much shock to apply meaning to it. For now, it was like something that had happened in a movie. Jessica was dead, but it wasn't real yet.

The wail of sirens drew closer, and several emergency vehicles converged on the intersection. Firemen and paramedics poured into the building as a pair of police cars pulled halfway onto the sidewalk. An officer approached.

"Agent Boucher?" he called. "Is there an Agent Boucher here?"

"Over here," she called, raising her hand.

She winced as pain shot across her right side.

"I need you to come with me for a debrief."

"Woah," called a paramedic. "She's not going anywhere until I check her out."

"This is a matter of national security," said the officer. "Could be an ongoing terrorist threat."

The hair on Shannon's neck stood on end. Something didn't feel right. Why would Honolulu PD take her away from the scene? Why would they be raising terrorism concerns? It wasn't their role.

"I'll get to her next," assured the paramedic. "Just hold tight."

"My phone," said Shannon.

"It has evidence on it."

"Where is it?" demanded one of the officers.

"Under that SUV in there," she said, motioning with her thumb.

He turned to his colleague and nodded.

"Don't worry. We'll find it for you," he assured. "Just wait here."

They rushed into the building while she pulled out her FBI-issued phone to make the call she hadn't had time to place before the crash. Holding her finger over the button for a moment, she thought better of it. Something was off, and she didn't know what. Struggling to her feet, she broke the phone in half and tossed it in a nearby trash can.

The busy paramedic wasn't paying attention as she started down the street towards the market against a throng of people coming to see about the commotion. The blood on her hands and face attracted a few second looks, but nobody tried to stop her. Looking back over her shoulder one last time, she ducked in among the vendor stalls and worked her way to the west side of the market.

There was a Starbucks on the other side of a watercress field flanking the parking lot where she could clean herself up and figure out how to get home to her gun and badge unnoticed. It wouldn't be easy. Her wallet, keys, and all the money she'd been carrying were underneath the mess back at the coffee shop.

Chapter 7

RICHARD WAS ENJOYING A leisurely cup of coffee in his backyard, feeling rejuvenated. He'd had a rare chance to sleep in after his wife volunteered to get up with the dog when it jumped on the bed at 6:30 AM and started sniffing at their faces to let them know he was hungry. By the time he got to the kitchen to make himself a coffee, it was already past 8:30. On a weekday—and plenty of weekends, for that matter—he'd already be sitting at his desk going over his agenda.

Today, he had time to take it slow because he and his youngest daughter weren't teeing off until 1:15. He was looking forward to some overdue father-daughter time, and an opportunity to get his mind off his Akindele problem while hooking a few balls into the rough. He hated golf, but he loved his daughter—and she loved golf. It reminded him he needed to ask someone on Delta to bring along a few balls and clubs so there'd be a robust golf culture for her to enjoy when they arrived centuries later.

"Another coffee, honey?" called his wife, Cecelia, poking her head out the patio door.

"I can get it, Sissy," he offered, rising to his feet.

"No," she insisted. I'll bring it out."

A few minutes later, she came out with two steaming cups, setting them on the glass-topped table.

"Thanks, sweetheart," he said.

She leaned over and kissed him before sitting down and taking a sip.

"I saw your old friend Spencer on the television this morning," she said.

"Admiral Daniels?"

"Yes. He was talking about the new submarine program."

"The Columbia class," said Richard. "Impressive piece of technology."

"He was with the captain who'll be testing the first one—talking about the crew controversy."

"Really? I haven't been following. What's going on?"

"It's going to be a nearly fifty-fifty split crew of men and women."

"They've had women on subs for a while now, if I recall."

"Yeah, but people are up in arms over it this time. Some senators and congressmen are freaking out about ruining the Navy with 'wokeness,' whatever that is."

"People will always find something to complain about," he shrugged. "Too many women, not enough women—it's just noise."

"What do you think about it?"

"I'm not in the Navy anymore," he replied, shaking his head. "Doesn't mean a thing to me."

In reality, it meant a lot to Richard after the Gamma disaster. Initially, the gender balance of Delta hadn't been much of a consideration, as they'd expected to be joining a healthy population of thousands where any imbalance would be easily absorbed. Now there was doubt about the nature and severity of the reset that might be necessary. Hopefully, Olena and the other SEALs had managed to keep things under control, but the simulations showed the possibility of some disturbing outlier scenarios that would require a harsh response.

"I bet you'd have liked that," teased Cecelia.

"What?" he asked, glancing up from his phone.

"Being locked in a submarine with a crew of fit young women."

"Sweetheart," he replied with a mischievous grin, "if I had to choose anyone to get locked into a pressurized steel cylinder with me, it would be you."

"Thanks," she laughed, leaning over to swat him playfully with the back of her hand. "I appreciate that."

His phone buzzed, and a notification slid down from the top of the screen. It was a hit from Rebecca.

"Shit," he said under his breath.

Need you at the Center
ASAP

What's up?

Emergency
Bunch of us are here

You on O'ahu?

Yes. Get over here

"Everything okay?" asked Cecelia.

"I've got to take care of something at work," he replied, rising from the table.

His heart skipped a beat, realizing Rebecca was on the island and he hadn't known about it. It was a worrying sign. He glanced at his watch, hoping he'd be able to deal with whatever it was in time to get to his game, but part of him already knew he was kidding himself.

"I hope it won't take too long. You're picking up Liz, remember?"

"I'm sure it'll be just an hour or two," he replied, rushing off to take a quick shower. "Tell her we might have to meet at the club."

***

Rebecca and Cal were involved in an intense discussion with a pair of techs from site security when Richard arrived in the third-floor conference room. Looking at several video feeds on the interactive wall, they didn't notice him come in. Instead, they were focused on a scene of devastation; a destroyed storefront flanked by emergency vehicles with flashing lights.

"What's going on?" he asked.

"We've got a situation," replied Rebecca. "And there could be fallout."

"What happened?"

"We uncovered some chatter about the Center and tried to shut it down."

"Why didn't you call me? This kind of thing is my deal."

"You have enough to worry about with Delta, so I decided to handle this without you."

"Yeah? And how'd that work out?" he asked with a snort, looking at the chaos displayed on the wall.

She glared at him without a word.

"I'm sorry, Rebecca," he offered. "That came out wrong. What, exactly, am I looking at?"

"This is a coffee shop in Waimalu—where an old friend of yours was meeting with an FBI agent."

"What?"

"Does the name Jessica Reyes sound familiar?"

"The OSHA bitch," he recalled with a sneer. "What's she up to now?"

"Well, apparently, her ex is an FBI agent. They were meeting for coffee this morning."

"*Was* an FBI agent," corrected Richard. "At least by the look of things."

"That was the idea. We had both of their phones locked into a three-foot radius, but Special Agent Boucher managed to avoid the crash."

"What crash?"

"We overrode the driver assist on an SUV and put it right on top of them."

"Jesus Christ! Do you know how risky that is? Cleaning up the traces of something like that is a nightmare."

"I've got the geeks on it," she assured, gesturing to the site security techs. "They say they've got everything covered."

"Except the FBI agent. How badly is he hurt? What hospital is he at?"

"*She* slipped away. We've got footage of her tossing a second phone before heading southwest, but we lost her in the market crowd. No new hits yet."

"Special Agent Boucher is a she? Should've known that OSHA bitch was a dyke."

Rebecca put her hands on her hips and glared at him.

"So, she's alive, on the loose, and suspicious enough to toss her phone?" continued Richard, ignoring her reaction.

"Seems so," replied Rebecca, still glaring.

"Shit. Assets on the scene?"

"She dodged them."

"This is a nightmare, Rebecca. A real fucking goat rodeo. Does Anton know?"

"I briefed him."

"Can we get him on a call? I'd like to know what he's thinking."

"I spoke to him. He's thinking about Epsilon," said Rebecca. "It's the only hope for humanity, and we have to defend it at all costs."

There wasn't going to be a call with Kamaras, Richard realized. Rebecca had become his gatekeeper over the last several years, effectively shielding him from any viewpoint but her own. Either she was hiding her screwup from him, or he'd said all he cared to say on the matter.

"Nuclear option?" asked Richard with a frown.

"Not yet. We've got to keep some powder dry. Things will scale up fast leading into Epsilon, and we'll need the distraction."

"Okay. What are the algos saying? What does she do next?"

***

Shannon wasn't sure she was acting rashly. After all, she'd just been through a traumatic event, watching the world around her disintegrate in an instant. Jessica was dead, for sure. Though she hadn't actually *seen* the impact or the body, there was no doubt about the result. It would be understandable—expected, even—if she was in shock. Victims of severe trauma often did crazy things. She once watched a woman trying to put her dead husband's arm back on in the aftermath of a police chase gone wrong. Was that her now? Was she the one incapable of rational thought?

On her way to the Starbucks on the other side of the watercress farm, she'd ducked into a wooden shed among the flooded canals. While she needed an opportunity to catch her breath, it was an overwhelming urge to hide that had driven her into the crude shelter. She could see no pursuers, but felt eyes everywhere. If she and Jessica had been lured into a trap by Anton Kamaras—an assertion that sounded insane and paranoid even as it materialized in her head—then he could have access to every camera phone and security surveillance system in the immediate area. Going to a crowded Starbucks would be like announcing her location with a bullhorn.

Her colleagues' phones—maybe even the secure FBI ones—would be targeted already. Anyone she knew who could come and help her was connected to her via Kamaras's app. So it would be naïve to think he wasn't already waiting for her to reach out. And those cops. Were they legit? What assets could a man of his wealth bring to bear? And, more importantly, what the hell could he be up to that would warrant a level of operational capability she'd typically associate with a hostile nation? It didn't make sense. She felt like one of those lunatics who called the FBI complaining that Bill Gates was reading their minds with his 5G microchips.

She couldn't hide out in the watercress forever, she couldn't reach out to a friend, and she sure as hell couldn't walk around looking like the survivor of a zombie apocalypse. If she walked up to a random cop without her FBI credentials, he'd probably think she was nuts and call it in. That, too, was out of the question. Where could she find an ally she could trust? Then she remembered the man that had set Jessica on the Center in the first place. Don something. The building inspector. A real winner, Jessica had said. Not likely the ideal ally, but at least someone she could reach out to—if she could get herself together and figure out how to find him.

Shannon waited in the shed until the early hours of Sunday morning, thankful no workers had stumbled upon her hiding place. Then, disguised with an old hat and a pair of overalls she found hanging on a peg on the back of the door, she crawled her way through the watercress farm, wishing it was a different crop that could have provided her with more cover. Even on her hands and knees, she felt exposed while working her way across the raised pathways between the flooded sections of the field.

She waded across the canal at the south end of the field and crawled up the bank to the sidewalk by the highway. Slinking about now would only make her stand out more. Relying on her disguise, she adopted a gait she imagined fitting for a drug addict or homeless person as she crossed the highway towards a gas station on the opposite side. She could see a phone booth, but had no idea if there would be an actual functioning phone there. She tried to remember the last time she'd used one—or even seen someone else using one.

Approaching the phone booth, she located the gas station security cameras and positioned herself to avoid them as much as possible. Then she picked up the phone, breathing a sigh of relief at the welcoming dial tone. There was even an intact phonebook—a relic from another age dangling from the end of a chain.

How many permutations of Don Lee, Donald Lee, or D. Lee could there be in the O'ahu phonebook? Considering the number of people with Chinese heritage, it could be a lot. She was relieved to find there were only eight. With her own phone, she'd be able to get some demographic information or compare the addresses with Don's office location to figure out where to start. The only option now was to work her way through the list one by one. She picked up the phone again and then cursed under her breath. She didn't have any quarters.

***

It took Shannon most of the morning to work her way to the fifth name on her list; a D. Lee with an address in the Kapalama neighborhood. Not wanting to be shooed away by the gas station attendant or, worse yet, have them call the police to report her for vagrancy, she'd taken her time quietly begging change from people who looked least likely to raise a fuss. The elderly tourist couple that had given her the last quarter even came out of the station with a cup of coffee and a prepackaged sandwich for her, handing over the much-appreciated meal as they expressed hope that she would be well, and one day seek salvation.

She took her time eating the sandwich—not because she was savoring it, but rather because it took a while to masticate the stale, dry bread with its stingy portion of condiments into a consistency she could force down her throat. Still, she was thankful for the generosity and compassion shown to her by a pair of complete strangers. After some of the cases she'd worked, small encounters such as these reminded her why she was an agent, and validated that at least some part of humanity was worthy of serving.

Shannon washed down the last of the sandwich with a gulp of coffee and jammed the wrapper into her empty cup before tossing both into a nearby garbage can. Then she headed over to the payphone to try her luck again. Picking up the receiver, she dialed the number and held her breath.

"Hello?" greeted the male voice on the other end of the line.

"Hello. Is this Don Lee?"

"Yes. How can I help you?"

"I'm looking for Don Lee, the building inspector. Is that you?"

"Yes, but I'm afraid I work for the city. I don't do private consulting," he replied apologetically. "I'm happy to recommend someone if you like."

"I don't need a building inspector. I'm looking for you."

There was a pause on the other end.

"Who is this?"

"I'm a friend of a friend," she replied, afraid to say her name—or Jessica's. "I need some help."

"I'm sorry, but I think you must have the wrong number."

"Wait!" pleaded Shannon. "Don't hang up. A couple of days ago, you asked a friend for a favor—over lunch."

"Jes—"

"Don't say it! Do you remember what you asked her to do?"

Again, there was silence.

"It's me, Mr. Lee," she continued. "The person she was supposed to contact."

"Sha—"

"Jesus Christ! Don't say it!"

"What the hell is going on?"

"I'll tell you everything, but I need your help first."

"You need my help? But you're an F—"

"Shut up and listen, Don! I need you to come and get me."

***

Thirty minutes later, Don Lee pulled up to the gas station. He patted the steering wheel nervously, looking around for Shannon, and nearly jumped out of his skin when she rapped a knuckle on the passenger window. Seeing only a disheveled vagrant, he waved her off and continued scanning the lot. She knocked on the window again and motioned for him to roll it down.

"I don't have any change," he said, shaking his head.

"Mr. Lee, it's me. Shannon."

He blinked a few times in disbelief before fumbling to unlock the door.

"Holy shit! What happened to you?"

She glanced around before sliding into the passenger seat.

"Let's get out of here," she advised. "I've already been here way too long."

Don eased his way into the eastbound lanes of the Kamehameha Highway and started driving, glancing wide-eyed at Shannon every few seconds.

"Where are we going?" he asked finally.

"Your place," she replied.

"My place? You're an FBI agent. Can't I take you to headquarters or something?"

"Not until I figure out what the hell is going on."

"What the hell *is* going on?" he demanded. "Why do you look like a homeless junkie?"

"They attacked us—I think. Jessica and me."

"What? Who?"

"I'm not sure," she admitted. "Your friends at the Center, I think. You hear about the crash at the market across from the gas station yesterday?"

"Holy shit! You were there?"

"Jessica and I. Yes."

Don's jaw dropped.

"Oh my God! Is she alright?"

He glanced at her with desperation in his eyes. Shannon took a deep breath and shook her head. Turning his attention to the highway, Don gripped the steering wheel so tightly his knuckles started turning white. Neither spoke for at least a minute.

"I'm sorry," said Shannon finally.

"You're sorry? I'm the one who killed her. Jesus Christ! I knew those guys were bad news, and I just couldn't let it go."

"It's not your fault," she assured, putting a hand on his shoulder. "You didn't know they would go this far."

"Didn't I?" he asked, turning to meet her eyes.

Again the pair fell silent, exchanging few words before arriving at Don's house. Inside, he got Shannon settled in, offering her a fresh towel and some clean sweats before showing her to the bathroom, where she could clean herself up.

"I wasn't expecting company," he called through the closed door. "I'm going to go out to grab a few things. You want anything in particular?"

The only response was the sound of the shower faucet turning on, followed by the gush of water.

Chapter 8

In the weeks following Luni's departure, Jayson found distraction in the fields by day and Jen's apartment by night. She didn't seem interested in a committed relationship, which was okay with him. He wasn't interested in one at the moment, either.

When he allowed introspection, he admitted to himself he was sleeping with her as a form of petty revenge against Luni for abandoning their budding relationship. Nothing to be proud of, he realized, but felt it must count for something that he could at least recognize it for what it was. He also recognized what it was doing to him. He paid for each moment of brief comfort with steadily increasing misery and self-loathing.

Seeking some time alone, he sat in a quiet corner of the lanai with a tablet after breakfast, gazing past the screen at the horizon on the other side of the harbor. Herman found him there and pulled up a chair.

"I have excellent news, my friend," he said, rubbing his hands together. "The first batch of ale is ready to try."

"That's great," replied Jayson. "How'd it turn out?"

He tried to sound more enthusiastic than he felt.

"I don't know. I wouldn't dream of trying it without the man whose barley and hops made it possible."

"So what's the plan?"

"Tonight. At my place," replied Herman. "Just you and me. We'll be the first to sample it."

"Zaina okay with you having a guys' night?"

"I'm sure she'll manage just fine."

"How much you got?"

"Almost twenty liters."

"I guess that'll just about do since there's only two of us," said Jayson with a forced laugh.

Herman nodded somberly.

"She'll come back, Jayson," he said.

"Who?"

"Be stoic if you want," said Herman, "but I'm ready to listen when you're ready to talk."

"And you were thinking the beer might help with that?"

"I didn't think it would hurt."

"Probably not," agreed Jayson. "I'm down for it."

"Excellent," said Herman with a clap of his hands. "After dinner at my place."

"I'll be there."

***

Jayson was grateful for the solitude his work afforded when he needed to be alone. Pruning the fruit tree saplings and checking them for signs of stress distanced him from the light banter of a group of people picking vegetables, among whom his brooding would have been noticeable.

He was lost for hours in his own world, absently snipping away at dead and damaged branches as though on autopilot. He'd built a considerable stack of twigs at the side of the orchard by the time someone finally called out to him, snapping him back to reality. It was Mano's wife, Anuenue, who'd become a fixture in the fields, and had a special gift for agriculture.

"Jayson, someone has come to the harbor."

The words didn't immediately register. Anuenue gestured for him to follow her and the others, already heading down to see what was happening.

"Luni!" he realized.

Had it been the security team, someone would have rushed up to tell him sooner. He slipped the pruners into his pocket, dusting his hands off on the front of his pants before jogging up to join the back of the procession.

By the time they arrived at the harbor, four men were already wading through the water, pushing an outrigger toward the beach. Four others remained in their seats. Jayson searched vainly for signs of more people, but there were none. Just eight; all men. His shoulders sank in disappointment, and he hung back to watch while the others hurried forward to greet their guests. He recognized most of them from the previous visit. Huaka'i had returned, along with Ino and some of the other warriors.

An older man he didn't recognize, elaborately dressed and adorned with a colorful headdress, stood in their midst. Solemnly, Huaka'i introduced him to Kai and Samaira. Jayson was too far away to overhear anything, but noted how they both nodded deferentially to the man. He must have some position of honor. Jayson hoped that didn't mean there would be another celebration. He wasn't in the mood.

In contrast to the others, Ino looked unhappy. Ignoring the introductions, he scanned the crowd, looking for someone. Jayson gulped involuntarily when Ino's eyes locked onto his, and the menacing warrior started towards him. He briefly considered leaving, but his curiosity got the better of him. Ino was obviously interested in Luni. If he felt he had a score to settle, Jayson wanted to know why. He took a deep breath to prepare for the confrontation.

"Aloha, Jayson," he said, extending a hand.

"Aloha, Ino."

They shook hands in the island tradition, gripping one another by the forearm.

"Makemake au e wala'au iā 'oe," said Ino.

"'Ae. Kali pokole," replied Jayson, looking around.

Jayson motioned for Ino to follow as he headed toward Serge, standing among those greeting the new arrivals. He almost always had a tablet with him.

"Hey, Serge," he said with a tap on the shoulder. "Can I borrow that tablet for a sec?"

"Sure," he said, handing it over with a polite nod to their guest.

The pair maneuvered out of the crowd to a quieter place before Jayson opened Kailani's app.

"Is everything okay? Is Luni well?"

"Luni is well," replied Ino with a somber nod.

"But something's wrong," he prodded.

"I know how you feel about her. I feel the same way."

"I—she's important to me."

"She asked me to tell you something for her."

"What?" demanded Jayson.

"She is sorry."

Jayson's heart sank, and he felt his extremities going numb.

"Why does she need to be sorry?" he asked, dreading the answer.

"She is to wed Moeanaimua, the eldest son of Paumakua, the ruler of Kaua'i."

"What? Why?"

"Kameha arranged it without her knowledge to seal their alliance."

Jayson was agape.

"I am sorry, too," added Ino.

"For what?"

"When I came with Huaka'i to get her, I did not know Kameha's purpose."

Kai and Samaira led Ino's companions toward the settlement, and the crowd gradually thinned out.

"Who's that guy?" asked Jayson, pointing at the man walking next to Kai, wearing the headdress.

"The high priest of Kaua'i. He is here on behalf of Paumakua as a sign of respect to your people. He offers an invitation for you to celebrate the wedding in one moon's time."

"Not sure I feel like going to see that."

"Nor do I," agreed Ino.

Herman broke away from the procession when he noticed Jayson wasn't following.

"It looks like we'll have to put off our plans for tonight," he observed. "We have guests."

"I was hoping we could just skip out," replied Jayson.

"Why?" asked Herman with a frown.

"You didn't hear? There's going to be a wedding. Luni's getting married."

"Oh. Shit," replied Herman. "I'm sorry, Jayson. Let's keep our plans, then. It'll be our secret."

"What secret plan do you have?" asked Ino, unable to follow the nuance.

"Actually, can I bring a date?" asked Jayson. "Ino's probably not in a mood to celebrate, either."

"Sure. Why not? I might bring one, too, then."

***

The sun disappeared behind the western mountaintops, and those gathered in the plaza heaped their plates with food laid out on a table near the common building before sitting down to eat. As Ino neared the end of the buffet, Jayson nodded toward the bakery and then ducked in behind it, carrying his plate of food. A moment later, Ino joined him. Sneaking off to Herman's apartment on the side of the crater to drink beer made Jayson feel like one of the cool kids at a high school party ducking out to smoke a joint.

When they arrived, Serge was already there, waiting patiently while their host slowly filled four gourds with foaming amber liquid. The smell was heavenly.

"Did you try it yet?" asked Jayson.

"Waiting for you," assured Herman, without looking up from his delicate work.

Jayson introduced Ino to Serge while Herman finished filling the gourds. When he was done, he offered them to his guests, taking the final one himself.

"Prost!" he said, raising his drink.

Serge and Jayson did the same, and the quick learning warrior needed no prompting to join in.

"Prost!" he said, following the others in downing a healthy portion of ale.

"Wow," marveled Jayson. "That turned out great."

"Yeah," agreed Serge.

They looked at Ino, who smiled before downing what remained in his gourd.

"Success!" cried Herman before following suit and draining his own.

"To your success," echoed Jayson.

He and Serge drank the rest of their beer, and Herman immediately refilled them.

A loud rap at the door startled him, causing him to spill a few precious drops.

"Scheisse," he huffed under his breath. "Who is it?"

Farzin opened the door without answering.

"What the fuck is going on here?" he demanded.

"Beer," replied Jayson, raising his gourd.

"Figures."

"What brings you by, my friend?" asked Herman with a grin.

"Jen noticed one of our guests had wandered off. She asked me to track him down to keep an eye on him."

"Looks like you tracked him down," replied Jayson. "Now you've just got to keep an eye on him."

Herman took a bowl down from the shelf above his basin and filled it.

"This'll help you pass the time while you do," he suggested.

Farzin looked at it doubtfully.

"A bowl of beer?"

"It's all I have, I'm afraid. Most of the cups and plates are in the plaza for our guests."

Farzin took the bowl and had a sip.

"Oh, that's good," he said, nodding in admiration. "Now I see why you kept it a secret."

"Not a secret," objected Herman. "Just a small-scale proof of concept before we go bigger."

Farzin took a large gulp.

"Consider the concept proven," he laughed.

"You might want to take it easy," suggested Herman. "I don't know the exact alcohol content."

"Please," he replied with a dismissive wave. "I was in the Navy. If you can handle it, I can handle it."

"You may have been in the Navy, but my mother weaned me from her breast on beer."

"What? At fourteen?"

Serge and Jayson both grimaced.

"Thanks for that visual, man," said Jayson, feigning a gag.

Ino was having difficulty following the conversation, even though it was being translated literally in real time. He nudged Jayson.

"What is happening?"

"Pissing contest," he replied, fully aware it would not translate well.

"What?"

"A dick-measuring contest," he added with a grin.

Ino wrinkled his brow, eyeing Jayson doubtfully.

"A childish disagreement about who is more of a man," explained Serge.

"Ah," replied Ino with a laugh. "We have those, too."

"What about you?" asked Farzin, sizing up the warrior. "Think you can keep up with a Navy man?"

Jayson glanced at Ino and shook his head slightly.

"I think I will watch," he replied.

"Anyone else?"

Serge and Jayson both declined. Farzin looked Herman in the eye before draining the rest of the bowl.

"That's gotta be worth at least two gourds," he said.

"Well, I guess that means you're just getting caught up," said Herman with a grin.

***

Samaira, Kai, and Jen sat across the table from Huaka'i and the Kahuna—the high priest of Kaua'i—discussing Luni's upcoming marriage to Moeanaimua. Huaka'i did all of the talking for his spiritual leader. The superstitious priest only whispered in Huaka'i's ear, not wanting his words overheard by the tablet and converted into something he could not understand. He also ignored the translations of any English conversation. Someone else needed to repeat them in his own language before he would whisper his reply.

"Why didn't you tell us Luni was to be wed?" asked Kai.

"She did not return to be wed," replied Huaka'i, repeating the whispers in his ear. "It was only when the Kahuna met her—and had a vision—that the arrangements began."

"What did he see?"

More private consultations followed.

"He saw Luni and Moeanaimua bound in marriage and the Nanaulu islands of Kauai and O'ahu bound by friendship. He saw us defeating Pa'ao together and returning the islands of Hawai'i, Maui, Lanai, and Moloka'i to the Ulu chiefs."

Jen reached for the tablet lying on the table between them to deactivate the translator app.

"That's a bunch of bullshit," she said to Samaira.

"While it may not be literally true, it may represent a truth."

"What?"

"As a priest, he could be speaking in allegory. The marriage is part of a strategy he's developing, embedded in mystical rhetoric to give it more authority."

"Yeah. That's what I said," insisted Jen. "Bullshit."

"We should hear him out. He might be on to something."

"You're unbelievable," said Jen, shaking her head.

"What?"

"Just a few weeks ago, you were the one talking about how Luni needs to be free to make her own choices. Now you're ready to sell her out."

"Give her some credit, Jen. She's a smart woman—and I think she might know exactly what she's doing."

"So you think this is legit?"

"I'm saying we should keep an open mind. Ignore the spiritual stuff and listen to what he has to say."

Kai put a hand on Samaira's forearm, nodding toward their guests. The Kahuna regarded her with a stern look.

"I apologize," she said after turning the app back on. "We needed a moment to discuss your vision."

He nodded after receiving the unnecessary translation from Huaka'i, and whispered back a response.

"We will discuss it further with chief Paumakua when you come as guests to the wedding," relayed Huaka'i.

"Who is to come?" asked Kai.

"The rightful chief of Hawai'i and his wife," replied Huaka'i. "And the leaders of O'ahu."

Jen raised an eyebrow.

"Thank you," replied Samaira. "We will discuss your gracious invitation among ourselves in the morning and give you an answer before you leave."

***

The other diplomatic efforts on the island were proceeding in a far less formal and dignified manner. Serge acted as DJ, creating a playlist on one tablet while a second served as their translator. It took some tweaking, but he'd finally managed to get Kailani's app to stop translating the lyrics to the hip-hop songs he'd queued up—unfortunately, not before it attempted to convey a particularly graphic metaphor for oral sex. Ino's twisted facial expressions revealed it had done a poor job of it—or perhaps done a little too well. The others were in hysterics as Jayson tried to explain the gist of it before giving up in a fit of laughter.

As the evening wore on, Herman and Farzin feigned enough maturity to avoid an outright drinking contest, but they were outpacing the others by a good margin. Neither would let a swig by the other go unanswered. Farzin's inability to properly judge Herman's tolerance for alcohol was only outdone by his inability to judge the volume of the bowl from which he drank. While he'd assumed it to be about double the size of Herman's gourd, it held more than three times the volume. After a few hours of laughing and drinking, he was showing the effects. He slurred his speech, an arm around Ino's shoulder, as he shared his philosophical views on life.

"You and me are brothers, man," he explained. "We're both warriors. These guys don't understand. They don't see the world the way we do."

Ino nodded politely and smiled, giving Jayson a sideways glance. He was buzzed enough to see the humor in the situation, but far from being on the same wavelength as Farzin.

"They just don't get us," he continued as he swayed back and forth.

"You feeling okay, Farzin?" asked Herman.

"Just gotta piss," he assured.

He slipped his arm from around Ino and stumbled for the door, banging his shoulder and cursing under his breath as he left. The others erupted in laughter as soon as the door closed behind him.

"What do you think, Ino?" asked Herman.

"We make a similar drink from the root of the ti plant. Yours is much better."

Herman tipped his head in appreciation of the compliment and took another swig.

"Farzin is going to have a rough day tomorrow," said Serge with a chuckle.

"We should try to make it worse," added Jayson. "I might make him some extra-runny eggs for breakfast."

"He's going to puke his guts out," laughed Herman.

The translator evidently had an answer for the colorful expression, allowing Ino to chime in.

"From the look on his face when he left, I'd say he's doing that right now."

"Shhh," said Jayson, raising a finger to his lips as he crept to the door.

He opened it slowly and listened for sounds of retching—trying unsuccessfully to suppress his giggling. The others leaned towards the door, straining their ears for signs Farzin had had too much to drink. There was nothing but the sound of insects and the indistinct chatter from the gathering below.

"Shit. Maybe we should check on him," said Jayson.

"Yeah," agreed Herman. "Let's get him to his bed. We've had our fun."

Suddenly, a short burst of automatic gunfire erupted from the direction of the plaza. A few screams followed—and then, silence.

Chapter 9

ANDREW PULLED INTO THE driveway of the Akindele home in the West Loch Estate neighborhood at 3:24 on Sunday afternoon, a few minutes early for tea. Getting out, he wiped his sweaty palms on his pants and took a deep breath before walking up to ring the bell. He still had no idea why he'd been invited, as the invitation did not explain the nature of the event. In anticipation of the inevitable handshake, he wiped his hands one more time as Mrs. Akindele opened the door.

"You must be Andrew," she greeted with a smile.

"Good afternoon, ma'am," he replied, extending his hand.

"Please, call me Tiara."

She ignored his outstretched hand, gripping him gently by the shoulders while nodding slowly.

"Andrew," she repeated.

He had the sense she was evaluating him.

"Please come in, young man," she offered, stepping aside.

The Akindele home was spacious and neat. A collection of colorful, oblong masks adorned the wall of the entryway. Through the glass-paneled door of the adjacent study, Andrew saw a table and several shelves hosting countless statues and busts of various sizes and shapes.

"Wow," he remarked. "This is quite a collection."

"Traditional Yoruba art," she explained. "I have a room full of ceremonial clothing upstairs as well."

Upstairs? Was she coming onto him? He blinked a few times, pushing the absurd notion aside as she led him through the kitchen and out into the backyard.

"Please have a seat," she said, motioning to an intricate wrought-iron table with two matching chairs.

"Just the two of us, then?" he asked.

"Just the two of us," she confirmed.

"What about Dr. Akindele?"

"He's at work. As usual."

Andrew pulled his phone out of his back pocket and set it facedown on the table before taking a seat.

"Let me put that somewhere safe for you," she offered, holding out her hand.

He cocked his head, unsure if he'd understood correctly. She wanted to take his phone?

"It's alright," she said with an assuring nod. "I'll give it back."

Reluctantly, he handed it over, and she disappeared back into the house.

A few minutes later, she returned with a tray of assorted biscuits and set them down in front of him.

"Please help yourself," she insisted. "I'll be back with the tea in a moment."

"Thank you."

Unsure how to pass the time without a phone, Andrew looked around the yard while munching on a shortbread cookie. It was large, by O'ahu standards, with a few leafy trees providing shade and privacy from the golf course behind. Manicured flowerbeds lined most of the fence and surrounded the stone patio where he sat. The blended fragrance of flowers and freshly mowed grass filled his nostrils. He sneezed.

"Bless you," remarked Tiara, returning with tea service. "I hope you're not allergic to anything out here."

"I'm fine," he assured as she set a cup in front of him and poured.

"I've got some sugar and milk—or lemon, if you prefer."

Not a tea drinker, Andrew didn't know what he preferred. He followed her lead, adding just a little milk before stirring it in with a tiny spoon unlike any he'd seen before. Watching her closely, he pinched the cup's likewise tiny handle between his thumb and index finger and placed his middle finger underneath it for extra support. His hand trembled as he raised the cup to his lips, and a drop or two splashed onto his pant leg.

"So, you work with my Jimi," said Mrs. Akindele, setting her cup delicately onto its saucer.

"Yes, ma'am."

"Tiara," she reminded him.

"Sure," he agreed, although he couldn't imagine calling her that.

"Do the two of you get on well?"

"Uh—"

She cracked a broad smile.

"I'm teasing you, Andrew. I know my Jimi. He doesn't get on well with anyone."

"He's fine," assured Andrew, unsure how to respond. "He's a very busy man."

"He makes himself busy because he likes work more than people."

"If you say so."

"He's been peculiar all his life, but I love him very much."

Andrew nodded, but had nothing to add.

"He's a capable man," she continued. "in ways I can't begin to comprehend. But in other ways, he is completely helpless."

"I don't think I'd describe him as helpless."

"You're not his mother," she said, narrowing an eye at Andrew and nodding sagely. "You don't see what I see."

"I guess not," he admitted.

"In fact, I'm not sure what he's gotten himself into over there at your Center."

She took another sip of her tea and then set it down again. There was a moment of awkward silence as she waited for him to offer something.

"You probably know we can't talk about it—what we do over there. It's sensitive stuff."

"Unlocking the secrets of nature and reimagining the universe," she said, as if repeating a mantra she'd heard dozens of times.

"I don't know anything about that. I'm just a systems tech."

"Hmm."

She picked a cookie from the tray, eating it in small, deliberate bites. Andrew shifted uneasily in his chair as afternoon tea turned into an unlikely interrogation.

"You might not know it, but we have a mutual friend," she said as she gently dabbed at the corners of her mouth with a cloth napkin.

"Really?" he asked, taking another sip of tea.

"A lovely young woman named Samaira."

Andrew choked on his drink and started coughing. A few drops of tea even dribbled out of his nose as he fought to regain his composure.

"Are you okay, dear? Have a napkin."

"I'm so sorry," he said as he took it and wiped his hands and face.

"No need to apologize. She's a remarkable woman. Hard for a man to forget, I imagine."

"She is," he agreed.

"I'll admit that I even thought about trying to set her up with my Jimi. But, of course, that would never have worked. He's only interested in physics."

"Hard to imagine."

"I knew she wouldn't interest him. A mother knows her son, but it doesn't stop her from dreaming," she said with a laugh.

"Well, he is a brilliant man," consoled Andrew. "Maybe the smartest man ever."

"God gives with one hand and takes with the other. As in all things, He balances His blessings."

"I suppose," replied Andrew with a shrug.

"You know, he's a sociopath?" she added as if it were a perfectly normal thing to say about one's child.

"What?"

"I mean that strictly in the clinical sense of the word," she added. "He's not malevolent or dangerous—at least not intentionally. It's just that to him, other people are nothing more than objects. I've had to act as his empathy his entire life."

"That—that must be hard."

"One day, when he was little, I found him ripping the wings off of flies and impaling them on a pin, three facing one direction and three facing the other. He was fascinated by how they just kept walking in an endless circle. He wasn't enjoying the torture or anything like that. It just never occurred to him they might be suffering. He might just as well have been tinkering with some mechanical toy."

Andrew couldn't hide a look of horror.

"It has not been easy," she continued, "but it is the challenge God gave me in this life, and I've accepted it."

"He's lucky to have you—if you ask me."

"I appreciate that, Andrew. But I'm not sure it's enough anymore."

"What do you mean?"

"I mean, the people he works for might find his lack of conscience beneficial in some way, and take advantage when I'm not there to be his moral compass."

Andrew shifted uncomfortably again.

"You know, she and I used to have tea like this," said Mrs. Akindele, changing topics abruptly, "but I haven't seen her for quite some time. How is she?"

"Who? Samaira?" asked Andrew, wrinkling his brow.

"Yes, of course. Samaira."

"Didn't, uh, Jimi tell you? She's joined a team of our researchers in a biodome experiment."

"Now that you mention it, I do recall something about that. Where is that, again?"

"Uh, some island. I'm not really sure."

"Well, that is strange," she said, shaking her head. "Because she told me you'd be able to help me understand a few things."

"What? When?"

"Just a few weeks ago."

"That's not possible."

She took another sip of tea, regarding him for a few moments before continuing.

"Do you play Mah Jongg, Andrew?" she asked in another abrupt change of direction.

"What?"

"The game," she clarified.

"I can't say I have."

"A friend here in the neighborhood introduced me a couple of years ago. You know, a well-crafted Mah Jongg set is a work of art? Would you like to see mine?"

"Sure," he said, trying to be polite. "But you were just talking about Samaira."

Clearly, Mrs. Akindele was losing her mind, unable to maintain her focus on a single topic. He'd seen it happen to his own grandmother before she'd passed.

"I'll get back to that," she assured with a smile.

She returned to the house again, giving Andrew time to pop another cookie into his mouth as he wondered what in the hell was going on. Moments later, she reemerged from the back door, carrying an ornate wooden box.

"I taught Samaira how to play one day when she agreed to sit in for one of our regular players at the last minute," she said, setting the box in front of Andrew. "She picked it up remarkably quickly."

"I don't doubt it," he replied.

"The last time I hosted, she even came over early to help me prepare—and then stayed to tidy up when it was over."

"She was quite remarkable."

"Was?"

Andrew gulped.

"It's fine, Andrew." she said with a disarming smile and a wave of her hand before continuing her story. "My friends and I take turns hosting a monthly game, but you know how things can be around the holidays. We missed getting together a couple of times, and before you know it, it's spring."

"Are we talking about the game or Samaira?" he asked.

"It's called Mah Jongg," she reminded him. "Take a look in the box, and you'll understand."

Andrew narrowed his eyes doubtfully before turning his attention to the box. Opening the latch gently, he lifted the lid and gasped. On top of the neat stacks of colorful tiles sat an envelope marked simply with the name 'Tiara.' The handwriting was familiar.

"What's that?"

"It's a letter from our friend. Except I didn't know she was your friend, too, until I read it."

"What'd she say?"

"Why don't you read it and find out?" she suggested.

Andrew, his hands shaking, picked up the envelope as if handling a priceless artifact from a lost world. He looked at her again before pulling out the letter, and she nodded for him to continue. Unfolding it, he set the envelope on the table and carefully read every word. When he finished, he placed it back in the envelope and returned it to the box.

"What now?" he asked.

***

Shannon opened her eyes and sat up with a start. Waking in unfamiliar surroundings, it took her a moment to recall where she was and how she'd gotten there. Her head slowly stopped spinning as she blinked a few times and looked around. The sky outside was growing dim, signaling it was late afternoon or early evening. Nearby, she heard the faint sound of a refrigerator door gently closing, followed by the crinkle of a plastic bag.

"I guess I passed out for a bit," she said, entering the kitchen.

Don spun around, holding a bag of pre-made Caesar salad.

"I'm sorry. I was trying to be quiet."

"It's fine," she said with a dismissive wave. "I needed to get up, eventually."

"Glad you were able to get some sleep, at least," he replied.

"That shower helped, too."

"I picked up a couple of things for you to try on," he said, motioning to a Walmart bag on the table. "I don't know your style, but I assume it's not my old sweats."

"Thanks," she laughed. "They're fine for now."

He looked at her awkwardly for a moment.

"So why call me?" he asked. "Why not the FBI?"

"Because I don't know who I can trust—or what systems I can trust," she replied. "Even if the people I talk to aren't compromised, it seems like they're pretty deep into the commercial networks—and maybe the government ones, too. If I pick up your phone and call the FBI—"

She left her thought unfinished and shook her head in dismay.

"How much danger are we in?"

"They crashed a car into us—Jessica and me. Who's to say they couldn't just decide to drop a seven-four-seven on our heads right now if they wanted?"

Don gulped, looking up involuntarily.

"Jesus Christ."

"What's the latest news on the crash?"

"I haven't been following today. Let's take a look."

He took out his phone and began typing.

"No!" said Shannon, grabbing his arm. "No online searches. Just turn on the TV."

"Shit. Really? It's that bad?"

"I don't know," she admitted. "But I don't feel safe even talking about it with a phone nearby. Can you put that thing away somewhere?"

"I'll turn it off."

"I'm not even sure that's enough. Just put it away somewhere. Please?"

"I know," he said, checking one of his drawers.

He pulled out a roll of aluminum foil, wrapped the phone, and tossed it in the freezer compartment of his refrigerator.

"That's what they did in that Snowden movie," he explained. "Turn on the TV while I get some dinner started."

Dinner turned out to be a frozen pizza to go with the pre-made salad. That was fine with Shannon. Don brought out a bottle of cheap red wine to go with it, proclaiming Sunday night Italian night at his house. She was grateful for the hospitality. Without him, she'd be dumpster diving for half-eaten KFC and trying to figure out where to sleep. With its out-of-date decor and bachelor menu, Don's house may as well have been a suite at the Ritz.

They sat quietly, surfing the channels for anything about the terrible accident at the coffee shop. At the top of the hour, one of the local channels offered a teaser for their upcoming weekend news broadcast.

"Stunning new developments in the *horrific* crash in Waimalu yesterday morning that left six people dead and several more injured," started the anchor. "Missing FBI agent Shannon Boucher, originally assumed to be a victim, is now being described by police as a person of interest. We've got the scoop from inside sources, and you won't *believe* what we're learning. Tune in to our broadcast later this evening or check out Action News Online to learn more."

"Shit," remarked Don. "They're going to drag you through the mud."

"Best way to take care of a loose end they haven't found yet," replied Shannon. "At least that's some good news."

"How is this good news?"

"It means they don't know where I am—yet. Otherwise, they'd just kill me."

***

Richard had spent his weekend dealing with Rebecca's clumsy attempt to prevent an FBI investigation into the Center. Facial recognition algorithms feasted on terabytes of data from all over the island for hours without a hit, and agent Boucher hadn't reached out to any of her colleagues or tried to go home. Without a target, his only option had been to drive her further underground to prevent her from making any kind of statement. He'd worked nearly around the clock with the security techs to engineer the false digital trail that would substantiate his narrative.

FBI agent Shannon Boucher was being extorted by her ex-wife. For years, the federal agent had been taking bribes from the human traffickers she'd been investigating for using Hawaii as the entry point for underage girls—and boys—procured for yet-unknown clients on the mainland. The numbered offshore accounts containing hundreds of thousands of dollars in unexplained wealth lent credence to the claim. Jessica Reyes knew about all of it—and she wanted her cut. Lured to the coffee shop by the promise of a payday, she was supposed to have been silenced for good. That's when agent Boucher's plan had gone off the rails.

Charles Hoang, the man they called St. Charlie, was anything but a saint. A trail of text messages on a secret burner phone found hidden in the wreckage showed a stream of text messages between Charlie and agent Boucher in the moments leading up to the crash. Though police hadn't discovered it yet, a separate evidence trail would reveal that the seemingly God-fearing pillar of the community was a pedophile—a regular customer of a local pimp supplied by the human traffickers. Agent Boucher had given him a choice to either die as St. Charlie or live out his life in prison as child-rapist Charlie. In a final act of defiance, he'd initiated his part of the plot a few seconds early in an attempt to kill the corrupt agent along with her ex-wife.

Richard was proud of his fiction. He imagined he was probably a writer in a parallel world—a famous weaver of tales. Of course, the entire story would eventually collapse, and agent Boucher would probably even end up fully exonerated. It didn't matter. Epsilon would be far too spectacular to hide, revealing the truth behind the Center for Sustainability Research. Then, all of his lies would fall apart after it was too late to matter.

All he needed to do was keep the chaos and confusion going until then. Not even that long, he realized. The aftermath of Delta was going to require a whole new level of distraction that would make the world forget about special agent Shannon Boucher for quite some time. With only months to go before the mission, the situation was manageable.

The best thing about Rebecca's mess was that it had given him a chance to once again prove his worth and, hopefully, prove they needed him around after Delta. She'd been genuinely impressed by his approach—particularly how he'd used it as a set-up for the nuclear option. A brilliant piece of foreshadowing, the tiny morsel slipped into the opening chapter of his work would only reveal its significance at the climax.

He was hopeful the rest of the plan to secure his position on Epsilon was now only an insurance policy. Still, he would make sure it was rock-solid—just in case. After a quick knock on Andrew's door, he didn't wait for an answer before walking in.

"Morning, Andrew," he greeted. "How was the weekend?"

"Boring," he replied. "You?"

"Same. You got an update on that security thing we talked about?"

"Yeah. I had it running over the weekend. It only took about ten hours to brute-force the password."

"Ten hours to come up with '100%MommasBoy?'" he snickered. "It would have been my first guess."

"It looks like a run-of-the-mill computer-generated key," replied Andrew, without a hint of humor.

"Write it down for me?"

"It's pretty long. Why don't I just email it?"

"Let's not create any more of a trail than we need to," suggested Richard. "I want to see if site security can figure out what happened—as a test."

"Am I going to get into any trouble over this?"

"Not at all, Andrew. This is sanctioned at the highest levels."

Andrew shrugged and peeled a sticky note from the stack on his desk, carefully writing out the twenty-character string to make sure he differentiated upper versus lower case, and letters versus numbers. Then, after double-checking, he handed it over to Richard.

"Wow. That's a good one."

"It took a lot longer than I expected for the stack to spit that one out," admitted Andrew.

"Remember, not a word," reminded Richard. "Let's see if the rest of our safeguards work the way they're supposed to."

He left the office beaming. After a rough few months, things were finally looking good for him. Andrew knew too much, of course, but he'd be easy enough to manipulate or otherwise neutralize—if it became necessary.

Chapter 10

SAMAIRA'S EYES WERE WIDE with fear. She grabbed Kai's thigh and pushed him back down onto his seat as he rose to meet the threat. Having arrived under cover of darkness, Josh and the rest of the security team were gathered at the top of the stairs on the southwest side of the plaza. His assault rifle was still pointed skyward, having just fired a few shots to get everyone's attention. At his command, the others took up positions spaced along the south and west flanks of the gathering, leveling their rifles at the crowd. Samaira stood to greet them while Kai quietly urged Huaka'i and the Kahuna to signal their warriors to stay calm.

"Welcome back," said Samaira, as calmly as she could manage. "There's plenty to eat if you'd like to join us."

She leaned over to close the translator app with a flick of her index finger.

"What the fuck is going on?" demanded Josh as he strode toward their table.

Jen and Kai rose to their feet next to Samaira.

"The tactical situation changed while you were gone," said Jen. "We had to make some decisions."

"And who the fuck is this guy?" he asked, seemingly uninterested in the explanation.

"I am Kai, son of Kapawa, and the rightful leader of the Ulu people. Who the fuck are you?"

Josh blinked several times, clearly not expecting the formidable-looking native to understand or respond to his question.

"Jen?" he asked again, still staring at Kai. "What's going on?"

"This man and his people helped save us from an attack," interjected Samaira.

"It's true," added Jen.

Josh took a deep breath and looked around, sizing up the crowd gathered for a meal in the plaza.

"Did these women and children help save you from an attack, too?"

"They're refugees," explained Samaira. "Here to escape the same men who threatened us."

"Judging from this little party, I'd say everyone is feeling pretty safe now. So maybe it's time to thank your friends for their help and send them on their way."

"It's not that simple," said Samaira.

She turned slightly, opening the sling across her chest. "Kai is my husband. And this is our son, Keanu."

"No," said Josh, raising his gun at Kai. "No fucking way. This is not going to happen. This is not the plan."

Though they'd never seen guns before, the visiting warriors understood the sudden, direct threat. First, Huaka'i, then the rest, rose from their seats. Even unarmed, they were an imposing sight. Only the Kahuna remained seated, looking calm yet severe. The security team flanking the group of tables released their safeties in a chorus of clicks.

"Please!" begged Samaira. "There are women and children here—civilians."

"That's a big part of the problem," said Josh, furrowing his brow.

"What does that mean?" demanded Jen.

"You know exactly what that means, Jen. Where is Olena?"

"Josh," pleaded Jen, "you need to get everyone to put their guns down so we can talk."

He cocked his head, narrowing his eyes at her.

"Where is Olena?" he demanded again.

"There is a lot we have to discuss," said Samaira. "And that's part of it."

"Where the fuck is Olena?" he shouted, flecks of spit flying from his mouth.

"She's dead," came a call from the north end of the plaza.

Josh swung his weapon around to face the new threat. Jayson marched toward him, carrying an assault rifle pointed casually at the ground. Ino was similarly armed, walking without expression at his side. The entire security team now had weapons trained on the approaching pair. They stopped a few meters from the table, standing silently with their guns still lowered.

"What. Happened. To. Olena?" demanded Josh, spitting the words out one at a time.

"She murdered Kailani, so I drove a knife through her heart," said Jayson.

"You? Bullshit. You're nothing but a pussy. I can see your hands shaking from here."

He turned to Jen.

"This is bullshit, right?"

She shook her head.

"And where were you when all of this was happening? And where the hell is Farzin?"

"He's hidden on the hillside behind me," indicated Jayson with his thumb. "With a sniper rifle locked on your head."

"Bullshit."

"And he's not alone," added Jayson. "Ino's men are in position all around the plaza."

Josh strained to see into the darkness beyond the clinic. He caught sight of two forms moving in the shadows. Another lay perfectly still against the wall with a weapon trained on their position.

"And we have the ship. By now, whatever's left of Scylla is at the bottom of the harbor—just like the rest you had stored up in the crater."

Josh's eyes widened, and he turned once more to Jen.

"What did you do?" he yelled in frustration.

"You didn't really think you'd just waltz back in here and catch us napping, did you?" asked Jayson. "We've been watching since you sailed in."

"He's right," added Jen. "You got careless and lost your tactical advantage."

"What is this? A coup?"

"This can't be a coup," said Samaira. "You were never in charge."

For the first time, Josh seemed unsure of himself.

"So, what do you expect to happen now?" he asked.

"We're all going to put down our guns and talk," she replied in a soothing voice. "There is a lot you need to know."

"I don't think we're ready to do that yet."

"What's the alternative?" asked Jen. "Nobody else needs to die."

"Fuck this," said Ted Park, lowering his gun. "There are kids here, man."

Jayson nodded at Ino before crouching to set his gun on the ground. The warrior followed his lead.

"I killed Olena because I didn't have a choice," said Jayson. "And I don't plan on killing anyone else—unless I have to."

Kai gave Huaka'i and the Kahuna a whispered update.

"What did you tell them?" demanded Josh.

"I told them there will be peace here tonight," he replied, adding a few more words to the warrior across from him.

Huaka'i and his men sat down. Josh took a deep breath and looked around at his team. With a sigh, he placed the assault rifle on the ground and signaled for them to do the same.

"Now, let's get you some food," suggested Samaira.

***

Though no one was at ease, the tension among those dining in the plaza gradually subsided to a point where everyone had at least stopped glancing at the weapons lying scattered on the ground every few seconds. Negotiating with Samaira and Jen, Josh eventually agreed to surrender them, provided the warriors lurking in the shadows would do the same. To ensure everyone's safety, they decided they'd work together to remove all of the magazines and clear any chambered rounds. Josh and Jen oversaw the activity, verifying the safety of each one as they added them to a growing pile.

"This one isn't even loaded," said Martina de la Cruz as she inspected the weapon Ino had carried.

"Really?" remarked Jayson. "We'll have to go over the security protocols again."

He glanced at Samaira with a shrug. She shook her head, trying to suppress a smile.

"Okay," said Josh after they'd cleared the weapons. "Time to call off your team."

"Guys," called Jayson. "Bring it in."

Herman and Serge stepped from the shadows on either side of the clinic with weapons slung over their shoulders. Joining the others, they presented the guns to Josh and Jen.

"What about that guy?" asked Josh, pointing to the prone form against the clinic wall. "And Farzin."

"That *is* Farzin," said Serge.

"Khan!" called Josh. "Get the hell over here."

"I don't think he can hear you," replied Herman, stifling a chuckle as he struggled to maintain his balance.

"Are you—? Are you drunk?" asked Josh.

Herman held his thumb and forefinger a few millimeters apart to indicate that he was, perhaps, a little drunk.

"What the hell is going on? And where are the rest of these guys?" he asked, pointing at Ino.

"Uh. There aren't any," admitted Jayson.

"You were bluffing?"

"Kind of. Yeah."

"And aren't you glad he did?" interjected Samaira. "Nobody got hurt."

Josh glared at her but said nothing. Instead, he jogged off to check on Farzin. They could see him shaking the prone figure by the clinic wall and then prying the gun away from him. He returned with a look of disgust on his face.

"He's passed out in a puddle of vomit."

"He's a bit of a lightweight," laughed Herman. "Can't handle his beer."

"Were any of these even loaded?" he asked, inspecting the sniper rifle.

"Mine was," said Jayson. "Just in case."

"Mine, too," added Serge. "But we were afraid Herman might accidentally shoot someone."

"So that was it? Just four untrained guys and sleeping beauty over there?"

"Yeah," shrugged Jayson. "Pretty much."

"Jesus Christ," said Josh, shaking his head.

"It really is for the best," said Samaira. "After you've had a few days to see what we've accomplished here, I know you'll agree."

"We'll see," he snorted.

***

Unlike the previous visit, the warriors from Kaua'i posted a few rotating guards around their encampment throughout the night. The security team opted to stay on the ship, a pair of them patrolling the dock at all times. Though they'd finished their dinner with assurances of peace and cooperation, nobody on Oahu slept with ease that night.

The following day, when Kai and Samaira went down to the harbor with Jayson to see off their guests, they did so under the watchful eye of those looming on the deck of Jasmine's Hope. They exchanged handshakes, and Ino offered Jayson a warm embrace. They had bonded first over their shared unhappiness with Luni's decision to wed Moeanaimua, then over their risky gambit the night before. Though Ino's only role had been to stand in silence with a menacing look—a role he was born to play, it seemed—it had taken enormous trust.

"Will you not come to the wedding?" he asked through the translator.

"No," replied Jayson. "I think I'll stay here."

Ino nodded.

"I understand. But someday, I hope you will visit so I can repay your hospitality."

"I will," promised Jayson.

After the guests boarded the canoe, Kai and Jayson waded into the water up to their knees to push them off. The pair stayed there, standing in the water, until the outrigger disappeared behind Sand Island. Josh, who'd been watching from the ship, clambered down the ladder and approached Samaira.

"So that's all the guests?" he asked. "The rest are staying?"

"That's right," confirmed Samaira. "The rest are part of our community."

"And this wedding?"

"Some of us will be attending."

"No," he said, shaking his head. "I don't like it."

"You're not in charge," she reminded him.

"Who is? You?"

She regarded him without answering as Jayson and Kai waded out of the water toward them.

"So, who's going?" he asked after a moment of awkward silence.

"Kai and I will go with Jen—and maybe Serge. We're not sure yet."

"I should go," said Josh.

Samaira and Kai looked at each other.

"Why you?" demanded Jayson.

"To assess the threat."

"Jesus Christ. You're a broken record."

"He has a point, Jayson," said Samaira. "This isn't just a wedding—it's politics. From what the Kahuna said, they want to discuss joining forces to defeat Pa'ao and send Pili back to where he came from. We'll need to talk strategy and commit forces if we're to have peace on these islands."

"Yeah," said Jayson, nodding toward Josh. "But that's not what he meant. He's not on the same mission as us."

"You're the ones off the reservation, not me," protested Josh.

"That's right, asshole," spat Jayson. "I'm off the reservation—and I'm not getting back on it."

Jayson turned and started up the pathway toward the settlement before Josh could respond.

"What's his problem?"

"He found out your job is to murder half the planet," said Samaira. "I guess maybe that set him off."

With that, she walked away. Kai eyed Josh sternly for several seconds before turning to follow.

Josh huffed his way back to Jasmine's hope at the end of the nearby dock. Several crew members had been watching the exchange from the deck, but hadn't been able to hear what had transpired.

"What was that all about?" asked Miroslava.

"Looks like I'm going to a wedding."

"Need a date?"

"Sorry. Jefferson is my date."

"But she's one of *them* now."

"That's perfect, actually. And I've got to do a better job of getting on board, too. We all do."

"What?"

"We need to play nice. All of us. *Really* nice."

"Why would we do that? This thing is off the rails."

"Getting it back on track won't be that hard. And this wedding is the perfect place to start."

***

The crew of Jasmine's Hope spent the morning unloading their cargo. Ingots of refined metals and barrels of saltpeter arrived at the stores in cartload after cartload hauled up from the port. Parth, Herman, and Zaina took particular interest in the steel and copper, imagining some of the immediate and longer-term possibilities offered by the precious commodities that could not be found in any significant concentration on the islands.

"This steel is probably the best on the planet right now," said Parth, hefting a sizeable ingot with two hands.

"And the copper looks pure," added Zaina.

Lisa Washington, one of the engineers among the Navy crew, arrived pushing another cart, stopping to wipe the sweat from her brow.

"Good stuff, right?" she said.

"Not bad," allowed Herman.

"We're going to need a foundry if we're going to do anything with it," she added.

"We know what we're doing," shot Parth. "We built all of this with no help from you guys."

"Calm down," said Lisa, showing her palms in a gesture of peace. "You're right. And it's time to change that."

"What do you mean?" asked Parth.

"We want to help with the foundry. Paul and I will pitch in with the design and construction."

"Oh?" he remarked, cocking an eyebrow.

"Have you thought about where it should go?" she continued.

"Serge has it planned," assured Parth.

"Let's all have lunch together, then. I'll get Paul, and you can find Serge."

She hauled a greenish block of oxidizing copper from the cart and handed it to Herman.

"Give me a hand stacking these?"

"Sure," he replied with a glance at his companions.

Both seemed surprised by her sudden interest in cooperation.

"Pass me one," said Zaina. "More hands can only help."

Luping, Riyoko, and Melinda watched with interest from a shaded bench in the plaza while their children played on a blanket beside them. It had been nonstop action at the stores all morning as they transferred cargo from the ship.

"Seems like they're getting on well," commented Melinda.

"What does Farzin think?" asked Luping.

"I don't think he's even out of bed yet," replied Riyoko.

She tried to pass it off as a joke, but the others could tell she was embarrassed by his drunken behavior the night before.

"I expected a lot more friction," admitted Luping. "I've been having nightmares about them coming back for months."

"Ezra, too," said Melinda. "With Kailani's death—and then all those men from the attack at the beach? I think he's been afraid it would start all over again."

She shook her head sadly.

"It almost did last night," said Riyoko. "I don't know what would have happened if Jayson hadn't figured out a way to get them to disarm."

"They wouldn't have done anything with families watching," said Melissa.

She didn't sound entirely convinced.

Ted Park huffed his way up the curving pathway next to the stairs to the plaza with a cart. A large wooden barrel lay strapped to the top. Herman greeted him as he arrived at the stores to help him lift it down to carry it inside. Emerging from the building, Ted caught sight of the women watching from the bench and waved. Melinda waved back. He took it as an invitation.

"Hey," he said, trotting over. "It's been a while."

"Hi Ted," offered Riyoko.

"Is that Jasmine? She's so big!"

"A lot changes in a year and a half."

Jasmine wobbled a bit as she pushed herself to her feet and ambled over to Riyoko.

"Mama," she said with a giant grin.

Just then, a young girl, maybe six or seven years old, ran up carrying two cups of water. Drops splashed over the side with every footstep.

"For Jasmine," she said, holding out a cup.

Jasmine took the cup and raised it to her mouth as she balanced herself against Riyoko's knee. Water ran down her face, splashing against the ground.

"And who is this little beauty?" asked Ted.

"La'akea," said Melinda. "And this is her mother, Anuenue."

Ted turned to see a woman approaching with a tray of fruit. Her eyes widened, and she froze in place.

"Ua maikaʻi nā mea a pau," offered Luping calmly.

Anuenue approached cautiously, her eyes locked on Park, and placed the tray on the bench.

"Some snacks for the children," she said.

Jasmine wasted no time. She dropped her half-full cup to the ground and picked up a piece of cantaloupe, biting into it with the new teeth erupting from her gums.

"Hello," offered Park with a warm smile.

Anuenue reluctantly shook his outstretched hand.

"Watch this," said La'akea to Ted, oblivious to the tension.

She walked over to one of the toddlers sitting on the blanket and held out her index finger. He grasped it in one hand, struggling unsteadily to his feet.

"Come on, Tyler," she urged.

He took a few hesitant steps forward and started giggling, causing him to lose his grip and plop to the ground. The toddler looked startled for a moment, then resumed laughing as he reached for La'akea's finger once more.

"Tyler, huh? Nice name," said Park.

"He's ours—mine and Ezra's," said Melinda.

"Ours is Leila," added Luping. "They're only a week apart."

"What's your name?" asked La'akea.

"I'm Ted."

"Nice to meet you, Ted," she beamed.

"You're very sweet," he replied.

"Want to see what Melinda taught me?"

"Sure."

She squatted down and then leaped into the air, leaning back and arching her body as she did so. Then, landing on her palms, she rotated onto her feet, completing a perfect backward handspring.

"Wow! What an incredible gymnast you are!" said Park, clapping his hands.

"Thanks. I can do other stuff, too," she said.

"You must be very proud of your daughter, ma'am," he said to Anuenue.

She nodded. An awkward silence followed.

"Well," said Ted finally, "I should get back to work. I just wanted to say hi."

He trotted back to his cart and wheeled it around to return to the harbor.

"Well, that was weird," said Riyoko.

"You think so?" asked Luping.

"Well, it *is* Park. So who can tell?" she shrugged.

***

Jayson and Jen walked onto the dock, sidestepping Isiah O'Neal as he pushed a loaded cart past them.

"Excuse me," he said with a polite nod.

"You two here to help unload?" called Josh from the deck above.

"Kind of," said Jayson.

"We're here to see what's left of—of the stuff," added Jen.

"You got it all last night."

It was the first thing Jayson had thought of the night before after he'd realized what was going on. While he and Herman gathered the weapons, Serge had sprinted down to the ship with a flashlight to get the rest of the Scylla. Of course, none of it was in the harbor, as he'd told Josh. Serge was incinerating it as they spoke. Still, he felt an inspection was in order—just to be sure.

"We just want to look around."

"Sure," invited Josh. "Come on up."

Jayson raised a doubtful eyebrow at Jen before taking a step onto the rope ladder hanging from the side of Jasmine's Hope. At the top, Josh offered him a hand to pull him aboard.

"Here's where we had it," he said, gesturing to a box sitting away from all of the others.

While Jen went off to explore the hold and the quarters, Jayson got down on one knee and opened the unlocked container. Inside, he found nothing but empty slots in the protective foam insert. He pulled it out to check for anything hidden underneath.

"That was all of it? The ones we grabbed last night?"

"That was it," confirmed Josh.

"So, you're giving up?" he asked, eyeing Josh suspiciously. "All the bull-shit is over—just like that?"

"What else are we going to do?" he asked with a shrug.

"How do we know we can trust you?"

He shrugged again.

"Part of me was relieved last night when you said you'd taken it."

"You didn't seem relieved."

"It took me a while to realize it. The stuff—what we're supposed to do with it—has been hanging over me since we got here. You've set me free, Jayson."

Jayson narrowed his eyes.

"Keep the box," offered Josh. "I don't need it."

"All clear," said Jen, emerging from the quarters. "No sign of anything else."

Jayson nodded and headed to the ladder with the empty box.

"Thanks, Jayson. I mean it," Josh called after him.

Jen stayed behind to talk.

"I'm surprised to see you accepting all of this," she said, gesturing around broadly.

"What's the alternative? Civil war?"

"It's better this way, Josh. It took me a while to get it, but I really think it's true."

"What do you get?"

"Kamaras was never our friend, and there's no guarantee he won't treat our descendants the same way he's having us treat the people already here."

"Why would he, though?"

"I've learned to ask it differently, Josh. The real question is, why wouldn't he? Men like him don't need a reason to exert control. They need a reason not to."

"Maybe," he allowed with a shrug.

"Think about it. I get why he wanted us to reduce the population and prevent large-scale industrialization, but why was he so insistent on isolating us from the natives here? They've never been a threat to the environment."

"I guess he figured it would mess with his plans."

"Yeah. His plans to make sure we're controllable when he arrives."

"Huh?"

"An immediate tripling or quadrupling of our population this far ahead of his arrival would make all of his simulations wildly unpredictable. Matteus and Serge ran a few of their own to show us the impact of cooperating with native societies."

"And?"

"Kamaras is expecting to find less than a hundred thousand people concentrated on these islands. If we play by different rules, we could be millions across two or three continents."

"That's nuts."

"We think it's the only way to guarantee our descendants are free people instead of his slaves."

"This is Samaira's doing, isn't it? She's the one who's got you all thinking this crazy shit."

"It's not that crazy, Josh," she insisted. "And even if it is—would it really be so bad?"

He sighed, saying nothing.

"We've got a good thing going here," she assured, turning to leave.

Halfway to the ladder, she turned back and added, "don't do anything to fuck it up, okay?"

"What can I possibly do now?" he replied.

Miroslava had been lurking nearby, trying to look busy. As Jen's head disappeared below the side of the ship, she approached Josh with purpose.

"I know you have a plan," she said. "You going to tell me what it is?"

"I have a lot to tell you," he assured. "Feel like going for a little hike later on?"

Chapter 11

JOSH GLANCED AROUND CASUALLY before disappearing down the pathway towards Diamond Head. He had some food in his pockets, and the canteen slung over his shoulder was hidden under his loose shirt. He didn't want to betray that he was on a mission. A few hundred meters down the trail, Miroslava popped out from behind a tree.

"Took you long enough."

"Got stuck chatting with a few people in the plaza," he explained. "Didn't want to look like I was in a hurry."

"Let's double-time it to get back before dark," she suggested.

"Plenty of time. It's not that far. Besides, we need to talk, and I don't feel like doing that on the run."

"How about you start by telling me why we're going to Diamond Head?"

"That's where our friend from the past had his base of operations."

"Van Zijl?"

"Yep."

"And how does that help us?"

"If he had any leftovers, they'll still be there."

"What's it been? Two hundred years? How do you expect us to find anything?"

"Because I know exactly where it is."

"What? How?"

"After Aiden died, Olena shared a few things with me."

Miroslava stopped walking and put her hands on her hips, furrowing her brow in frustration. Josh turned to face her.

"Like what?" she demanded.

"Relax. I'm telling you now."

"Why now?"

"Same reason Olena told me after Aiden died. In case something happens."

"Why did Aiden and Olena need to keep anything secret from the rest of us?"

"Listen," he said. "I trust you, and I'm going to tell you everything. Let's just keep moving, okay?"

"Okay," she agreed, resuming her place beside him as he continued down the path.

"Kamaras always knew there was a possibility that people like Farzin and Jen would fall out of line, and things could go south. So he had a plan for it. A long-term plan."

"How long term?"

"Centuries," replied Josh. "We'll spend our lifetimes doing the work, but that's not enough to bring about what he envisioned. We need the generations that follow us to continue what we've started—to prevent any more of this bullshit we've got going on right now. We're to maintain a secret society that controls key positions as our civilization develops."

"Like Freemasons?"

"I prefer to think of us as Knights Templar."

"Alright. So why not just tell the rest of the team?"

"Because we'd already be screwed if we had. Farzin and Jen, remember? And would you really feel comfortable telling Park? No way he's a solid as you or me. This has got to be done carefully—deliberately—over decades and centuries."

"How the hell are we supposed to do that?"

"It's all planned out for us—recruitment, rituals, how to stay hidden in plain sight—everything."

"And it's just you right now?"

"No. It's just us," he corrected. "I'm giving you access to everything in case something happens to me at this wedding."

They worked their way to the north side of Diamond Head as Josh explained the long-term mission of their secret society. Miroslava absorbed it all with fascination. Kamaras wasn't leaving the centuries before his arrival to chance—there were guardrails in place to make sure things didn't devolve into rule-by-mob chaos just because they'd laid down their arms that night in the plaza.

After cresting the north rim of Diamond Head and ambling down the gentle inner slope to the crater floor, Josh began searching for the landmarks described to him by Olena. He found one of the large volcanic formations exactly where she said it would be.

"Stand here," he instructed.

"And then what?"

"Gimme a yell when I am directly between you and that outcropping just beyond the clearing," he said, pointing at a distant rock feature.

He then located the second pair of markers and began walking in a straight line between them until she called out. He motioned her over and then dropped to his knees, digging away at a thin layer of soil. The top of the first plastic container was visible by the time Miroslava arrived at his side.

"Bingo," said Josh, clearing away the rest of the dirt.

He unlatched the lid, breaking an airtight seal that had been intact for nearly two centuries.

"What is all of this?"

"There's a pair of these containers where Van Zijl was supposed to put anything that wouldn't decompose. If he had any of the stuff left, it would be in one of these."

"The weapons might still work," said Miroslava, catching sight of a handgun. "We should grab them, too."

"No," he warned. "Don't bring back anything we'd have to explain."

"What about the stuff?"

"That's between you and me for now."

Finding nothing of interest in the first container, he unearthed the second and immediately found what he was looking for.

"Moment of truth," he said, unlatching the smaller container.

Three stainless steel cylinders remained nestled in the pockets of the foam insert.

"Yes!" exclaimed Josh. "One Scylla and two Charybdis."

"Great! Let's grab 'em and go."

"I just need one for now. There's no reason to think the other two won't be safe here for another two hundred years."

He slipped the last Scylla into his pocket and closed the containers before carefully covering them with dirt.

***

In the weeks leading up to the wedding, the Navy crew continued their charm offensive. They gradually moved off the ship into the quarters prepared for them on the slopes of Punchbowl among the other recruits. Most even volunteered to help with the daily chores and the ongoing infrastructure projects intended to offer steady improvements to their quality of life.

At mealtime, they dined among the others and learned to pronounce the names of their newest community members. A few even made an effort to learn basic greetings in their language. Josh always sought Samaira and Kai in the common building, choosing to dine with them whenever he could.

Days before the wedding, they sat discussing their plans.

"So how is this going down?" asked Josh. "When do we leave?"

"Tomorrow afternoon, our escorts will arrive by canoe," replied Samaira. "We'll host them overnight and then depart the next morning."

"We don't need escorts to get to Kaua'i. Besides, we'll be able to go a lot faster on our own."

"We're not following," said Kai. "We will travel with them."

"On a canoe? But we've got our own ship."

"It's tradition," he explained. "We are being treated as guests of honor. That is why the Kahuna traveled here to invite us himself."

"So we're completely at their mercy? No way back without them?"

"Nobody said you had to come," reminded Samaira. "You're perfectly welcome to stay here."

"No," he said with a frown. "You won't be able to talk strategy on your own. This fight with Pa'ao is going to be a naval engagement."

"Then I guess you're getting in a canoe with us."

"Shit. How long does that take?"

"Two days," said Kai.

"So, we're gone about a week, then?"

"Sounds right," said Samaira. "We'll be on Kaua'i for a few days, and there'll be four days of travel in the mix."

"Shit."

"You're a Navy man, Josh," said Samaira with a thin smile. "I didn't expect you to be so soft."

"Fair enough," he snorted. "You won't hear anymore bitching from me."

***

At sunrise the following morning, Josh knocked on Miroslava's door, letting himself in without waiting for a response.

"Mira? You up?"

"I am now," came the groggy reply from the bedroom. "What time is it?"

"Early," he admitted.

A moment later, she came out, still slipping a t-shirt over her head.

"What's up?" she asked.

"Things are going sideways with this wedding."

"Huh?"

"They're ferrying us over as 'guests of honor' or some crap. We're not taking the ship."

"Can we just follow along?"

"I don't think so," he replied, shaking his head.

"Shit. What are you going to do?"

"I'm not sure yet."

"You'll have to smuggle it aboard somehow."

"Yeah. But that's not the biggest problem."

"Huh?"

"I've got to jab someone without causing a fuss if I expect to leave in one piece. And I've got to get the timing right for Kai. If he shows symptoms before we get back, they'll put him in isolation."

"What if you don't have to jab anyone?"

"Okay. I'm listening."

"Scylla can't hurt us, but that doesn't necessarily mean it can't infect us."

"What do you mean?"

"You could be patient zero."

"Would that even work?"

"I don't know," admitted Miroslava. "But Simmons should be able to tell us."

***

As the team's biomedical researcher, Annette Simmons's role, at some point, would be to establish and oversee the facility where they would cultivate new batches of antibiotics and synthesize medicines. She'd also received much more detailed information about Scylla and Charybdis's characteristics than her colleagues. Josh joined her and a few others for small talk over breakfast. When they'd finished, he followed her into the plaza.

"I need to ask you a couple of things about Scylla," he said quietly.

"Here?"

"Yeah. It'll be quick. Just take that serious look off your face, and nobody will pay attention."

"Okay. Shoot."

"Can we carry it? As hosts, I mean."

"Sure. If we still had any."

"I stashed one as a failsafe," he explained. "Do I just jab myself with it?"

"Yeah. But I wouldn't recommend it."

"Is it dangerous?"

"Not in theory. But I wouldn't volunteer to find out for sure."

"How long after the jab before I could spread it?"

"Twenty-four to forty-eight hours, based on what I know."

"So you're not sure?"

"It's not a scenario we studied," she admitted.

"And how long would I stay infectious?"

"Three to five days?" she said with a shrug.

"Hmm. And how long before someone with secondary exposure shows symptoms?"

"About twenty-four hours. *That* I know for sure. What's this all about?"

"I'm flying solo to the wedding. No ship. No backup," he explained.

"Okay, but I don't know how you expect to smuggle it over there."

"Let me worry about that. I just need you to figure out how the timeline plays out."

***

The escorts arrived in a much larger canoe than they had on the two prior occasions. The massive outrigger was more like the ones Pa'ao had used to chase the refugees from Moloka'i the year before. The crew was much larger, as well. The extra paddlers would work in shifts to stay well rested so the trip could be as short as possible.

A small crowd gathered to see them off on the morning of their departure. Samaira stepped into the canoe first, with Keanu snug at her breast, as always. Two men steadied her as she found her way to a seat. Kai followed, waving off his escorts. He'd grown so accustomed to the prosthetic blade in place of his left foot that he maneuvered on the unsteady craft with ease.

Jen leaped aboard with such confidence and ease that none of the warriors dared offer her support. The Navy recruits snickered among themselves, seeing the looks of surprise among the crew of the war canoe.

"Smart guys," remarked Park, standing just behind Sirotkin and Simmons.

Finally, Josh stepped gingerly into the canoe, holding tightly to the edge as he did so. After the first few uneasy steps, he lost his balance. One of the warriors caught him. He nodded politely and lowered himself onto the seat next to Jen. She cocked an eyebrow, giving him a sideways glance.

"What's wrong with Josh?" asked Miroslava Sirotkin.

"I guess his cargo isn't sitting right," replied Annette Simmons, stifling a chuckle.

"No way! He didn't."

"Yep. The old prison pouch," confirmed Simmons.

"Got to admire his dedication."

"Not to mention his dilation," she replied with a snort.

Park cocked his head, having overheard the cryptic conversation. Whatever they were talking about, they both thought it was funny.

***

Ted Park spent most of the day coming to terms with what was happening. That Simmons was in on a secret plan left little doubt about what it could be. Josh was taking Scylla as his uninvited guest to the wedding. It wasn't exactly a precision weapon. The briefings they'd received before leaving had made it clear their immunizations provided no inherited immunity to the pathogen. None of the natives—or even the children of the recruits—would be safe from its horrifying effects if anyone brought it back to O'ahu after the wedding. Not only was it possible many of the inhabitants could die, it seemed a likely part of the plan that they would.

Arriving for dinner, Ted felt sick. Anuenue and Mano sat with their charming daughter La'akea, who'd asked his name and shown off her gymnastics skills. Across the table, Tyler was sitting on Dr. Kitzinger's lap, picking away at their shared plate with his fingers. Farzin and Mano were laughing about something while Anuenue tried to help Riyoko convince Jasmine to try some unfamiliar food. It was the same at all of the tables. The original recruits and the new arrivals talked and laughed like old friends. Scattered among them were Park's Navy brethren. He wondered if any of *their* interactions were genuine.

Without the stomach to join the families, Ted headed to one of the other tables.

"Joining us tonight, Ted?" asked Serge as Park sat down.

"Yeah. Why not?" he replied, glancing at Malo. "You're Mano's twin brother, right?"

"Yes," nodded Malo.

"Very astute, Park," said Herman. "What gave it away?"

"Come on, man. I put up with enough of that shit from my crewmates. I was hoping to have a break for once."

Zaina shot Herman a disapproving look, elbowing him in the ribcage.

"I'm sorry, Ted," he said. "You're welcome to eat with us."

"What are you guys talking about?"

"Just commiserating with Malo about some of the finer points of learning English," said Serge.

"It can be confusing," added Herman. "Too many homonyms and no discernable rules."

"At least we don't sound like we're hacking up a lung when we talk," said Jayson, still chewing on a mouthful of food.

"German is an elegant language," he insisted.

"Elegant?" replied Serge. "I'm never sure if someone is speaking German or choking to death."

"Wow," remarked Park. "Didn't realize I was stepping into World War Three here."

"It's all in good fun," assured Herman. "What brings you to our table?"

"Nothing. Just looking to catch up on what I missed over the last year."

Jayson stopped chewing and swallowed what was left in his mouth, glancing sideways at Park.

"You want to know what you missed?" he asked with a sneer.

Park gulped, and the rest of the table went quiet.

"That came out wrong," he said quickly. "I'm sorry about Kailani. I really liked her."

"And Olena?" asked Jayson.

"I didn't like her as much."

Jayson didn't break eye contact.

"We got a lot done around here while you were gone," said Herman, attempting to change the subject. "You must hardly recognize the place."

"How about you, Ted?" continued Jayson. "What did you get done last year?"

Parked nodded in resignation.

"I just wanted to stop by and say hi," he said, rising from the table. "I don't really feel like eating."

***

Ted Park barely slept that night. When he did, he was plagued by nightmares. He awoke covered in sweat in the predawn hours after one particularly troubling one. La'akea led Tyler and Leila by the hand as the toddlers took tentative steps across a distorted version of the plaza. Weeping red sores opened on the young girl's neck, oozing thick pus. They spread across her face and body, moving down her arm, where they soon began infecting her obliviously giggling charges. None of them seemed to notice. They kept laughing even as the sores went black, and pieces of their dead flesh flaked to the ground.

"Watch us, Ted!" exclaimed La'akea, as she continued her transformation into a grotesque, disfigured monster, walking toward him with the others still in tow.

He tried to back away, but his legs would barely move. They resisted his attempts to escape as though caught in thick mud. Finally, he tripped and fell to the ground. The once-beautiful little girl and the decaying toddlers were on top of him, still playfully giggling as they grabbed at his clothes. He sat up in bed with his heart thumping so loudly he could hear it over the sound of the singing night insects outside his apartment. Afraid the horror would revisit him if he tried, he didn't go back to sleep.

Instead, he waited for the sun to rise before slipping outside, heading for the path to the harbor. There, he chose a spot in the dry sand just out of reach of the breaking waves and sat down. When he closed his eyes, he imagined himself on summer vacation with his parents on the beaches on the Outer Banks of North Carolina.

They'd made the drive from Arlington to stay in a rental house a block from the water a few times he could remember. Maybe they'd even done it a few times before that—when he was still too young to form lasting memories. He imagined his older sister leading him by the hand, like La'akea had done with Tyler and Leila in his dream, as they searched for shells on the beach. But he wasn't sure it was something that had really happened.

Someday, almost a thousand years in the future, his sister, brother-in-law, and their kids would arrive in this new world along with his parents. The first thing they'd do, he imagined, would be to explore the historical record to find out what great things he had accomplished on their behalf. What would be written? What would they think? Would he be a hero or a monster?

"You're up early."

The sudden intrusion startled him from his daydream, and he looked up to see Serge standing beside him, huffing. He was dripping with sweat.

"Couldn't sleep anymore," explained Park. "What about you?"

"I like to go for a run in the morning before it gets too hot," replied Serge, taking a seat on the sand.

They stared at the waves in silence for a few moments.

"Are you upset about dinner last night?" asked Serge finally.

"I deserved it, I guess."

"Yes. You did."

"So you didn't stop by to make me feel better, I see."

"There are some things you shouldn't feel better about."

Park sighed and shook his head, still looking out at the water.

"Is this what it's going to be like from now on?"

"It doesn't have to be," replied Serge with a shrug. "It all depends on you and your crewmates. We have different ideas about our place in this world."

"And if we can't all come to the same conclusion? What then?"

"We will fracture apart," he said. "None of us will be a party to genocide."

"What if you don't have a choice?"

"You have to understand that we are not the same naïve kids you left behind. We've seen violence, war, and death up close. Your guns don't scare us anymore."

"We didn't have to put them down that night in the plaza, you know."

"And yet, you were the first one who did," said Serge.

"I guess I was."

"Maybe you're getting your humanity back. It happened to Farzin and Jen, so there's hope for you, too."

Neither spoke for several minutes as they enjoyed the last moments of quiet before the rest of the community slowly came to life.

"It was nice talking to you, Park," said Serge finally. "I'm going to have a shower and some breakfast."

He stood up and started for the pathway back up to Punchbowl.

"Wait," called Park.

"What is it?" he asked, turning back.

"You said you're not afraid of our guns anymore."

"Yes?"

"What if we're not planning to use guns?"

Chapter 12

RICHARD REMAINED AT THE Center late that Tuesday evening. In fact, it was the early hours of Wednesday morning before he finally realized he desperately needed sleep and closed the lid of his laptop. He was beyond frustrated. After getting the password from Andrew, he'd rummaged through Akindele's files to find something he could put on a flash drive to convince Rebecca the physicist was stealing company information.

It was a simple enough plan, but he'd run into a snag. He couldn't figure out the meaning behind Akindele's latest work. He could hardly go to Rebecca to claim it was valuable information if he couldn't even explain it. Of course, he could choose some files he *did* understand, but if Jimi's new work was important, Richard would have to prove he was smart enough to continue it on his own. So far, it seemed he wasn't.

The baffling matrices of equations were based on the Akindele Space-Time model. That much he could tell. He put a great deal of effort into understanding how to calculate the convergences between their own reality and the ones created during a transfer. The characteristic eight-dimensional space—which they'd represented visually as a torus to illustrate the illusion of time travel to the Gamma recruits—revealed itself in Akindele's latest work. But it wasn't looking at convergences at all. It seemed to be an attempt at modeling the relationship between realities beyond the confines of the convergence windows.

With a sigh, Richard rose from his desk, tucked the laptop into his shoulder bag, and headed to his car. Perhaps his mind would make sense of it all, sorting through the endless matrices as he slept, and he would waken to a sudden revelation. Doubtful. His mind already had too many tasks to juggle. Nevertheless, he maintained a close watch on the efforts to track down Agent Boucher while developing the strategy to undermine her should she slip through their fingers and make some noise.

Rebecca was still on site, insisting on in-person briefings twice a day, and, of course, he still had to keep Delta on track. In two days, the last of the components from the warehouse would be loaded onto a cargo ship to make their way south to the vast open waters of the equatorial Pacific Ocean for final assembly. If anything went wrong, Rebecca would lose her mind, and he would lose his chance to join *either* of the remaining missions.

He didn't want to admit it, but the stress was getting to him. He ignored the heart palpitations and dizzy spells with the irrational conviction that any imagined problem could only become real if confirmed by a doctor. The next few months were the home stretch, he told himself; then everything would calm down, and the problem would disappear on its own.

As he approached his car, the now familiar thumping sensation of something misfiring in his chest and the accompanying shortness of breath returned. He steadied himself against the door as his vision narrowed into a black-walled tunnel. After a few deep breaths, his heartbeat normalized, and his peripheral vision returned. He shook his head in disgust before getting into his car. There was no time for this kind of weakness. Not now. He'd overcome it by sheer force of will, he decided, and everything would come together. By the time he left the parking lot, he almost believed it.

***

For the second day in a row, Don Lee was eating lunch alone at the Ruby Tuesday in Kapolei, far from his office and usual haunts. After a disappointing chicken salad the day before, he sat at a table with a view of the entrance, enjoying the guilty pleasure of a hamburger. He glanced towards the door every few seconds, hoping to recognize Assistant Special Agent in Charge Nathaniel Clyburn from his many recent press conferences about the incident at the coffee shop. It wouldn't be hard. At six-foot-five and a little over two hundred and eighty pounds, he would be hard to miss. Shannon had described his build as that of a retired linebacker—imposing but a bit out of shape. His inexplicable preference for Ruby Tuesday among the many eateries near the Honolulu field office probably had something to do with that.

The day before, Don had nursed his iced tea for two hours, waiting for the agent to show up. It was almost a relief when he didn't. The plan to intercept him, though sound, made him feel more than a little uncomfortable. Despite Shannon's assurances he was the most trustworthy man she'd ever met, Don couldn't help but worry there was a chance he'd be arrested, shot, or beaten to a bloody pulp. Unfortunately, he couldn't think of a better way to approach the agent without drawing the attention of anyone in the FBI field office who might be compromised. On the second day of reconnaissance, he wasn't so lucky. ASAC Clyburn walked in with two other agents just before 1:00PM—and Don ordered another drink to sip on while he waited for his moment.

The group of agents put in their orders, enjoying a lively discussion while they waited for drinks to arrive. Don watched with increasing anxiety, knowing that eventually, ASAC Clyburn would excuse himself to use the restroom, initiating the planned intercept. All the while, he regretted ordering the third glass of iced tea, which was rapidly making him feel very uncomfortable. He crossed his legs and shifted in his seat, wondering how long he could wait before his bladder exploded from the building pressure. None of the men seemed in a hurry to get back to work—or to use the facilities. Instead, they took their time, talking and laughing as they ate.

An hour after they'd arrived, his sandwich long gone, Clyburn picked away at a few remaining fries. When he finally popped the last one in his mouth, Don started whispering silent prayers that he would excuse himself from the table. Instead, he pointed to the small pile of fries remaining on the plate of the agent opposite him. With a nod of approval from his colleague, Clyburn started eating them one by one with maddening deliberation.

By now, Don was screaming silent obscenities at the man, urging him to get up and go to the bathroom. Though he'd stopped drinking himself, each time Clyburn raised his drink to his lips, Don felt his own discomfort harder to ignore. Finally, he could take the pressure no more. He shuffled awkwardly to the restroom as quickly as possible to avoid doing any permanent damage to his plumbing. Rushing for the nearest urinal, he barely unzipped in time to unleash the desperate torrent, ringing it musically off the porcelain bowl. He sighed as the pressure eased, and marveled at how good it could feel to do something as simple as taking a piss.

After a quick shake, Don zipped up and turned around to find Clyburn glaring at him.

"You want to tell me why you've had me under surveillance for the last hour?" demanded the agent.

Petrified, Don didn't say anything. Instead, he reached for his pocket with a trembling hand. Clyburn grabbed his arm, nearly pulling it out of the socket, and spun him around. Before he knew what was happening, the agent had Don spread eagle with his face against the bathroom wall and was patting him down. Clyburn pulled a note from Don's right front pocket.

"Is this what you were reaching for?" he demanded, shoving the folded piece of paper in his face.

"Yes," he gulped. "It's just a note."

"Don't move," replied the agent.

"I was sent by a friend."

Clyburn ignored him as he read.

"This legit?" he asked finally.

Don nodded.

"Got a number where I can reach you?"

"No phones," he whispered hoarsely. "She says it's not safe."

The agent regarded Don like a wolf evaluating a wounded rabbit.

"Meet me here at noon on Monday," he said, pocketing the note.

He left without another word—and without using the facilities.

***

If Andrew had been nervous about coming to the Akindele home the week before, this time, he was terrified. Jimi's mother planned to reveal all she knew about the Center, Samaira, and Andrew to her son. Despite assurances she could handle him, Andrew knew what was at stake if she was wrong. He rang the bell, and Mrs. Akindele—Tiara, she still insisted—relieved him of his phone before leading him to the backyard, where a stern-faced Jimi was fidgeting impatiently in one of the wrought-iron chairs.

"Hello, Dr. Akindele," he greeted as he wiped his sweaty palm on his pants and extended a hand.

The physicist didn't take it. Andrew shrugged and sat down opposite him. Tiara Akindele, ever the gracious host, ignored the awkward silence while bringing out tea and biscuits for her guest. Getting down to business without the requisite niceties would not be proper.

"It's so nice to have you here again, Andrew," she said with a warm smile as she maneuvered into her chair and pulled it up to the table.

"Thank you, ma'am."

"Tiara," she reminded him.

"Thank you, Tiara."

Dr. Akindele narrowed his eyes but said nothing.

"Jimi?" coaxed Tiara. "Have you welcomed our guest?"

"Welcome to our home," said Jimi without a hint of sincerity.

Andrew had visions of childhood when his own mother would correct his behavior in front of guests at the dinner table. The grown man across from him was getting the same guidance, seemingly unaware of how absurd it was at his age.

"It is a lovely home," he replied, unsure of what to say.

"Can we get on with this?" implored Jimi.

"Alright," his mother said with a sigh. "I asked Andrew here because I'm worried about you, Jimi."

Andrew's eyes widened at the realization that Akindele's mother hadn't prepared her son for the conversation. He was taking part in an intervention.

"You are always worried about me," replied Jimi with a dismissive wave. "And why is *he* here? I barely know this man."

"Andrew is here because I want to talk about what they have you doing at work."

Akindele swung his head around at Andrew and glared.

"What have you told her?" he demanded.

Andrew opened his mouth to reply, but Tiara cut him off.

"He didn't tell me anything. One of your other colleagues did."

"Who?"

"Samaira Adams."

"Dr. Adams?" he asked, cocking his head. "When did this happen?"

"A few weeks ago."

"That's impossible," he snorted.

"And why is that, Jimi?" she asked.

Andrew noticed a hint of self-satisfaction as she asked the question.

"We cannot have this conversation," said Dr. Akindele, rising from his chair. "There is too much at risk."

"Sit down, Jimi."

She didn't raise her voice or look angry, but Andrew felt a sudden chill. He gulped. Jimi froze momentarily before lowering himself back into his chair.

"I know what you are trying to do for the world," she continued. "Samaira told me everything. It's lovely, Jimi. It really *is* lovely. You are a good man."

Andrew watched with fascination as Jimi calmed down at her soothing words and rhythmic, almost sing-song delivery. He wondered if it was exhausting for her to interact with him, or if it had become second nature from decades of practice.

"If you know what I am doing, then you know Samaira is gone. She couldn't have told you anything."

"She left me a letter explaining everything. It is truly amazing what you are capable of, Jimi. I've always thought so."

"And him?" asked Jimi, tilting his head toward Andrew. "Why is this fool here in our garden?"

"He's a guest, Jimi," she reminded him.

He sighed.

"Why is Andrew here?"

"Samaira told me he would help me understand what they've gotten you into over there."

"*They* haven't gotten me into anything. There is no *they*. It's *me*. The Center is all about *my* work."

"I know that, Jimi," she assured. "And it really is the most incredible thing. But there are things you don't know about."

"Like what?"

"Andrew?" she prompted.

He gulped. He'd been more than happy to sit silently on the periphery of the conversation, and wasn't sure how he'd fit into their unique dynamic. What he was about to say could not be taken back. If Richard found out, he was as good as dead.

"Someone died, Dr. Akindele."

"We are not certain of that," cautioned Jimi. "And Aiden was a volunteer. He knew the risks."

"What? Aiden? What happened to Aiden?"

"This is about the Gamma incident, correct?"

"No. What incident?"

"If this isn't about Aiden, then what are you talking about?" deflected Akindele.

"Hitarthi," said Andrew. "She was murdered."

"Which one was she?" asked Dr. Akindele, seemingly unfazed by the declaration.

"Hitarthi Srinivasan."

Dr. Akindele shrugged and shook his head.

"Sri Lankan girl," continued Andrew. "Materials science."

"Oh yes," he recalled. "She decided to leave the program."

"No. She didn't," said Andrew. "She's dead."

"How?"

"They made it look like an accident, but it was murder. I have proof."

"Does Richard know about this?"

"I think he might have ordered it."

"Impossible," huffed Akindele, rolling his eyes. "The man is a spineless, incompetent weasel. There is no way he had someone killed."

"Maybe," allowed Andrew with a shrug. "But for sure, he knows about it."

"Even if this is true, what has this got to do with me?"

Andrew recalled the gruesome experiment Tiara had described the week before; the impaled flies walking in an endless, circular death march. Statistically speaking, he knew he'd interacted with sociopaths before. Probably Richard, he imagined. What made Akindele different was his inability to understand when and how to feign empathy.

"Jimi," said his mother, shaking her head. "You cannot separate yourself from these actions. You said yourself that your work is the very reason for the existence of the Center. You must take some responsibility for everything that happens there."

"How can I take responsibility for something I didn't even know about?"

"Well, now you know," she said simply.

"So what do you want me to do about it, mother?"

"Help us stop it."

"No," he replied, shaking his head. "I can't do that."

"Why not?"

"Because we'll be stuck here."

"What do you mean, stuck here?"

"Can't you see what is happening around you? Humanity has failed. Our only chance is to start again."

"That doesn't explain anything, Jimi. Where, exactly, do you think you're taking me?"

"Why do you think I created a new world? As a plaything for Dr. Adams and the others? It's for us, mother. You and me."

For the first time since Andrew had met her, Tiara seemed to lose her composure. She tried to find words, but none came as she stared at her son in disbelief. She took his hands in her own and shook her head. It was heartbreaking—and awkward. Andrew wished he could just get up and slip away unnoticed.

"My dear, sweet boy," she said finally. "I'm sure no mother has ever felt as proud as I do right now."

Andrew was agape. Of the dozens of possible scenarios he'd imagined before arriving, this was not among them. Either she was manipulating her son, or she was just as nuts as he was. Neither thought was particularly comforting. His future—his survival—was now inextricably linked to both of them.

"So, we're just forgetting about Hitarthi, then?" he asked. "You know—the dead girl?"

"Of course not," said Tiara. "But I believe Jimi didn't know."

"But what do we do about it?"

"It is in the past, Andrew," replied Dr. Akindele. "There is nothing we can do."

"Then what's the goddam point of this meeting?"

"Andrew!" scolded Tiara. "You may be a guest, but I will not have you speaking like that in my home."

"I'm sorry, ma'am. It's just that—"

He paused.

"What is it?"

"Richard scares the crap out of me, and I'm pretty sure he'll have me killed if he finds out what I know."

"You don't need to worry about Richard for long," assured Dr. Akindele. "In a few months, he'll be gone for good."

"Oh shit," said Andrew.

Tiara shot him a disapproving look.

"Sorry, ma'am," he said sheepishly before turning back to Dr. Akindele. "Are you talking about the submarine thing?"

Jimi's eyes narrowed.

"How do you know about that?"

"Richard told me about it. I'm supposed to be on the mission."

"You're going on Delta with Richard?"

"That's what he's calling it," confirmed Andrew. "But he's not planning to go."

"What do you mean?"

"I mean, he made it pretty clear to me he's not going."

Dr. Akindele was silent for a few moments. His mother regarded him with growing concern.

"What's wrong, Jimi?" she asked finally.

"The incident I mentioned during Gamma," he started. "As punishment for letting it happen, Richard was relegated to Delta."

"What do you mean by *relegated*?" demanded Andrew. "What's wrong with Delta?"

"Nothing is *wrong* with Delta," he shot. "You should count yourself lucky to be involved at all."

"How did Richard get out of it?" asked Andrew, setting aside his doubts for the moment.

"He didn't. Not as far as I am aware."

"Richard is a physicist, Jimi," reminded his mother.

"Barely," he snorted.

"But he understands your work?"

"If I speak slowly enough, yes, he now understands some aspects of my work."

Andrew and Tiara shared a look of horrified recognition.

"What?" demanded Dr. Akindele.

"So, what would happen if you weren't able to continue your work for some reason?" asked Andrew.

"What sort of reason?"

"Like, maybe you go paddle boarding and accidentally drown?"

"Don't be ridiculous. I don't paddle board."

"Neither did Hitarthi," replied Andrew with a shrug.

Dr. Akindele frowned, nodding slowly.

"Richard would take over," he realized.

"He's planning to kill you, Jimi," said Tiara.

"I don't think so," said Andrew. "He's got something else in mind."

The hack request made much more sense now that Andrew understood the intent. He explained to his hosts how he'd provided Richard with access to Akindele's account by bypassing the brute-force safeguard to figure out the password.

"Why would you do that, Andrew?" asked Dr. Akindele.

"Like I said, Richard scares the shit out of me."

He winced at Tiara, but she didn't seem to have noticed his colorful language this time.

"It's done," she said with a wave of her hand. "The only question now is, what can we do about it?"

Chapter 13

His name was Don Lee—a building inspector. A nobody. A query on his plates and a look at the associated license photo confirmed it. Had he not waited until after the man had emptied his bladder to confront him, ASAC Clyburn was convinced he would have pissed himself with fear. He was no fame-seeking narcissist, inserting himself into the investigation just for the fun of it. He was telling the truth.

Even before the encounter in the men's room, he had doubts about what he'd been forced by circumstances to say in press briefings; that one of his agents was a person of interest in the deadly crash at the Waimalu coffee shop. The unsourced allegations about Shannon's secret offshore account were both accurate and bullshit simultaneously. The account *did* exist, but it was so clumsy and obvious that routine internal security audits would have caught it easily.

The joke in the office was you couldn't even take a dump at the FBI without the correct paperwork. The most recent audit gave credence to the crude axiom. The audits were documented and included the requisite signatures from the auditor and a supervisor. He'd called both into his office to look them in the eyes when they swore they'd followed the procedures to the letter. Then they went through the process again. The system flagged the offshore account for a deeper forensic audit, just as it should have on prior occasions when it had apparently failed to do so.

His own suspicion, supported by the audit team, was why he hadn't dragged Don out of the restroom in handcuffs the week before. The message from Shannon aligned with what he already suspected; she was the victim of a highly sophisticated setup. Now, he sat alone at his usual table in Ruby Tuesday, waiting for Don to reappear. It was early enough that nobody else from the field office was likely to be there, but not so early the place was deserted. A few retirees were beating the lunch rush, and a table of hungover tourists was having a late breakfast of steak and eggs with Bloody Marys.

Clyburn knew he was treading on dangerous ground. He'd probably already done enough to get himself disciplined—maybe even fired. Following through on his plan with the building inspector might even raise the risk of getting himself arrested.

A protector by nature, he couldn't turn his back when one of his agents needed him. It started in middle school, where he'd used his size to intimidate bullies when they tried to pick on the kids that were different. His interventions were almost always without reward. A black kid in a very white suburb of Salt Lake City, his punishment when things got physical was often more severe than that meted out to the bullies who had started it.

His reputation as a troublemaker was forgotten in high school when he showed promise on the football field. True to his nature, he was a star on the offensive line, protecting the quarterback that led them to a state championship before heading to BYU, where he was part of the line that propelled the legendary Ty Detmer to the only Heisman trophy in school history.

Though a giant among regular people, Clyburn was smart enough to realize he didn't have the size or skill to translate his college success to the NFL. He studied hard, got a law degree, ending up at Quantico on his way to a bright career in the FBI—and a coveted position in the Honolulu field office. It was a career he was proud of. Now, he was putting it at risk by trusting some pencil pusher to stay quiet.

The base-model Civic pulled into the lot at 11:35. Don Lee pulled a baseball cap low over his forehead, looking around nervously before heading for the entrance. Clyburn snorted with amusement at the clueless building inspector's amateurish attempt at counter-surveillance.

"You have a phone on you?" asked Don as he slid into the booth opposite the agent.

"Left both on my desk, as requested," he assured.

"She wants to come in," said Don. "But she's scared."

She wants to come in. It seemed Don had spent at least part of the weekend preparing cliches for the encounter.

"She *should* be scared," replied Clyburn.

"But you could keep her safe, right?"

"I'm not sure I can."

"She's not even safe in FBI custody?"

"She'd be safe from physical harm," assured Clyburn. "But I can't control how the legal case will unfold. Whatever she's up against here has some pretty long tentacles."

"I can't keep her at my place."

"And if she comes out of hiding, I have to take her into custody."

"What the hell am I supposed to do?"

"Relax, Mr. Lee. You've done your part."

He handed Don an envelope.

"What's this?"

"A key to a rental condo I own near Waikiki and some cash. Just get her there quietly and forget everything—especially talking to me."

Don breathed a sigh of relief.

"I mean it," cautioned Clyburn. "Forget *everything*, or we're *both* in trouble."

"Already forgotten," assured Don. "I wish I'd never even heard of the Center for Sustainability Research."

***

After a frustrating weekend reviewing Dr. Akindele's latest work, Richard had to admit defeat. He took solace in knowing he'd found a way to turn that defeat into a small victory for himself. He would go to Rebecca and use its very existence as evidence of his own value. Without Richard's diligence, who could say if Akindele ever planned to share it with its rightful owner, Anton Kamaras? Once he exposed the deception and established what the data was for, he'd force Jimi to explain the math. He grabbed his laptop from the desk and headed for Rebecca's office, prepared to show her what the physicist had been up to.

When he arrived, he was surprised to find Dr. Akindele was already there, sharing something on the interactive wall. He knocked lightly on the glass door. Rebecca looked up with a smile, motioning for him to enter.

"You're just in time, Richard," she said. "Dr. Akindele has some good news to share. I'm going to need a translator to put this into words I can understand."

"Great," he replied, trying to hide his frustration as he looked at the equations on the wall, realizing it was the same work he was about to expose. "What are we looking at?"

"It's a way to develop the precise relative coordinates of two parallel worlds in eight-dimensional space," explained Dr. Akindele.

"And why is that such good news, Rebecca?" asked Richard, his mind racing to catch up.

"I haven't the faintest idea," she admitted. "But Dr. Akindele assures me it is."

"So far, the interactions with our parallel world have all occurred at what we call convergences," the physicist continued.

"Which makes the most sense," interjected Richard, desperate to demonstrate his expertise, "because that is where we get the best mass transfer rates."

"Actually, the main reason is that we don't know exactly where it is before convergence," corrected Akindele. "Before convergence, and immediately after, the parallel world is in one of an infinite number of potential locations relative to our own."

"How is that possible?" asked Rebecca.

"Because of our limited information."

"Think of it like this," tried Richard again. "If I told you A plus B equals ten, what are the possible values of A and B?"

"There are an infinite number of combinations that would work," she said, nodding in recognition. "But how do we suddenly know the answer at convergence?"

"Because that's what convergence means. The coordinates relative to our own universe are all zeros."

She eyed Richard doubtfully, looking to Dr. Akindele for clarification.

"Think of it geometrically," suggested Akindele, touching his finger to the interactive wall to draw a dot. "If our world is this point, you can think of the parallel world as being one of an infinite number of points around it."

He drew a circle around the dot to represent the infinite number of points.

"Before convergence, we don't have enough information to know which of the points on the circle represents our other world. At convergence, the radius of the circle of possibilities is zero, and both worlds occupy the same point. Infinite choices become one, and we can do our transfer."

"And that's rare," stated Rebecca.

"Yes. Very," he confirmed. "It took a long time to identify a reality with enough appropriate convergences for our needs."

"And your new work? What's the significance?"

"He's trying to pinpoint the parallel reality before convergence," said Richard.

"How?"

Akindele started to answer, but Richard cut him off in an attempt to remain relevant in the conversation.

"Remember A plus B equals ten?" he asked.

"Yes."

"Well, what if I told you four times A equals B?"

She thought for a moment before answering, "A is two, and B is eight."

"Correct," he said. "It's just a matter of having enough information."

Grateful he'd studied the data without Jimi's knowledge for almost a week, Richard struggled to stay relevant in the conversation while deciphering the implications on the fly.

"This is all very confusing," said Rebecca, shaking her head.

"That's because Richard is making it confusing," said Akindele. "Forget his A plus B nonsense and think geometrically."

He returned to the interactive wall with the point and surrounding circle he'd drawn.

"We know convergence is coming. But, so far, we have not been able to calculate what direction it is coming from."

He drew a line from the convergence point and tapped where it intersected the circle.

"If we can calculate the direction of this line, we will know the exact position of the parallel reality relative to our own."

"That seems easy enough."

"This example has only two dimensions," reminded Dr. Akindele. "Now, imagine yourself standing at the center of a sphere—like you are inside a giant, inflated balloon. We know the reality we are looking for is somewhere on the balloon's surface."

"But we don't know where?"

"Correct. We lack the necessary information."

"Which is?"

"The vector to its location."

"In English, please."

"Point your finger from where you are standing at the center of the balloon. The direction you are pointing is our vector, and the spot on the surface of the sphere you are pointing at is our parallel world."

"And we didn't need this vector before because we've been waiting for the convergences," interjected Richard quickly. "That's when the balloon collapses to a single point."

Rebecca turned to him.

"So, what's different now? What does this all mean?"

"Uh—"

Richard glanced at Jimi, hoping to get bailed out, but the physicist said nothing.

Rebecca snorted, turning back to Dr. Akindele.

"Go on, please," she said.

"Of course, it is not so simple as pointing. We represent Akindele space-time visually as a toroid—a donut—because it is a convenient way to illustrate something that is finite, yet has no boundaries. The mathematical model behind it has eight spatial dimensions, so we must develop an eight-dimensional vector to calculate its intersection with the space-time model."

"I can't visualize that," admitted Rebecca, "but I get the idea. What I *don't* get is why this is such good news."

"It means we have opportunities before Delta to influence what is happening in our parallel world."

Richard's eyes went wide with sudden recognition.

"When?" he demanded.

"In less than two weeks. We'll reach the smallest offset we can hope for outside of convergence."

"It'll never happen," he said, shaking his head. "We don't have any extra capacitor networks, and Fusion B hasn't been completely reassembled after Gamma."

"We can use the capacitor network for Epsilon," replied Akindele. "There is plenty of time to get another one to replace it, and it will only take a day or two to get Fusion B ready."

"You don't have a crew to run another event. Everyone's in the middle of the South Pacific preparing for Delta."

"Once all of the numbers are in, they mostly watch. I just need a bit of help to push buttons."

"We can't spare anyone," insisted Richard. "The schedule is too tight."

"Any monkey will do. I can use that fool, Andrew, from IT. He's not doing anything of value."

"Take him," decided Rebecca. "He's yours."

"This is chaos. We can't work like this," protested Richard.

"Chaos seems to be your area of expertise, Richard," said Akindele with a grin. "The only reason a course correction is necessary is because of your Gamma disaster."

"How much can we get over?" asked Rebecca, ignoring their bickering.

"Quite a bit less than Gamma," cautioned Akindele. "Even with a smaller time difference, we need considerable energy to overcome the spatial mismatch."

"How much?" she asked again.

"He doesn't know," realized Richard. "He hasn't been able to calculate the intersection yet."

"I won't know for sure until I have all eight spatial components of the vector."

"So Richard is right?" she demanded. "You don't actually know how to do this yet?"

"I will know in less than a week," he promised. "But I can safely estimate a three-to-five-second window with a transfer rate between one fifty and two fifty kilos per second."

Rebecca nodded thoughtfully.

"This is excellent news for us, Richard. And especially for you."

"Why is that?"

"It looks like your chance to atone has come early."

"What?"

"Pick some SEALs and saddle up. You're going for a ride."

"It's too soon—," he started. "I can't."

"You will," she insisted.

"The FBI shit show," blurted Richard in desperation. "Boucher is still out there. You need me."

Dr. Akindele cocked his head.

"FBI?" he asked.

"It's nothing you need to worry about, doctor," said Rebecca with a wave of her hand. "Why don't you get back to your work while Richard and I review some logistics?"

Richard gritted his teeth and glared as Akindele excused himself.

***

After an hour of argument, Rebecca hadn't budged an inch. Surely an extra SEAL would be a better option than wasting precious mass on somebody who'd never even carried a gun as part of his Navy service, he'd pleaded. However, she insisted it would be too late to rely on force alone. The situation called for flexibility and planning that only someone with Richard's knowledge could handle. There was no outright threat, but Rebecca had implied that his family's safety upon their arrival as part of Epsilon would hinge on his success.

His vision narrowed to a tunnel in front of him as he stormed his way back to his office. A disorienting mix of intense anger and desperate fear gripped him. He had less than two weeks to figure out how to neutralize Akindele, or he'd be heading through the aperture early—without his family.

"Fuck!" he screamed as the outer door slammed behind him. "I'm going to murder that motherfucking son of a bitch!"

He flung his laptop at the glass door of his inner office, shattering it to pieces. His heart fluttered in his chest as he struggled to draw full breaths. Richard was still a few steps from the couch when the room started spinning, and everything went black.

Chapter 14

KAMEHA STOOD BESIDE HIS sister, Luni, on a raised platform overlooking the bay. After receiving word their guests were approaching, they'd taken their positions along with Chief Paumakua, his son Moeanaimua, and the Kahuna. Kameha and Luni stood behind, barely able to see past their hosts' ornate, feather-adorned ceremonial garb. Though Kameha had been relegated to a supporting role, it was only temporary. Within days, he would reveal the full extent of his ambition, assuming a position of far more prominence than the one he'd sought to usurp after Kai's disappearance.

He resisted the urge to stand on his toes or crane his neck to get a better view. It was undignified—unbecoming of a man who would be chief. Still, he was curious to see the new arrivals. The Kahuna had assured him the Dark Witch, the one who had defeated Pa'ao with her magic, would be among the guests from O'ahu attending the wedding—and Kai would be with her.

He caught glimpses of the approaching canoe through the plumes of feathers crowning the heads of the trio in front. When it was close enough that he could hear the splashing of their paddles, he could take it no longer. He nudged Luni to one side, pushing her forward next to Moeanaimua. Then he shuffled his way to the other side of the platform and assumed a position beside the Kahuna. He caught a disapproving sideways glance, but they exchanged no words.

A group of warriors rushed forward to help pull the outrigger ashore, while a priest raised a conch to his lips to sound a welcome. Kai stepped from the canoe, and the chief whispered something to his son—probably remarking on the prosthesis, Kameha imagined. The witch, a baby slung across her chest, took Kai by the hand to steady herself as she followed him into the shallow water. Kameha momentarily lost his composure before closing his gaping jaw. He'd heard a description of the witch, but it hadn't done her credit. She was stunningly beautiful and seemed at ease despite being surrounded by dozens of warriors.

At first, the news Kai had married the witch, and that she had borne his child troubled him greatly. It didn't take him long to realize it was a blessing he could use to get what he needed from her. Now, after seeing her in the flesh, doubts began creeping in once more. His plan relied on being able to control her. He'd have to scale back his ambition if he had to kill her instead. At least that was still an option. He hadn't exposed the full extent of his duplicity to anyone but his closest allies, and was still in a position to profit from either outcome.

The other two guests from O'ahu disembarked. Warriors escorted the group to the platform where their hosts awaited.

"Hau'oli mākou e ho'okipa iā 'oe ma ke 'ano he malihini," greeted Chief Paumakua.

He maintained a severe gaze, but the glint in his eye revealed his sincerity. His son smiled and uttered a similar greeting.

"Masalo. No makou ka hanohano," replied the witch.

"Masalo," agreed Kai with a polite nod.

To the fascination of the chief and his heir, they made further introductions with help from the translator. In a break from protocol, Moeanaimua stepped down from the platform to approach Kai.

"Hiki ia'u ke pa'a?" he asked, reaching out his hand.

To his delight, the tablet translated his request into unfamiliar sounds. "May I hold it?"

Kai handed the tablet to Moeanaimua.

"Ke kilokilo o Akindele," he remarked as he examined the strange device.

"Hōʻoiaʻiʻo," confirmed Kai.

The magic of Akindele. Moeanaimua handed it back.

"It is good to see you again, Kameha," continued Kai in his native tongue as the translator provided commentary for the benefit of his companions. "I was glad to hear you escaped Moloka'i."

"Indeed," agreed Kameha. "It was only by the grace of the gods that we escaped Pili."

"And also because Kai diverted Pa'ao and half of his warriors to O'ahu," suggested the witch—Samaira, she'd called herself.

"Also that," conceded Kameha with a nod. "Where you gave him a most unkind welcome, I understand."

She answered with only a smile.

Neither of their companions had offered anything more than a few polite gestures and smiles up to that point. The man, in particular, seemed uncomfortable—shifting back and forth on his feet while glancing around anxiously. He finally interrupted the witch, tapping her on the shoulder to ask a question. Kameha couldn't help but laugh when the device translated his request for directions to the latrine.

***

They'd spent the day frantically recruiting help and gathering supplies—all while doing their best to maintain the appearance of routine. Matteus had some sailing experience as a child in Denmark, and was among the first enlisted in the effort to foil Josh's plan. He, Park, and Farzin were the only ones with any knowledge of sailing. They would have to guide the others in the workings of the ship as they pursued the canoe that was already more than a day ahead.

Having been the one to sound the alarm, Serge would join the crew, along with Jayson, Herman, and Malo. Mano argued with his brother about being left out, but the others eventually convinced him the people remaining on O'ahu—including his wife and child—would need strong protectors should anything go wrong. He would prepare a cache of weapons and stay behind in case there was a second prong of attack Ted wasn't aware of.

Park managed the weapon requirements for the mission. Most of what they needed had been returned to the secure facility in the crater following the tense standoff the night of their return. The contents were inventoried twice daily by a pair representing both factions to keep everyone at ease. Park had arranged to be the Navy team representative for the evening inspection, and Serge had warned Dr. Kitzinger, the community representative, to expect irregularities in the routine.

Jayson, naturally, was in charge of provisioning the food, while Serge helped Herman fill a couple of large containers with fresh water to hide in dense foliage not far from the dock. Once everything was ready, there was nothing to do but wait.

Jayson tried his best to get a few hours of sleep before the start of the pre-dawn operation to steal Jasmine's Hope from the harbor. It was nearly impossible. When he closed his eyes, all he could think about was Luni. If Josh managed to deploy Scylla before they arrived, she would likely suffer a horrible death. Maybe they'd be able to isolate her in time, but from what Park had told them, the spread was likely to be rapid and thorough. Some on Kaua'i would survive, but most would not.

The tablet beside him vibrated, emitting a ping. Startled, he sat up in his bed with the realization he'd actually managed to fall asleep. It was just after five in the morning and still dark outside. He gathered his things and quietly opened his door. A shadow slipped through the dim light where the pathway disappeared behind the clinic below. Serge, probably, he thought. They'd agreed to staggered, predetermined times to slip down to the dock while avoiding suspicion. A single person heading down to the plaza could easily be written off as someone needing to use the communal latrine. A group was harder to explain. Jayson waited two more minutes before following.

Twenty-five minutes before sunrise, Ted Park arrived at the rendezvous point in the tree line near the harbor carrying a fully laden pack. He had an assault rifle over one shoulder and an RPG launcher over the other.

"Holy shit, Park," said Jayson. "What are you planning to do with that?"

"No such thing as too much firepower," he explained.

As if on cue, Farzin arrived with a second load of light arms.

"Okay," said Park. "This is all of us. Let's get this show on the road."

He unshouldered his weapons and glanced up the pathway towards the settlement to make sure it was clear. Taking a deep breath, he set off at a jog towards the dock. The others peered nervously through the trees, hoping their plan would work—and hoping Park didn't have a sudden change of heart. They could hear his footfalls on the wooden dock over the sound of the waves. He stopped at the rope ladder slung over the side of the ship and slapped the hull a few times.

"Hey, Paul," he called out. "You in there?"

Paul Suryana emerged groggily from the crew quarters.

"What the hell, Park? What's going on?"

"There's a bunch of weapons missing, and we can't find the geeks."

"What?"

"They're gone. Sirotkin needs us in the plaza—*now*."

"Jesus Christ. What are they up to?" he demanded as he swung onto the ladder and clambered down.

"Come on," urged Park. "Let's go."

He sprinted off towards the pathway with Paul at his side. As they reached the tree line, Park lunged at his unsuspecting companion, tackling him to the ground and clamping a hand over his mouth. Within seconds, Farzin, Jayson, and Serge were on top of him as well. Securing his hands and feet with rope, they gagged him so he couldn't raise an alarm. He wriggled desperately as they dragged him into the trees and tied him to a thick acacia. A stream of muffled profanities flowed from behind the gag.

Wasting no time, Farzin and Park gathered up the weapons while Serge and Herman took either end of a water barrel. The stocky warrior, Malo, shouldered the second one himself while Jayson and Matteus followed with the other provisions. Within minutes, they'd loaded the cargo and were ready to cast off as the first rays of sunlight crested over the water southeast of Diamond Head. The timing was perfect. They had no intention of maneuvering out of the harbor in darkness with an inexperienced crew.

Park manned the helm while Farzin untied the lines and pushed off. Matteus was already in position by the mainsail halyard to receive instructions by the time Farzin scampered up the ladder to join him at mid-deck. As the ship nosed its way downwind, the pair worked in unison to hoist the mainsail, watching closely as it inflated in the gentle morning breeze. Jasmine's Hope slipped seemingly undetected from Honolulu harbor and turned west towards Kaua'i.

"How long's this going to take?" asked Jayson as he secured the boom vang with Farzin's guidance.

"We could be there in as little as twenty hours if we push it."

"Then let's push it."

"No point arriving in the middle of the night. There's probably nowhere to dock this thing, anyway. We'll have to moor offshore and wait for morning. Maybe they'll send a canoe to get us or something."

"Screw that," replied Jayson. "I'll swim over myself as soon as we get there. We don't know what Josh plans to do with that shit."

"You'll either drown or get yourself speared through the chest," said Farzin, shaking his head.

"I'll take Malo. He's a good swimmer. He can let them know we're friendly."

"You ever do a night op, Jayson?"

"You mean besides the one we just did?"

"In the water?"

"No," he admitted.

"We're taking it easy and going ashore in daylight," insisted Farzin.

"What if we're too late to stop him?"

"What would you do if you were him, Jayson?"

"Kill myself out of self-loathing?"

"Seriously, though. He's not gonna do anything until just before they leave, so nobody shows symptoms while he's still on the island. Otherwise, it'd be suicide."

"I guess not," allowed Jayson.

"So let's not get ourselves killed. We're going to make it in time."

At that moment, Herman stepped onto the deck from the crew quarters with a tablet in hand. Ignoring Park at the wheel, he worked his way unsteadily towards Farzin, holding tightly to the railing as the ship porpoised its way through the waves.

"We've got a problem," he called.

"What is it?" demanded Farzin.

"A hit from Diamond Head. We've got canoes inbound."

"What?"

Herman handed over the tablet, and Farzin regarded the screen with a frown. Serge and Jayson squeezed in beside him to take a look.

"It's from Parth," observed Jayson. "He started his watch shift yesterday afternoon."

"I can't believe he's actually up this early," marveled Serge.

"Shit," said Farzin as responses began filling the screen.

Anyone who wasn't already awake soon would be.

The tablet buzzed in his hand as a notification appeared that Sirotkin was initiating a video conference. He moved his finger to select the option to join, and Jayson grabbed him by the wrist.

"What are you doing?"

"We have to find out what's going on," he replied. "Besides, it's too late for anyone to stop us now."

"I guess," allowed Jayson, releasing his grip.

Farzin joined the call as a tiled array of faces filled the screen. Parth was already delivering a panicked summary of what he was witnessing.

"Lot's of them. Like a half-dozen."

"How far out?" demanded Miroslava.

"I don't know. Pretty far, I guess."

"Where are they headed?"

"Too soon to say, but they're spread out."

"Don't panic," she advised. "Just keep updating us. We'll intercept as many as possible by sea while you direct land-based teams to anything that gets through."

"Okay," he replied in a shaky voice.

Sirotkin walked briskly as she spoke, pounding on doors and calling out the Navy recruits by name.

"Farzin! I need you out here."

He glanced at his companions on the deck of Jasmine's Hope with a shrug as he unmuted the device.

"Already out."

"Where the fuck are you?" demanded Sirotkin, focusing on the tile he occupied on her screen for the first time.

"On the ship."

"Okay. You and Paul get her ready to sail while I pull together the ground teams. I'll meet you down there in ten minutes."

"Uh, we're already out of port."

"What? Who?"

"Me and Park—and some of the others."

He tilted the screen to the left and right to reveal Jayson and Serge standing at his side. Jayson waved an awkward greeting.

"You're taking the geeks for a fucking joyride? Jesus Christ, Khan. Get the fuck back here!"

"Can't do that, I'm afraid."

"What? Let me talk to Paul."

"You're welcome to talk to Paul. He's tied to a tree near the dock."

"What the hell is going on?" she screamed at the tablet.

"We know about Josh," shot Jayson. "And that stuff he's got shoved up his ass. We're going to stop him before he can do anything with it."

"We're under attack, you idiot! We need that ship—now!"

Sirotkin directed a torrent of spit-flecked profanities at the tablet, and Farzin disconnected from the conversation.

"She's right, you know," he said.

"What do you mean?" demanded Jayson.

"Half a dozen war canoes could mean a thousand warriors are headed this way. If even a tenth of them make it into the jungle, things will get ugly."

"What Josh is doing isn't ugly enough for you?"

"Whatever happens, we won't let him bring Scylla back here."

"What about the people on Kaua'i? Kai? Luni? Keanu?"

"Listen. It's not like there are any easy choices here."

"So we just abandon them?"

"We're not abandoning anyone, Jayson. We'll get there as soon as we can."

"And if we're too late?"

"Jen and Kai can take care of themselves, and you, of all people, should know not to underestimate Samaira. We have to trust them to do their part while we do ours."

"He's right," added Serge. "We can't leave our friends here to face this alone."

Without further discussion, Farzin reconnected to the videoconference.

"We're turning around to intercept the canoes," he announced.

"You need a crew that knows what the hell they're doing," shouted Sirotkin. "Get back to the dock!"

"Not gonna happen," he replied before disconnecting again.

"Serge, man the boom. I'll tell Park we're bringing her around."

Miroslava Sirotkin hurled all manner of threats and profanities at the screen in front of her. It was no use. Farzin was gone.

"O'Neal," she ordered, "get down to the harbor and find Paul. The rest of you bring every weapon you can find to the plaza. I'm going to find out how many of these natives know how to use them."

***

Less than fifteen minutes later, a crowd of SEALs and warriors stood around a table outside of the bakery, listening while Sirotkin detailed the plan. A row of weapons leaning against the wall glinted in the early morning sun.

"We have no idea where they're planning to land, or even if they'll all land at the same place," she explained. "According to Parth, they're currently in a spread-out formation, indicating they might split up."

She held her tablet aloft, revealing a map where Parth had added several red circles to show the approximate positions of the approaching canoes.

"We need to double-time it eastward, and then wait for guidance from Diamond Head," she continued. "If they split up, so do we."

"How far can we realistically get before they land?" asked O'Neal.

"Aiden Point is doable, but it'll be a hell of a push."

"Nobody's landing a canoe there," he replied. "No beach."

"Probably not," agreed Sirotkin, "but there are some good spots in the bay just north of there."

"And if they go farther? To Waimanalo?"

She shook her head and frowned.

"Then they come ashore. No way we get there before they do."

"Shit."

The native warriors chattered among themselves as the translator filled in what they'd missed.

"Grab your weapons and ammo, and don't forget water and rations. Let's move!"

They grabbed their weapons without hesitation and headed for the trail. Dr. Kitzinger stepped forward from a group of onlookers, grabbing Sirotkin by the arm as she loaded a few extra magazines into her pack.

"What about the rest of us?"

"Bring food, water, and medical supplies up to the crater. If they break our lines, we'll fall back on your position to make a stand."

Chapter 15

Jasmine's Hope sliced her way through the relatively calm waters of Māmala Bay, heading for the southeast corner of the island as quickly as conditions allowed. The wind was mostly out of the east, requiring the crew to tack their way in a zig-zagging pattern off the southern coast of the island to intercept the approaching canoes.

Matteus and Serge established a rhythm with Park to manage the sails, and after a few turns, Farzin was confident enough to leave them to it while he focused on the tactical situation. Herman and Malo stood on the bow, scanning the water ahead, but saw no sign of the enemy force. Their canoes were still either below the horizon, or hidden behind Diamond Head. Parth sent Farzin an annotated map showing their approximate locations.

Heading?

Spreading out on southern part of east coast

Farzin cursed under his breath. He knew it had been a mistake to release the prisoners Dr. Kitzinger nursed back to health following the battle at Waikiki. They knew where the settlement was, approximately how many lived there, and where they should come ashore to avoid getting ripped to pieces. Experience had taught them their koa wood shields could provide some protection from the gunfire they believed was magic. This time, they'd use an entire jungle of koa to shield themselves. It would be guerilla warfare—and if history was any guide, it would be ugly for both sides.

How long before they land?

Maybe 2 hours

Tell Sirotkin

It was going to be close.

***

Miroslava Sirotkin glanced at the tablet in her right hand without breaking stride and saw the short message from Parth.

"Forget Waikiki," she called out. "We're going east. Keep pace if you can."

She kicked into another gear, opening a small gap to those behind before they reacted to close it again.

***

"I see them!" shouted Herman from the bow an hour later as they neared the tip of Aiden Point. "Three of them."

Farzin strained his eyes against the light of the still-rising sun, scanning the horizon in the direction Herman was pointing until he spotted them.

They appeared to be no more than a few kilometers from shore, but the perspective made it difficult to be sure.

"We'll intercept in about thirty minutes," he called out.

Park motioned frantically at Jayson to take the wheel.

"Just hold her steady. I'll be back before the next tack," he said, scampering toward the hold and disappearing below deck.

He reemerged a few moments later with two assault rifles over one shoulder and the RPG launcher over the other. In his hands, he carried a crate of RPG rounds.

"Keep one of these and give the other to Herman," he instructed, pushing the assault rifles on Jayson.

He pulled a pair of extra magazines out of his pocket, handing them over, too.

Jayson nodded and made his way carefully to the bow.

A few minutes later, they cleared the point, and several more canoes came into view.

"Ready about," called Park in preparation for the next tack.

"Ready," answered Matteus.

"Hard a lee!" announced Park as he cranked the tiller.

Matteus and Serge worked in unison to bring the boom around, quickly re-inflating the mainsail before pulling over the jib. Jasmine's Hope rounded the point on course for the first group of targets.

"What's the count now, Herman?" yelled Farzin over the sound of the wind.

"Still three," he called back. "Shit. Now four—one on the horizon. I think they've seen us."

The canoes accelerated towards the safety of Hanauma Bay, trying to outpace the intercepting sailboat in their race to the shore, still at least a kilometer away. Farzin went back to the tablet to check with Parth.

Confirm the number?

Seven

Where?
Only see four

Don't know
All below the mountains now

Shit. Parth was blind. He hit Sirotkin.

Where are you?

He looked back and forth between the tablet and the horizon for several minutes before she replied.

Six clicks out from the point
Stopped for water

Send a team to Waimanalo

You kidding?
Can't get there

"Shit," said Farzin to himself.

Of course, they couldn't get to Waimanalo in time. He should have known that.

New plan
We sideswipe canoes hitting Aiden Point
To slow them down
You pin down the ones that make it
Don't let them off that point

And you?

Going to hit the canoes heading for Waimanalo
Stop them from landing
If we can

Ok
We'll clean up stragglers

The tack completed, Park called out, motioning once more for Jayson to take the wheel. Jayson handed his assault rifle to Malo and made his way back.

"Almost in RPG range," explained Park. "Just keep us on an intercept course."

Then, he set up position midway along the starboard side of the boat, where there was the least amount of up-and-down motion to complicate the targeting.

"What are you doing, Park?" demanded Farzin.

"Setting up for a shot at these guys," he replied.

"How many rounds you bring?"

"Six."

Farzin shook his head.

"That's not enough."

"Listen, I wasn't expecting to re-enact the Battle of Trafalgar."

"Save 'em for the boats heading to Waimanalo. We can't afford to let any of 'em land."

"Alright," agreed Park with a sigh almost loud enough to be heard over the wind and waves.

He secured the crate to the deck on his way to the hold for a rifle.

"Grab me the SR," called Farzin after him, referring to the sniper rifle he'd used to devastating effect in the first battle with Pa'ao's forces.

Park nodded as he disappeared below deck. By the time he returned, they were only a few hundred meters from the first group of westbound canoes—and the distance was closing fast. The canoes were running on parallel courses, about two hundred meters apart.

"Get as close as you can, Jayson," yelled Park.

He held up a pair of grenades in one hand to explain his intent before scurrying off toward mid-deck.

The others on deck, except Matteus, who was unarmed, rushed to the starboard side and readied their weapons.

"We're not slowing down or doubling back for any of these guys," reminded Farzin. "This is a drive-by."

Jasmine's Hope pushed through the water perpendicular to the track taken by the invading canoes. As they approached the nearest one, several warriors aboard threw aside their paddles, trading them for heavy wooden shields. They'd learned from their first encounter they offered at least some protection against whatever magic guarded the island.

"Don't waste ammunition on those shields," said Farzin. "Wait until we're right on their bow."

He opened fire as they passed directly between the approaching canoes and the shoreline. The others followed suit. Bullets splashed into the water or splintered against the hull as they found their range, and soon, most were finding their mark among the helpless men. The warriors shifted the wall of shields from port to starboard as Jasmine's Hope passed in front of them. There were now several open gaps where men had fallen. Farzin continued pumping shots into them with his sniper rifle while the others turned to find the next target.

"Closer, man!" yelled Park. "You're too far."

Jayson eased the wheel to the right, adjusting course as they bore down on the next target. This time, they were much closer. Only fifteen meters separated them from the canoe as they slipped in front of its bow. Several warriors rose to their feet amid the barrage to launch spears at their attackers. Malo shoved Herman out of the way of an expertly thrown projectile, diving for the deck as it lodged itself in the wooden planks between them.

Park yanked the pin from one of his grenades and tossed it into the chaos of the canoe. Jayson gaped in horror, turning back to watch as the grenade exploded among the warriors. Those closest to the blast were sent flying over the sides. Pieces of splintered wood and shattered bodies flew further still. Screams filled the air, and injured men thrashed about in the water as they called for help. The damaged canoe listed to one side, tossing the remaining occupants into the sea.

"Jayson!" screamed Park at his distracted colleague. "Hard a port!"

"What?" he yelled, snapping his head around.

"Turn left!"

"Oh, fuck!"

They were closing quickly on the next canoe—on a collision course.

"Brace for impact!" called Farzin, grabbing desperately for the railing.

Spears came flying over the bow. The enemy was close enough for those aboard Jasmine's Hope to hear their terrified screaming, followed by the splintering of wood and the sickening crunch of breaking bones. The bow heaved into the air before crashing down again, splitting the canoe beneath them in two. The two halves of the broken craft rose simultaneously, throwing warriors into the sea. In just a few seconds, the ship was already clear of the dead, injured, and stranded men in its wake.

"Well, that was pretty goddam effective," said Park as he pulled himself to his feet and stared at the devastation behind them.

"Matteus, take the wheel," instructed Farzin. "We're lucky we're still in one piece."

Matteus nodded and released his death grip on the carbon fiber mast, making his way aft.

"Farzin wants me at the wheel," he explained, reaching out to take it with trembling hands. "Sorry, I don't have a weapon for you."

"No worries," replied Jayson, holding up his own violently shaking hands. "Probably wouldn't work out much better than my steering."

Matteus answered with a sympathetic nod. Neither man was cut out for battle.

By now, they could see the four remaining canoes ahead of them racing northwest, where the vast white beaches of Waimanalo lay hidden beyond Makapu'u Point. Farzin glanced up at the sails, checking the wind direction to see if there was anything they could adjust to coax a bit more speed out of their ship. Matteus and Serge had done a good job, he realized, and they were making about eight knots against craft that were managing less than half of that.

"We'll intercept in about an hour," he announced before pulling out the tablet to update Sirotkin.

Took out two canoes
Strafed another pretty good
Where are you?

Message failed to send

"Shit," he said, glancing east.

Diamond Head was no longer visible behind the ridge above Aiden Point. Sirotkin and the others would need to figure it out on their own. At least he and his novice crew had reduced the strength of the attacking forces by half. More importantly, they'd bought their ground forces more time to get into position. Those remaining in the undamaged canoe had doubled back to pluck their surviving comrades out of the water.

***

On the morning of the wedding, Huaka'i gathered the rest of the Ulu warriors on a secluded beach for a final practice of the performance they would give at the evening feast. As Kameha's most trusted friend and advisor, he was to ensure the men performed their traditional dance flawlessly—as befitting such an important celebration. The men had sharpened their skills under his critical eye for many days and were now ready to reveal the results to Kameha, determined to prove they were worthy of representing the Ulu traditions to their hosts.

Huaka'i said a final few words of encouragement as Kameha approached the beach with Chief Paumakua's Kahuna at his side. Ino rocked back and forth nervously. He and the others waited in their starting positions for the drumbeat to signal the start of their final practice. Kameha and the Kahuna took Huaka'i aside for a few private words while the warriors murmured among themselves, waiting for instructions. When the men finished conferring, Huaka'i called everyone into a circle for an unexpected address by their leader. Ino positioned himself next to his mentor to find out what was happening.

"What is this about?" he asked in a whisper.

"You will know soon enough," assured Huaka'i.

The Kahuna took a position at the center of the circle to recite a prayer.

"But you know already, don't you?" he prodded.

"I do," he admitted.

"What is it, then?"

Huaka'i glanced sideways at the younger man before turning his focus back to the Kahuna.

"The Ulu people no longer have a home," he said. "Kameha has a plan to change that."

"And the Kahuna? He is not Ulu. Why is he here?"

Huaka'i snorted.

"He is here because his ambition is even greater than Kameha's."

Ino narrowed his eyes at his older companion.

"What do you mean?"

"Just listen," advised Huaka'i.

Kameha approached the center of the circle and embraced the Kahuna. Then, he addressed his people to explain what was to unfold.

"By now, the island of O'ahu is under attack by the forces of Pa'ao and Pili. The strangers there, and those of our brethren foolish enough to join them, are outnumbered and outmatched. Without the protection of their witch, they will soon die. As our reward for luring the witch here, Pa'ao and Pili have pledged to help us take Kaua'i for ourselves."

Murmurs rose from the circle of warriors. Ino turned to Huaka'i in disbelief.

"We cannot trust them! When they finish with O'ahu, they will come here to kill us."

"Kameha is smarter than you give him credit for," assured Huaka'i. "Keep listening."

Then the Kahuna spoke. Ino was agape by the time he'd finished explaining the rest of the plan.

"I told you he was ambitious," said Huaka'i.

"He's insane," protested Ino. "He will get us all killed."

"Perhaps. But at least our fate will be in our own hands, and we will die as warriors."

***

They'd closed the distance to five hundred meters, still out of range for the RPG, before briefly losing sight of the canoes behind Makapu'u point.

"There's a small beach on the other side of the point," said Farzin, looking at a map on the tablet. "Another thousand meters, and they're ashore."

"How's the depth looking?" asked Park.

"Good to about a hundred meters offshore. Charts call out a couple of rocks, but nothing crazy."

"Okay. I'll show Matteus. We'll get a nice tailwind to run them down around the corner, but we can't wait too long to drop the jib if we don't want to be pushed into shallow water and run aground."

"I know what I'm doing, Park," assured Farzin. "Just be ready to hit 'em."

Ted took the tablet and returned to the tiller to show Matteus the charts. They looked over them for a few moments, agreeing on a route that would bring them as close as possible to shore while still allowing time and distance to make the turn away from the coral on the north side of the small beach. By the time the short briefing was over, they were clearing the point, and the four canoes racing for shore were visible once more. The chase was on.

"Ready about," yelled Matteus.

"Ready," came the call from Farzin.

"Hard a port!"

Farzin brought the boom around as Matteus cranked the wheel. Serge pulled over the jib sheet, and the crew could feel the acceleration as the wind grabbed hold of the sails. Only four hundred meters separated them from the canoes, and they were gaining fast. They could see the men aboard occasionally glancing over their shoulders as they drove their paddles desperately into the water. Park, the RPG launcher slung over his back, grabbed Jayson by the arm.

"Come with me," he demanded, leading him towards the bow.

On the way, he stopped to unlash the box of rocket-propelled grenades from the deck, shoving it into Jayson's arms.

"You just keep handing me rounds."

Jayson nodded silently and followed.

As soon as Farzin finished securing the boom, he swung his rifle around, ready to engage.

"When we reach two hundred meters to target, I need you to haul in the jib."

"Got it," confirmed Serge.

Farzin, Park, Herman, and Malo lined up across the bow with Jayson right behind them. Though the calmer, protected waters along the shore made for smoother sailing, the bow still heaved too much for them to line up their targets. Farzin squeezed off a few shots, only to see them splashing harmlessly into the water.

"Now!" he called back to Serge.

As the jib dropped, they could feel Jasmine's Hope slow down. The bow steadied, allowing Farzin and Malo to place their shots into the group of canoes with deadly accuracy. Here and there, warriors slumped over as the bullets found their marks. Park turned back to Jayson.

"You're not gonna want to be directly behind me for this," he said, motioning Jayson to move aside.

Moving into a crouch, he shouldered the launcher for a shot at the nearest target. A blast sounded, and a cloud of smoke enveloped the bow of the ship.

"Shit," said Park, as the round exploded in the water between two canoes. "Still too much movement up here."

"Let out the sheet a bit!" yelled Farzin.

"I don't know what that means," replied Serge with a desperate shrug.

"Shit," said Farzin, scampering back to help Serge level out the ship.

Park unslung the assault rifle hanging awkwardly over one shoulder, shoving it at Jayson.

"Hold this for me." he said. "And give me another grenade."

Jayson passed Park another round. Flames shot from the back of the launcher once more as the grenade leaped forward and found its mark.

"Jesus Christ!" said Jayson, putting his hands over his ears. The canoe exploded in a ball of flames, sending warriors flying into the water.

"Give me another one!" yelled Park.

Farzin raced back to the bow, strafing the survivors in the water while Park lined up his next shot. A second canoe disappeared behind a wall of fire and debris as the RPG impacted amid the men paddling their craft desperately for the shore.

"Pass me another grenade!" shouted Park.

Jayson didn't respond. He stared at the men thrashing in the water all around them as Jasmine's Hope plowed through a mass of bodies. They hit the hull with a series of cracks and thuds. Park shuffled back on his hands and knees to grab a grenade from the box. Rising to a crouch, he took aim and fired again. Another direct hit.

"Hell yeah!" he yelled, pumping a fist in the air.

By now, Malo and Herman had stopped firing. Both were looking back at Jayson, their eyes wide with horror.

"Jayson! Grenade me!" commanded Park.

Jayson snapped his head around, staring blankly.

"Grenade!" repeated Park.

As Ted reached back to grab it for himself, Jayson slammed the lid shut and slid the box out of reach.

"What the fuck are you doing?"

"There has to be another way," pleaded Jayson. "This isn't war. This is a massacre."

"They came to *our* home," reminded Park. "Fuck 'em."

He lunged for the box of grenades. Jayson snatched it up and scrambled to his feet, grabbing the railing as he backed away slowly.

"You're on a ship, idiot. Where do you think you're gonna go?"

Farzin soon realized he was the only one firing.

"What's going on?" he asked, turning back.

"Dipshit took my grenades," said Park.

"What are you doing, Jayson?"

"I don't know. Not this," he said, motioning to the bodies in the water.

Park lunged again, almost getting a hand on the box.

Jayson pulled it back with both hands and heaved it over the side of the boat.

"You fucking idiot! You've just killed everyone back at Punchbowl."

"There's got to be another way."

"Yeah? And what's that, genius?"

"We don't have time for this," yelled Farzin. "Keep shooting."

He gave Malo a shove and pointed at the final remaining canoe. It was now less than a hundred meters ahead—and only a few hundred meters from shore. Farzin opened fire. The warrior joined in, squeezing off a few reluctant rounds.

"Give me my gun, Jayson," said Park, moving on him like a cat stalking its prey.

"There's another way. I know it," said Jayson with a gulp. "Save Luni and the others."

He took a deep breath and threw himself over the railing, into the water.

"Man overboard!" called Matteus. "Hard a starboard!"

Matteus immediately cranked the tiller, throwing Serge off balance. He stumbled backward a few steps before regaining his footing and getting into position to move the boom over. Farzin ignored the chaos, swinging his gun around to put as many rounds as he could into the last canoe as the ship veered to the right.

"We're bringing her all the way around," announced Matteus.

"No, we're not," said Park. "Look."

Jayson was swimming towards the shore, already among the coral in dangerously shallow water.

"We can't just leave him."

"He made his choice," said Park. "We can't help him now."

"What was he thinking?" asked Farzin, striding towards mid-deck.

"No idea," replied Park, shaking his head.

After securing the boom, Serge came running back to join the others.

"What do we do?" demanded Matteus.

"He's on his own," said Farzin with a shrug.

As if in answer, they heard a splash from the starboard side and spun around to see Malo was gone. Farzin looked over the edge to watch as the warrior resurfaced and swam for shore, the assault rifle strapped across his back.

"At least Jayson won't die alone," lamented Park.

There was no hint of attempted humor in his words.

Chapter 16

IT TOOK RICHARD A moment to realize where he was. He blinked a few times and sat up slowly amid chunks of broken glass. Luckily, his office door was made of safety glass that crumbled into mostly harmless chunks instead of shattering into jagged shards. Otherwise, he could have impaled himself and bled out on the floor. What an inglorious end that would have been, he thought to himself. He took a few deep breaths, noting the beat of his heart. It was back to normal.

Stepping through the remains of his inner door, he picked up his laptop and set it down gingerly on the desk. It was comical, he realized, to treat it with such care now after hurling it through the window. He opened the top, and it sprang immediately to life, displaying his login screen.

"Son of a bitch," he said, shaking his head in disbelief. "You really are indestructible."

He wiped a few crumbs of glass from his chair before sitting down to log in. Immediately, he tried to access Dr. Akindele's files to see if he'd made any progress calculating his vector. A message appeared on the screen; access denied.

"Shit."

He'd changed his password.

As his agitation grew, Richard felt his heart skip a couple of beats. After losing consciousness amid a pile of broken glass, it was time to admit he had a serious health problem. He took a deep breath and reminded himself to calm down. He'd need to keep his shit together if he expected to outsmart Akindele and avoid a life in primitive exile without his family.

He went down to Andrew's office, already opening the door as he knocked a few times in rapid succession. The gangly IT tech jumped in his seat and slammed the lid of his computer closed. Richard eyed him suspiciously.

"Sorry, boss. I didn't know it was you."

"What are you working on, Andrew?"

"The Columbia data," he replied. "Stuff's top secret, remember?"

"Of course," realized Richard with a nod.

"What can I do for you?"

"Any way Akindele could have figured out we compromised his password? He say anything to you?"

"No. Why?"

"He changed it this morning."

Andrew regarded his boss for a moment.

"Are you okay?" he asked, furrowing his brow.

Richard took another deep breath. He realized he was talking a mile a minute and his hands were shaking. His shirt, drenched with sweat, was clinging to his body.

"Too much coffee, I guess," he said with a shrug. "So, can you do it?"

"Do what? You haven't asked me anything."

"The password. Akindele's new password. Can you crack it?"

"For the security audit?"

"Yes. Exactly."

"I can have it for you by the end of the day."

"Thanks, Andrew. I'll stop by later to see how it's going."

He excused himself and left Andrew's office, heading for the stairwell instead of the elevator. Inside, he leaned against the wall and slid down into a squat to catch his breath.

"What the hell was that?" he asked himself.

Usually, Andrew would be the one sweating and looking uncomfortable. Richard could only imagine how bad he must look to draw questions about his well-being from *Andrew*, of all people. He had to get out of the office before someone who actually mattered saw him in such a state. And he needed to admit it was time to see a doctor. All the plans and ambition in the world meant nothing if he didn't live long enough to see them to fruition.

***

Andrew waited for an hour after Richard left before going to search for Dr. Akindele. Renewed activity at the site of Fusion B made it easy to track him down. The physicist was checking on the technicians' progress in bringing the facility back to life.

"We gotta talk," said Andrew, pulling him aside.

He looked around nervously.

"No need to skulk about," chided Akindele. "Rebecca has assigned you to help me ramp up for Gamma Prime."

"Gamma Prime?"

"Delta was already taken," he explained. "Now, what's wrong?"

"That FBI thing you asked me about? I looked into it. It's bad. Really bad."

"Spit it out," urged Akindele with a scowl.

"The accident at the coffee shop wasn't an accident. It was us—the Center."

"What do you mean, it was us?"

"The FBI agent—the one the cops are looking for—was onto something," he explained. "That whole thing was a hit job meant to kill her."

"In a car crash? That's absurd."

"It was kind of genius, actually. A couple of security techs pulled it off by hacking into the over-the-air software update system through the owner's cellphone. They overrode the controls and sent it flying into the coffee shop like a goddam missile. Not a trace left on any of the onboard systems or cell networks they compromised."

"Then how did you find out?"

"They didn't bother cleaning the logs on *our* system yet."

Akindele considered what he was hearing.

"Was Richard involved?"

"I'm not sure, but he's definitely running the smear campaign they're using to go after the agent now."

"This is excellent news, Andrew. We can use this as leverage," said Akindele, nodding slowly. "Please tell me you have the evidence."

Andrew looked around again before producing a flash drive from his pocket, holding it out for Akindele to see. The physicist took the drive and examined it.

"I was copying the data when Richard came to see me," explained Andrew. "I just about shit myself, you know?"

"He came to see you again? Why? Is he suspicious?"

"I don't think so. He just wanted me to crack your password again."

"I'm still days away from a solution," replied Akindele. "I can't keep changing my password every day without arousing suspicion."

"That's why I cloned your account," said Andrew. "As long as there's a reasonable amount of activity on the original, he'll have no reason to suspect anything."

Akindele nodded thoughtfully.

"Excellent idea, Andrew. You're smarter than I realized."

Andrew knew that was as close to praise as he could expect.

"Are you certain he didn't notice you acting suspicious?" continued the physicist.

"No. He was in worse shape than me, for a change. He seemed really off."

"Off? How?"

"You know. Sweaty, nervous, disheveled—and he was shaking. What the hell happened with Ms. Steinman this morning?"

Akindele smiled broadly.

"He was squirming like a worm impaled on the end of a hook."

Andrew had the discomforting impression Jimi may have drawn the grotesque simile from firsthand experience.

"Do you think it's smart? To push him too far? I've never seen him like this—and we know he's dangerous."

"I'll push him until he breaks. Then Rebecca will see just how weak a man she's been relying on."

"A cornered animal is most dangerous," warned Andrew. "That's what they say where I'm from."

"Perhaps. But we have our animal on a short leash," he said, holding up the flash drive.

"What are you going to do with that?"

"Give it to the only person I trust."

***

Makapu'u Beach was two hundred and fifty meters of white sand southeast of the more well-known stretches of Waimanalo. If it wasn't the original plan to land there, Pa'ao's warriors must have diverted their canoes as soon as it became clear they could not outrun their pursuers. Jayson immediately regretted his rash decision to jump into the water. On such a small beach, he'd be among the landing warriors the moment he made it ashore.

"Jayson," came a call from behind him.

He stopped swimming, treading water as he looked around with surprise.

"'O wau pū me 'oe."

"Malo? No ke aha eia 'oe?"

He swam up to Jayson and pointed to a low outcropping at the base of a cliff a couple hundred meters east of the sandy beach.

"E hele kāua i laila."

Jayson nodded. Even without the translator, he understood. It was far safer to risk climbing onto the sharp volcanic rock than to face the shark-tooth spears and sharpened stone knives of the warriors leaping onto the beach from the last remaining canoe. Malo kicked up his bare feet and headed for shore. Jayson, still wearing his boots, struggled to keep up.

Malo scampered up the east side of the outcropping, out of sight of those on the beach. Trailing behind, Jayson's boot slipped on some algae as he struggled for a foothold, driving his bare right knee down onto the rock.

"Shit," he said.

Blood was running all the way down to his sock by the time he was safely atop, crouching against the cliff beside Malo to stay hidden from the enemy warrior still in the water.

"He aha kā mākou e hana ai i kēia manawa?" asked Malo.

"I don't know what we're gonna do," admitted Jayson. "I didn't think that far ahead."

All around, torn bodies bobbed lifelessly in the water among men swimming for safety and the injured still clinging to the wreckage of their canoes. A pair of survivors from one of the doomed boats hauled a barely conscious colleague onto the beach. Upon realizing the attacking ship was breaking off, the warriors who'd landed safely rushed into the water to retrieve their injured comrades in a frantic rescue operation.

"We should help," said Jayson, edging his way back to the water.

Malo shook his head sadly, pulling Jayson back.

"Ikaika loa keia mau mea kaua," said the warrior with a frown.

"I know," agreed Jayson. "It's terrible."

He turned away from the grisly scene to examine the steep wall of black volcanic rock behind them.

"We've got to get out of here before they notice us," he said. "Get some high ground over this beach and convince them to leave."

"Ma 'ō," replied Malo, pointing to a narrow washout lined with loose rocks.

It was still steep, but potentially a passable route to the top of the cliff. Jayson crept towards it, awkwardly maneuvering his bleeding knee so it wouldn't drag across the ground. Malo crawled along behind him.

At the bottom of the washout, Jayson slowly eased into a standing position before hauling himself a couple of meters up the wall. Stretching for his next handhold, he transferred his weight too quickly and lost his footing. He slid down the washout, his injured knee glancing off the rough volcanic stone.

"Fuck!" he spat through gritted teeth.

Behind them, an excited yell rose from the water. Jayson swiveled around to see one of the survivors pointing at him.

"Ma 'ō! Ma 'ō!" the warrior shouted.

A clamor rose as the others spotted Jayson and Malo pressed against the cliff wall on the rocky outcropping.

"Oh, shit," said Jayson, turning his attention back to the narrow washout.

He clawed his way desperately up the wall, only to lose his footing at the same place and slide back down again. Looking back, he saw men armed with spears running from the beach into the shallow water. Those swimming nearby pulled up and treaded water, waiting to see what would happen.

Malo urged Jayson to try again, this time pushing him by the feet to propel him upward. He barely made it higher than his first two attempts before losing his footing again.

By now, the approaching warriors were less than fifty meters away—and closing quickly. Jayson started climbing again, but Malo grabbed him by the wrist, solemnly shaking his head.

"Kaua mākou," he said, reaching for the assault rifle slung across his back.

Jayson grimaced and looked again at the approaching warriors. The water was now up to their thighs, slowing their progress only marginally. They would soon be close enough to let loose their spears with deadly accuracy.

"Hōʻike iā lākou?" panted Jayson, pointing up.

Malo nodded. Aiming his weapon skyward, he pulled the trigger. The gun emitted only a single underwhelming click. He'd emptied it while still aboard Jasmine's Hope.

"Shit," said Jayson, scrambling to swing his gun around.

He fumbled to find the safety before holding it aloft and squeezing off a short burst. The approaching warriors froze in place and went silent, standing in the hip-deep water.

"Tell them they don't need to die," urged Jayson. "Tell them to go home."

Malo called out to the men to relay Jayson's plea. He could tell before his companion attempted a translation that the angry reply was not a concession.

"He said they follow orders only from Pa'ao."

The front line of warriors did not advance, but behind them, more continued to creep toward the outcropping. More than a hundred men armed with shark-tooth spears faced off against the cornered pair. For a moment, everyone was silent. Then, with a loud cry, one of the warriors lofted his spear and hurled it at Malo. He dodged it easily, leaving it to fly past his torso and clatter harmlessly against the rocks.

Several more men raised their weapons. Before they could let loose a deadly barrage that would be impossible to evade, Jayson lowered his gun and began firing. The front line of warriors shuddered from the impact of the bullets, dropping their weapons and falling into the water. Immediately, the rest turned to flee for the beach, flailing and shouting in terror.

"Fuck!" shouted Jayson over the sudden clamor.

He threw the weapon aside with disgust, and Malo quickly retrieved it.

The nearby enemy warriors who had been helping the injured ashore also fled for the beach, abandoning their charges to drown or bleed out while clinging to pieces of their shattered canoes.

"I'm going in," declared Jayson. "Cover me."

He pulled off his boots and stripped down to his underwear before gingerly making his way to the edge of the outcropping to dive into the water. Malo shook his head in disapproval. Many of the warriors who had rushed ashore were already heading for cover in the trees north of the beach. Those trailing behind stopped at the tree line to stare at the scene unfolding in the water.

Jayson hooked his arm around a man struggling to stay afloat, pulling him toward the shallows. Finding the sandy bottom with his toes, he continued dragging the man until he could sit himself up with his head out of the water. Then he ran back towards the next victim. Men on the beach started shouting, and two of them ran into the water to finish dragging their colleague to dry ground. Then, one by one, those who had fled into the trees returned to see what was happening.

As Jayson pulled a second, and then a third victim towards the shallows, a pair of warriors cautiously approached him, stopping where the water was up to their knees. Jayson took a few steps toward them, his chest heaving from the exertion. The men stared at each other for several moments while Jayson caught his breath. Moving no closer, Jayson heaved the injured man towards his waiting colleagues and backed away. They nodded, stepping forward to haul their comrade to safety.

The remaining uninjured warriors, watching cautiously from the beach, then streamed into the water to join the effort while Jayson swam back to the outcropping. Malo helped him up, and he collapsed onto the rock in exhaustion.

"Ua hana maikaʻi ʻoe," said Malo.

"It's not enough," he panted. "They need to leave."

"Yes," agreed Malo. "They do."

He dropped his empty weapon and slung the loaded one over his shoulder before slipping into the water on the hidden side of the outcropping.

***

Malo made a show of retrieving a few survivors farther out in the water and handing them off to the rescuers—all while keeping a careful distance and exchanging only a few words. Gradually, he worked his way across the bay, finally coming ashore at the north end of the beach. Too late, the enemy realized what had happened. With the high cliffs walling off the south end of the beach, he'd cut off their only avenue of inland retreat.

Sensing they were about to be attacked, the warriors abandoned the rescue effort and picked up their weapons instead. Malo lowered himself to the ground, sitting cross-legged on the sand in a show of peace. He placed the assault rifle across his lap as a group of warriors cautiously approached.

"Save your friends, and leave this island," said Malo. "If you stay, you will die."

"How is this island still protected?" demanded one of the warriors. "Your witch is not here."

Malo narrowed his eyes.

"What do you know about her?"

"Chief Kameha told Pa'ao he had lured her to Kaua'i so we could safely attack O'ahu."

"Chief Kameha?" snorted Malo.

He turned his head and spat in the sand.

"Go back and tell Pa'ao he has made a deal with a fool, not a chief," he continued. "And tell him you are the last of his warriors that will set foot on the sands of O'ahu and live."

He picked up the gun and punctuated the sentence with a short burst of gunfire into the sky.

"Save those who can be saved, and go," he added.

The startled warriors retreated to the grim task of sorting through the injured to determine which ones could survive the journey home. They showed those that would not the mercy of the knife, giving them a quick death on the beach where they lay.

***

After the departure of the lone overloaded canoe, Malo crossed the blood-stained beach to rejoin Jayson on the outcropping and find a way up the rock face, onto the plateau above. From there, they watched until the enemy warriors disappeared from sight behind the ridge of Makapu'U Point. The pair then followed the plateau southward to connect with Sirotkin's ground team.

Another canoe appeared below the horizon to the southeast as they made their way towards the coastline, retreating to Moloka'i from the direction of Hanauma Bay. Considering how far offshore they were already, they must have abandoned their attack a couple of hours earlier.

The steep walls of Koko Crater, extending all the way to the sea, cut off the coastline route to Aiden Point. The pair changed course, opting instead for the inland route along the bottom of the crater's northwest slopes. Neither spoke more than a few words as they sought their colleagues while contemplating the day's horrors. Suddenly, Malo froze, grabbing Jayson by the arm.

"Ua lohe au i kekahi mea," he said.

Jayson held his breath while straining to listen.

"Footsteps," he replied, turning to his companion with alarm. "Coming this way."

Before they could react, a figure appeared among the trees ahead. It was Miroslava Sirotkin, jogging towards them.

"Hey!" called Jayson. "It's us."

She slid to a quick stop, raising her weapon. Jayson threw his hands in the air and stepped forward.

"Don't shoot! It's us. Jayson and Malo."

Sirotkin held her stance, staring at him through the sites.

"Give me one reason not to," she replied with a sneer.

She quickly lowered the gun as Isiah O'Neal and Mano ran up behind her. O'Neal stopped at her side, breathing heavily, while Mano rushed past them both to embrace his brother.

"No ke aha eia 'oe?" he asked.

Several more armed team members joined the group, seeming grateful for the opportunity to catch their breath after the exertion of trying to keep up with Sirotkin.

"What the hell are you guys doing here?" asked O'Neal.

"Trying to find you," replied Jayson.

"He means, why are you on the island at all?" clarified Sirotkin. "You stole our fucking ship."

"We didn't steal anything. We were just borrowing it."

She snorted.

"So why aren't you still on it?"

"One of the canoes managed to make it to the beach," he explained. "Malo and I stayed behind to deal with it."

"Shit. How many made it into the trees?"

"None."

"Bullshit," she spat. "No way you two got 'em all."

"We didn't need to. Malo just told them to go home."

"What?"

"He told them to go home."

"And they just left?"

"Yeah. Pretty much."

"E ha'i iā lākou e pili ana iā Kameha," advised Malo.

"Shit. Yeah," realized Jayson.

"What?" demanded Sirotkin.

Pa'ao's men knew Samaira wasn't here. That's why they thought it was safe to attack."

"How did they know that?"

"Pa'ao and Kameha are working together to kill us—and take Kaua'i."

"Do Farzin and Park know that?"

Jayson frowned and shook his head.

"Christ," spat Sirotkin. "What a clusterfuck."

Chapter 17

PARTH HAD RELAYED NEWS of the outcome back to Honolulu, and the people were already gathered in the plaza when their defenders began returning from the pathway to Diamond Head in small groups. It was past midnight, and Jayson was exhausted. Trudging across the stones with Malo at his side, he heard running footsteps approaching from behind. He turned around just as Paul Suryana pulled up and shoved him to the ground.

"Hey, asshole," he spat. "Let's see how tough you are when you're not jumping someone from behind."

Malo swung around and made a move, but Suryana had his gun raised in an instant. The warrior backed off slowly while the rest of the weary defenders suddenly came to full alert, some reaching for their weapons.

"Calm the fuck down," ordered Miroslava Sirotkin, arriving the scene of the commotion. "Lower your gun, Paul."

"No problem," he replied, setting it down. "Jayson and I can work this out the old-fashioned way."

He raised his fists in invitation.

"I didn't have any other choice," said Jayson, still sitting on the ground.

"Choices have consequences, asshole. Now get up and show me again how tough you are."

"Did you know about Josh?"

"Enough, Paul," interjected Sirotkin. "We can talk about this later."

"We can talk about it now," insisted Jayson.

"What about Josh?" demanded Paul.

Sirotkin looked around nervously at the gathering crowd, aware it wasn't just her team that was armed.

"Not now," she hissed at him.

"He went to Kaua'i with a tube of Scylla jammed up his ass," continued Jayson. "He was going to kill everyone there with it—including Kai and Keanu."

Paul shot a wide-eyed glance at Sirotkin.

"Is that true? Jesus Christ. I thought we were done with this shit for now."

She said nothing. De la Cruz shook her head and turned away.

"Seriously? You didn't think to tell the rest of us about this?" demanded O'Neal. "What the fuck?"

"We took the ship because we had to stop him," explained Jayson. "I only hope it's not too late."

Paul shook his head and extended a hand to Jayson, hauling him to his feet.

"I didn't know, man," he said. "Sorry."

"You must all be starving," announced Dr. Kitzinger in an effort to ease the tension. "We've prepared a meal for you inside—after you check in your weapons, that is."

Paul shot another angry look at Sirotkin as he retrieved his gun from the ground. He handed it to the doctor before walking into the common building without another word.

"Here you go, doc," sighed Jayson, holding out his weapon.

"Everything went okay today?"

"You mean other than a few hundred people getting ripped to shreds? Yeah. Just fucking peachy."

***

Sunlight sparkled off the water in the secluded bay on the southeast side of Kaua'i. Luni sat in the shade of an open-walled pavilion near the shore while her sister and several other women fussed over her. They'd helped her don her finest attire and bedecked her in fragrant blossoms of awapuhi keokeo and ma'o hau hele. Her brother, Kameha, oversaw the preparation of the twin-boomed outrigger that would ferry the bride's party to the ceremony on another nearby beach where similar preparations were underway for the groom.

"You are the most beautiful woman I have ever seen," gushed Palila.

"And you will be even more beautiful on your wedding day, little sister," she replied with a tender smile.

"I'm glad Kai and Samaira are here to see it."

A slight frown betrayed something was bothering her.

"What is it, Palila?"

"Jayson has been such a good friend to us. Why did he not come?"

"I'm sure he is very busy with his fields."

Palila put her hands on her hips and cocked her head.

"Tell me the truth. Is he angry with us?"

"No, Palila," assured Luni. "He is not angry with us. I think maybe he is just sad."

"Because he wanted to marry you."

It was a statement, not a question.

"You are growing up quickly," replied Luni.

"And you didn't want to marry him?" she persisted.

"It's not so easy as that. When you get older, you will learn that sometimes things are not as simple as you would like."

Palila considered her sister's cryptic words.

"So, why are you marrying Moeanaimua if you don't want to?"

"I never said I don't want to. I just said it's not simple."

"Oh," replied Palila.

She didn't seem convinced.

"Listen, Palila," said Luni, taking her sister gently by the shoulders, "Moeanaimua is kind and loving, and his father gave our people a home when we had none."

"We had a home. On O'ahu."

"I wish it was as easy as that. I really do."

Palila relented and let out a sigh.

"I hope we'll see Jayson again."

"Me too, sister. Me too."

***

Just to the north, preparations for the ceremony were nearly complete. As the son of the chief, and a future chief himself, the celebration of Moeanaimua's wedding ranked among the most significant occasions the people of Kaua'i had seen in their lifetimes. The ceremony would honor the traditions of both the Ulu and Nanaulu people to symbolize their unity against the threat from Pa'ao and Pili.

A temporary pavilion erected close to the water's edge was festooned with all manner of flowers. There, the Kahuna would say a blessing before binding the couple—and the people they represented—in an undying commitment to one another.

In the shade of the nearby trees, groups of men and women prepared for the feast that would sustain the celebrants throughout an entire afternoon and evening of festivities. Smoke and steam rose from the sand-covered pits where fish and fowl had been cooking since before dawn.

More than a dozen raised koa wood planks covered with ferns and flowers were arranged to accommodate the many guests. Woven mats were laid out on the sand where the guests would sit to enjoy the meal. At the conclusion of the ceremony, a host of women would place the fish, poi, and an abundance of berries and fruits on the planks to signal the start of the feast—and the entertainment.

First, Nanaulu women of marrying age, who had yet to be promised, would perform the hula kahiko in a display of grace and beauty. Hopefully, they'd also catch the attention of appropriate suitors. Then, the Ulu warriors would perform the ha'a koa—a war dance—to demonstrate their fighting prowess to their new allies. Finally, retellings of the islands' history and stories of the gods, acted out in choreographed displays by costumed dancers, would follow long into the night.

As the hour of the ceremony approached, a line of men filed onto the beach, pounding rhythmically on long, thin wooden drums topped with sharkskin to signal it was time to start. They arranged themselves at either side of the pavilion, still playing as the celebrants gathered around.

Warriors escorted the guests from O'ahu to a place of honor next to the chief and his family as two of the Kahuna's priests, standing on either side of the pavilion, announced their arrival with long blasts from conch shells. Along with the other guests, they formed a large semicircle around the platform where Moeanaimua and Luni would commit to one another in front of their people, and under the watchful eye of totems representing the god Hulihonua and his wife, Keakauhulilani.

The Kahuna approached the pavilion, trailing two of his priests and two lines of priestesses bearing stacks of leis. They positioned themselves on either side of him and, after a brief prayer, proceeded to greet the attendees. Working their way from both ends towards the chief and his honored guests, they placed a lei on each person while saying a few words of blessing.

The Kahuna himself solemnly approached Chief Paumakua and those nearest him. The priestess trailing him bore a small stack of especially ornate leis to adorn the most honored among the celebrants. He placed the first bulky wreath of multi-colored flowers over the chief's head as he whispered an incantation. The chief's immediate family, on his left, were next.

Finally, he approached the visitors from O'ahu. One by one, they bowed their heads to accept their lei and blessing. He greeted Samaira last of all, giving her a slight smile and a deferential nod. For her, he'd reserved a special lei of pure white flowers, placing it carefully over her head and arranging it so that it would not disturb the sleeping baby held snugly against her chest in a sling.

The Kahuna returned to the pavilion, standing alone in the center, while his priests and priestesses gathered on either side. The conch shells sounded their call once more, and the guests turned their heads expectantly to watch as Moeanaimua, bedecked in an elaborate headdress of multi-colored feathers, walked deliberately across the beach toward the pavilion. When he arrived, the Kahuna placed a lei of white flowers around his neck.

The priests blasted another long note as a canoe came into sight from around the point at the south end of the bay. The twin-boom outrigger, adorned with flowers, glided through the water. Two rows of warriors paddled in rhythm with the drummers ashore. Luni sat alone on a raised platform at the center with her brother, Kameha, standing behind her, carrying a spear to symbolize his duty as her protector. The audience began chattering excitedly among themselves as the canoe drew slowly closer in the carefully choreographed approach.

"She's beautiful," whispered Jen.

"Yes, she is," agreed Samaira.

Josh stood nervously beside them, scanning the crowd.

When the canoe reached the shallow water, the paddlers disembarked in a single, synchronous movement and slowly walked the craft forward until the bow made gentle contact with the sand. Then Kameha stepped into the water, holding his spear aloft as he called out to Moeanaimua.

"He is asking Moeanaimua if he will accept the spear and pledge his life to Luni's protection," explained Kai.

"Kind of like giving away the bride?" asked Josh.

"I guess so," said Samaira with a shrug.

Moeanaimua stepped from the pavilion and waded into the water to greet Kameha, followed by one of the Kahuna's priests. Kameha held out his spear to the groom, and both men gripped it while they exchanged customary words, binding them forever as ohana—family. Then Moeanaimua turned to the crowd, holding the spear aloft, and repeated his promise to Kameha for all to hear. The conch shells sounded again as he handed the ceremonial weapon to the priest.

Luni stood from her seat on the elevated platform in a signal that the requisite promises had been accepted and the ceremony would go forward. Kameha and Moeanaimua waded together to the canoe, interlocking their arms to form a seat for the bride. She stepped down from her platform and gingerly lowered herself into their arms so they could carry her ashore. The warriors followed behind, pushing the outrigger onto the sand while Moeanaimua led Luni to the pavilion. The priests and priestesses encircled them, chanting and dancing to the rhythm of the drums, while Kameha retreated to join the honored guests.

Facing each other, the bride and groom held hands as the Kahuna carefully bound their wrists together with braided green vines interwoven with small, white flowers, chanting a prayer as he did so. When he finished, the dancing stopped, and the drums went silent.

"He alo a he alo," said the Kahuna, loud enough for everyone to hear. "E ka'ana like i kou hanu mua ma ke 'ano he kāne a he wahine."

Moeanaimua and Luni gazed into each other's eyes, leaning inward until their foreheads touched.

"Is he going to kiss the bride, or what?" whispered Josh.

Kai furrowed his brow as if the suggestion was somehow scandalous.

"They are sharing their first breath as husband and wife," he explained.

"It's beautiful," said Samaira.

Jen wiped a tear from her eye and glanced around to see if anyone had noticed.

The couple embraced as the conch shells punctuated the end of the ceremony, and the drums resumed their intoxicating rhythm. Young women ran onto the beach behind the pavilion from both directions and started dancing. Meanwhile, the semicircle collapsed into a mass as people rushed forward to greet the couple, carefully leaving a clear path for Chief Paumakua and his wife to be the first to offer congratulations. The guests from O'ahu hung back and watched.

"Short and sweet," commented Josh. "I like it."

"What did you think, Jen?" asked Samaira.

"It was fine, I guess," she said with a sniff.

Samaira couldn't help but chuckle.

"I guess this is the receiving line?" said Josh. "Should we get in there and greet the couple?"

"I'm going to wait until they've had a chance to catch their breath," said Samaira.

"So what happens next?"

"Looks like dinner and a show to me," replied Jen, looking around at the preparations.

Behind them, a team was arranging food on the low koa wood planks that served as tables. A group of men had already disassembled the pavilion and were carrying the pieces away as others arrived with armloads of firewood. Before long, a fire was blazing in a shallow pit dug into the sand where the pavilion had stood. The dancers encircled the growing tower of flames, continuing their skillful display as the celebrants dispersed to find seats on the woven mats flanking the tables.

"Where should we sit?" asked Josh.

Kai exchanged a few words with the warrior that served as their chaperone.

"We are to join chief Paumakua and Kameha with the newlyweds," he explained

The warrior led them to a large, centrally located table with an especially ornate centerpiece of food and flowers. Unlike the other tables, arranged around it in a haphazard semicircle, it had mats only on one side, so everyone could enjoy an unobstructed view of the entertainment. They sat together at one end, assuming the middle of the table was for the newlyweds and their family.

Finally, once all the guests were seated, Luni and Moeanaimua approached the main table with Paumakua, his wife, and some other family members. Samaira stood to embrace her. Kai, Josh, and Jen followed her lead.

"I am so happy for you, Luni," she said.

"Thank you, Samaira. And thank you for coming."

Moeanaimua, too, seemed overcome with emotion. He was beaming with joy as he hugged Samaira with too much enthusiasm for baby Keanu, who was sandwiched awkwardly between them.

"E kala mai, e ke keiki," he apologized, kissing Keanu gently on the forehead.

Then he and Kai exchanged a friendly greeting, gripping one another by the forearm in their version of a handshake. He greeted Josh the same way before he found himself standing face-to-face with Jen, seemingly unsure of the appropriate way to acknowledge her. She grabbed him by the arm without hesitation.

As the greetings took place, Kameha and Paumakua seemed to be having some kind of disagreement a few paces away. Both men were clearly frustrated with one another, but maintained calm tones as they spoke. Finally, they approached the table to exchange brief pleasantries with the guests from O'ahu. Kai and Kameha shared only a few words in a noticeably tense exchange.

"I thought they were friends," whispered Josh as they took their places on the mat.

"A long time ago, maybe," replied Jen. "But there was a bit of a power struggle last year."

"I'd say it's not over yet."

Jen shrugged.

"I don't think Kai has any interest in power."

"Maybe not," he allowed. "But Kameha sure as hell does."

Chapter 18

Assistant Special Agent in Charge Nathaniel Clyburn had one last opportunity to reconsider his actions in light of the attention the case was getting from D.C. He'd received a rare phone call from the assistant attorney general to check on the progress of the investigation, calling Shannon's actions a stain on the reputation of the bureau. There was no presumption of innocence, only an expressed interest in wrapping things up as quickly and quietly as possible.

By the letter of the law, there was no question what he needed to do next. The envelope full of cash and the key to his condo could all be explained as part of a brilliant trap if he went in and immediately took Shannon into custody. If he delayed, even by a day, he'd be crossing the line that defined aiding and abetting—putting both his career and his freedom in jeopardy.

Under normal circumstances, it would have been an easy call—make the arrest and then work like hell to prove his agent's innocence. Everything by the book. The current circumstances were anything but normal. His review with the forensic accountants and an examination of Shannon's cell phone records made it clear he was either dealing with corruption and incompetence on his own team, or someone who could manufacture evidence at will. His gut told him his team was neither dirty nor incompetent. If Clyburn had to choose between his career and his people, it was no choice at all.

Wearing a baseball cap, he kept his head low to avoid the security camera as he swiped his card to access the lobby of the downtown high-rise where he'd bought a rental property during the real estate crisis more than a decade earlier. His disguise wouldn't save him if anyone ever had reason to examine the footage closely. Clyburn's stature would give him away immediately. At least there was no security guard to note his arrival, and he knew the access cards were all the same. The system wouldn't link the entry—or Shannon's earlier arrival—to his unit.

Arriving at the door to the tenth-floor condo, he pulled out the key and moved to unlock the door before thinking better of it. Instead, he knocked a few times in rapid succession. A shadow moved across the peephole before he heard the chain sliding out of its slot. Shannon opened the door and embraced him.

"It's good to see you, too," he said. "Let's get inside and close the door."

"Yeah. Of course," she realized. "Sorry about that. It's just so good to see someone I can trust."

"You doing okay here? Got everything you need?"

"It's great. Thanks," she replied with a wave of her hand. "Did you get the chat logs?"

"Yeah. Didn't even have to subpoena them. They're cooperating fully with the investigation."

"And?"

"No surprises. The logs don't match what you're saying about the messages."

"What about the phones? Did you recover them?"

"Yep. Pulled them out from under the wreck. The guys in the lab managed to recover everything."

"Let me guess," said Shannon with a sigh. "The data matches the logs from Hitz-It."

"You know it."

"Shit. They must have changed it all just before the crash. What do we do?"

"I'll start by paying a friendly visit—let them know a rogue agent was looking into them."

"Be careful," she warned. "I just did a few searches—nothing too crazy—and look where I am."

"This place isn't *that* bad," laughed Clyburn. "Maybe a bit small, but look at that view of Waikiki."

"You know that's not what I meant," she replied with a wry smile.

"Oh, and I got you a burner—so we can message," he said, producing a phone from his pocket. "And I've written down a few code phrases for when you need something. The only number programmed in there is my burner."

"Thanks."

"And no voice calls or uncoded messages," he warned. "I think that goes without saying."

"Of course," she agreed.

"Hang in there, agent. I'll be back in a couple of days with more food and supplies. Anything special you need?"

"Richard Vandergroot's head in a box?"

"Hmm. How about ice cream instead? Best I can offer for now."

"Rocky road," she said with a smile. "But I'm going to get his head, too—one way or another."

***

Ino shifted nervously from one foot to the other as he watched the Nanaulu women dance the hula kahiko in front of the blazing fire. He was too preoccupied with his own upcoming performance to give the alluring display the attention it deserved. Around him, the other Ulu warriors were preparing themselves in various ways. Some stood in contemplative silence, some jumped up and down, shaking their arms to loosen up, and one pair even exchanged open-handed slaps to the face to get them in the right frame of mind for the war dance choreographed to intimidate as much as it was to entertain.

It was a tradition as old as the stories they told about the far-off island home of their ancestors. As a child, Ino often mimicked the fearsome moves and chants of the ha'a koa as he watched his father and the other warriors of Hawai'i perform for Chief Kapawa on special occasions. His mother, though smiling, would always assure him that he was a truly terrifying sight to behold. Tonight, he would finally dance the ha'a koa for real—and it would be more terrifying than anything his mother could ever have imagined.

The sun vanished behind the mountains, and the young women doing the hula were lit only by the light of the fire. The movements of their elongated shadows, exaggerated by the dancing flames, added an extra dimension to the performance by creating the illusion they were among their audience. The interplay of light and shadow had a mesmerizing effect.

"Are you ready, Ino?"

It was Huaka'i.

"Yes," he assured. "I'm ready."

"Good. It's almost time," said the older man with a nod as he slapped Ino on the shoulder.

The drumming ended with a flourish, and the exhausted hula dancers made a final circle of the fire before rushing off to make room for the next act. Cheers and shouts of appreciation from the crowd were quickly replaced by hushed chattering as a new drumbeat rose, and two rows of

Ulu warriors shuffled in unison towards the fire, one from each flank. With each synchronized step, they raised one knee high in the air and hopped forward a half step. Thrusting their spears in the air, they roared out in a single voice each time they switched from one foot to the other.

The lines of warriors converged directly in front of the fire, forming two staggered rows. They spun to face the audience and punctuated the move with a war cry before assuming identical squatting stances. The drums stopped, and the men held their positions in silence. The audience, too, was silent—anticipating the next part of the display. The only sound was the crackling of the flames.

After a long pause, Huaka'i, positioned in the middle of the front row, stepped forward and issued a loud, guttural yell. His eyes bulged, and his face was contorted in a grotesque expression of madness. Pumping his spear in the air in one hand, he slapped himself on the chest and thigh while the other men sneered and snarled. Moeanaimua stood from his place on the mat next to his father, Chief Paumakua, and faced the Ulu men. He stomped his feet and slapped his own chest and thighs, mimicking Huaka'i, before answering back with the savage call of the Nanaulu warriors. The challenge had been issued and answered. The ha'a koa would commence.

As dictated by tradition, all of the men in the audience then stood with Moeanaimua to face down Huaka'i and the Ulu men. They had to prove they were worthy allies who could not be intimidated. Ino noticed the woman from O'ahu—the warrior called Jen—did not hesitate to rise with the men.

The drums started again, and the Ulu warriors resumed their dance, moving towards the audience with their knees bent, sweeping their feet across the sand. Every few steps, they fell back into a squat to stomp their feet and rhythmically slap their bodies before sliding forward again. All the while, they chanted in unison. Some crossed their eyes while others stuck out their tongues or twisted their faces to make their appearance more unsettling. The Nanaula men—and Jen—stood stone-faced and steadfast against their advance.

When the staggered lines of warriors were less than an arms-length away from the honored guests, they stopped once more, thrusting their spears in the air and stomping their feet as they stood in place. Finally, the drums stopped, and they froze, holding their contorted facial expressions while staring down the Nanaula men with wild eyes. Ino stood directly opposite Kai; his arms and legs quivered in anticipation of what would come next.

Huaka'i raised his spear without warning and thrust it into Chief Paumakua's chest. Kameha and the Kahuna immediately grabbed the newlywed couple and hauled them through the lines of Ulu warriors, toward the fire. Moeanaimua tried to fight back, but the oversized lei around his neck obstructed his vision and movement. Luni shrieked at her brother, struggling against his grip, as panic erupted among the guests.

Josh took half a step backward, assuming a defensive position. It was too late. A spear found its mark at the base of his sternum, ripping through him until the tip emerged next to his spine. He fell backward and hit the ground as his attacker retracted the weapon to prepare for his next target—the imposing warrior-woman from O'ahu.

Ino cocked his spear and leveled it at Kai, but hesitated for a moment as he faced the man that would have been his chief under different circumstances.

"Kumakaia," spat Kai with a look of disgust.

The word, betrayer, hit Ino like a fist.

All around, Ulu warriors were engaging with their unarmed hosts and the visitors from O'ahu. Jen spun to one side, narrowly avoiding the spear thrust at her by the warrior who had just killed Josh. She grabbed the weapon by the shaft before he could retract it for another attack. Then, planting her left foot in the sand, she drove her right foot into his crotch with all of her considerable strength. The resulting crack was audible above the din of the sudden melee. He dropped to the ground, leaving her holding his spear.

Three of the Ulu had thrown down their weapons to engage Samaira while two others covered their assault. One man held her arms and another clasped his hand over her mouth to stop her from uttering any magical incantations that might undo their advantage. The third was trying to pry baby Keanu from his sling.

"'A'ole! Kū!" shouted Kai, moving in to help her.

Ino tracked him with his spear, but still could not find the conviction to attack.

Jen and Kai rushed to Samaira's aid as two armed attackers stepped in to protect the men grappling with her. Jen lofted the spear she'd taken and launched it at one of them, penetrating the base of his throat. The doomed man clawed at it desperately as he fell to the ground. Kai nearly managed to avoid a spear thrust from the other warrior. The shark-tooth tip glanced off his ribcage, and he quickly pinned it to his side with his arm. He grimaced in pain as the warrior wrenched and pulled on the spear in an effort to retract it for another attack. Before he could, Jen was on top of him, tackling him to the ground before delivering a single, deadly strike to his Adam's apple with her bare fist.

While the Ulu attack was going mostly as planned, Huaka'i noticed the commotion developing on his left flank and moved in to support. He shoved Ino aside, sending him sprawling to the ground, before hurling his spear at Jen. It pierced the left side of her abdomen, tearing a jagged hole as it passed through her flesh. Her eyes went wide with shock. She managed to yank the weapon out before collapsing, clutching her side in agony.

Kai, bleeding from his left arm and ribcage, had his right arm wrapped around the neck of one of the men trying to subdue Samaira. The man gasped for breath, clawing at Kai in desperation. The distraction allowed Samaira to pull her arms free, and she hammered her fists against the man who was wrestling Keanu out of his sling.

Despite her frantic blows, he pulled the infant free and took a few steps backward before stumbling and falling onto his back. Keanu wailed in distress, but seemed unharmed. Kai let out a scream as he wrenched the man in his grasp, snapping his neck and tossing him aside. Samaira wrestled herself free from her last remaining attacker to set upon the man who had taken her son. Kai was only a step behind.

Huaka'i drew a stone knife from the folds of his wrap without breaking stride as he went after the pair. Swinging the blade with a broad backhand sweep, he caught Kai by surprise, cutting a deep gash across his shoulder. The enraged father spun around just in time to dodge the next attack.

As he shuffled backward, his prosthetic blade caught on a shallow root, and he toppled over. Huaka'i was about to finish him off when he noticed Samaira overpowering the man who had taken Keanu. The look of rage and madness on her face made the posturing of the ha'a koa seem tame. She kicked him repeatedly before falling down on top of him with her fists flailing. He raised both arms against the blows, allowing Keanu to wriggle free and roll onto the sand at his side.

By now, Samaira had grabbed a nearby rock and was trying to smash the man's skull. Huaka'i ignored the plight of his comrade and instead scooped Keanu up in one arm.

"Kū. A i ole ia, e pepehi au ia ia," he shouted, holding the stone knife to the infant's neck.

Samaira froze. Kai's eyes widened in terror. He rose slowly to his feet and took a step toward Huaka'i.

"Mai hōʻeha iā ia," he pleaded.

"Pani hou," warned Huaka'i.

He pressed the knife against Keanu's skin to demonstrate he was serious about the threat. Kai backed off a couple of steps towards the spot where Jen was panting on the ground with a hand pressed against her wound.

The warrior who had ripped Keanu from his mother's arms struggled to his feet. He was bruised and bleeding. He moved as if to strike Samaira, but Huaka'i intervened with a harsh rebuke. He nodded in obedience and retrieved his spear from the ground.

By now, the Nanaulu warriors who'd survived the initial deception had armed themselves and had the area surrounded. They were unsure what to do. Their chief was dead, his son held captive behind a wall of Ulu, and their Kahuna was calling for them to put down their weapons. The cacophony of battle had ceased, and the only sounds were the crackling of the fire and baby Keanu's screams.

"Please!" begged Samaira. "Don't hurt him!"

She looked first at Huaka'i and then at Kai, still backing slowly away toward Jen. She shook her head as tears welled up in her eyes and began rolling down her cheeks.

"Pepehi iā lākou," ordered Huaka'i, pointing at Jen and Kai.

A pair of warriors began advancing on them, their spears cocked back and ready.

"'O ʻoe kekahi," he added with a scowl as he glared at Ino.

Ino gulped. Raising his spear, he advanced cautiously toward Kai. He noticed the injured warrior-woman from O'ahu was clinging to his leg. No. She wasn't clinging to him, he realized. She was unwrapping the fabric that bound the strange-looking prosthesis. He cocked his head curiously and paused while the other two warriors moved within striking distance of their short-range thrusting spears.

Ino's eyes went wide with sudden recognition as the warrior-woman pulled something out from the fabric just below the stump of Kai's leg. Though smaller than the one he'd been given by Jayson during the standoff on O'ahu, it was unmistakably one of their weapons. A blinding flash spat from it, and two successive blasts louder than thunder rocked his head. He had to blink a few times before he could see anything again. The two warriors were down, lying motionless on sand stained with their blood—and now the weapon was trained on him. He dropped his spear and took a step back.

"Samaira," urged Kai. "Take Keanu."

She nodded and, still shaking from the adrenaline, took a step towards Huaka'i. He backed away towards the group of warriors huddled by the fire as she continued stalking him.

"It's a trap, Samaira!" yelled Jen, still on the ground wincing in pain. "Let's get out of here!"

"I'm not leaving without Keanu," she replied without looking back.

"We need help, Samaira. We need to get back to O'ahu."

"Then go. But I can't go with you."

Jen tried to stand using Kai as a crutch but fell back in agony."

"I'm not going to make it back," she said to Kai. "You need to go. You need to get help."

He took the gun from her hand and leveled it at Ino.

"E kokua mai oe ia makou," he ordered.

Ino, still trembling from shock, nodded and edged warily closer to the pair. He felt Huaka'i's glare, but didn't dare look at him. Instead, he focused only on the smoking weapon aimed at his head, and the smell of sulfur stinging his nostrils.

"E hoʻokiʻekiʻe iā ia i kona wāwae," said Kai.

Ino crouched down and lifted Jen to her feet, throwing her arm over his shoulder for support. Kai sat down in the sand, the gun in easy reach, while he re-tied the bindings of his prosthetic foot. When he finished, he stood up and slowly backed away into the trees, with Ino and Jen following closely behind.

"We're coming back for you, Samaira," he called.

Then he issued a grim warning to Kameha before disappearing from sight, telling him every Ulu man on the island would die if anything happened to his wife and son.

Chapter 19

RICHARD FELT ONLY MARGINALLY better after leaving his doctor's office. After several tests, including an echocardiogram which had required him to contort into all manner of uncomfortable positions while a nurse jammed a probe under his ribcage, the prognosis was supposedly good. An electrical fault rather than a plumbing problem, the doctor had explained; and easily fixable. Despite his doctor's confidence, it was unsettling to realize his heart was essentially a time bomb ticking away in his chest.

His cardiologist prescribed a blood thinner to prevent clotting leading up to the routine procedure that would correct his newly diagnosed atrial fibrillation, and they would meet again in a week to schedule it. Although the idea of sending a pulse of high-voltage electricity through his heart wasn't exactly comforting, he'd been assured it happened hundreds of times a day across the country with very few complications.

The only good news, as far as he was concerned, was the timing. He wouldn't be able to have the procedure for at least a couple of weeks; too late to participate safely in the surprise mission. He'd debated whether to share the diagnosis with Rebecca, but ultimately decided it was a common enough affliction that it wouldn't reflect poorly on him. There was no reason to expect it would impact his future performance. He still had to get out of Delta, but at least he had time to rework his plan to get Akindele out of the picture before then.

He knew he'd eventually have to get more serious about that, and the security techs who'd taken out the OSHA bitch had enlightened him to a new world of possibilities. They'd pushed the boundaries much farther than Richard had thought possible. They didn't just manipulate data, as he had done. They'd used the system's power to physically manipulate the outside world, having done so to devastating effect. Richard wondered what other vulnerabilities he could exploit.

He considered the possibilities as he walked to his car. An internet-connected smart oven, for example. Did Akindele have one? Was there a way to open a gas valve and delay the ignition long enough to blow his house to pieces? What about taking over the autopilot of a jet leaving Inouye Airport? The flight path wasn't far from Akindele's house.

Of course, something that spectacular would get international attention, and it would be hard to pretend such a statistically unlikely event was an accident. Something at work, maybe? There was a lot of potentially dangerous equipment on Center property. No matter what he chose to do, there'd be no way to exploit the required systems without leaving a trace that would point back to him. The security techs would catch him for sure. Unless—.

A thought struck him as he slid into the driver's seat and slammed the car door shut.

"Andrew," he said with a grin.

***

Rebecca scheduled a meeting the next morning to discuss progress on planning the mission that Akindele had dubbed Gamma Prime. Richard arrived in the spacious meeting room adjacent to her office a few minutes early to get comfortable and go through a self-calming routine his doctor had recommended.

He sat with his eyes closed, taking deep breaths while focusing on how each part of his body felt. He started with his toes and worked his way up, taking time to consider the sensations in every muscle and joint. Mindfulness, his doctor called it. Horseshit is what Richard would have called it just a few weeks earlier. Now, he'd try anything to keep himself relaxed and under control.

Whatever it was called, it wasn't working. His mind leaped haphazardly from one thought to the next despite his best efforts to focus. He'd been advised to cut back on caffeine to improve his meditative abilities, but he wasn't ready to give up his coffee regimen just yet. Maybe that accounted for some of his jitteriness.

"What the hell are you doing, Richard?" demanded Rebecca as she walked into the room.

He opened his eyes and jerked to attention.

"Just some relaxation exercises."

"Well, get your shit together. There's a lot to do."

"Do you have an update from Akindele?"

"That's what we're here to find out," she replied.

Moments later, the physicist entered the room, plopped himself down in a chair as far away from Richard as the room's layout allowed, and opened his laptop.

"What have you got for us, doctor?" asked Rebecca.

Her tone was neither hostile nor pleasant.

"Significant progress," he replied.

He shared his display on the interactive wall, filling it with an array of incomprehensible matrices and equations.

"If you're trying to impress me, doctor, this is not the way to do it."

"Of course," he said with a deferential nod. "This is for Richard's benefit."

"I trust your work, doctor," assured Richard. "Just tell us what it boils down to."

"In the interest of time, I've decided on an iterative approach to solving the problem."

"What does that mean?" asked Rebecca.

"It means he's just going to start guessing," said Richard.

"It most certainly does not," chided Akindele. "And you, of all people, should know that."

"So what *does* it mean, then?" demanded Rebecca again, narrowing her eyes at the physicist.

"It means our nearest point to convergence is only a week away—sooner than I thought. And I do not believe I will have time to complete a direct solution. An iterative solution, using all of the power of the quantum stack, is our best hope."

"I don't understand what that means, doctor."

"You don't have to," he assured. "You just have to give me what I need."

"If it means we can move forward? You can have it," she assured.

"I need everyone off the stack—starting immediately. Shut down all guest researchers, and any other activity using our quantum resources. Converging on an eight-dimensional problem iteratively in such a short time will take absolutely everything we have."

"Done. How do we do it?"

"Andrew can shut everyone out. You just need to ask."

"Everyone but me, right?" asked Richard, leaning forward and putting a fist on the table. "I have requirements."

"Everyone," repeated Akindele.

"Relax, Richard. It's just a week," assured Rebecca with a sideways glance. "Spend the time assembling your team and equipment instead."

For Richard, the updated timeline was good news. Akindele could have the stack for a week. When he was done, Richard would use it to plot his demise. It was time to reveal his hand.

"Unfortunately, I won't be able to go," he announced.

He sighed and shook his head to demonstrate his immense disappointment.

"What?" demanded Rebecca, glaring at him. "What makes you think you can make that call?"

"It's not my call. It's my doctor."

She raised an eyebrow.

"A doctor's note? Really? That's pathetic, Richard."

"I'm not well," he insisted. "I could have a stroke at any minute."

That was an exaggeration. Although that was the main risk associated with his condition, they'd already ruled that out as an immediate danger, since the echocardiogram revealed no evidence of clotting.

"I think you're having a stroke right now," laughed Akindele.

Rebecca rolled her eyes.

"So what's the problem?" she asked.

"Afib. Atrial fibrillation."

"Seriously?"

"Yes. I was diagnosed yesterday."

"No," she said, shaking her head. "I mean, you seriously think that's enough to get you out of the mission?"

"I need a procedure to fix it, Rebecca. It'll take at least two weeks to get it scheduled."

She laughed and raised her eyes to the ceiling, still shaking her head.

"You've watched Kamaras move mountains to ensure the success of this mission, and you think *this* is a problem?"

"I'm no good to the mission if I stroke out over there."

"Nobody's stroking out, Richard. Be at Wheeler tonight by midnight. We'll have the jet take you to Kamaras's private facility in Seattle for the procedure, and you'll be back here in time for lunch tomorrow."

Richard's jaw dropped. How could he not have seen this coming?

***

Richard was in a state of near panic by the time he reached Andrew's office. Before going in, he leaned against the wall to catch his breath, even trying his mindfulness exercises to calm down. It was no use. The more he tried not to think about his predicament, the more it invaded his thoughts. He needed access to the stack to have any chance at all of getting out of Gamma Prime. After a few more deep breaths, he imagined he looked as composed as possible under the circumstances. He knocked on the door and stepped inside.

"Hey, Andrew," he announced with a disarming smile.

"Hey. What's up, Richard?"

"Need another quick favor."

"Shoot."

"Rebecca's going to ask you to lock everyone out of the stack."

"Okay. Why?"

"Akindele needs all of our computing power for a few days."

"I can do that in just a few minutes," he assured as he started clicking away at his keyboard.

"Wait!" said Richard, sounding a little more desperate than he'd wanted.

Andrew stopped typing. His fingers hovered, shaking slightly, inches above the keyboard.

"Wait," repeated Richard, more calmly this time. "I still need just a tiny bit of capacity for the security audit."

He held his thumb and forefinger close together to demonstrate the insignificance of his request.

"Rebecca knows," he added. "But it's got to stay hidden. That's why it won't be in her request."

"No problem," replied Andrew. "I've got you covered."

"Thanks, Andrew. You're doing great work here."

"I appreciate that, sir," he said with a nod. "Let me know if there is anything else I can do to help."

Richard was back in the hallway before he allowed himself a deep breath. Step one had been a success.

***

Kameha was furious. Most of the plan had gone as expected, but Kai's escape was a disaster. Only the son of Kapawa had the legitimacy to challenge him for the leadership of the Ulu people, and he was still alive somewhere in the surrounding jungle. No such concerns remained on the Nanaulu side. Chief Paumakua and his brothers were dead, and Moeanaimua was under his control. By the time the Nanaulu warriors had taken up weapons against the unexpected treachery, Kameha and his men had formed a defensive position around the fire with their captives at the center.

The angry men were held at bay by the threat of harm to Moeanaimua, their de facto chief. One of his captors had tied his hands and now held a knife to his neck. The witch, with murder in her eyes, was bound and gagged beside him. Even Luni had to be restrained. The moment they'd tried to release her, she'd assaulted her brother with a barrage of kicks and punches, tearing a piece out of his forearm with her teeth. She hurled insults at threats at him until she, too, was tied up and gagged—left to thrash about on the ground beside her husband.

After the initial confusion and threat of immediate violence had passed, the two groups settled into an uneasy standoff. As the sun rose over the beach, Kameha and the Kahuna broke from the protective circle to approach the leaderless warriors with an offer of dialog. The Kahuna was the first to speak.

"Our chief, Paumakua, was not the man to lead us in these dangerous times. His time has passed."

"And how did you come to decide this for all of us?" demanded one of the warriors.

"I did not decide. The gods did," declared the Kahuna. "I serve the gods and the Nanaulu above all else."

The men grumbled among themselves.

"Our chief is dead, and our own Kahuna conspires with an outsider to hold his son hostage. How does this serve the Nanaulu?"

"In a dream, the gods showed me our future. I saw this beach where we now stand stained red with our blood. I saw Paumakua die at the hands of Pa'ao while his men ravaged our wives and murdered our children. I saw the end of the Nanaulu."

"Your dream is coming true," challenged the warrior. "The sand is red with our blood, and Paumakua is dead."

"But it is not the end of the Nanaulu," assured the Kahuna. "It is a new beginning."

The Kahuna took a half step back, leaving Kameha face-to-face with the crowd of warriors.

"Today marks the end of our retreat from Pa'ao, and the return of the Nanaulu people to O'ahu. Your new chief, Moeanaimua, with my sister at his side, will rule O'ahu and Kaua'i while I rule Hawai'i, Maui, Lanai, and Moloka'i for the Ulu."

"What of him?" asked a warrior, pointing at the Kahuna.

"He will unite the priests of the islands and maintain our favor with the gods."

"We cannot bring the fight to Pa'ao," scoffed another man. "Our only hope is to defend ourselves here on Kaua'i."

"Don't you see what we have done?" asked Kameha, sweeping his arm towards the captives by the fire. "We have the Dark Witch of O'ahu and her child!"

"How does that help us? You have only made her angry."

"Then she can take her anger out on Pa'ao, who is right now killing her people on O'ahu."

"She will take her anger out on us, you fool!"

"Not if she wants her child to live."

Huaka'i stepped forward to Kameha's side, holding Keanu in his arms. The baby squirmed uncomfortably, trying to soothe himself with his thumb.

"You must hide him away where she cannot find him," explained Kameha, "under the care of a nursing mother."

The Nanaulu warrior recoiled in shock as his brethren chattered among themselves.

"You would threaten the witch with the death of her child? This is madness!"

"We cannot turn back now. It is done."

"We could kill you to regain her favor," suggested the warrior.

"Then Moeanaimua and his bride will die, too, along with as many Nanaulu as my warriors can kill."

"You would have your own sister killed for your ambition?"

"If necessary, yes," replied Kameha with a cold stare. "It is the only way we will survive Pa'ao's onslaught."

The Nanaula warriors retreated to discuss the bold plan among themselves. Kameha returned to the fire with Huaka'i and the Kahuna, the wall of warriors closing behind them.

***

Kai sat among the low bushes on a dune overlooking a small bay north of the main village, catching his breath. They hadn't made it very far since the evening before, but he was already exhausted. After only a few minutes on the run, Jen had slipped out of consciousness, and he'd had to help Ino carry her through the dense trees.

Ignoring his own injuries, he'd forced Ino to remove his wrap and tie it around Jen's waist to staunch the bleeding. It hadn't worked. Blood was still oozing from the tear in her abdomen, and the cloth was soaked through by the time they'd collapsed behind the dune. Ino gazed at the horizon, watching the sun rise in silence. Between the two men, Jen lay motionless, taking shallow breaths that were barely perceptible.

Most of the fishermen had already left the bay, but a few late-rising stragglers were still arriving on the beach with their gear and enough provisions for a few hours out on the water. Kai heaved in a deep breath and winced, reaching down to check the injury to his ribcage. Though the bleeding had stopped, the cuts on his side and arm still hurt badly.

"Let's go," he said.

He waved the gun at his captive, but it wasn't necessary. Ino had no will to fight. Together, they took Jen by the arms, raising her to her feet and dragging her toward a small group of men preparing a pair of outriggers on the beach.

The men stopped talking and stared in disbelief when they noticed the odd trio approaching. Ino was naked, having been forced to give up his wrap, and Kai and Jen were covered in blood.

"Give us your food and water, and leave," ordered Kai.

They set their provisions on the ground without protest, backing away a few paces before turning to run. Kai and Ino placed Jen gently into an outrigger and pushed off. Ino got into the front and started padding while Kai propped Jen on his legs. When he was satisfied she was in a comfortable position, he put his paddle in the water and matched Ino's pace.

"She will not make it to O'ahu," said Ino.

"We have to try," replied Kai.

"Even if she does not die on the way, you'll find no help when we arrive."

"You know nothing of the people there. They can still help her."

"By now, they are dead, Kai. I'm sorry."

"What do you mean?" he demanded.

He stopped paddling and glared at the back of Ino's head.

"Last year, the day you left Moloka'i, Pili attacked us. Many men died, and many more were trapped in the river valley with no chance of escape. Kameha was negotiating a surrender when Pa'ao returned from O'ahu. Those of his warriors that were not badly injured had defeat in their eyes."

"Tell me what he did, Ino," said Kai, his voice rising in anger.

"He used Pa'ao's defeat to his advantage. What started as a surrender became a negotiation. He convinced Pa'ao he could use Luni to learn more about the witch who had torn his men to pieces, and figure out a way to defeat her."

"You visited our home with treachery in your heart, Ino? Your father would be ashamed."

"I swear to you, Kai, I knew nothing of Kameha's plans until yesterday morning."

Kai ignored his plea of ignorance.

"What was Kameha to get from this bargain?"

Ino stopped paddling, turning to face Kai.

"He negotiated Kaua'i for the Ulu people. In exchange for help to defeat the witch, Pili promised to take this island from Chief Paumakua, and to leave our people here in peace."

"But the Kahuna," said Kai, cocking his head. "Why did he turn on his own people?"

"Kameha realized the witch—"

"She is my wife, Samaira," interrupted Kai.

"I'm sorry. Kameha realized Samaira could be a powerful weapon. He sought the Kahuna's advice on how to control her, and use her against Pa'ao and Pili."

"So when the Kahuna came to visit, it was not to honor us. It was to find her weakness."

"Your son, Keanu," confirmed Ino.

Kai shook his head and looked at the sky.

"They will be safe," assured Ino. "The witch—"

He stopped mid-sentence to rephrase the statement.

"Samaira and Keanu will be safe—if she does what is asked of her."

"What will be asked of her?"

"To do what is best for all of us, Kai. To destroy the men who took our islands and drive them back into the sea from which they came."

"And Kameha believes she can do this?"

"Of course she can. Just as she did when they chased you from Moloka'i."

"There is no magic, Ino. You were there—with Huaka'i and the Kahuna. What magic did she show when her own warriors turned on her? If not for you and Jayson, she might already be dead."

"It seemed that way," admitted Ino. "But then we learned the truth—she was hiding her power from us."

"Why would you believe that?" asked Kai.

He was afraid he already knew the answer.

Chapter 20

REBECCA'S PREDICTION TURNED OUT to be uncannily accurate. It was not yet noon when Kamaras's private jet touched down at Wheeler on the return trip from Seattle. Richard peeked out the window to see Cecelia's Mercedes waiting for him as the plane rolled to a stop at the end of the taxiway. After spending the morning messaging with him for constant updates on his condition, she'd insisted on picking him up herself.

She rushed from the car as he descended the stairs, embracing him the moment his feet touched the ground.

"Thank God you're okay," she whispered in his ear.

"I'm fine. It was completely routine."

"How are you feeling now?"

"Better," he said.

She pulled away, furrowing her brow.

"That didn't sound convincing. What's wrong?"

"Nothing is wrong," he insisted. "Everything went as planned. Heart rhythm is better than ever, and my resting rate is even down twenty beats per minute."

"Then why are you still so tense?"

He sighed. She'd been on him for months about the extra stress he was carrying around since the Gamma disaster. He wanted so badly to share his burden with her, but it was impossible. It would only endanger her—and their children—and put their place on Epsilon at risk.

"It's just work stuff. Nothing to do with my heart."

"The work stuff has *everything* to do with your heart," she chided as they walked towards the car. "Is it worth it?"

"You know it is."

"You say it like you're the only person who can save the world. Can't you give up some of your responsibility? Or even just take a leave of absence? When was the last time we had a vacation?"

"It's not that simple," he replied.

"You always say that, Richard, but I can't believe it's worth your health—and maybe your life."

He opened the passenger door, gesturing for her to get in. Instead, she walked around to the other side.

"I'll drive. You need to rest."

"I'm fine," he insisted.

"Just let me baby you a bit, okay? It makes me feel good."

Richard smiled as he slid into the passenger seat, marveling at how lucky he was.

"This stuff at work—it's all for you, you know," he continued. "And the kids."

"We never asked for any of it. Did you ever consider maybe we just want you around a little more? To live a little longer instead of dying from stress?"

Richard winced. If everything went as Rebecca wanted, he only had a few days left with his family. He wouldn't even be able to say goodbye. Maybe they'd let him make a video or something, but it would probably end up the same way the recruits' videos had—deleted and forgotten.

"I want to be around for you, Sissy. I *will* be."

"Okay, but—"

"But what?"

"If you try to hide anything like this heart thing from me again, I'll kill you myself."

She glanced over and cracked a smile.

"I wouldn't dare," he assured.

***

By the next day, Richard was already back at work. He'd spent much of the early morning watching the ships sail in and out of Pearl Harbor. For him, it was another form of attempted meditation—and much more effective than the mindfulness garbage. He felt renewed. Aside from the oddly regular, matching burn marks on his chest and back from the electrodes, he'd suffered no ill effects from the cardioversion.

The night before, as Cecelia rubbed an aloe ointment on his burns, he'd tried to imagine his life on the other side without her. The line of thought triggered a momentary panic, forcing him to shut it down. He knew it was silly and cliché—especially for a man of science—but she was his soulmate.

He was still desperate, but resolved to keep the outright panic at bay so he could focus on what he had to do. He wasn't going anywhere—not without his family—and there was only one way to guarantee that. Akindele had to die. Whether or not Richard could figure out his latest equations was irrelevant. Without Akindele, he was still the next best hope Kamaras had to make sure Delta and Epsilon didn't go off the rails.

To protect himself from repercussions, it would be best to make it seem like he wasn't responsible; but it wasn't critical. He'd walk up to the prick and shoot him in the head right in front of Rebecca if that's what it took to avoid being sent on the mission. It just meant he'd need to maintain his leverage until he finally *did* go through the portal. Then, if Epsilon was successful, and the new world wasn't too much of a mess, he was sure all would be forgiven. Still, he hoped none of that would be necessary. He'd made a plan and found a patsy to take the fall for him.

Richard picked up his phone and dialed. It was best not to leave a trace of text messages on the system.

"Hey, Andrew. Good news. Rebecca was impressed with the results of the security audit. I need you to document everything you know about the vulnerability you used to compromise the passwords."

He listened to the response and continued.

"As soon as possible. I'll be down to pick up a hard copy in an hour."

Before he put the phone down, a hit arrived from the Waipio Point Access Road security gate.

FBI here to see you
What should I tell them?

Richard's stomach twisted into a knot as he stared at the screen. Then a smile crept slowly across his face.

Send them in.

***

By late morning, Kameha had grown impatient with the pace of the Nanaulu warriors' deliberations. He broke from the protective circle around the remains of the fire to see if they were any closer to making a decision about his proposal. Nearing the large group of men, he realized they weren't deliberating at all. They were staring at a pair of fishermen in the distance and didn't even notice his approach.

"What is more important than deciding the future of our people?" he asked.

"Look there," said one of the men, pointing in the distance.

"They're just fishermen."

"No. Farther out. On the horizon."

Kameha strained to see a distant white peak rising out of the water like the fin of some enormous shark.

"What is it?" he demanded.

"We don't know. But it is getting closer."

The Ulu men, noticing their distracted leader, followed his gaze to see what had caught his interest. They whispered among themselves about the meaning of the unfamiliar sight as they edged toward the water, leaving Samaira, Luni, and Moeanaimua unattended. Movement in the corner of Luni's eye caught her attention. She looked up and realized with horror it was Palila creeping in from the dense foliage of the nearby jungle.

Luni shook her head vigorously to urge her sister back into hiding. Palila ignored the silent plea as she scurried toward the trio of captives, taking advantage of the distraction out at sea to avoid detection. As she passed the body of one of the fallen warriors, she retrieved a stone-blade knife from the folds of his wrap before continuing towards the fire pit and ducking down behind her sister.

"You should not be here!" whispered Luni as soon as her sister removed the gag.

Palila didn't respond. She focused instead on cutting the rope binding Luni's hands behind her back. Then she moved immediately to Samaira while Luni untied Moeanaimua.

"We need to get away from here," pleaded Luni.

"No," whispered Samaira, rubbing her sore wrists. "I am not leaving without Keanu."

Though Moeanaimua could not understand their exchange, he seemed to agree with Samaira. His eyes locked on the distracted men, he crawled slowly forward to retrieve a spear left carelessly lying beside the fire.

"Give me that, please," whispered Samaira, pointing to the crude stone knife in Palila's hand.

The young girl handed it over without hesitation.

"Take your sister and hide somewhere safe," she instructed Luni.

"No," replied Luni. "I want to help. This is my fault."

"No, it's not. Kameha did this."

"He did it because of me."

"What?"

"When I returned here, Kameha wanted to know if it was true you had magic that had killed Pa'ao's men. I told him it was. I told him I had seen you summon the power of a thousand knives with nothing more than a whisper, and fling them at Pa'ao's warriors like you were throwing a pebble."

"Why would you do that?"

"I thought it would keep you safe—prevent him from ever harming anyone from O'ahu."

Samaira sighed and shook her head.

"It's not your fault," she assured. "Now, please take your sister and hide."

"Pono 'oe e hele," added Moeanaimua, pointing to the trees where Palila had been hiding.

Luni nodded and took Palila by the arm. Staying low, she led her sister to the forest. Moeanaimua repeated his warning to Samaira, asking her to take cover. She shook her head and held up the knife, pointing it at the man who held her child. Moeanaimua nodded, understanding immediately he would not win the argument with the angry mother.

Huaka'i stood facing the water only a dozen paces from the smoking remains of the fire. Keanu fussed and wriggled in his arms, doubtlessly hungry after so long away from his mother's breast. Distracted by the distant sail of Jasmine's hope and the frustrated cries of the baby in his arms, he didn't notice Moeanaimua and Samaira creeping up behind him.

Samaira leaped up, striking first. She drove the stone blade into his back, just to the right of his spine, aiming for his heart. The crude weapon tore through his skin and muscle, but failed to penetrate his ribcage. Huaka'i howled in pain as he spun around to face his attackers. His eyes widened at the sight of the witch glaring at him with fiery hatred in her eyes.

Moeanaimua drove his spear into the lower part of Huaka'i'iʻs gut to avoid endangering Keanu. The warrior gasped, falling to his knees. Samaira pulled Keanu from his arms and was already running for the safety of the trees before Huaka'i expelled his last breath and collapsed face-first onto the sand.

The sudden commotion drew the attention of everyone on the beach. Kameha realized in an instant of horror that his leverage had vanished. Moeanaimua was free, and the witch was escaping with her child.

"E hoʻomākaukau i ka hakakā," he cried out, quickly distancing himself from the Nanaulu warriors and retreating to the remains of the fire.

"E pepehi iā lākou a pau," yelled Moeanaimua to his men.

He glared at the Kahuna, hiding behind a wall of Ulu warriors.

"E pepehi au i ke kumakaia," he spat, reserving his right to kill the traitor personally.

Then, with a cry, he led his men into battle.

***

Kai and Ino, looking like any other fishermen, paddled across the mouth of the bay mostly unnoticed. They, too, had been distracted by the approaching ship on the horizon, and had adjusted course to intercept. Kai knew immediately upon seeing the shape of the sail that it was Jasmine's Hope, and realized it could mean salvation for Jen.

Though he had been determined to try, he knew Ino was right. She would never have survived the two-day journey to get help on O'ahu. He redoubled his effort with new hope in sight, glancing back every few minutes to see if they'd been noticed. He expected canoes to come racing after them at any moment. Instead, he saw a commotion on the beach.

"Something is happening ashore," he said.

Ino dragged his paddle on one side of the canoe, turning it so he could get a better look.

"It's a battle," he realized. "That is not part of Kameha's plan."

"What does it mean?"

"The Nanaulu have rejected his bargain, or he has lost his leverage."

"Samaira and Keanu!" realized Kai.

He looked down at Jen, still lying in his lap, frantically trying to decide what to do. It didn't take long. He would always choose his wife and child first.

"Take her to the ship for help," he ordered. "I'm going back."

"Of course," agreed Ino with a nod.

Kai wriggled his way from underneath Jen as gently as possible and sat up on the side of the outrigger.

"If you betray me again," he warned, "I swear I will kill you."

He grabbed the gun from the bottom of the canoe and rolled backward into the water without another word.

***

The melee on the beach pitted dozens of Nanaulu warriors against their Ulu cousins. Moeanaimua and Kameha stood at the front of their respective sides, trading attacks and parrying blows from one another. On either side of them, a growing number of dead and injured lay on the sand. Battle cries rose from both sides of the chaotic front line, drowning out the sound of the waves.

Even the din of battle could not compare to the gun's deafening report. The warriors fell silent as they turned in unison toward the bay where Kai was wading through knee-deep water toward them. A wisp of smoke rose from the barrel of the handgun, still pointed skyward.

"Enough of this madness!" he cried. "You do Pa'ao's work for him by killing each other."

"You do not lead the Ulu people," spat Kameha. "You lost that right when you abandoned them for your witch."

"Look how you lead them, Kameha. Your ambition will cost them their lives."

By now, Kai was on dry land, only a few arm's lengths away from his former friend.

"Kill him!" shouted Kameha.

The Ulu men exchanged looks, but not one raised his weapon. Kameha lofted his spear and cocked his arm back, ready to launch his own attack. Before he could take even half a step, Kai raised the gun and fired again. The nearest warriors recoiled in fright as fire leaped from the barrel, and Kameha's chest exploded in a cloud of blood. He crumpled to the ground, his lifeless eyes staring at the sky.

"What manner of magic is that?" asked Moeanaimua with wide eyes.

"It is not magic. Only a weapon," assured Kai. "And I'll not hold it while I talk of peace among our men."

He tossed the gun to the ground and positioned himself between the two groups of men, holding his arms apart and exposing his chest to the new Nanaulu chief.

"I prefer peace," said Moeanaimua with a nod, "but some treacheries cannot be forgiven."

He quickly raised his spear, hurling it forward. It flew past Kai's shoulder and found its mark at the base of the Kahuna's sternum. The holy man, still bedecked in his finery from the wedding, toppled over. He gasped for breath and gurgled blood for a few moments before going still.

"Put down your weapons," called Moeanaimua to his warriors. "This fight is over."

***

The crew aboard Jasmine's Hope noticed the approaching canoe when they were still a few kilometers from shore. Every few minutes, the lone man at the front of the small outrigger waved his paddle in the air, trying to get their attention. They'd altered course to intercept.

"Is that Kai?" asked Park.

"No. It's Jayson's friend, Ino," replied Farzin, lowering the binoculars.

"Why the hell would he be out here alone?"

Farzin shook his head and frowned.

"No idea. But I doubt it's good news."

"You think we're too late?" asked Herman.

"I don't know," replied Farzin. "But we did the best we could."

He raised the binoculars for another look.

"Shit. He's not alone."

"What is it?" demanded Park.

"I think it's Jen. She's lying down behind him. She must be hurt."

As they closed in on the approaching canoe, Park scurried to mid-deck and grabbed the line to haul in the jib.

"Luff the sails," he called to Matteus.

Matteus handed the wheel to Serge and adjusted the mainsail until it fluttered inefficiently in the breeze, causing the ship to slow down. Farzin grabbed a rope and jumped into the water. Taking a few strokes to reach Ino, he handed it over before pulling himself up on the side to get a better look at Jen. Everyone on deck rushed over to see what was happening as the small outrigger drifted past. Still firmly in Ino's grasp, the rope went taut, and the small canoe came around, now trailing Jasmine's Hope. Park grabbed the line and started frantically hauling it in.

"Is she okay?" he called to Farzin.

Farzin looked up and shook his head. Tears were running down his face.

"Fuck!"

Park kept pulling the rope, tying it off only once the outrigger was alongside them. It swayed back and forth in the ship's wake, bumping rhythmically against the side of the wooden hull. He kneeled on the deck, looking down anxiously while Farzin gently removed the bloody wrap around Jen's waist to examine the wound.

"There was a fight," he announced. "With the locals. This wasn't done by a modern weapon."

"You!" said Park, leveling a finger at Ino. "Get up here and tell us what the hell happened."

Ino cowered in fear at the sudden aggression. He waved his hands in front of his face and slid back into the canoe.

"There's nowhere to go, dumbass."

"He doesn't understand you," explained Herman, placing a calming hand on Park's shoulder. "Let me try."

Herman opened the translator app.

"Do you remember me, Ino?" he asked.

Ino nodded.

"Let us help you onto the ship."

The naked warrior nodded again and clambered towards the rope ladder. Herman and Park each grabbed a hand, hauling him aboard Jasmine's Hope. Park snatched the tablet from Herman and began interrogating him.

"What happened to Jen? Where are the others? Are they okay?"

"Give him a break, Park," said Serge. "He's traumatized. Get him some water and something to cover himself up before you go full inquisition on him."

"Screw that. I'm going to make this asshole squeal."

"He brought Jen to us," reminded Serge. "He's a friend."

Park snorted and backed off.

"Fine," he said. "Get him some water. But I'm not done with him."

Serge handed the wheel back to Matteus and went below to find something for Ino to wear.

In the meantime, Farzin had pulled the wrap out from underneath Jen and draped it over as much of her body as it would cover. Herman helped him onto the deck, where he collapsed with his head in his hands.

Chapter 21

ANDREW FINISHED THE SECURITY audit report in less than thirty minutes, documenting the steps he'd taken to deactivate the safeguards before brute-forcing Akindele's password. The hardest part of the request for a hard copy was finding a printer. Nobody at the Center printed anything, not even the old guys like Richard. Tablets, laptops, and digital whiteboards abounded. Printers? Not so much. He dug one out of a storage closet, still in its original packaging, and went through the excruciatingly complex setup instructions, denying its requests for network access and opting instead for a hard-wired connection. After all, it would go back into the box the moment Richard's document was ready.

His concerns about the complexities of printing a hard copy were only secondary. He understood what was happening. Richard didn't want to rely on him as the conduit for sneaking around in the system. It was a concerning development, but nothing he couldn't deal with. He hadn't documented *all* of the log files and other telltale signs of misuse that he had to clean up after every breach. He'd still be able to tell if his boss was up to something.

***

The dark SUV pulled into the circular drive in front of the Center's main building and came to a stop in the fire lane. Richard walked toward it, arriving to greet the agents just as they got out.

"Dr. Richard Vandergroot," he said with a smile. "Managing Director of the Center for Sustainability Research."

"Assistant Special Agent in Charge Clyburn and Special Agent Tanaka" said Clyburn. "Thanks for seeing us."

"Of course," replied Richard. "How can I help you?"

"Can we talk inside?"

"Sure. Let's head up to my office."

On the way through the lobby, Richard stopped at the reception desk.

"Monica, can you please let Rebecca know we have some guests from the FBI? We'll be in my office."

"Rebecca Steinman?" asked Clyburn. "Hitz-It.com Chief Operating Officer?"

"That's right," replied Richard, leading them to the elevator.

"Is she usually here?"

"No. But she does come by regularly. This operation may seem modest, but it's one of Anton Kamaras's top priorities. She likes to stay involved—on his behalf."

Clyburn glanced at his colleague, raising an eyebrow.

"Will we be able to speak with her?"

"I'm not sure if her schedule will allow it. She's quite busy."

In his office, the two agents took their seats across the desk from Richard.

"Now, how can I help you?" he asked.

"Special Agent Shannon Boucher," started Clyburn. "You've heard of her?"

"Of course. I'm pretty sure everyone on O'ahu has heard of her."

"What about Jessica Reyes?" asked Agent Tanaka. "You know her?"

"One of the victims. Your agent's ex-wife, I believe."

"And an acquaintance of yours, Dr. Vandergroot."

"Not that I am aware of," replied Richard, furrowing his brow.

"She's an OSHA inspector—was an OSHA inspector," added Clyburn. "She tried to have a project of yours shut down for some safety violations last year."

"Oh? I didn't make the connection. But I can assure you there were no safety issues."

"It got pretty heated, from what we've heard."

"If the Center or I are subjects of your investigation, I'm going to have to escort you out and ask that you contact me through our attorneys."

Richard stood and motioned toward the door.

"Nothing personal," he added. "Just company policy."

"Please have a seat, doctor," replied Clyburn. "You're not under investigation. It's Agent Boucher we're after."

Richard lowered himself back into his chair.

"What's this got to do with me?"

"Were you aware Agent Boucher was looking into the Center?"

"I thought you said we weren't under investigation."

"It was unofficial and unsanctioned," clarified Tanaka. "Looks like it might have been on behalf of the ex-wife. Maybe she held a grudge?"

"I don't know anything about that. I never interacted with Ms. Reyes after she left our site."

"What can you tell us about Hitarthi Srinivasan?" interjected Clyburn.

"Materials scientist—brilliant," replied Richard. "Shame what happened to her. What's that got to do with your agent?"

"We were hoping you might tell us. Agent Boucher was reviewing the incident report before she went AWOL."

Richard frowned and shook his head.

"I can't help you there."

A knock at the door interrupted their conversation. It was Rebecca.

"Richard? Can I speak with you for a moment?"

"Ms. Steinman," interjected Clyburn. "Do you think you could spare us a few minutes today?"

"I'm afraid that won't be possible," she replied. "In fact, I need to steal Dr. Vandergroot away from you now so we can attend to an urgent matter."

"We can—"

"I'll have someone from security show you out. My apologies."

She ushered Richard out of the office and closed the door. Leading him down the hallway at a brisk pace, she didn't say a word until they were in her office with the door shut.

"What the fuck were you thinking?" she demanded. "You invited the FBI into the building?"

"It's under control," he assured. "I just figured it was an opportunity to see what they know."

"No matter what over-inflated opinion you might have of your abilities, you cannot out-interrogate the fucking FBI, Richard."

"I don't think—"

"Next time you hear from them, direct them to the lawyers. Do you understand?"

"Of course," he replied with a deferential nod. "I was just trying to help."

"You want to help? Stay in your lane."

He nodded again and left. Walking down the hallway, he could barely suppress a smirk.

***

Andrew looked up with a start as Richard burst into his office without knocking. He seemed different. No. Not different; back to normal. His swagger was back, and he didn't seem as anxious. That couldn't be a good sign.

"You got that report ready?" he asked without pleasantries.

"Here you go," said Andrew, handing over the eight-page document.

"That's it?"

"It's not that complicated, sir. It all comes down to access."

"I'm going to need that. The access, I mean. To demonstrate the vulnerability to Rebecca."

It didn't really make sense, but Andrew knew better than to expose his suspicions by pointing it out.

"Sure."

"One last thing. This is sensitive stuff. Dangerous, even. I need you to delete every trace that this document ever existed."

"Of course. No problem."

"Thanks," said Richard with a curt nod before turning to leave.

Andrew slumped down in his chair as the door clicked shut. Delete every trace? Richard clearly had a plan to avoid Akindele's trap, and Andrew was no longer part of it. He'd given his boss everything he needed to be self-sufficient, leaving himself as the only remaining loose end that could expose whatever he was up to. The taste of bile filled his mouth.

***

The crew anchored Jasmine's Hope two hundred meters offshore from the battle scene, where the water was deep enough to ensure they wouldn't run aground when the tide went out. Kai beckoned them ashore. Despite his invitation, and the apparent cessation of hostilities, Farzin and Park waded through the water with weapons slung across their backs. Ino joined them, along with Serge, armed only with his tablet.

"How is Jen?" demanded Kai, rushing to meet them at the shoreline.

Farzin shook his head and frowned in response.

Kai hung his head.

"She saved my life," he said.

"What's the deal here?" demanded Park.

"What?"

"What's going on?" he tried again, gesturing around at the carnage on the beach. "And what happened to Jen."

"Kameha," replied Kai. "He betrayed the people of Kaua'i after they offered our people a home. He attacked us at the wedding."

"That one, right?" asked Park, pointing at one of the bodies.

"That one," confirmed Kai with a nod.

Park unslung his weapon and let loose a short burst of fire, causing Kameha's body to shudder grotesquely on the ground. The nearby warriors gasped and recoiled at the grisly sight.

"It's over," admonished Kai. "There is nothing more to do here."

At that moment, Samaira, Luni, and Palila came rushing in from the trees.

"Kai!" shouted Samaira. "Thank God you're alright."

He embraced her and gave Keanu a kiss on the head.

"Is he okay?"

"Yes. He'll be fine. Just a little hungry. Where is Jen?"

Kai frowned, shaking his head.

"She gave her life to save us."

Samaira dropped her head against his shoulder and sobbed.

Luni approached Moeanaimua with caution, her head hung low in shame.

"I am sorry for what my brother did to you and your family," she said. "I promise I didn't know."

"I know," he assured her, opening his arms.

She fell against his chest and wept.

Palila, in the meantime, crouched beside her brother's body and took his hand, tears streaming down her face. Kai approached and kneeled down beside her.

"I am sorry I had to kill him, Palila. I hope you know I had no other choice."

"I know," she replied with a weak nod.

While Kai stayed by Palila's side to offer comfort, Samaira spoke with Serge.

"What are you doing here?" she asked, wiping a tear from her face.

"Kameha wasn't the only one with a plan," he explained. "Josh smuggled a container of Scylla with him and was going to do something at the wedding. We came to stop him."

She shot a look at Park, who was standing nearby.

"Who else knew about this?" she demanded.

"Relax," said Serge, taking her by the shoulders. "Park is the one who warned us."

"Were we too late?" asked Park. "Where is he?"

"Kameha's men got him. He's dead—over there."

Park's eyes followed where she was pointing. He beckoned to Farzin, and the two men jogged off towards the collection of bodies near the remains of the feast. They quickly found Josh, his clothing, fair skin, and blond hair standing out among the dead natives. Searching his cargo pants, they located the cylindrical container in one of the large pockets near his thigh. Park unscrewed the top and let out a sigh of relief upon discovering the pathogen had not yet been prepared for delivery.

"Thank Christ for small miracles," he said.

"Yeah. At least something went right."

"Anything worth taking?"

"Just the boots, I guess."

Farzin unlaced them while Park patted down the rest of the pockets for anything of value. After a moment of consideration, Farzin unrolled the socks and stuffed them into the boots as well.

"Hand me the stuff," he said, holding out his hand. "I don't want to have to explain what it is."

He took the cylinder of Scylla and tucked it all the way down to the toe of one of the boots.

"Should we bury him or something?" asked Park.

"I suppose we should help clean this mess up," replied Farzin, gesturing around.

"Yeah," sighed Park. "I suppose so."

"Let's find out if they have any kind of special ceremony, or something, before we start moving bodies. I don't want to piss these people off any more than they already are."

Park nodded and followed Farzin back to the beach.

Samaira closed her eyes and exhaled in relief as Farzin approached and gave her a thumbs up. He patted the boots slung over his shoulder to let her know he had the Scylla.

"What's going on over here?" he asked, sliding up beside her.

"I don't know. Serge just turned on the translator, and we're trying to catch up."

"Didn't you guys have a tablet?"

"Yeah. I think Jen had it."

"It's not with her now," said Farzin, looking around. "We'll have to find it later."

By now, Kai and Moeanaimua were standing face to face. Luni stood next to her husband, with Palila clinging to her side. Though they'd diffused the immediate crisis, the surrounding warriors still held their weapons, warily eying one another as their leaders conferred.

"How can the Nanaulu ever again trust the Ulu people after such a betrayal?" asked Moeanaimua.

"They can't," replied Kai.

The warriors on both sides stiffened upon hearing the words.

"What the hell is he doing?" asked Farzin as the translation emerged.

He reached involuntarily for his rifle to make sure it was still over his shoulder.

"I don't know," admitted Samaira.

Moeanaimua remained stern-faced and motionless as he waited for an explanation.

"Kameha has destroyed the honor of our people," continued Kai, turning to face his men. "But we are not without fault. I abandoned you to his leadership far too easily, just as you abandoned your honor far too easily for him."

Many of the Ulu warriors shuffled uncomfortably and stared at the ground.

"I reclaim my birthright for one purpose only," he continued. "To declare my father, Kapawa, the last of the Ulu chiefs. The Ulu are no more."

The warriors on both sides began murmuring among themselves while Moeanaimua betrayed nothing by way of reaction.

Farzin cocked one eye and glanced at Samaira. Still focused on the new Nanaulu chief, she didn't notice.

Moeanaimua finally broke his silence.

"Kai is right. This world is not the same one we knew only a year ago. We must face the threat to our existence—the threat from Pa'ao—as one people. What I say now, I say with the deepest respect for my father. As Kapawa was the last of the Ulu chiefs, so Paumakua shall be known as the last of the Nanaula chiefs."

His people gasped collectively and started chattering among themselves.

"The legacies of our forbearers—of Kapawa and Paumakua—are not dead," he continued. "Today, they can become something greater. Today we are all Kanaka Mokupuni."

"We are all people of the islands," repeated Samaira after hearing the translation. "It's brilliant."

Then Moeanaimua turned to face her.

"E hui pū anei kou poʻe me mākou?" he asked.

"Will your people join us?" came the translation.

***

They spent the day on Kaua'i preparing to honor the dead. Those without the stomach to gather bodies and cleanse the beach gathered firewood instead. After a short debate, the recruits brought Jen's body ashore to mark her death in the same way as the other warriors who had fallen as a result of Kameha's betrayal. Herman and Matteus joined the rest of the crew ashore to watch as the priests gave their blessings and set the massive pyre ablaze as the sun disappeared behind the mountains.

They watched mostly in silence for hours as flames consumed the flesh of the unfortunate wedding guests and their attackers. When all that remained of the fire were glowing embers, Moeanaimua approached the visitors from O'ahu, sitting with them on a large woven mat.

"Tomorrow, we will take the bones to a sacred place for burial," he said via the translator. "I hope you will stay."

"We will," assured Samaira. "But we would like to take our warriors' remains home. There are people on O'ahu who will need to mourn them."

"Of course. I will instruct the priests to set them aside for you."

"Luni told me about your magic," he revealed to Samaira, pointing at the tablet that made their conversation possible. "That it is not really magic at all."

Samaira looked at the others. Their dejected faces all said the same thing; lies had not served them well.

"No. It is not magic," she replied.

Moeanaimua nodded as he considered her admission.

"But she could not explain how you came to these islands."

"Neither can we."

"Not with that ship?" he asked, pointing to the harbor.

She shook her head, and Moeanaimua narrowed his eyes—examining her for a few moments.

"You are here now," he said finally. "And without your tools and weapons, Pa'ao will soon overpower us. So I ask again—will you join us as one to defend our islands?"

Park leaned in and paused the translator app.

"We don't even know what that means," he protested.

"Then let's find out," suggested Serge.

"I agree," said Samaira. "We eventually need to figure out how we're going to integrate with other societies and influence their development. If we can't figure out how to do that with our neighbors—people with a philosophy of environmental stewardship similar to our own—what chance do we have at fulfilling our mission?"

Park sighed and nodded.

"Makes sense, I guess," he admitted. "But there are people back on O'ahu who won't like it. Shit, we'll be lucky if they don't shoot us dead the moment we step onto the dock."

Samaira activated the app before turning to Moeanaimua.

"We need time to speak with our people," she said.

"I understand," he said with a curt nod. "But I am not sure how much time we have left."

Moeanaimua rose, leaving his guests to consider the offer.

"He seems pissed," said Farzin.

"No. Just worried for his people, I think," replied Samaira. "We can't fault him for that."

"You think he's angry? This is going to cause another shitstorm with the security team," said Park.

Chapter 22

THE RESIDENTS OF HONOLULU rushed to the harbor to greet the returning ship after several tense days of waiting for word from Kaua'i. As it approached the dock, their excited chattering fell silent. The glum faces of the crew betrayed things had not gone well. Matteus guided Jasmine's Hope into her slip under luffed sails, fluttering in the light breeze, while Park and Farzin prepared the lines. The two sailors leaped onto the dock moments before the ship made contact.

Miroslava Sirotkin pushed her way to the front of the crowd and caught Park by the arm just as he finished tying off the bow line. Farzin shot her a deadly look. Immediately, she softened her stance and let go.

"How'd it go?" she asked.

Park glanced at Farzin, but said nothing.

"Pretty fucking bad," said Farzin. "Luckily for you, it had nothing to do with that shit you tried to pull."

The others were disembarking from the ship, and Sirotkin scanned the deck to see who was among them.

"What happened?" she demanded. "Where's Josh?"

"He's dead. Jen, too."

"Jesus Christ! What did you do?"

"Happened before we got there," he replied, shaking his head. "The whole wedding thing was a setup."

Kai and Samaira, with Keanu clinging to his mother's neck, were next to step off the ship. There were some audible expressions of relief among those gathered when they saw the baby was unharmed.

Jayson, who had been taking time to decompress in solitude in the days following the battle, was tending the coffee and cacao plants he'd established in the higher elevations near Kaaikahi Spring when he saw the ship's sails appear off Ewa Beach. He arrived at the dock panting as Serge and Herman climbed down the ladder with the charred remains of their colleagues bundled in woven blankets. He worked his way through the crowd towards them. Surveying the scene as he caught his breath, he noticed the subdued nature of the reunification.

"What's going on?" he asked. "What's wrong?"

"It's Jen," replied Samaira, wincing sympathetically. "She was killed."

Jayson was silent for several moments, trying to make sense of the words.

"Jen?"

"I'm sorry, Jayson," added Kai. "Kameha attacked us without warning. He killed Josh, Jen, and most of the chief's family."

Jayson's eyes went wide.

"Where's Luni?" he demanded.

"She's fine," assured Samaira. "Luni had nothing to do with it. She's safe with her new husband—and Palila."

Jayson hung his head. When he finally looked up, he pointed to the bundles carried by Serge and Herman.

"Is that what I think it is?"

Serge nodded solemnly.

Jayson shook his head and turned away. Pushing his way through the crowd, he headed back toward the settlement. Serge dropped Josh's remains unceremoniously to the ground and went to follow. Samaira grabbed him by the arm.

"Give him some time," she advised. "He'll be okay."

***

Richard was ready for the last-minute meeting request from Dr. Akindele. He'd been monitoring progress surreptitiously using the password he'd gotten from Andrew, and had seen the solution for the eight-dimensional vector converge. He arrived purposely late as part of his plan to reassert some level of dominance over his former underling.

"Sorry I'm late," he announced, striding into the room. "I was just verifying with the admiral that the Reagan will be here in time to support our mission next Wednesday evening."

Akindele raised an eyebrow, a smirk barely perceptible beneath his stoic facade.

"Dr. Akindele has already shared his results with you?" asked Rebecca with surprise.

"No. I've been working on an independent solution to verify his calculations. So how did I do, doctor?"

"That is correct. The moment of nearest alignment will arrive just a few seconds before 8:45 on Wednesday evening. Were you able to determine the mass flow rate?"

"One hundred and seventy-seven kilograms per second for five-point-three seconds."

"Agreed," nodded Akindele. "I'd like to have the Reagan hooked up a few days in advance since we have limited staff support."

"That won't be a problem. It's arriving on Sunday afternoon."

Rebecca had her phone out, working the numbers in the calculator app.

"Almost a ton. That's excellent news. You've got your wish list, Richard?"

"Me, Two SEALs, and gear," he confirmed with a nod.

He didn't add the details of the backup plan he'd prepared for when Akindele fell victim to a tragic insider betrayal.

***

After nearly a week without contact from Jayson, Samaira and Serge hiked up to Kaaikahi spring to find him. He'd taken one of the tents they'd lived in during their first months on the island and set up a campsite among the rows of coffee plants, opting to isolate himself from the others. Nobody had seen him for several days after Serge had come to tell him there would be a funeral for Jen and Josh. He hadn't attended.

When the pair arrived to check on him, he was kneeling next to one of his plants, pruning away some branches. They watched silently for a few minutes as he carefully selected which ones to remove.

"The crop is looking good," offered Serge when he could take the silence no longer.

"I've neglected these little guys too long," he said with a frown. "They should have been pruned months ago. Probably not going to have any fruit for another year, at least."

"Are you doing alright?" asked Samaira.

He stopped pruning and sighed before turning to face her.

"No. No I'm not."

"I know it's hard to lose someone, Jayson. We're all feeling it—but we can support you through this. We can support each other."

"Yeah? And what about the next time? And the time after that?"

"We'll be there for those, too."

"So you admit this is going to keep happening?"

Samaira didn't respond.

"You had all these great ideas about how we were going to integrate with the locals once we got the security team on board," he continued. "But it's been nothing but a mess. Do you know I had to kill a bunch of Pa'ao's men? I had to shoot them, Samaira. Dozens of them."

"I heard. I'm sorry about that."

"Me too," he said with a frown. "And the ones I just injured? I watched their friends finish them off before they left."

"That must have been terrible for you."

"It was. But I can only imagine how much worse it was for them. I keep imagining what it would be like if I had to do that to you—or any of the others. Slit your throats to stop your suffering."

"That's not going to happen, Jayson."

"No? So what happens next time Pa'ao shows up, or when Moeanaimua decides to betray us like Kameha did?"

"Moeanaimua has offered to join us—not as an ally, but as one people. He's coming here with a delegation to discuss it in a month or so."

"Is Luni coming, too?"

"I don't know," replied Samaira. "But we could use your help."

"Me? What can I do?"

This time, it was Serge who answered.

"There is a lot of work to be done," he replied. "We need to develop a constitution and a system of representative government everyone can accept if we are to span our culture across multiple islands."

"And go to war with Pa'ao," added Jayson.

"We need to eliminate the threat," said Samaira. "He'll be back to try again if we don't."

"What if we negotiate?"

"Without making him pay for what he's already done? That's appeasement—and it never works. It only buys time until the next attack."

Jayson sighed and returned to his coffee plant, clipping away another branch with his pruners.

"What if there is another way?" he asked.

"What did you have in mind?"

"This," he said, gesturing around. "Farming."

"You want to defeat Pa'ao with farming?"

"Kind of. Yeah."

Samaira glanced at Serge and raised an eyebrow. He shrugged back.

"Okay. Let's hear it."

***

As scheduled, the U.S.S. Ronald Reagan arrived at Pearl Harbor with its carrier group on Sunday afternoon. Some of the support ships were docked across the channel at the naval base so the sailors could enjoy some well-deserved leave while the rest anchored offshore due to a lack of berth space. Smaller vessels ferried some of their crews ashore in shifts so they, too, could spend some time on the terra firma of their home country.

There was no opportunity for rest for many of the men on the Reagan itself. Those experienced with the setup required for Fusion B worked to haul the massive cables ashore and affix them to the facility. They also hooked up the capacitor network, which was sitting on a nearby barge with a tugboat at the ready in case the fire got out of hand.

Andrew walked down the pathway toward Fusion B carrying an armload of cables and gear. None of it was necessary. With Richard's office commanding easterly views overlooking all the activity along the water, it was a necessary pretense to make his frequent visits with Akindele seem less suspicious.

"What did Tiara say?" he asked, walking into the control room.

The physicist scowled, and Andrew bit his lip. After a few semi-regular visits, and her continued insistence on more familiar greetings, he'd grown used to using her first name.

"She agrees with your assessment that Richard's sudden change in behavior is bad news."

"And?"

"She thinks he'll wait until the last moment to show his hand, so Rebecca has no time to adjust."

"Do you think he'll double-check the convergence data?"

"I doubt he could figure out how," replied Akindele with a snort.

The convergence data in Akindele's hacked account was off by twenty-four hours. According to the *real* calculations, the ones done in secret using his cloned account, the optimum transfer time would be Tuesday evening. It would be late Tuesday afternoon before Richard and Rebecca learned about the mistake.

"What do you need me to do?" asked Andrew.

"Nothing here—for now. Just keep an eye on Richard to see if you can figure out what he's up to."

"Already on it," he assured.

***

Rebecca would figure it out, of course. Richard knew that. He bargained the gift he would offer her in exchange for his salvation would be enough to make her look the other way. It was such a good deal, she might even play along and pretend not to know the truth. He would stay at her side and join Kamaras on Epsilon as the only physicist who could run the preparations for the remaining events. In exchange, Richard would put an end to the FBI investigation into the Center by offering up a suspect in the terrible deaths at the coffee shop, and the murder of renowned quantum computing pioneer Dr. Olujimi Akindele.

He watched from his office window as Andrew, returning from Fusion B, disappeared beneath the canopy of a shade tree in the plaza below. He had been a useful pawn, and it pained him to lose the advantage the unsuspecting computer tech had given him over the last few weeks. But ultimately, the role of the pawn was to be sacrificed in service of the greater goal.

Using the knowledge in Andrew's security report and the newly acquired system access, he'd uncovered the secret behind how the security techs had taken over Charlie Hoang's vehicle controls, and sent him careening into the coffee shop at full speed. He'd brute-force Andrew's account to do something similar to Akindele—only he wouldn't be so careful about cleaning up the traces in the vehicle's systems. They would lead the FBI to a rogue employee of the Center for Sustainability Research. The Center, of course, would cooperate fully in the investigation, handing Andrew over on a silver platter.

There was still some groundwork to do. He had to create a link between Andrew and the child trafficking ring that had allegedly entangled Charlie Hoang, the FBI agent, and her bitch ex-wife. It wouldn't be hard, either. He already had a reputation as a bit of a creeper, and there were several women on the Center staff who would be happy to share their firsthand experience of lewd exchanges. The evidence that would come to light—after his death, of course—wouldn't surprise anyone. This led to the final missing piece of the plan; how to make sure Andrew wasn't alive to provide testimony.

***

"This isn't a plan," complained Farzin. "It's suicide."

"I don't think it is," countered Samaira. "Not if we do it right."

"We'll go in armed to the tits," assured Park.

Samaira frowned.

"Do you mean armed to the teeth?"

"Is that how it goes? Makes more sense than tits, I guess."

Samaira rolled her eyes and turned to Jayson.

"Are you okay with that?"

"Yeah," he nodded. "I know what we have to do."

"We can mitigate the impact, Jayson," offered Serge. "We could prepare some floatation devices for the survivors."

"Good idea."

"Is it really worth the risk?" asked Farzin.

"We can save thousands of lives," replied Jayson. "To me, that's worth the risk."

Farzin shook his head in dismay.

"Who else?"

"Me," replied Kai, thrusting his arm in the air.

"No," replied Jayson. "You have a family. Malo and Ino have already agreed."

Kai started to object, rising to his feet, but Samaira pulled him back down to her side.

"Paul wants to come, too," said Jayson. "He told me this morning."

"Suryana?" asked Park with surprise. "You think we can trust him?"

"O'Neal's had enough, too," added Farzin. "And de la Cruz."

"I don't buy it," replied Park, shaking his head.

"I do," said Samaira. "This is what recovery from brainwashing looks like."

Everyone looked at her.

"Men, it has been well said, think in herds," she quoted. "It will be seen that they go mad in herds, while they only recover their senses slowly, one by one."

"What the hell does that mean?" asked Park.

"It means we're winning," replied Samaira.

He shook his head in frustration.

"So, do we bring him or not?"

"I'd say so. It'll help develop trust and bring us together."

"Fine with me," he shrugged. "When do we go?"

"As soon as possible," replied Jayson.

***

Two days later, at Honolulu Harbor, Jayson and Serge loaded several small woven bags into a single-boom outrigger on the beach near Jasmine's Hope. Farzin and Park had some weapons laid out on the dock and were doing an inventory while Paul helped Matteus and Herman haul rations down from the settlement.

The inhabitants of Honolulu, who, by now, were used to the comings and goings of the ship, mostly ignored their preparations. Miroslava Sirotkin was the only one observing. Even Simmons, who had shared knowledge of Josh's plans for Kaua'i, had opted not to join her at the dock.

"What's going on, Paul?" she demanded as he walked past her with a barrel of fresh water on his shoulder.

"Jayson has a plan to end the war with Pa'ao," he replied without breaking stride.

"So you're taking orders from the fucking farmer now?" she chided as he walked away.

Farzin and Park glanced up for a moment before returning to their preparations, but neither said anything. She approached them with a scowl on her face.

"Is anyone going to share this little plan of yours?"

"Nope," replied Farzin without looking up.

"Park?"

"Nah. We're good."

"So now anyone can just take the ship whenever they want?"

"We posted a signup board outside the bakery," said Jayson, walking up from behind. "You can have it next Tuesday."

"Fuck you, smartass."

"Right back at you."

Sirotkin snorted and shook her head.

"Fine," she said, throwing her arms up and walking away.

The others finished their prep work as Farzin attached the outrigger to Jasmine's Hope with a thick, braided rope. Malo and Ino then helped Jayson and Serge haul the loaded canoe off the beach and into the water. With the rest of the provisions now safely in the ship's hold, the crew boarded and pushed off.

Farzin raised the mainsail into the light morning breeze while Paul manned the wheel, guiding them away from the dock. The line to the outrigger went taut, turning the small craft into the ship's wake, where it remained, bobbing and zigzagging behind them as they left the harbor and headed for Moloka'i.

Chapter 23

IT WAS THE FIRST time Andrew had ever been aboard the Reagan. The techs that had worked the checklist for all of the previous missions were a thousand kilometers away in the middle of the Pacific Ocean, leaving him to manage the preparations with his Navy counterpart. The eager young ensign couldn't have been more than nineteen or twenty years old, but his rigid formality and manner made him seem older.

It made Andrew feel like an underachiever to see someone younger than him acting with such maturity and apparent diligence. The answer to every question was a smart 'yes, sir' or 'no, sir.' It was amusing at first, but by the time they'd neared the end of the checklist, it had become grating.

"Okay," said Andrew, holding his tablet in front of him. "This is the last step. I'm sending the test signal."

"Yes, sir. Receiving the signal now," assured the ensign. "Transferring reactor output in three, two, one—transferring."

He put his hand on a massive lever on the console and counted slowly to ten.

"Well? Are you going to do it, or what?" asked Andrew.

"No, sir," replied the ensign. "We don't actually transfer power as part of the pre-check. It disrupts operations."

Andrew referred to his tablet.

"Oh, yeah. You're right."

The young man nodded smartly, but said nothing.

"I guess we're done here, then," he continued. "Thanks for your time."

"Of course, sir."

Andrew nodded as he turned to leave the control room.

"Wait, sir! I need to escort you off the ship."

"I can find my way," assured Andrew.

"No, sir. It's the rules," explained the ensign. "You can't be on the ship without an escort."

"Ah, right," sighed Andrew. "Lead the way."

It was a straightforward walk through a few passages and down a flight of stairs to get to the top of the gangplank. When they arrived, Andrew turned to shake his host's hand.

"What's your name, by the way?"

The sailor looked confused.

"Uh, Ensign Butler, sir."

"I know that. I meant your first name. And enough with the sir crap. I'm barely older than you."

He glanced around.

"It's William," he said.

"Billy Butler," replied Andrew with a smile. "It has a nice ring to it."

"I prefer Ensign Butler, if you don't mind, sir," replied the young sailor.

"Alright. Well, thanks for your help, Ensign Butler. I'll reach out before the event later today to validate the comms."

"You mean tomorrow, right, sir? It's only Tuesday."

"Right," said Andrew, biting his lip. "Tomorrow."

He grimaced to himself as he turned and walked down the gangplank. His slip up was probably harmless enough, but he'd need to be more careful around Richard.

***

Richard didn't want to take any chances with an unfamiliar system. The security techs had created a blueprint for taking over Charlie Hoang's hybrid-electric SUV, and the safest course of action was to find the same make and model for his attack. It was popular enough among the ride-share drivers, so it hadn't been difficult. At 6:30 on Wednesday morning, one would be waiting to pick up a fictional passenger at the home of Jimi's neighbor in West Loch Estate; five minutes before he and his mother typically backed out of their driveway in her Toyota Prius for the daily drop-off at the Center.

Investigators would eventually trace the Uber reservation to an account created under an alias by one Andrew Jorgensen. Along with all of the other evidence linking Andrew and his victims to St. Charlie's sex trafficking ring, it would put a nice little bow on things. The Center would cooperate by providing all of the logs showing how Andrew had pulled it off. The final touch would be Andrew's suicide—helped along by a Navy Seal who would then vanish forever into the portal. By the time the FBI could unravel the mess, Epsilon would be over.

With so many variables, the plan was fraught with risk. He needed to mitigate as much as possible by practicing his technique. Pulling out his phone, he opened the Hitz-It app to hit Andrew.

Need you to check on some things

Sure
What's up?

Capacitor controller diagnostics for event

Did them
Yesterday

Do them again

On it

Richard smiled to himself. The diagnostics would keep Andrew busy for at least an hour. Plenty of time to get into his recently hacked account and test drive a new SUV. He picked random VINs from the manufacturer's shipping logs until he located one that was online. According to the GPS, it was heading southwest out of Omaha on I-80, heading for Lincoln. It was already getting dark in Nebraska, and he could see the orange light of the setting sun on the distant horizon through the forward-facing camera.

His new SUV had its lights on, as did the oncoming traffic sweeping into view from around a bend in the highway. There was a slight bounce in the camera view as the vehicle passed over an expansion joint marking the transition to the bridge over Platte River. Richard realized he could send the driver—and any passengers that might be onboard—careening over the side and into the river, if he wanted to. As far as they were concerned, he was God. He imagined who might be inside the vehicle. A woman like his wife, perhaps, ferrying her daughter back to med school after a well-deserved long weekend at home with her family.

He pushed the thought aside, turning to the system diagram in a separate window on his screen next to the camera display. He expanded the pedal and steering inputs and requested an increase in speed to eighty miles per hour. In the video feed, he could see the vehicle lurch forward. The driver applied the brakes, but Richard overrode the command. He could see the repeated, panicked braking attempts flashing through the pedal input dialog box in red text to indicate they were being rejected by the controller.

Next, he used the steering input to change gingerly into the passing lane. The counter-steer data from the driver showed up in red, too. Richard was in complete control. He held steady for a few moments before changing back to the right lane and fully engaging the brakes. The car juddered to a stop as quickly as possible under the guidance of the anti-lock braking system. He could have overridden that as well—if he wanted to have some real fun.

He realized the poor woman and her imagined daughter must be scared to death. He didn't need to traumatize them any more than he already had. Relinquishing control of the vehicle, he removed all traces of his practice run, and logged out of Andrew's account. Then, he went to the main system log to delete the evidence that he'd been in it at all.

Richard stared absently at the screen for a few minutes, thinking of all the ways his plan could go wrong. No matter what, he was determined he would not go through the portal. A loaded sidearm would be among the equipment he and the SEALs would receive before departure, just in case they encountered resistance on the other side. If necessary, he'd use it at the last minute to make sure he was indispensable to Kamaras on *this* side of the portal.

His phone buzzed on the desk, snapping him out of his daydream of splattering Akindele's brains all over the chamber wall. It was a hit from Rebecca.

Emergency meeting
My office
Now

"What now?" he muttered to himself.

He wasn't surprised to find Akindele waiting with Rebecca in her office.

"What's the emergency?" he asked.

"I'm sorry to say I made a mistake in the calculations, Richard. The maximum transfer rate is sooner than I thought."

"When?"

"Just a few hours from now, I'm afraid."

Richard fought the immediate panic welling up inside him. He'd appeared weak in front of Rebecca far too often lately, and was determined not to show any outward signs of distress.

"How could you fuck up so badly, Jimi?" he demanded.

"It wasn't just him, Richard," interjected Rebecca. "You confirmed the results yourself at our last meeting."

Richard narrowed his eyes at the physicist. Was it really a mistake, or had Akindele outplayed him?

"I guess I did," he conceded.

"Are your SEALs ready to go?" asked Rebecca.

"We're always ready for anything," he said with a thin smile, not taking his eyes off Akindele.

"Good. Get your shit in order. We meet in the chamber in four hours."

***

They sailed due east out of Honolulu Harbor, traveling around the north side of Moloka'i to the bay where Jayson had first met Luni a year earlier. Scanning the beach with binoculars, they could find no evidence of a significant force. Only a few fishermen and their families remained. The island was sparsely populated to begin with, so it was unsurprising to find it had been deserted by Pa'ao's men following the departure of the Ulu warriors.

According to Kai, the most likely place to find the warrior priest and his men would be Wailuku. The small village, nestled in the crook of the northeastern coastline of Maui, had adequate resources to support them, and a protected bay from which they could launch their canoes.

The crew of Jasmine's Hope spent the night anchored off the coast of Moloka'i and set sail for Maui at first light. After only three hours, the village appeared in the distance. They trimmed their sails to watch from a safe distance. Ashore, the fishermen, just starting their daily routine, spotted the ship immediately.

"Seems like we're causing quite a fuss," observed Farzin, gazing through the binoculars.

A throng of people gathered on the shore to witness the unfamiliar sight.

"Anything interesting going on?" asked Jayson.

"Just fishermen, as far as I can tell. Some women and children now, too."

"Should we check out Lahaina instead?"

Farzin, still focused on the excitement ashore, held up his hand.

"Wait," he said. "More people coming now. A few warriors, it looks like."

"How many?"

"Four? Maybe five?"

"E nana ma o," interjected Ino, patting Jayson on the shoulder and pointing farther up the shore.

"North," instructed Jayson.

Farzin panned the binoculars up the beach.

"Oh, shit."

Scores of warriors splashed through the shallow water, dragging a half dozen war canoes into the sea with them. Scrambling aboard, they took up their paddles, speeding away from the shore. Jayson took the binoculars from Farzin to have a look.

"Oh, shit is right."

"Well," said Farzin with a shrug. "This is what you wanted."

"In theory, yeah," agreed Jayson. "The real thing is a little scary."

***

Andrew sat at a console in the control room overlooking the chamber. Although he'd always known the modular building as Fusion B, he learned in a secret letter from Samaira only five months earlier that it had nothing to do with energy research. Officially, he'd only been aware of the *real* purpose of Fusion B for about a week, and the spectacle below him still made his skin crawl. The walkway to nowhere, terminating at the twin-ringed apparatus that had transported Samaira and the others away, was hardly a comforting sight.

Andrew had grown up on Harry Potter, and imagined something magical from Samaira's description—kind of like Platform nine-and-three-quarters, taking her to a world of new possibilities. The sterile reality of the equipment reminded him more of a high-tech abattoir. All the math in the world couldn't convince him it didn't just atomize its victims—or dump them into some eternal void where their bodiless consciousnesses were trapped forever and doomed to go slowly insane. That thought scared him even more than death.

He jumped at the sound of the door handle cranking behind him and turned to see Richard walk into the room. He ignored Andrew for a moment as he looked around.

"Where's Akindele?" he demanded.

"Down there," replied Andrew, pointing through the window. "Just double-checking some stuff."

Richard didn't bother walking over to the window for visual confirmation. Instead, he turned around and left without another word. Andrew hit the intercom button.

"Incoming," he said. "He looks pissed."

Akindele tapped his ear and pointed up. Andrew nodded. The physicist wanted him to activate the ceiling microphones to listen in.

Moments later, the chamber door flew open, and Richard walked up to Akindele, a menacing sneer etched on his face.

"You think you're pretty fucking smart, don't you?" he spat.

Akindele backed away a couple of steps in the face of Richard's aggression—something Andrew had never seen him do before.

"I don't know what you're talking about."

"You expect me to believe you just made a mistake about the timing? I'm not an idiot, Jimi."

"You made the same mistake," protested the physicist.

"Bullshit. You know damned well I didn't do any calculations. You fed me a bunch of shit."

"I wouldn't even know how to go about doing such a thing."

Richard stared at him for a moment without saying a word. Suddenly, he shot a look up at the control room and glared at Andrew.

"Shit!" said Andrew under his breath, quickly looking down at the panel.

Richard looked back at Akindele, nodding slowly.

"And here I thought you didn't know how to make friends. I have to admit, I didn't see this coming."

"I don't know what you are talking about, Richard," he insisted. "You're losing what's left of your mind."

Richard thrust out his palm and shook his head.

"Shut the fuck up, Jimi. It doesn't matter. Let me tell you how this is going down."

He pulled out his phone and held the screen to Akindele's face.

"This look familiar to you?"

Akindele's eyes went wide.

"Why don't you tell your friend up there what it is?" he added.

"My house," he replied, glancing up at Andrew.

"It's a live shot," added Richard. "Taken from a car parked across the street."

"What is the meaning of this?"

"You know, I met a lot of interesting people when I was recruiting for Beta. Van Zijl was one of the more stable ones. That's why we went with him, in the end."

"What is this, Richard?" demanded Akindele again, pointing at the screen.

"Let me make this simple for you. If I go through that portal—if I'm not around to call off my man—*Mrs.* Akindele is going to have a very rough evening."

"You wouldn't!"

"No? Remember the accident at the Beta site? It wasn't an accident. I did that," he spat.

Akindele pulled out his phone and started to dial.

"You call anyone, and I give the order," warned Richard.

He spun around and pointed at Andrew.

"That goes for you, too," he added.

"What do you want?" asked Akindele.

"I just need you to screw up the transfer. No superposition and no waveform."

"Fine," he relented. "No transfer."

"Don't fuck with me," warned Richard. "If either of you so much as set one foot outside of this building before it's over, I will have your mother peeled open, layer by layer, like an onion."

Arranged against the far wall were three backpacks, a couple of plastic cases, and a table neatly stacked with assorted gear. Richard walked over to grab a sidearm and made sure it was loaded. He held it up in an unspoken threat before stuffing it into the inside pocket of his sport coat. As Richard left the chamber, Andrew wondered momentarily if he should run. It was a stupid thought. There was no way to exit the building without passing him. He gulped as he heard the handle turn again, and Richard stepped halfway through the door.

"You?" he said, leveling a finger at Andrew. "You're fucked."

He left, slamming the door behind him. Akindele waited a few minutes before returning to the control room to check on his co-conspirator.

"What did he say?"

"He said I'm fucked," replied Andrew with a blank stare. "We have to tell Rebecca what's going on."

"What about my mother?"

"He was bluffing, right?"

Akindele shook his head.

"I'm not sure," he replied. "But someone is watching outside my house."

"So we give in and let him stay? Then what?"

"We take our time to figure out another way," replied Akindele with a shrug.

"We? He told me quite explicitly that I'm fucked," reminded Andrew. "I'll be dead—and so will you. How else do you think he plans to get out of Delta?"

The physicist was silent for a while.

"First, we figure out how to keep my mother safe, and then we tell Rebecca everything," he said finally. "She'll send him through at gunpoint if she has to."

"Well, we can forget about calling or sending her a hit," said Andrew. "He'll be tracking our comms, for sure."

"And we can't leave. He's watching the entrance."

Andrew buried his head in his hands.

"We are so screwed," he lamented. "Unless you have any great ideas."

Akindele didn't answer.

"Ninety minutes to window," announced the soft robotic voice from the speakers in the ceiling.

The disembodied voice jolted Andrew out of his daze.

"I have an idea," he said, raising his head from his hands. "We still have the cloned account. If he hasn't found it yet, we can get a message out."

Chapter 24

THE WAR CANOES HEADED directly for Jasmine's Hope, their bows heaving as they nosed into each successive wave. The ship's crew raised the mainsail to close the distance even faster. If there was any fear on the part of the approaching warriors, they didn't show it. For all appearances, they were moving forward at full speed. On the distant beach, one figure stood apart from the throng of fishermen watching the spectacle unfold.

"It's him," said Farzin, staring through the binoculars. "It's Pa'ao. I recognize him from Waikiki."

He passed the binoculars to Jayson. The man, adorned with tattoos and a feather headdress, stood motionless with his arms crossed over his chest.

"That whole thing is a blur to me," he said. "I'll have to take your word for it."

Park had taken up position on the bow just in front of them as the only one with experience firing rocket-propelled grenades in naval combat.

"You're not going to freak out this time, right?" he asked, looking back at Jayson.

"No. I'm good. But just until they stop, right?"

"Just until they stop," confirmed Park.

"Make 'em count," added Farzin.

It took less than fifteen minutes for the first of the canoes to close within range. Paul steadied the ship as much as possible, asking Matteus to drop the sails as he lined up with the waves. Park took a few deep breaths, laying belly-down on the deck. He took a moment to get used to the rhythmic rise and fall of the waves before squeezing off a shot. A bright flame shot from the back of the launcher as the grenade leaped forward in a wisp of smoke. Seconds later, the nearest canoe erupted in a violent explosion.

"Raise the sail," directed Suryana.

At the same time, he cranked the wheel to port to alleviate their immediate threat and give the enemy a chance to reconsider their actions. The crew of Jasmine's Hope held their breath, waiting to see how the other warriors would react to the fate of the lead canoe.

"Don't do it, assholes," urged Jayson under his breath. "Just stay where you are."

They'd stopped paddling at the moment of the explosion, and there was confusion among the men on the remaining canoes. They yelled at one another in an apparent disagreement over their next move. With Jasmine's Hope pulling away to the south faster than they could pursue, they finally elected to help the survivors thrashing about in the water.

"Thank Christ for small miracles," said Jayson.

"It's not over yet," reminded Farzin.

After they'd put a few hundred meters between themselves and the canoes, the crew came about with a starboard turn towards the shore, lowered the mainsail, and dropped anchor.

"What now?" asked Park, still lying on his stomach with a new round in the launcher.

"We wait to see if they decide to do anything stupid," replied Farzin.

***

Tiara sat in an armchair in her study reading. Aside from her backyard, it was her favorite place to sit. It was bright and cheery by day, and hosted the favorites among her personal treasures. A fan of classic fiction and history, she was lost in a biography of Nigerian author Chinua Achebe when a beep from the living room caught her attention. It was followed by the familiar whirring sound of the robotic vacuum cleaner starting its rounds.

"What the devil?" she wondered aloud.

It had already run its pre-programmed duties for the day hours earlier while she'd busied herself in the garden. There was an app on her phone, she knew, that could send it back to its charging base, but she was too engrossed in her book to bother finding it. Besides, things could never be *too* clean.

She heard the sound fade into the kitchen briefly before it started getting louder, approaching the door of her study. She swung her chair around, using her toe to push the door shut and keep the noisy intruder from disturbing her any more than it already had.

The robot bumped against the door. After a brief pause, it backed up and bumped it again, repeating the pattern over and over until Mrs. Akindele couldn't stand it any longer. She rose from her chair with a huff and went into the hallway.

"Why are you being such a little pest today?"

She picked it up without noticing the message on the top display panel and flipped it over. Locating the main power switch, she turned the robot off, setting it back on the floor before settling back in to resume reading.

Within a few minutes, another less familiar sound caused her to sit up in her chair.

"What is it now?" she huffed, getting to her feet again.

She followed the noise to the kitchen to find her refrigerator ice maker spilling its contents onto the floor. The cubes hit the ceramic tiles and burst into pieces, creating a dangerous, slippery mess. She hurried to the hall closet for a bucket to put under the dispenser before examining the control panel to figure out how to turn it off. A strange message greeted her.

Open and close the fridge door twice if you can read this

She shook her head and sighed. She'd just wanted an ordinary refrigerator to replace the one that had died a few months earlier, ruining everything in the freezer compartment, but Jimi had insisted on getting the most expensive model that would fit in the opening. It did all sorts of things he thought were incredible.

He'd excitedly demonstrated on his phone how he could display live pictures of the interior from anywhere in the world to see how much ketchup they had left. It even had a built-in calendar and weather display. She'd never wanted any of it. And now her refrigerator had been hacked—just as they'd warned on the evening news. She took a deep breath and decided to find out what the hackers wanted in exchange for not ruining her milk. Cautiously, she took hold of the handle and did as instructed.

Thank God
It's Andrew
I need you to do something.

She blinked at the message in disbelief.

"Why are you on my refrigerator?" she asked.

There was no response. Apparently, he could not hear her. She opened and closed the door again.

Look outside
Open and close the door twice if there is a car you don't recognize
Do it once if there is nothing

Tiara scurried quickly to the front door and peered outside. There *was* a car parked directly across the street; a high-end white Mercedes with tinted windows. Returning to the kitchen, she answered by opening the door twice, and then waited for the response.

You are in danger
Do exactly as I say

***

Wrestling with panic, Richard barely managed to hold it together. The confrontation had been the only choice left—he was sure of that. But it meant he'd have to keep the illusion of leverage alive until after the window closed, and then get rid of Jimi before Rebecca learned what was going on. She wouldn't just fire him. She'd have him killed—and probably his family, too—to protect the secrets he carried.

His SEALs were on the way, and he wracked his brain to come up with a way he might convince them to do his dirty work. He put the thought aside as his phone buzzed with a hit from his wife.

How long do you need me to stay here?

Just a couple more hours, honey
Sorry

And the live stream?

Keep it going
Prop the phone against the window if your arm gets tired

Why am I doing this?

Tell you later
Promise

He sighed as he put the phone down. Of course, he could have found someone who really *was* willing to gut Jimi's mother on a live stream, but not with only an hour's notice. That was okay. The bluff only had to stand another couple of hours—and then Richard could focus on the next problem.

***

Dr. Akindele heaved a sigh of relief and collapsed into his chair, his hands still shaking.

"That was brilliant, Andrew. Thank you."

"Yeah, but now what? He's still going to kill us."

"No, he won't," assured the physicist. "He's going through in less than two hours."

"You heard what he said. If he goes through, your mother dies. I'm pretty sure he's amended that order to include me by now."

"There is nothing Richard can do that Rebecca can't undo. We just have to stay here at the Center until she can have Anton call off whatever he's set in motion."

"Yeah," nodded Andrew. "Okay."

***

Tiara changed out of her floral pattern dress into a dark-colored tracksuit and put on a pair of running shoes. That hadn't been part of the instructions, but it seemed prudent under the circumstances. She'd been told to put a few necessities into a backpack, as well, because she might not be able to return home immediately. Of course, that meant she should probably water her plants, too.

After double-checking she hadn't left anything dangerous plugged in, she slipped out the back door and pushed through the trees and bushes separating her yard from the adjacent golf course. From there, she made her way through the twilight shadows along the edge of the fairway toward Kapapapuhi Point Park. The streetlights were on by the time she got there, allowing her to easily navigate the trail to the parking lot.

She crossed the main street quickly, mindful not to spend too much time in the open, and then slunk quietly through a backyard to get to a cul-de-sac opposite the park. Now safely away from her own street, she could use the sidewalk to get to her friend Irene's house. Although hardly a comfortable thing, sneaking about was the easy part of what she had to do. The hard part was having to lie to a friend.

She rang the doorbell and waited anxiously for Irene to answer, hoping her unpracticed story would be convincing.

"Tiara!" greeted her friend with surprise. "Was I expecting you?"

"Hello, Irene. No. My apologies for coming over unannounced. I'm having a bit of trouble."

"Oh no," she replied, knitting her brow. "What's wrong?"

"Nothing serious," assured Tiara with a dismissive wave. "I need to get my Jimi from work, and my car won't start. I was hoping I could trouble you for a ride."

"Of course, dear. Let me get my keys."

Irene disappeared into the house. A minute later, the garage door opened, and she backed out in her red Honda CRV. Tiara got in, discretely shielding her face as the small SUV navigated the streets of West Loch Estate and headed for Fort Weaver Road.

"I really *do* appreciate this," said Tiara as they merged onto the Farrington highway heading east towards Waipi'o.

"It's no trouble at all," assured Irene. "This is what friends do."

Tiara winced at the words, aware her own dishonesty was at odds with the spirit of friendship she was taking advantage of.

"How is work going for Jimi? Has he made any more progress on that fusion thing they're working on?"

"I can't say. I don't really understand any of what he does."

At least that was less of a lie.

"Well, if anyone can figure it out, your Jimi can."

"I believe you are right about that," she replied.

Finally, something truthful.

"Mah Jongg this Sunday?" asked Irene, changing the subject.

"I'm not sure. Jimi has something going on I might have to help him with. I'll let you know."

They pulled up to the guardhouse off Waipi'o Point Access Road and came to a stop. The guard lumbered out to greet them.

"You can drop me off here," said Tiara, opening the door. "I'll borrow a car from the Center until I get mine fixed."

"Are you sure? I don't mind taking you both home."

"I'm sure. Thank you so much, Irene."

She gave her friend a smile, waving as she backed out onto the road and left.

"Mrs. Akindele," said the guard with surprise. "Is everything all right?"

"I should say not, Makani," she replied, placing her hands on her hips.

The guard laughed, and Tiara cracked a smile.

"Tiara," he corrected himself. "How can I help you?"

***

Jimi's mother pulled up to the charging station in the golf cart she'd borrowed from the guard and got out, trying to look as casual as possible. So familiar was her presence at the Center, the few people still walking around took no notice as she made her way to the path toward Fusion B. She'd never been to the building before, but the description Andrew had provided on the screen in her refrigerator door allowed her to find it with ease.

In his office above, Richard had the Fusion B entrance security camera live feed displayed in the corner of his screen. He caught sight of movement and strained to make out the approaching figure.

"Oh, shit," he gasped to himself. "No, no, no!"

Someone opened the door from the inside, and he switched to a different view to see what was happening. Jimi, his mother, and Andrew were embracing in the small foyer of the most secure building on site.

"Fuck!"

He grabbed his phone to check on the live stream. It was still focused on the front door.

What happened?
When did she leave?

Nobody left

Are you sure?

Yes
I've been watching the whole time
What's going on?

Glancing back at the security camera, he saw Jimi pulling out his phone.

"Fuck!" said Richard again as he started for his door.

Running down the hall as quickly as he could, he burst through Rebecca's outer office door and caught sight of her through the inner glass wall, sitting at her desk with her phone to her ear. She was staring directly at him, her eyes wide with shock.

Richard was out of options. He pulled out the gun and sprinted toward her, his teeth gritted. Rebecca dove over her desk in a last-minute attempt to lock her door, but Richard got there first, kicking it open violently. The edge of the glass panel caught her in the forehead, sending her reeling back onto the floor. When she sat up, blood was running down her face.

"Rebecca! What's happening?"

It was Jimi, his voice emanating from the phone now lying at Rebecca's feet. Richard kept the gun trained on her as he picked it up.

"Stay right where you are, or I will kill her."

"This has gone too far, Richard. You can't kill Rebecca."

"Why not? She's not critical to any of Kamaras's plans."

"He'll kill you."

"Not if he needs me."

Jimi was silent. Richard put the phone down to close the blinds in Rebecca's inner office. When he finished, he picked up the phone and continued.

"I'm in charge now, Jimi. Without Rebecca, people take orders from me."

"I'll call Anton myself, then."

"Right," laughed Richard. "When's the last time he answered a call from anyone but his right-hand bitch? He'll ignore you just like he's been ignoring me for the last five years."

"You don't know what you're doing, Richard," cautioned Rebecca, shaking her head.

"You didn't leave me any choice," he replied, stepping over her. "You had no right to take me off Epsilon."

He back-handed her across the temple with the butt of the gun, knocking her unconscious.

"You hear that, Jimi?" he asked over the phone. "That was the sound of your last hope disappearing. Sit tight. I'm on my way."

Chapter 25

The crew of Jasmine's Hope watched anxiously as the rescue effort transitioned into a recovery operation. The grenade had impacted low on the bow of the outrigger, sparing most of the men aboard any serious injuries. Those in the first few rows, however, hadn't a chance. Their comrades pulled their bodies from the water to be brought back ashore. One canoe took up a defensive posture between the sailing ship and the rescuers, the warriors aboard watching for signs of another attack. They remained in position even as their comrades retreated.

"What do you think they're going to do?" asked Jayson.

Farzin shook his head.

"No idea."

"What would you do if you were them?"

He lowered the binoculars and considered the question.

"Stand my ground and try not to shit myself."

"What about when we try to go ashore? What would you do then?"

"Your guess is as good as mine," he shrugged.

Jayson nodded somberly as Malo approached with Serge and Ino carrying a folded cloth.

"What's that?" asked Jayson.

"Anuenue made it," he replied, unfurling it. "It's a sign of peace."

The woven square bore a turtle design, similar to some tattoos he'd seen on the Ulu men.

"Are you guys ready for this?" asked Farzin. "You can still back out, you know."

"No," sighed Jayson, shaking his head. "We're not backing out. Let's do this."

He put his hands on the railing and took a deep breath before vaulting over the side. Malo, Serge, and Ino followed him, one at a time, swimming back to board the small outrigger trailing behind the ship. Serge untied the rope, and Farzin hauled it in.

"You sure you don't want this?" he asked, holding a rifle aloft.

"No," replied Jayson. "They've already seen what those can do."

"Alright," he said with a doubtful shrug. "Good luck."

The four men on the outrigger took up paddles and turned for shore.

"Should we follow them in closer?" asked Suryana.

Farzin shook his head.

"They don't want us to look like a threat. We'll hold here."

The warriors in the remaining enemy canoe set off on an intercept course.

"They're not even going to make it to the beach," said Park.

"If they engage with weapons, take 'em out."

"Not likely, at this range."

"Just raise the sail and go in another couple hundred meters," suggested Paul.

"We'll hold," insisted Farzin.

***

Serge was the first among those heading ashore to notice the approaching outrigger.

"We need to pick up the pace," he warned. "They're coming for us."

"Stay calm," urged Jayson. "Slow and steady—nothing aggressive."

Serge glanced over his shoulder and took a deep breath.

"Putain de merde," he muttered to himself.

"Show them the flag, Malo," said Jayson.

The warrior placed his paddle at his side and picked up the piece of cloth his wife had given him. Holding it aloft, he rose unsteadily to his feet, displaying the turtle symbol to the approaching men. After some discussion among themselves, Pa'ao's men turned onto a parallel course less than fifty meters away and matched their pace. Jayson breathed a sigh of relief.

"That's a good start," he said.

As they drew closer to shore, they could see the stone-faced leader had changed neither position nor expression. He remained on the beach with his arms crossed in front of him. The warriors who had already returned to shore were gathering at his side.

The inky black water beneath their canoe transitioned gradually to a transparent aqua as Jayson and the others entered the shallow water of the bay. The warriors shadowing them arrived at the beach first, leaping from their canoe and pulling it ashore. Pa'ao issued a short command to his men, and a pair of them ran out into the water toward their uninvited guests.

"This is it," said Serge with a nervous glance at Jayson.

"They're unarmed, at least," he replied.

The warriors regarded them cautiously as they splashed through the knee-deep water. Jayson nodded in greeting, and Malo offered a few words in his own language. The men looked at each other, but said nothing as they grabbed the canoe and dragged it ashore.

Half a kilometer away, Farzin peered through the binoculars.

"So far, so good," he assured the rest of the crew.

"I still wish we were a bit closer," said Park.

Though he'd laid the RPG launcher on the deck, he still had a hand on it, ready to pick it up at a moment's notice.

***

"We can call onsite security and tell them what he's done," suggested Andrew, who'd been listening in on speakerphone along with Tiara.

As if in reply, red lights began flashing on and off, and the low, repetitive tone of the emergency warning emanated from everywhere.

"Looks like he beat us to it," said Dr. Akindele. "There is no telling what lies he's told them."

"We're out of options," replied Andrew. "I'm calling 9-1-1."

Jimi looked at his mother, but neither could think of a reason to disagree.

"Shit!" said Andrew. "No bars."

He held up his phone for them to see.

"Same here," said Jimi. "The security alert must have jammed all the signals."

Through the double doors, they could see three people approaching the building, realizing with horror it was Richard and the two SEALs who were supposed to be going through with him.

"What now?" demanded Andrew.

Jimi was agape. Watching the approaching men, he froze in fear. Andrew looked around frantically for anything that could delay his inevitable death and noticed a fire hose cabinet on the opposite side of the hall. He yanked it open and unreeled the hose, wrapping it around both door handles as many times as its girth would allow before tying it off in a triple knot.

"There are weapons in the chamber," he added quickly. "It's our only hope."

The trio retreated to the chamber, and Andrew ran straight to the table where the gear for the mission was laid out for the SEALs. He grabbed one of the unloaded assault rifles and a magazine—fumbling to fit them together with shaking hands.

"Anyone know how to do this?" he asked, still trying to jam the magazine in.

He hadn't been able to get it to catch properly, and it kept sliding back out.

"Don't look at me," replied Tiara, holding her hands up.

Jimi shook his head and said nothing. Instead, he looked frantically around the room for any other solution that might come to him. Finally, his gaze fell on the portal.

"We have to go through," he said. "It's our only hope."

Andrew spun around to see him staring at the twin-ringed device at the far end of the elevated walkway.

"Are you crazy? I'm not going through that!"

"What other choice do we have?"

"You could help me figure out how to use these goddam things," he said, gesturing to the weapons in front of him.

"To what end? To fight off trained Navy SEALs—and who knows how many other security personnel headed this way?"

"What does that mean?" demanded Jimi's mother. "If we go through?"

"It means we leave here," replied Andrew with a gulp. "We follow Samaira and the others."

"Does it really work?" she asked her son.

"Yes," he nodded. "It works."

"Even if it does, there's not enough time," said Andrew. "It's still an hour to the convergence."

"Near-convergence," he corrected. "It's an hour until the maximum transfer rate, but we can go earlier with less mass."

"How much less?"

"It would take time to adjust the calculations."

"Time we don't have, I assume?"

"It will be tight," he admitted.

"Is there any other way?" pleaded Tiara.

Andrew shook his head.

"I can't think of anything."

"I'll get to work on the calculations," said Jimi. "Secure the chamber door to buy as much time as you can."

"What about the control room?" asked Andrew, pointing up at the glass wall above them. "Don't we need it?"

Jimi considered the question for a moment, as if running through the transfer process in his head.

"Yes," he realized. "We will need to initiate the sequence from the control room."

"I'll take care of it," assured Andrew. "Just do your thing with the math."

Jimi nodded and returned to the cart, where his laptop remained connected to a diagnostics port. Andrew ran over and grabbed a handful of screwdrivers. Then he took a chair and dragged it over to the double doors.

"Stick the legs through the handles as soon as I'm out," he instructed Tiara.

Bursting through the doors and heading for the stairs, he could hear banging from the main entrance as Richard and the SEALs worked to get into the building. Once inside the control room, he jammed a chair between the exit handles just as he'd instructed Tiara to do in the chamber.

He scurried over to the plexiglass windows to examine the metal strips holding them in place. Fumbling through the tools, he found the Torx head driver that looked like it would do the job. He fought against his own shaking hands to remove the screws holding the metal strips surrounding one of the panels. Then, with a flat-tip screwdriver, he pried out the strips and dug under the edge of the plexiglass. Once the panel was out far enough, he slipped one hand behind it and pulled it out. It fell to the floor with a reverberating twang, but did not break.

His hands still trembling, he sat down at the control panel and tried to remember the sequence. Only then did he notice the flashing red light next to the hard-wired comms link to the Reagan.

"Shit!"

He'd forgotten about the manual power transfer sequence that could only be done from the ship. He shook his head as he picked up the phone.

"Hello?"

"I've been trying to get a hold of you for ten minutes," complained Ensign Butler. "I was about to come over."

"No!" said Andrew, trying to regain his composure. "No. We're all good here."

"Could have fooled me, sir. The whole site is lit up light a Christmas tree. Red lights flashing everywhere. What's going on?"

"Miscalculation," replied Andrew. "The window is moving forward, and we're scrambling to get everything ready."

"Again?"

"Sorry," said Andrew. "We're going to need you to redirect power now."

"That's not the procedure," complained the ensign. "You need to synchronize the countdown clock with me first."

"Uh, we don't have it calculated yet. And there might not be time once we do."

"I have to run this up the chain."

"There's no time," said Andrew, raising his voice. "If you screw up our one shot at this, you'll be on latrine duty for the rest of your career."

He slammed down the phone to end the debate, waiting for the power transfer indicator. He'd invented the threat to the ensign based on limited knowledge of Navy culture gleaned from movies and television, and had no confidence it would actually work.

***

Pa'ao offered no greeting as he glared at the men from O'ahu. Though he tried to maintain a look of stoic indifference, Jayson noticed him glancing periodically at the tablet at the ready in Serge's hand.

"We're here with an offer of peace," he started, watching Pa'ao's reaction to the translation.

"So, this is the magic I've been hearing about," he replied.

"No," said Jayson, shaking his head. "No magic. Only tools."

Then he pointed back at the waiting ship.

"Tools and weapons," he added.

Pa'ao narrowed his eyes.

"And what have you brought with you?" he asked with a nod at the laden outrigger. "Tools or weapons?"

"Neither," replied Jayson. "It's food. We're here to share a meal with you and your men while we discuss peace."

"Why would I offer you peace?"

Malo stepped forward before the translation finished.

"You are not in a position to offer anything," he said. "You can only accept or reject what we offer you."

Several of the warriors around Pa'ao grew restless, murmuring among themselves.

"There is no need for posturing," assured Serge. "Let us talk—and eat."

Pa'ao glanced at the outrigger again and nodded. He issued a command to his men. Several rushed over to unload the contents. Then he sent another of his men over to a collection of dwellings nearby.

"Okay," he agreed, turning to Serge. "We will talk. Come with me."

He led them to a clearing among the dwellings where three frightened-looking women had arranged mats and were pouring out gourds of fresh water. Pa'ao invited his guests to sit as his men, returning with the packages from the canoe, searched through the unfamiliar offerings with interest.

"Let me help," offered Jayson, reaching for one of the bags.

He spread a collection of fresh fruits, vegetables, and nuts on the mat. From another bag, he produced a number of sweet pastries stuffed with a gooey strawberry sauce.

"And that one," he said, pointing to an especially bulky sack. "You're going to love this."

Their eyes went wide as Jayson revealed the first cantaloupes the men had ever seen. He pulled out his pocketknife and began slicing them into wedges, exposing the bright orange flesh. Pa'ao regarded the shiny folding knife with far more interest than the melons.

"What is your blade made from?"

"Steel," said Jayson.

The translator repeated it unchanged, as there was no equivalent in their host's language. Jayson flipped it around, offering it to Pa'ao by the handle. The warrior examined it with curiosity.

"Let me show you how it works," he said, taking it back.

He depressed the blade lock and folded the knife shut before demonstrating how to open it again. Then he let Pa'ao practice a few times for himself.

"This is a beautiful weapon," said the warrior-priest.

"A tool," corrected Jayson. "Our weapons are much more dangerous than this."

Pa'ao cracked a thin smile at the translation, nodding as he handed back the knife.

"Of course."

"Please," insisted Jayson, sweeping a hand over the offerings on the mat before him. "Try something."

The warriors seated alongside their leader, whose intricate tattoos and fine clothing revealed them to be among the upper echelons of society, glanced doubtfully at one another.

"Eat," commanded Pa'ao.

They took a few hesitant bites—as if expecting some duplicity on the part of their guests. Their trepidation soon turned to excitement as they sampled more and more of the unfamiliar foods.

One warrior closed his eyes in blissful enjoyment as the nectar from a slice of cantaloupe rolled down his chin. Another did a double-take at the jam-filled pastry after taking the first bite, as if unable to believe a single morsel could contain such flavor. He urged a companion to try it. As the other man took a bite, some of the sweet strawberry filling escaped his lips, falling onto his leg. He scooped it up with a finger and licked if off.

Jayson took a swig of ale from a gourd and offered it to the man across from him. The warrior took a sip before passing it around among his colleagues.

"It's delicious," he said, wiping the back of his hand across his face.

After a few minutes of silent observation, Pa'ao began tentatively sampling the food. He nodded appreciatively when one flavor or another struck a chord with him, but never offered a smile or a word of approval. Finally, after he'd exhausted his choices, he motioned for the gourd of ale and took a swig.

"Tell me about your offer of peace," he said.

"This food is part of it," replied Jayson. "If we are at peace, we can trade food and goods with one another—and teach you how to grow these things for yourself."

"I can have all these things by defeating you in battle."

"You have attacked O'ahu twice without killing a single one of our people. You will take nothing from us in battle."

"Tell me, then," he said, leaning forward. "If I am the one who is weak, why are you the one asking for peace?"

It was a question Jayson hadn't anticipated.

"Because we're tired of killing your people," he replied.

Everyone went silent. Pa'ao sat upright and furrowed his brow. The remark could easily have been interpreted as bluster, but he seemed to recognize the underlying earnestness.

"So, if we agree to end our hostilities, you will trade your food and tools with us?"

"No," replied Jayson, shaking his head. "It's not that easy."

He and the others had already discussed it. Offering Pa'ao peace without demanding significant concessions was appeasement. Any peace achieved through such means would only be temporary.

"What, then?"

"We will trade food and knowledge—and maybe some of our tools—but you must first agree to leave Maui, Moloka'i, and Lanai. You will have only the island of Hawai'i for yourselves."

Pa'ao leaned back and crossed his arms.

"And if we refuse?"

Jayson glanced at his colleagues, taking a deep breath before answering.

"We will drive you from these islands by force."

The warriors began murmuring among themselves as the tablet delivered the translation. Pa'ao cocked his head to one side, evaluating Jayson through narrowed eyes.

"Or I could take hostages," he suggested. "Perhaps your people would offer better terms in exchange for your safety."

Pa'ao smiled broadly as Jayson and the others exchanged uncomfortable looks.

***

Richard and the two SEALs finally burst through the outer doors of Fusion B after one of them had managed to slip the blade of his K-Bar through a narrow slit and slice the firehose securing the handles. Andrew watched from the control room as they began their assault on the chamber door below. It moved under their repeated blows, but the chair legs jammed through the handles held fast.

"What's the word, doc?" he called through the opening where he'd removed the plexiglass panel, his eyes fixed anxiously on the door.

"Be patient," Akindele shouted back. "I will send the solution the moment I have it."

"We don't have much time."

"You can't create more by rushing me."

Tiara motioned calmly at Andrew to back off. He nodded. Slumping into his chair, he looked at the power transfer indicator light. It was still off.

Suddenly, the door to the control room shuddered violently, and he leaped to his feet. He could see shadows moving outside through the reinforced frosted glass panels. Frantically, he began looking around for more things he could use to strengthen his crude barricade.

Almost everything in the room was bolted to the floor. Besides, if he moved any of it, he risked making the whole facility inoperable. Instead, he gathered whatever might be helpful on the other side of the portal and stuffed it into an empty trashcan. Any loose pieces of tech, like his laptop and a couple of tablets, went in as well.

"Come and grab this," he called to Tiara. "It might come in handy."

She stood under the opening and reached up. It was just beyond her fingertips.

"Just a moment," she said, rushing back to the table on the other side of the chamber.

She swept the weapons and other gear onto the ground before dragging the table over. Gingerly, she maneuvered onto it and stood to take the trashcan from Andrew.

"I've got the numbers!" called Dr. Akindele. "I'm sending them to you now."

Andrew pulled up the data to enter the time and spatial offset coordinates into the device controller. Automatically, it translated them into the inputs required for the portal, the walkway LEDs, the capacitor discharge, and the power draw from the Reagan.

Numbers flashed up on the screen, and the countdown timer started ticking down from four minutes and twenty-three seconds. Andrew stared at it. The numbers ticking down in the upper right corner of the screen triggered something in his brain. The reality of what he was facing hit him. He'd either be stepping into the unknown or facing almost certain death in less than five minutes. He searched around desperately for the trashcan before remembering he'd already passed it down to the chamber. Instead, he ran to a corner of the room and vomited on the floor.

"Andrew!" called Dr. Akindele. "Have you started the sequence?"

"Uh, I think so," he replied, rushing back to the console.

"That's not good enough, dammit. You need to be sure."

He looked over the checklist one more time.

"Shit."

The Reagan still hadn't initiated the power transfer. He needed to synchronize the countdown clock with by-the-book Ensign Butler. With the push of a button, it was done. Butler had taken just more than five minutes to run through his practice procedure, leaving Andrew to wonder if there were any rules against doing it faster.

He turned to the doors with a start as the frosted glass panel on one of them shattered. The axe head protruding through was withdrawn, and Andrew could see Richard peering in at him.

"Open the fucking door, Andrew," he called through the opening.

Andrew stared at him in frozen silence. Then, Richard shoved his gun awkwardly through the small hole and aimed it in Andrew's direction.

"Open up, or I'll shoot."

"Why should I? You're going to kill me anyway."

"Probably," admitted Richard. "The only question is, how painful do you want it to be?"

The transfer light from the Reagan blinked on as the hum of the power sequence filled the room. Richard's eyes went wide with recognition.

"What the fuck are you doing?" he demanded.

"Leaving," replied Andrew.

"No, you're not," he said with a sneer. "You have to get past me first."

"Already thought of that."

Andrew eased first one leg, then the other over the ledge where he'd removed the plexiglass pane. Rolling onto his belly, he took hold of the edge and lowered himself until he was dangling by his fingertips with his feet hovering just above the table. Then he let go. The table wobbled from the impact of his uneven landing, and the legs collapsed underneath it, sending Andrew and the table crashing to the floor.

Chapter 26

FARZIN HAD BEEN WATCHING for more than an hour, looking for signs of how the talks were going. He'd seen the warriors empty the contents of the outrigger and haul them out of sight, but hadn't seen their colleagues since Pa'ao had led them off the beach. So when he saw them appear from among the trees, he breathed a sigh of relief.

"I see them," he said to the others. "They're coming down to the beach."

"How do they look?" asked Herman.

"It's hard to be sure, but everything seems friendly enough."

He stared through the binoculars as two warriors helped drag the now unburdened outrigger into the water.

"Looks like they're coming back," he added.

"Oh, thank God," said Herman.

Park's hand edged away from his weapon for the first time since they'd engaged the enemy canoes.

"Wait. Something's wrong," said Farzin.

Park's hand snapped immediately back to the rocket launcher.

"What is it?" he demanded.

"Looks like only two of them getting back into the canoe. Serge and Malo, I think."

"What? That wasn't the plan. What the hell is going on?"

"Should we move in?" asked Paul.

Farzin considered it for a moment.

"Yeah. Let's find out what this is."

Matteus raised the mainsail as Suryana hauled in the anchor. In less than fifteen minutes, they'd closed nearly all the gap. They dropped the sail to ease up alongside Serge and Malo.

"What happened?" grunted Farzin as he hauled Serge aboard. "Why aren't Jayson and Ino with you?"

"Pa'ao said he needs to confer with his chief—Pili—on Hawai'i. He asked for someone to come with him to explain our position."

"And they agreed?" asked Herman.

"Uh, I'm not sure it was an invitation—exactly," said Serge.

With a nod, he deferred to Malo for his opinion.

"Pa'ao is the one with power, I think. He needs Pilikaʻaiea only for his bloodline."

"What are you saying, then?" asked Farzin. "It's bullshit?"

"He wants Jayson and Ino for leverage while he tries to decide what to do about our offer," said Serge.

"So they kidnapped them?"

"Not exactly. Jayson wanted to avoid escalation, so he didn't really insist on leaving with us."

"Shit. This wasn't part of the plan."

"We knew the risks," reminded Serge. "Of all the things that could have happened, this is not the worst outcome."

"We'll see about that," snorted Farzin.

***

Shannon stood by the window of Clyburn's tenth-floor condo, staring at the twinkling lights of the boats out in the bay. She'd watched the sunset more than an hour earlier and then lingered there with the lights out as the sky transitioned from the burned-orange hue of twilight to the purple-blackness of a moonless night. Though she'd only been captive there a few days, she was already starting to feel disconnected from the world outside the window.

The buzzing of her burner phone on the coffee table snapped her into focus. Finally, something from Clyburn.

Turn on the local news
Something going on with your friends

She fumbled for the remote and turned on the television, spending almost a minute trying to figure out how to get out of the streaming services menu on the unfamiliar system. Once she finally had access to live television, she flipped through the channels until she saw the familiar logo of KHON2 news, stopping to listen as the breathless anchorwoman recapped the story.

"Again, you're watching live aerial footage of some kind of incident now underway at the Center for Sustainability Research on Waipi'o Peninsula. Although not much is known about the activities at the Center, we *do* know at least *some* aspects of their work involve experiments with nuclear fusion."

The scene accompanying the commentary came from a helicopter hovering just outside the restricted military airspace surrounding Joint Base Pearl Harbor-Hickam and the Center. It showed flashing red lights on several buildings, and some sort of commotion near the harbor where the Reagan was moored.

"Although nearby residents have brought up concerns, the Center and their partners in the Navy have assured us that the small-scale fusion testing poses no risk to the surrounding area. But with the scene unfolding now, local residents will undoubtedly be asking more questions."

Shannon quickly composed a reply to Clyburn.

What do we know?

Nothing
No info getting out
But this could be a way in

Hope so

Not going to leave you hanging
We'll get these SOBs

She turned her attention back to the television.

"—and with one of the Navy's most advanced aircraft carriers in the middle of whatever is happening at the private facility, terrorism has *got* to be a concern."

***

Tiara rushed over to the collapsed table and fell to her knees at Andrew's side.

"Are you alright?"

He sat up and rubbed his shoulder.

"I think so."

He tried to stand, but fell back on the table, grimacing.

"Crap," he said, grabbing for his right ankle.

"Broken?" she asked.

"No. Just sprained, I think."

He got up gingerly, putting a little weight on his right leg to test it out. Tiara offered her arm as he started hobbling toward the far wall where Jimi was already sorting through the mess of weapons and backpacks scattered on the ground. He waved her off.

"It's fine. Really," he assured.

"Is everything set?" asked Dr. Akindele, oblivious to Andrew's injury.

"Yeah. I double-checked everything," he replied, limping over. "The countdown's on. Systems are waiting on input from the controller."

The pounding on the chamber door intensified suddenly. Realizing what was going on, Richard had abandoned his attempt to gain access to the control room and was now working furiously to get into the chamber to stop them. The door heaved and began to buckle under the assault. The steel rods anchoring it withdrew fractionally more from their sockets with every blow.

"We've gotta hurry," urged Andrew.

"Hurrying will make no difference," reminded Akindele, the sweat beading on his forehead betraying his anxiety. "The countdown is set."

Andrew glanced up at a display. One minute and thirty-one seconds. In the current context, that was an eternity.

"Take this," said Tiara, offering him a backpack.

"Pack only what you need," warned Dr. Akindele. "I didn't have time to calculate a precise transfer rate."

Andrew dumped the pack out on the ground and looked helplessly at the collection of gear.

"How the hell do I know what I need?"

Nobody answered. They were too busy trying to sort that out for themselves.

He stuffed the rations and canteen back in and began sorting through the trashcan from the control room. He wanted his laptop and the pair of tablets, for sure, but hesitated to figure out what else might come in handy in whatever kind of world awaited on the other side of the portal.

A terrible creaking noise got his attention. He looked over to see the head of an axe wedged in a growing opening at the top of the double doors. The upper steel rod had given way, leaving only the one anchored in the concrete floor keeping the SEALs at bay. Desperately, he grabbed as many technical manuals as possible, stuffing them into the pack until they were sticking out of the top.

"Is this going to be too heavy?" he asked.

"It's probably fine," replied Akindele with a glance. "Just mind your pace as you go through."

"Mind my pace? What the hell does that mean?"

"Just walk at a normal pace, and you'll be fine."

"And if I don't?"

"It's best not to think about that."

Andrew stared at him and blinked in disbelief, wondering why he'd suddenly forgotten what a normal pace was. Then, movement in the corner of his eye diverted his attention to the portal apparatus. The twin rings were starting to rotate in opposite directions, the low whirring noise barely perceptible over the commotion of the SEALs attempting to breach the doors. The emerging pattern of interfering concentric rings was mesmerizing. He stood frozen in place, gaping at the spectacle.

"Come on," urged Akindele, clapping him on the shoulder.

He led his mother toward the ramp as he hoisted a pack over her shoulders.

"How does that feel?" he asked.

She nodded wordlessly as she marveled at her son's creation coming to life in front of her.

Andrew slung his pack over one shoulder and limped over to join them.

"Okay. Up we go," instructed Akindele, taking a step onto the ramp.

From the top, he turned back to see the others were still standing at the bottom.

"I don't know if I can do this, Jimi," said Tiara, shaking her head.

He pointed toward the entrance. The chair legs were still jammed firmly between the handles, but the upper set of hinges had given way, and the doors were folding in. Andrew could see a red-faced SEAL, beads of sweat running down his face, wind up for another swing of the fire axe.

"There is no choice, mother. These men will not let us leave here alive."

"This is where Samaira went, right?" asked Andrew with a glance over his shoulder.

"She and many others," confirmed Akindele.

"Without any problems?"

"Mostly without problems," he assured with a nod.

Andrew gulped, putting a comforting hand on Tiara's shoulder.

"We can do this—together."

She nodded and took one step forward, then another, until she stood next to her son at the top of the ramp. They made room for Andrew, who squeezed in between them. The row of LEDs on the platform turned red and started advancing toward the portal.

"What's going on?" asked Tiara. "Is it starting?"

"Calm down, mother. These lights show us how fast to walk. When they turn green, we need to keep pace until we're through to the other side."

"And what happens on the other side?"

"Nothing," he said in a calm voice. "Just count to ten and keep walking."

Andrew noted the dramatic change in roles compared to his first encounter with the odd pair in their back garden. Now it was Tiara who'd lost her composure while Jimi did his best to soothe her. They were like a married couple, instinctively adopting complementary behaviors in a time of stress.

"Here we go," said Jimi as the soft, feminine voice began the final five-second countdown.

The lights went green, and he pushed her gently onto the walkway, stepping onto it behind her. He held the strap of her pack, controlling her speed as he watched the lights out of the corner of his eye. Ahead, the whir of a servo motor indicated the start of the final alignment of the wave patterns.

Andrew was about to follow when he heard a heavy grunt and a clattering sound. He looked back to see that the SEAL with the axe had finally managed to dislodge the chair by splitting it in half.

"They're through!" he called.

With one final kick, the doors flung apart, sending pieces of the chair sliding across the floor. The two SEALs burst into the chamber, followed by Richard. Jimi and his mother were halfway to the portal, but Andrew remained frozen at the top of the ramp, staring at Richard.

"Keep calm and keep moving," called out Akindele without looking back.

Andrew snapped his head around and stepped tentatively on the walkway. Looking down at the advancing lights, he did his best to match their pace.

"Stop right where you are," yelled Richard.

Instinctively, Andrew froze in place, throwing his hands in the air at the order from his boss. Dr. Akindele had no such conditioned response. He continued ushering his mother toward the portal without looking back.

"You too, Jimi," he added. "I *will* shoot."

Akindele took two more measured steps before Richard raised the gun and fired. A bullet whizzed past the pair, ricocheting off the opposite wall of the chamber.

"Jesus Christ!" yelled Andrew.

The green rows of advancing LEDs passed under his feet. He took a couple of quick steps forward to get out of the red zone before finding his pace again.

The SEALs retrieved their weapons from the floor, hastily loading magazines as they ran for the walkway.

"Hurry up!" urged Richard.

He fired two more shots from his pistol. The first one buried itself in Akindele's backpack, ringing off something metallic. The second caught Tiara in the shoulder. She yelped in pain and grabbed at it with her opposite hand. Only a meter ahead of her, the glowing wave patterns finally converged into the characteristic standing wave, confirming the connection with another world.

"Fuck!" cried Richard as Jimi shepherded his mother through the aperture before vanishing in a flash of blue light.

Andrew was still a few paces behind, fighting the urge to break into a run. Richard took aim at him, squeezing off the last of his rounds just as the SEALs reached the top of the ramp. The bullet tore through the flesh above Andrew's left knee just as he put his weight down. His leg collapsed, sending him lurching forward onto his hands and knees.

Wincing in pain, he unslung the backpack from his right shoulder and hurled it wildly toward the portal. It hit the ground and slid forward with enough momentum to carry it through to the other side. Now unburdened, he crawled forward as quickly as possible, aware of the footsteps approaching from behind.

"Forget him!" called Richard. "Get through and kill that other motherfucker!"

As the first SEAL vaulted over him to catch up with the quickly vanishing green LEDs, Andrew stabbed his arm wildly into the air, catching the soldier by the foot and throwing him off balance. The SEAL stumbled and fell onto the walkway, his head and torso disappearing into the glowing waves. The rapidly spinning inner ring caught his belt and flung the lower half of his body across the room, spraying blood and gore as it sailed through the air.

The second SEAL put two rounds into Andrew's back as he sidestepped him, not wanting to share the gruesome fate of his colleague. Then, he hurled himself at the portal just as the final row of green lights turned red and the waveform collapsed. It was too late. He bounced off the back wall of the chamber and fell back into the contra-rotating rings. His body tumbled and bounced, the terrible thudding punctuated by the occasional cracking of bone until his ragged, lifeless body was ejected onto the floor.

"Fuck!" screamed Richard, flecks of spit flying from his mouth.

Chapter 27

AMONG NATIVE HAWAIIANS, O'AHU is known as The Gathering Place. It was appropriate, therefore, that the residents decided they would call their neighbors to Honolulu at the next full moon to discuss the future of their cluster of islands. Though Moeanaimua was quick to accept the invitation, after many days, there was no word from Pa'ao. By the eve of the full moon, they'd still heard nothing from the warrior priest and his chief—or from Jayson and Ino. Their friends began to worry they'd miscalculated in the gambit to negotiate a peace.

Luni, who'd come along as part of the delegation from Kaua'i, was especially distraught. While her husband and the others toured Honolulu to see the many marvels of technology and medicine, she'd spent much of the time since she'd arrived sitting on the lanai behind the common building, looking out towards the sea for signs of Jayson's return.

She hadn't seen him since leaving for Kaua'i, and had been looking forward to the opportunity to explain her decision. Though it had remained unsaid, she knew they'd parted with the expectation they would be together again as more than friends. She felt an obligation to tell him why it had been necessary to marry Moeanaimua and why, after her brother's treachery, it was more important than ever to stay true to him. Now it seemed she might not get the chance.

"Luni?"

She looked up to see Samaira offering a drink, and forced a smile.

"Thank you," she said, taking the cup.

"There's still no word from Diamond Head," said Samaira with a frown. "I think we have to accept they might not be coming."

"What will you do?"

"That's part of what we need to decide tomorrow."

"Moeanaimua will fight with you to get them back."

Samaira hung her head and let out a deep sigh.

"Isn't that what you wanted?" asked Luni.

"No. It's not what I want—and it's not what Jayson wanted. But it might be the only way."

"How could he be so foolish?"

"It wasn't foolish to want peace," countered Samaira. "To him, it was worth the risk—if he could stop the killing."

Luni looked out at the horizon, shaking her head.

"My husband says there are some people who cannot abide peace—and so those who want it most must always be ready for war."

"I am afraid he might be right," replied Samaira.

***

After breakfast the following day, they gathered on the lanai. Moeanaimua and his delegation from Kaua'i sat facing the sea so Luni could keep her vigil while still at her husband's side. Samaira, Kai, and Dr. Kitzinger joined on the opposite side of the table, having been chosen as the community's trusted proxies.

Sirotkin had argued for representation from the security team, but after the disaster with Josh, the residents of O'ahu had ultimately voted against it. They tried to ease her concern by agreeing that anything they negotiated would be ratified through another vote. Despite the concession, her anger at being left out was evident when she'd fumed back to her apartment alone.

And so, there was only a small group on hand when Samaira took a few pictures and a short video to commemorate the start of the discussion. Then, placing the tablet in front of her for translation, she welcomed the guests.

"We are honored to have you here with us, Chief Moeanaimua, to decide how we will come together as Kanaka Mokupuni—The Island People."

"The honor is mine," he replied. "You and your people have been gracious hosts."

"There are two things I hope we can achieve over the coming days," she continued. "The first is to decide why the Kanaka Mokupuni should exist—what we and our children should live for. The second is to decide on the principles by which we will live."

Moeanaimua laughed lightheartedly.

"You ask us to do in a few days what cannot be done in a lifetime," he said.

"Most of the work has already been done over many lifetimes," assured Samaira. "By your ancestors and mine."

"Perhaps," he allowed. "But of what value is the work of my ancestors to people like you?"

"The life your people have created here on these islands can help guide the future for all of us."

"What we have created is nothing compared to the marvels you have shown me here."

"These marvels are meaningless if they do not serve some purpose. Without guidance, they can do great evil as easily as they do great good."

Moeanaimua pondered her words before turning to Kai.

"What would our fathers think of us now? Do we betray their legacy?"

"We are not here to betray the legacy of our fathers," he assured. "We are here to make sure it survives."

"I hope you are right," said Moeanaimua. "I have spent many sleepless nights weighing the cost of my rash decision to announce the end of the Nanaulu, and I know there is much worry among my people about what we will lose in these negotiations."

"Then let's make sure you sleep well tonight," said Samaira, placing her hand on his.

Moeanaimua let out a deep breath as his shoulders relaxed.

"Please," he urged. "Explain what it is you think I have to offer."

"We are not the perfect society you imagine," said Dr. Kitzinger, leaning forward. "It is not a lie nor an attempt at flattery to say we need your people. We offer you defense from Pa'ao, but you offer us something equally valuable—your ethos."

The tablet struggled with the last word, pausing before eventually translating it as 'pono.'

Moeanaimua looked at Kai with puzzlement.

"They wish to live as we do?"

"Not exactly," explained Kai. "They want to live *why* we do—in righteousness and in harmony with our world."

"Where we are from," added Dr. Kitzinger, "men trade the world's future for possessions. They poison the earth and the sea only to gain more wealth than can be used in a thousand lifetimes."

"There are those among us—those like Pa'ao—who would do the same," replied Moeanaimua, shaking his head. "It is not enough to speak of pono—one must *live* pono."

"We agree," said Samaira. "That is why we must also build the guidelines and laws to support our ethos."

Moeanaimua opened his mouth to reply just as Luping burst onto the lanai and interrupted the meeting.

"We just got word from Diamond Head," she panted. "There's a canoe inbound from Moloka'i."

"Jayson!" said Luni, rising to her feet.

"They can't tell yet, but yeah—that's what we're hoping."

"Just one canoe?" demanded Kai.

"Yeah," she confirmed. "Just one."

"At least it doesn't sound like another attack," said Dr. Kitzinger.

"Nor does it sound like a delegation," said Kai.

"What does that mean?" asked Luni, knitting her brow.

"We'll know soon enough," replied Samaira. "Let's prepare an appropriate greeting in case it *is* a delegation."

***

As she had done for the arrival of the guests from Kaua'i, Samaira arranged for a few people to gather at the beach with food, drink, and leis of fresh flowers. A crowd of curious onlookers joined nearby, hearing the rumors that Jayson and Ino were returning with news from Hawai'i. Farzin raised a pair of binoculars from a vantage point at the end of the dock as the canoe entered the harbor. Everyone fell silent in anticipation.

"I see Ino!" he called finally.

"And Jayson?" asked Kai.

"I'm looking," he responded, still staring at the approaching outrigger.

As the seconds passed without confirmation from Farzin, worried murmurs rose from the crowd of onlookers. Eventually, he lowered the binoculars and turned away, shaking his head. The canoe drew steadily closer, and everyone went silent again as they strained to find Jayson among the men aboard. The warriors pulled up their paddles as the canoe glided silently past the dock toward the sandy beach.

Farzin glared down at them as he kept pace, walking alongside them on the dock.

"Auhea 'o Jayson?" demanded Kai as he waded into the water with Mano and Malo at his side.

"Ua palekana 'o ia—i Hawai'i," replied Ino.

Ino stood shakily, grabbing the side of the outrigger to steady himself as he leaped into the shallow water and waded towards the shore.

"He says Jayson is okay," explained Kai to those nearby.

Kai reached for the bow of the canoe to help drag it ashore when one of the warriors aboard smacked his hand with a paddle. Enraged, he tore it from the man's grip and swung it at him. Ino caught it by the shaft before it could land.

"Mai," he said softly, taking the paddle and handing it back to the warrior.

Then he gave the canoe a shove, and his escorts began paddling backward until they were far enough out to turn around. They continued toward the mouth of the harbor, leaving O'ahu without looking back.

"What the hell is going on?" demanded Farzin. "Where is Jayson?"

Serge rushed forward, fumbling to open the translator on his tablet.

"What happened to Jayson?" he asked.

"Nothing happened to him. He is still on Hawai'i."

"Then let's go get him back," said Farzin, pointing at Jasmine's Hope, swaying in the breeze on the other side of the dock.

"He is not their prisoner," explained Ino. "It was his choice to stay."

"Why the hell would he want to stay?"

"He negotiated it—with Pili."

Luni pushed her way through the crowd until she was face to face with Ino.

"How could you leave him behind?" she demanded, shoving him in the chest.

He stumbled back under the unexpected force of her anger.

"Please, Luni. He sent me back with news of what he negotiated."

She crossed her arms, glaring as she waited for him to explain.

"It worked," he said. "Jayson's idea worked. Pili has called his people to Hawai'i."

***

The delegates reconvened the meeting on the lanai, but were too distracted by the news from Ino to make any notable progress in their discussions. At Samaira's suggestion, they offered the returning warrior some time to compose himself and have a meal after his long journey. Then he would join them to explain the details of what had happened on Hawai'i. Farzin, having joined them to learn of the security implications, paced back and forth along the railing as the others sat at the table.

"He should have come back," he said, shaking his head. "He's given them too much leverage."

"He's just one person," replied Samaira. "That's not much leverage at all."

"This is Jayson we're talking about here—one of our own," he shot back. "How can you say he's just one person?"

"Relax, Farzin. I didn't mean it that way. I just meant that from Pa'ao's perspective, it can't seem like he's got much of an advantage."

Farzin frowned and looked out to sea without responding.

"How can we trust these invaders not to harm your friend?" wondered Moeanaimua.

"It doesn't matter," said Farzin. "We'll blow them to pieces if they try to fuck with us."

By now, the translator algorithm had learned to handle some of the more colorful phrases it was required to interpret. Moeanaimua seemed satisfied, nodding at the response.

"Let's try taking them at their word before we start talking about blowing anyone to pieces," admonished Samaira.

"Where the hell is Ino?" asked Farzin. "We need to find out exactly what happened over there."

As if conjured by his name, Ino walked onto the lanai.

"I am sorry to make you wait," he said to Farzin.

He glanced around at the others, looking away sheepishly as soon as his eyes met Moeanaimua's. It was the first time they'd seen one another since the chaos at the wedding. Samaira rose to grab a chair and placed it at the head of the table. Then, pouring a cup of water, she invited him to sit.

"Tell us what happened after Malo and Serge left," she urged. "When you're ready."

"I'm ready," he assured, setting down his cup. "We stayed the first night at Wailuku—under guard—and left before sunrise. Pa'ao pushed his men to arrive at Hana before dark."

"How many warriors did you see in Hana?" asked Farzin. "Did you count the canoes on the beach?"

"Hana is still a very small settlement," he replied. "We saw only Ulu fishermen and their families. They fed us—and gave us shelter, but mostly tried to stay away from Pa'ao and his men."

Farzin nodded as he made a few notes in his tablet.

"The next morning," continued Ino, "We left early again—to make the crossing—and paddled south along the coast of Hawai'i until sunset. There were no villages, so we camped on the beach near the mouth of a stream until morning. By the next evening, we were in Hilo."

"And the forces there? Warriors? Canoes?"

"Many warriors and many large canoes. It has grown much since I was forced to flee with you and your father," he said, looking at Kai. "I think even more of Pili's people have arrived from his homeland."

"What of those we left behind?" he asked.

"Alive—mostly," confirmed Ino. "But they live on the fringes, apart from the newcomers."

Kai shook his head in dismay.

"What happened in Hilo?" asked Samaira.

"They took Jayson's knife and tablet and led us to a hut. The family that lived there was forced to leave, and guards were posted outside while we slept. We did not see Pili that day, nor the next, nor the one after that. When Pa'ao finally came to summon us, he was angry. He had his men escort us to Pili with spears at our backs. We said goodbye to one another, believing they were leading us to our execution."

He reached for his water again. This time, his hand was shaking noticeably as he took a sip and put it back on the table.

"Pili examined the two of us in silence—especially Jayson—touching his clothing and caressing his hair and skin. After some time, he retrieved the tablet and asked us to show him how it worked. Jayson used it to speak with him."

"How did he react?" asked Samaira.

"Without surprise or fear. He was prepared for what to expect, I think. He asked Jayson where the people of O'ahu came from, and your intent—and then he asked everyone else to leave the hut."

"Everyone? Even Pa'ao? And his guards?"

"Everyone. Pa'ao did not hide his anger from Pili, but he did as he was told."

"I thought Pili was just a figurehead—and Pa'ao held the real power."

"Pa'ao whispers in his chief's ear," agreed Ino, "but Pili has royal blood. If there is disagreement, he is the one the people listen to."

"So, what happened?"

"Jayson relayed the terms for peace—and accepted a new condition demanded by Pili."

"What condition?" asked Farzin.

"He agreed to stay to teach them what he knows about agriculture."

"What?" said Luni, rising to her feet. "He is staying with them?"

"Only for a short time," added Ino quickly, holding up his hand as if he feared she would leap over the table at him. "He will return."

"When?"

"I don't know—exactly. He said three or four moons."

Luni slumped down onto the bench, her eyes wide in disbelief.

"Three of four months?" repeated Farzin. "This is ridiculous. We should go and get him."

"You're sure it was his idea to agree?" asked Samaira, narrowing her eyes at Ino.

"Yes."

"And you let him stay alone?" asked Luni.

"I wanted to stay, but he insisted I return with news so you would not worry."

"Well, I *am* worried."

"We have to honor his choice," said Samaira with a shrug.

"Your friend is a brave and honorable man," said Moeanaimua, putting an arm around Luni. "A living example of pono. I look forward to meeting him one day."

A smile crept across Samaira's face.

"He is, isn't he?" she said.

"Who is what?" asked Dr. Kitzinger.

"Jayson. A living example of pono. We can use that."

He raised an eyebrow at Farzin. The former Navy SEAL replied only with a shrug.

Chapter 28

IN THE MONTHS AFTER the founding of the Federation of the Kanaka Mokupuni, the comings and goings of canoes among the islands became so commonplace that Jayson's return from Hawai'i went almost unnoticed. Barefoot and wearing only a wrap instead of his usual cargo shorts and t-shirt, it was easy for him to blend in with the primarily indigenous men and women on the new dock designed to accommodate their outriggers. His black hair, which he hadn't cut for more than a year, flowed loosely to his shoulder blades in the fashion of the natives.

He'd been ferried to Hana by Pili's people and then borrowed a small outrigger to make his way to Wailuku over a couple of days. From there, he'd arranged passage with a group heading to O'ahu in a larger seafaring canoe, discovering on the way they were going to help with a construction project and learn building techniques from their mysterious new allies.

After so long among the people of Hawai'i, he communicated without using his tablet, which he kept tucked safely away in a woven bag with his other few belongings. He didn't tell his fellow passengers he was one of the new allies of which they spoke, nor did they suspect he was anything other than a traveler from another island. As a result, he enjoyed candid conversations about their hopes and concerns for their new civilization.

He'd anticipated an enthusiastic greeting upon his return—and maybe even a celebration in the plaza—but realized quickly from the level of activity on the dock why nobody had noticed their approach. He found it more amusing than disappointing that he'd been lost in the bustle of an active and growing port. Making his way up the pathway to the settlement with a bag slung over his shoulder, he passed several people who paid him no attention. It was only as he walked across the plaza towards his apartment that Parth noticed him and did a double take.

"Jayson?"

"Hey, Parth," he replied with a grin.

"Jesus, man. You look like—like Jesus."

He came over and greeted him with a hug.

"Nice tatts," he added, admiring the artwork adorning Jayson's shoulders and upper torso. "What do they mean?"

"Hopefully not their equivalent of 'kick me,' or anything like that. Talk about it over a beer after I get cleaned up? Assuming you guys haven't drunk it all."

"Oh, we tried," assured Parth. "But Herman insisted on making more for when you got back."

"Things are changing fast around here," marveled Jayson, looking around.

"Yeah. Lots going on now that Honolulu is officially our capital city. We're adding more housing for guests and diplomats, and moving the clinic so we can start building the capitol complex."

"Wow! That's at least a few generations ahead of schedule."

"So are we. There are probably thousands of us now. Kai and Samaira are out with a delegation trying to figure out how many people there are on the islands, and how they want to be represented."

"The birth of a nation," said Jayson, shaking his head. "I never imagined being part of something like this."

"Tell me about it. As a civil engineer, this whole thing is like a dream come true. You won't believe what we've got going on up top," said Parth, pointing to the crater wall. "We're building a reservoir—a whole freakin' lake as a centerpiece for the university campus."

"A lake? You're kidding."

"Nope. We'll fill it with pumps, at first—but we're going to build an aqueduct all the way back to the source of Moleka stream," he replied. "A fucking aqueduct, man! Just like the Romans. We're gonna use it to run water to the apartments, and even put a fountain in the center of the plaza."

Parth was a run-on sentence, barely pausing to breathe in his excitement.

"Show me later?" suggested Jayson. "Then we can get together with everyone."

"Not much of the gang around right now, to be honest—but Luping and I can meet you for dinner on the lanai."

"Where is everyone?"

"They went over to Kaua'i to check things out. Herman and Zaina are setting them up with the second wind turbine, doc is doing a health assessment, Serge is surveying their settlement and infrastructure to plan for some modernization, and Melinda is trying to figure out how we're going to scale up our education system for all of the new kids we've got to teach."

"Wow. This is really taking off, isn't it?"

"Like you wouldn't believe. In fact, I've got a whole crew of new people helping out on the reservoir to learn our construction techniques. I've got to get back up there to see how it's going. Come and check it out once you're settled in?"

"Yeah. Sure," promised Jayson. "I'll come up and take a look."

"Incredible," he marveled to himself as Parth scampered off. "Just incredible."

He made his way up to his apartment without encountering anyone else, finding it waiting as tidy and clean as he'd left it. Evidently, someone had been coming in regularly to dust and chase away the insects, spiders, and centipedes that would have otherwise reclaimed it for themselves. Flinging open the shutters, he took in the breathtaking view of the harbor and the glittering waters beyond. It felt both familiar and alien at the same time—a strange inconsistency he attributed to the changes that had taken place while he'd been away.

In the clearing below the plaza, grasses and wildflowers were reclaiming the land where the newly arrived recruits had set up camp over two years earlier. In those first months, they had worked from dawn until dusk preparing the fields and building the settlement, stopping only to share a meal around the fire before collapsing into sleep. They were good times. The camaraderie of working side by side and the gratification they found in the tangible fruits of their labor kept spirits high. It was as Samaira had said; with purpose came happiness.

Jayson was overwhelmed by the sweet melancholy of nostalgia as he pictured himself and the others gathering in the clearing after a day's work. It was like leafing through some old photo album or yearbook. There was joy in recalling those memories, but they were tempered by a sense of loss that things would never be the same. Kailani and Jen were both dead; their laughter forever silenced, and Luni had decided not to return to him. Herman would soon start a family with Zaina, and Matteus and Serge probably wouldn't be far behind.

Even the version of himself that had arrived on the island barely a man, naïve and unprepared for the brutality of an unsheltered life, was gone. He'd witnessed considerable pain and death, and had even been forced to take life himself. The work on Hawai'i was part of a penance he felt he needed to pay for that. Whether he'd saved one life or a thousand as a result didn't matter. It was worth the risk he had taken for any chance at peace with their neighbors. But what would happen next? How would they be greeted by the next culture they encountered? And the one after that? He wondered if they'd always have to shed so much blood before they could have peace.

Exhausted from the journey, he lay down on the bed, but sleep wouldn't come. After an hour of restlessness, he grew frustrated with staring at the ceiling, deciding instead to survey the fields to see how Anuenue and the others had managed without him. Even there, the changes were considerable. The fruit trees had grown fuller in his absence, having been carefully tended. Someone had kept up the pruning, and the soil around their trunks was still moist from a recent watering. Most noticeable were large swaths of newly tilled soil on either side of Nu'uanu Stream. He saw a group of workers extending the irrigation channels into the new fields while others planted rows of seeds.

He passed by the men digging the channel, acknowledging them with a nod as he smiled to himself. There was not a single familiar face among them. The anonymity of living in a bigger world was a strange comfort—something he'd missed from time to time. It didn't last long. Anuenue looked up from the row of seeds she was planting and, after taking a moment to process the juxtaposition of Jayson in native garb, screamed in delight.

"Jayson! You're back!"

"It is good to see you," he replied with a broad grin, taking her in his arms. "You have been busy here."

"Yes," she agreed. "Many people are joining us here in Honolulu, and we need to feed them."

"And you have many new helpers."

She nodded with satisfaction at the activity all around them.

"Some will stay, and others will take what they learn back to their communities—along with seeds and saplings to start their own crops."

"You have learned so much in our time together, Anuenue," he marveled. "It seems you were meant for this purpose."

"Thank you," she said, blushing. "I am so grateful for everything you have shown me."

As they looked around, she suddenly turned to him, narrowing her eyes.

"The translator," she said. "You don't need it anymore?"

They'd gone past simple pleasantries, speaking her native language the whole time, without the awkward pantomiming that usually accompanied his attempts to communicate without the tablet.

"Not as much."

"I see I am not the only one who has learned a lot."

"I guess not," he laughed. "Take me on a tour? I want to see what else you've done while I was gone."

***

By mid-October, everyone had returned to Honolulu in anticipation of rougher seas and more difficult travel. Kai and Samaira's census revealed the Kanaka Mokupuni comprised nearly two thousand people in dozens of communities scattered across their islands. Representatives from each would spend the winter in Honolulu ratifying a constitution and developing a basic set of laws to bring back to their people in the spring.

The people of Kaua'i had electricity, lighting, and pumps to supply fresh water directly to their main village. And they had Ino. He had insisted on taking what he'd learned from Anuenue and Jayson to help them start their agricultural development. It was in payment of a debt to Moeanaimua that would never be settled—a penance for his role in Kameha's betrayal.

Though everyone was back, Jayson still felt unsettled. He often felt the need to separate himself from the others and spend his downtime alone, reading or tending the small garden next to his apartment. It was there that Samaira tracked him down one afternoon as he sat outside, absorbed in something on his tablet.

"Hey, Jayson," she greeted. "What are you up to?"

He looked up in surprise.

"Hey. Just reading."

"What about?"

"The history of my people," he replied, turning the tablet to show her.

"Learn anything interesting?"

"Just how little I actually knew," he said with a laugh.

"How long have you been studying them?"

"Since I got back from Hawai'i. Living among the natives there—you know, without all our technology and stuff—got me thinking about my ancestors."

"That's only natural, I guess. I think about mine, too."

"And what's coming? What's going to happen to them?"

"All the time," she admitted. "Come for a walk with me? There's something I want to show you."

"Sure. Where to?"

"Just down to the plaza," she said, motioning to the pathway.

"Alright," he agreed. "I could use a walk."

He set the tablet down and followed as she led the way. Descending the stairs to the plaza, she walked to the collection of shaded benches in the middle before turning back to face the extinct volcano that served as a backdrop to the center of their community. Large sections were a mess of rubble and tools where excavation for the foundation of the capitol building was already underway.

"Have you seen the updated plans from Serge and Parth?" she asked.

"Yeah. Pretty impressive."

The pair had proposed a structure, married into the living rock, that would tower more than eighty meters over the plaza—all the way to the crater rim. Water from the lake above would cascade down the rock face in the central atrium before disappearing below the floor to be recycled for more practical purposes.

"We're going to carve our guiding principles—the Pono Mokopuni—right into the rock," she continued. "At the heart of our capitol."

"Pono Mokupuni," repeated Jayson. "The Ethos of the Islands. It has a nice ring. Have you defined it yet?"

"We'll work on that throughout the winter. Then, the representatives will ratify it with their communities back home in the spring."

"Getting them invested," realized Jayson.

"You're learning," she said with a laugh.

"So, what did you want to show me?"

She gestured up at the crater rim, continuing her description of the future capitol.

"At the top, there's going to be a gallery with ten-meter arched ceilings supported by columns, open on all sides. We're calling it The Hall of the Founders."

"Sounds impressive. What's going in there?"

"The story of our arrival and the founding of our community. It will be written out on plaques—along with stone carvings depicting the major events."

Jayson closed his eyes, trying to picture the space in his mind. He imagined the columns topped with soaring arches supporting the ceiling above, and the echoing footsteps of awed visitors walking among the displays in a Parthenon-like structure.

"Wow."

"There will be statues of our heroes, too—larger than life—Kailani and Jen."

She paused and took his hand, looking him in the eye.

"And you, too," she added.

"What? You're joking, right?"

"Why not?"

"Well, I'm not dead—for a start," he protested, pulling his hand away.

"But where would we be without you? If you hadn't saved Kai's life, or gone with him to Moloka'i, would we have this community we have now? And the deal you negotiated with Pili? Who else could have done that?"

"Anyone could have done that."

"Even if that's true, they didn't. You did."

"Come on, Samaira. This is crazy. I don't need a fucking statue."

"I know that—but it's not just about what you need. *We* need this. We need to establish our mythology alongside our ethos if we're to create something that will last."

He looked again at the top of the crater, shaking his head.

"I—I don't know what to say," he stammered. "You want to turn me into some kind of George Washington?"

"Let's not inflate your ego too much," she laughed. "More of a Paul Revere, maybe?"

"What's the Canadian conversion on that? Am I like a Laura Secord or more of a Chief Tecumseh?"

"I've never heard of either of them."

"Of course not," he sighed, shaking his head in mock disappointment.

"You're too hard to categorize, anyway. Warrior, diplomat—"

"Farmer," he added.

She laughed again.

"But, seriously," continued Jayson, motioning up to the rim. "How am I supposed to live up to something like that?"

"I'm not sure anyone lives up to their legend."

"Keanu Reeves?"

"Okay. Maybe *some* people do," she conceded with a smile. "But you're not done building yours. You've shown yourself to be a skilled diplomat—and we still need that."

"So, what are you thinking? Ambassador to Hawai'i, or something?"

"Nothing so official as that. In spring, we're sending a crew out to make contact with the Americas. I think you should be part of it."

"So soon? You think we're ready for this?"

"We're just going to say hello for now. Let them know we're out here—and we're friendly."

"That's a long time at sea. I don't know if I'm cut out for it," he replied with a shrug.

"You have plenty of time to think it over," she assured him. "It's a few months away, yet."

She put her arm around his waist, giving him a gentle squeeze.

"I've got to get back to *my* Keanu," she said. "Think it over?"

"Yeah," he agreed. "Sure."

Samaira walked off and left Jayson standing alone in the middle of the plaza, staring up at the blank rock face of Punchbowl Crater.

Chapter 29

THE START OF THE exodus of humpback whales in their annual migration to the nutrient-rich waters of Alaska marked the arrival of spring—and the calmer seas that made travel among the islands more routine. The representatives from Maui, Kaua'i, and Moloka'i, who had spent the winter months on O'ahu, were rightly proud of their work to craft a first draft of the Pono Mokupuni. They had also agreed on a set of principles to guide the creation and administration of their laws—a constitution of sorts. Soon, they'd return to their communities to share them with their people.

Springtime also meant Jasmine's Hope could venture into the open ocean for another mission far from home. A crew of volunteers would head east to the lands that would never officially be called the Americas. There, they would establish friendly relations with coastal natives from Ecuador in the south to Vancouver Island in the north, initiating trade agreements that would eventually provide a source of the raw materials needed to continue the development of their society.

The dock bustled with activity on the morning of May 13th, 1176, as the ship's crew prepared it for a second transoceanic voyage. Nearby, a canoe bound for Maui slipped into the water amid tremendous cheers and wishes of good fortune. All morning, canoes had been arriving almost as regularly as they'd been departing. As those who had gained experience working with Luping, Parth, and Serge over the winter left to apply their new skills at home, fresh crews were arriving—filled with excitement at their first glimpses of the wonders of Honolulu.

Every time another canoe paddled into the harbor, Jayson scanned for signs of Luni or Ino. He hadn't seen Ino since they parted ways on Hawai'i, and was eager for news of how his crops were faring on Kaua'i. As for Luni, the last time he'd seen her it was with the belief that she'd return to be with him. He wasn't sure what to expect if he *did* get a chance to see her again. He wasn't even sure how he'd react. Would he be overjoyed or filled with sadness?

Walking along the dock with a load of provisions, he saw an outrigger arriving in the harbor from the west—a sure sign it was inbound from Kaua'i. He set down the bag he was carrying, pausing to watch as it got closer. With a mix of relief and disappointment, he noticed only unfamiliar faces among the crew paddling their way toward the beach.

Ashore, the crowd of well-wishers seeing off the diplomats from other islands turned their attention to Jasmine's Hope. Some women had made leis for the brave explorers, and lined up with the others near the dock to ensure everyone got a few words of traditional blessing to go with the string of flowers placed around their necks.

Jayson left his bag in a pile with the rest of the supplies near the ship and jogged back to the beach where the official sendoff was taking place. He walked the gauntlet of handshakes, hugs, and kisses with good humor, even though he didn't necessarily feel the same excitement as everyone else.

Then, the crew filed their way down the dock, occasionally turning to wave back at the cheering crowd. All that remained was to get the last of the supplies loaded. Jayson hoisted a bag of seeds over his shoulder and took hold of the ladder, ready to climb aboard.

"Wait!" called Serge, dodging his way down the dock.

"I have something for you."

Jayson stepped aside to make room for the others boarding the ship.

"What is it?"

"Here," said Serge, producing a tablet. "I've been working on the translator, feeding it whatever I can find about native North American languages."

"Thanks. But Farzin already has a tablet with everything we need for the coastal tribes."

"This one is for you. It has everything."

Jayson eyed him suspiciously.

"Why would I need that?"

"Because I think maybe you're not coming back," replied Serge.

"What makes you think I'm not coming back?"

"Samaira told me."

Jayson set down the bag, shaking his head.

"Of course she did."

"So it's true?"

"Maybe," he replied with a shrug. "I don't even know yet—not for sure—and I sure as hell didn't tell her I wasn't coming back."

"She has a way of knowing things."

"I'm not sure about that either. I think maybe she has a way of making things turn out the way she wants."

Serge nodded somberly, but didn't respond.

"Anyone else know?" asked Jayson.

"I had to tell Herman and Zaina—so they could make you this."

He handed over a device a little smaller than a loaf of bread.

"They tried to make it as light as possible," he added.

"What is it?"

"Here," said Serge, demonstrating the folding crank. "It's a manual generator made from one of the spare motors. Just plug in your tablet and turn the crank."

"This is too much, Serge," protested Jayson. "You need this stuff here."

"We have plenty here," he assured. "We all agreed you need it more."

"We *all* agreed? Who else knows?"

"Just a few of us. I didn't think you'd appreciate a scene."

"Thanks," he replied with a sigh of relief. "I don't want people making a big deal of this—in case I chicken out."

"But it is a big deal. You realize that, right?"

"It's a long shot that I'd even make it ten kilometers from the coast, let alone pull off some kind of reverse-Lewis-and-Clark."

"But if you do? It will change the course of our history—and the history of your people."

"Yeah. No pressure," he laughed.

"This is a serious thing," reminded Serge, gripping Jayson by the shoulders.

He looked his friend in the eyes and drew him into an embrace.

"If the rest of your people are half as brave as you, then I have great hope for this world of ours."

"Thanks, Serge. That means a lot."

Jayson took the tablet and the generator, stuffing them into the bag of assorted seed packets.

"Oh, and Farzin knows, too," added Serge, pointing up to the deck.

Jayson glanced up to see Farzin looking at him. The former SEAL gave a quick nod and turned away.

"He'll give you basic survival training during the trip and then set you up with a proper backpack and some other supplies before you head off."

"Wow. You guys have given this way more thought than I have," he grinned.

"How will you manage without us?"

Serge tried to smile as he asked the question, but the corners of his mouth began to twitch. A glossy film built up in his eyes.

"That's my cue," said Jayson. "No way I'm going to stand here crying with you."

He hoisted the bag over his shoulder and ascended onto the deck. Looking back, he caught Serge wiping away a tear with his knuckle.

"Love you too, man," he said with a grin before disappearing below deck to stow his things.

Serge rejoined his small group of coconspirators as the crew of Jasmine's Hope prepared to cast off. It was a perfect morning for it. The seas were calm, and a light breeze in the harbor assured a smooth start to the journey. The crowd cheered again as the mainsail rose, and the ship eased silently from its slip. Jayson and a few others stood on the stern waving, acknowledging the calls of encouragement and wishes for a safe, successful journey. By the time the top of the mast vanished behind the trees to the east, only Jayson's closest friends remained at the dock. They lingered there silently for a time, each lost in their own thoughts.

***

I hope you enjoyed The Gamma Effect. If so, please consider leaving a review on Amazon and Goodreads. Your feedback helps indie authors get noticed!

Use the QR code below to visit my blog and sign up to my reader list for exclusive updates and offers.